OTHER BOOKS BY PIERS PLATT

Combat and Other Shenanigans

The Janus Group:
Rath's Deception
Rath's Gambit
Rath's Reckoning
Rath's Trial
Rath's Rebellion
Rath's Redemption

The Falken Chronicles:
Escape from Oz
Escape from Olympus
Return to Oz

Viral

PIERS PLATT

CONTENTS

CHAPTER 1

In my first battle, I made fourteen thousand dollars in five minutes. I didn't go viral, not technically ... I needed another two million views to hit that mark. But I came damn close, and I got a taste. And I liked it.

I was also scared as hell, of course. As the saying goes, there are two kinds of deathstreamers: those who admit they're scared ... and liars. Me? I straight up peed in my suit (a little) on my first ride down. It's a good thing StreaMercs designed our suits to be able to recycle that stuff.

I was still shaking in fear when the space elevator jolted to a stop. In front of me, over the helmeted heads of the first rank of streamers, I saw the ramps crack open at the top, swinging down to give me my first view of an alien planet. Beneath a grimy yellow sky, the ground was rust-orange mud, which eventually gave way to a set of distant mountains. I saw a white-red gout of flame reach across the battlefield, and a hail of tracer rounds replied. Then the first rank of streamers hurried forward. My clan – me, Arliss, Naja, Taalib, Dhia, and Johnny – stood near the back. I know: stupid move. We didn't know any better. We had called ourselves "Clan Demonium." It had seemed like a funny name when we came up with it the day before, up in the safety of the barracks. But it turned out to be a bit too prophetic.

I found myself running, following the streamers in front of me, and just like that, my vac-suited boots slipped off the worn titanium of the ramp and into muddy soil – slick, with the consistency of day-old oatmeal. I cleared my throat.

"That's one small step for woman," I said, hoping my viewers couldn't hear the fear in my voice. "One giant: 'Oh fuck, what did I just get myself into?' "

Somebody must have been watching, and thought the joke was funny – I got a notification in my heads-up display of a twenty dollar tip. I had made my first buck as a deathstreamer.

"Thanks for the tip, guys," I said. "Stick around. If you like dry humor accompanied by a complete lack of fighting skill, I'm your girl."

I surveyed our section of the battlefield through my visor. The firing had stopped, abruptly, and I saw no sign of the enemy. The other clans were taking advantage of the sudden lull, and were all heading toward the perimeter that the first wave had hastily established, about a hundred meters beyond the ramps. I continued turning in a circle, and saw a handful of casualties from the first wave being helped back onto the elevator by other streamers. One girl was hopping on one leg, her arms across the shoulders of two clan mates. Her other leg dragged along the ground behind her, bumping and twisting, dangling from a thin strand of fabric that was all that remained of her suit's knee pad. My stomach lurched. Her friends set her down on the floor of the elevator, gave her a reassuring pat on the shoulder, and then hustled back outside as the ramps began to close. The doors weren't even fully shut, and the massive doughnut-shaped elevator was slipping rapidly upwards again, disappearing up along the thick cable into the haze above.

No turning back now, I thought. *Not until the third wave gets down, at least.*

"So that's an Ocho," I heard Dhia say, over my suit's internal speakers.

I turned and found the rest of Clan Demonium standing in a loose semi-circle around a mud-spattered form in the dirt at our feet. I hadn't noticed it before, but Dhia was right – it was indeed an Ocho, the first we had seen in the flesh. A dead one, thankfully – some streamer from the first wave had holed it repeatedly along one of its long, sinewy flanks. The creature's corpse twitched, suddenly, and we all flinched.

Arliss laughed nervously. "It's dead, right? It's bigger than I thought."

"Look at its legs," Johnny said. "That's one ugly motherfucker."

A burst of gunfire from the far side of the elevator cable caused us to jerk our heads up. *This is a battlefield, and we're just standing around gawking like a bunch of morons.*

"What now?" Taalib asked, about a half second before I could.

"Everybody else headed for the perimeter," Arliss said, jerking a thumb over his shoulder. "I think we should join them."

"I agree," Naja said. Her streamertag appeared in my heads-up display when I looked at her, hovering just over her helmet: *StarKillah*. "We need to be where the action is."

Naja had been a moderately successful video game streamer before she traded in her joysticks for real guns. Most of her fan base had followed her to see if she could hack it as a deathstreamer; she had become the de facto leader of our clan given the rest of us were completely new to streaming. She set off across the slippery earth, heading toward a section of the perimeter. The five of us followed.

We found a spot of open ground between two other clans and prostrated ourselves, peering out over the terrain. I snugged my e-rifle into my shoulder, letting the barrel rest on my left hand and scanning the terrain ahead through the weapon's scope. As usual, the company had anchored the space elevator on a roughly circular rise – a small patch of high ground with good visibility in all directions. If you're thinking, "Well that makes good tactical sense, it's easier to defend the high ground," then ... *sigh*.

You sweet, summer child.

While you are *technically* correct, StreaMercs picks its landing sites based on two factors alone. Factor one: is it physically possible to anchor the space elevator into the bedrock at that site? Factor two: is it a nice picturesque location with good sightlines for shooting streaming videos? This is show business. Whether streamers stand a good chance of seizing and holding the site with minimal casualties is entirely irrelevant.

I'm no geologist, but the elevator's base seemed to be well anchored. And they had certainly picked a scenic spot for our first landing on Pentares. Ahead of me, the ground sloped gently away from our position, and continued for several rolling miles, split at intervals by what I could only guess were small chasms. In the far distance, I could see a set of jagged mountains, their deep red sides streaked with white and yellow ore deposits. Above, the mountains' craggy tops faded into the planet's hazy yellow cloud layer. Well, not so much *clouds* ... Pentares' atmosphere didn't really have distinct clouds, per se, just a gradually thickening layer of toxic gases. Our arrival briefing had talked about which specific gases were in the air, but I had promptly forgotten the details. "Don't take your helmet off" was the key takeaway, and all I really needed to know. We weren't there to terra-form and colonize – those folks would come along well after we were done.

I turned and glanced over my shoulder, eyeing the dead Ocho with curiosity. Its armored shell, spattered with Pentares' mud, was a deep brown, smooth, but segmented into sections. Each of its eight legs were as long as my own legs, and the thing's cylindrical thorax stretched a ways along the ground –if I had laid down next to it, it would have been nearly twice as long as I was. Not that I was gonna get anywhere close to it. *It's like some mad scientist crossed a centipede with an anaconda.* I shuddered, and turned back to watch my sector.

A drone camera zoomed by, streaming third-person footage of the perimeter for the viewers. I thought about waving to it and saying something silly, like, "Hi, Mom!" but it was gone before I could do so. And my Mom was almost certainly not watching, having made it clear to me that she had no wish to see her only daughter star in a 'glorified snuff film'.

Fair enough.

I wondered idly what I looked like to my viewers – they could opt to see what I was seeing, or a close-up feed of my face, and most fans choose to watch both, at the same time, via picture-in-picture. I hoped I looked like a badass, but I felt like I was going to hurl.

Next to me, Arliss shifted on his stomach, trying to get comfortable. He held an ancient Thompson sub-machine gun in one gloved hand, an antique from the early twentieth-century. The weapon looked comically undersized compared to our bulky armor, like some kid had mixed up the accessories for his toys, and given his space marine the gun that was supposed to go with a much smaller, cigar-chewing gangster in a fedora and trench coat.

That was Arliss' shtick: he was hoping to get history buffs to watch his stream by showcasing famous weapons from different eras during each battle. Hence his streamertag: OldSchool. He'd convinced some military museum to lend him a good chunk of its inventory, in exchange for plastering the museum's logo and URL all over his armor. I had to admit it was a cool idea, especially as I had no such gimmick of my own. And when I had checked the clan's viewer counts during the elevator ride down, Arliss had far and away the most fans watching, even more than Naja. The fans had a good idea of what was coming, even if we didn't – they love to watch a dumb noob get schooled.

"Heads up," Naja said. She was a few meters off to my right, but had broadcast the message to our clan's radio frequency. I focused through the scope of my e-rifle, scanning the ground below us. A flicker of movement caught my eye – something had popped up, briefly, out of one of the chasms several hundred meters away. But it was gone before I could identify it.

"Was that an Ocho out there in the chasm?" I asked.

"I didn't see it," Taalib replied.

Arliss' voice came in over my speakers next: "Okay, so for my first battle, we're testing out the forty-five caliber Thompson sub-machine gun, also known as the 'Tommy gun' and affectionately nicknamed the 'Trench Sweeper' by G.I.s in World War Two—"

"You're on the clan channel, Arliss," Naja told him, curtly. "Save that crap for the viewers on your own stream; we don't want to hear it."

"Oh, right – sorry," Arliss said, adjusting his audio controls.

I realized I should be giving some running commentary of my own for however many viewers had mistakenly stumbled across my stream (I checked quickly: a measly twenty-two thousand), but before I could open my mouth, the chasm I was watching simply erupted. Octipedes – *hundreds* of them – poured over the edge, like angry hornets whose nest had just been given a particularly ill-advised whack.

"Oh, fuck," I said, and opened fire, along with everyone else in my clan.

I squeezed the trigger convulsively, not even attempting to select individual targets, just pumping rounds into the thick mass of writhing creatures surging toward us. At that stage in my career, and at that range, hitting individual Ochos would have been pretty unlikely, anyway. Along with my own fire, I could see a deadly network of tracers zipping down the hillside, converging on the Ochos. The aliens in front stumbled and fell under the withering fire, but they were immediately replaced, and still the wave rolled at us. I heard Arliss open up next to me, and the submachine gun was shockingly loud compared to the more efficient cycling of my electromagnetic rifle. I would have yelled at him in annoyance, but the Ocho horde was covering ground fast, and a warning indicator had just appeared in my heads-up display:

>>>*Last 5 Rounds – Reload – Last 5 Rounds – Reload* …

With fumbling fingers, I dropped my magazine, then rolled onto my side, scrabbling at the pouches mounted against my armored stomach for a replacement. Arliss was reloading, too, I saw. The volume of fire from our whole sector had tapered off noticeably. *Are we all fucking reloading at once? Shit!*

Arliss had pushed himself up onto one knee to swap out mags on the "Trench Sweeper," and as I finally levered one of my own magazines out of its pouch, he slammed his new magazine home. I felt a scorching heat pass between us, and plasma beams crisscrossed the sky. A quick glance down the hill told me that the Ochos had stopped briefly, holding their forelegs up to deliver a withering plasma volley. Then they were back on all fours – or all eights, I guess – and skittering at us again with shocking speed.

Arliss screamed. The plasma bolt that I thought had gone between us had amputated his right arm at the shoulder.

"Arliss is hit," I yelled, and in my shock, like a dumbass, I dropped the fresh magazine I had been about to load. It hit the mud with a wet *smack*. I grabbed for it, shook it roughly in a vain attempt to clear the mud out of it, and jammed it optimistically into my e-rifle.

>>>E-Rifle Malfunction. Remove Foreign Debris.

Some vindictive, extremely annoyed portion of my brain chose that moment to remind me that I had willingly opted *not* to carry a pistol into combat, for reasons that boiled down to: *I barely know how to handle this e-rifle … how am I going to learn how to use a pistol, too?*

And then one of the Ochos reached us, and I stopped having higher-order thoughts altogether, and instead focused on thoughts like: *ohmyfuckinggod* and *getmeoutofherenow.* The Ocho ignored me and hit Arliss in the chest – he was still kneeling and staring at the cauterized stump of his shoulder in disbelief, and the creature just punched its forelegs through his torso armor, knocked him onto his back, and pinned him to the ground, like a giant, malevolent stapler.

A productive thought finally penetrated my mental circuits, and I realized that although I had dropped my first magazine a few moments ago, my e-rifle hadn't *technically* been empty at the time, which meant that there was still a round in the chamber. So I pushed myself off the ground, stuck the barrel into the side of the Ocho's thorax-thingy, and pulled the trigger.

… and promptly learned that a lightly wounded Ocho is infinitely more scary than just about any other kind of Ocho. It let go of Arliss, whirled around, and a single swipe from one of its razor-sharp legs neatly severed the last four inches of my e-rifle's barrel. I fell back in surprise, landing unceremoniously on my butt. The Ocho reared up over me, bearing an uncanny resemblance to a giant cobra, poised to strike, which immediately reactivated all of those Neanderthal-level thoughts in my head. *Oh fuck oh fuck it's going to staple me too.* But just then, a notification appeared in the clear plastic of my visor:

>>>You have 3,000,000 viewers! Congratulations on a new personal best! [Champagne glass emoji][Party hat emoji] Keep it up, Valkyrie6!

CHAPTER 2

"Eventually the weight of scientific evidence was just too great to ignore: universal basic income's potential to improve society became indisputable. Then, once the first few countries committed to it, it was only a matter of time before all countries had to follow suit. And the predictions were right: governments handing out free money to every citizen had a massive – and lasting – positive impact.

"But the thorn on that rose was sharp, and certain mental health conditions became much more prevalent. In short, without a 'job' to center their identity around, many people struggled to find their *raison d'être*. With little incentive to find employment – and few jobs remaining that weren't automated – a growing number of people became listless and depressed. And eventually they found each other, formally organized, and started to protest publicly. But what else could their governments give them? They had food, they had healthcare, they had money. How does a government give its citizens a sense of purpose?"

-Dr. Suzan Weinberg-Shen, "Aimless: The Birth of the Roamer Movement"

U p on the stage, behind a massive wooden podium sporting the university's crest, the dean smiled and leaned forward into the microphone.

"And with that, I'd like to formally congratulate the graduating class of two thousand, two hundred, and thirty-one!"

We all whooped, and I threw my cap up into the air, watching as it spun through a high arc, lost among hundreds of other looping black squares in the sky overhead. It landed somewhere off to my left; I thought about trying to find it, but quickly gave up on that idea, and turned instead to wave at my parents, up in the bleachers. As I was looking for them, Paul caught me by the elbow.

"Sam!" He hugged me, and I squeezed him back. "We did it!"

"I know, hard to believe, right?" I said, smiling.

He laughed. "Don't forget – happy hour at The Dive. Remy's coming, too."

"I'll be there." I tried to spot Remy in the crowd, but she had been sitting farther back and across the main aisle, with the rest of the English majors.

Paul disappeared; I threaded my way through my grinning classmates, and hurried across the track encircling the football field's bright green turf. Outside the stadium, after a few false starts, I managed to find my parents waiting for me under a lamp post – not the one I had told them to meet me at, but they were in the general area of where they should have been, at least. I pushed through the crowded sidewalk to them.

"Congratulations, honey," my dad said, hugging me.

"Thanks."

"We're very proud of you," my mom echoed, giving me a hug as well.

Dad pushed his glasses up the bridge of his nose and sniffed, and I could tell he was about to get sentimental.

"Dad …," I warned.

"Oh, let him cry," Mom said. "It's not every day your only daughter grows up."

Grows up. I mentally tallied up how many years it had been since I had first gotten drunk, and how long I'd been sexually active (actually the same exact number of years, not coincidentally), and a handful of other milestones besides, but decided to just smile and let them have their moment.

"Paul's speech was very nice," Mom said. "He's a very intelligent young man."

"Yeah," I agreed carefully, seeing where this was going.

Mom seemed to be waiting for me to say something else. I sighed, and rolled my eyes. "We're just friends, Mom."

She wrinkled her nose at me, causing the freckles on her dark skin to bunch up. "I'm just saying, you could do a lot worse."

"Margret, she's twenty-two!" Dad protested. He wagged his finger at her. "You wouldn't even talk about marriage with me until we were *forty*."

"I'm not saying she has to get married right now," Mom said.

"Can we talk about my love life somewhere besides the middle of a crowded street?" I suggested, nodding toward the press of graduates and their families passing by on the sidewalk. *Or better yet, not talk about it at all?*

"Yes," Dad agreed. He checked his watch – an antique Casio that I had given him for his sixtieth birthday, complete with a calculator pad and everything. "We have a table in twenty minutes at the Moroccan restaurant on Walnut Street."

"This way," I said, and we set off.

Lunch was actually fun, once we got Mom to start talking about work instead of Paul's qualifications as a potential mate. She was getting ready to retire by that point – partly her choice, partly an automation initiative at her department. She comes from a long line of social workers, and had kept the Ombotu family tradition going strong – hell, as a psychology major, I had intended to do the same, or close enough. But we stayed away from the topic of my future, by mutual, silent agreement.

After dessert – crisp, flaky baklava dripping in honey – Dad surprised me with a graduation gift: a small white box, tied with a bow. I opened it, frowning. There was a thin, gray cartridge nestled in the tissue paper inside. I gasped.

"Metroid II!?"

Dad smiled at me. "An original edition, for your Game Boy," he said. "It has a nineteen ninety-one serial number and everything."

"Oh man …," I leaned across the table and hugged him, then Mom. "Thank you."

"'Metroid'? " Mom asked. "Is that a game about numbers?"

Dad laughed. "No. It's a classic shooter."

"Sounds like fun," she managed.

I stroked my fingers across the plastic case, examining the faded sticker. Then I frowned. "These go for thousands online … you guys must have been saving your basic income for a couple months for this."

Dad shook his head. "I found a seller willing to trade. I'm doing a series of custom prints for his home, mixed calligraphy and landscape stuff."

That, too, is a family tradition, at least on the Chen side – Dad's side. He learned it from his parents, when he lived in Shenzhen, before he came to the States for college and met Mom. Dad tried to teach me, but I just didn't have the patience for it.

"Well, I can't wait to play it," I told them.

"I get dibs after you," Dad said. Mom rolled her eyes. She tolerates our vintage electronics obsession, because she thinks it gives the two of us, in her words, 'a strong father-daughter bond,' but there were plenty of times growing up where a MiniDisc player or first-generation smart home device was sentenced to a month-long detention in the back of her closet for interfering with family dinner time. And it wasn't always my fault.

"Have you thought more about … what you're going to do?" Mom asked.

I shook my head. *I thought we had all decided we weren't gonna talk about this.*

"I, uh … I'll need a little time to move my stuff back from school, and find a place of my own," I said.

"Of course," Mom agreed, a little too quickly.

"Take your time," Dad said.

Mom reached across the table, and took my hand. "You've probably been thinking about Lucie these days."

Well, I was trying not to, Mom. "I guess."

"We're here, if you want to talk about it," she continued.

"I'm good." This was quickly turning into the lunch conversation that veered directly into the path of every uncomfortable topic she could think of. "What time are you guys heading home?"

"We have a hypertube at four," Dad said, happy to help me change the subject.

"I'll walk you guys to the station," I said.

* * *

I didn't *ditch* them. I just left them at the station with plenty of time before their 'tube boarded. Which also allowed me to get over to The Dive and grab a table before the rush, and drink most of a gin and tonic before my friends arrived. I needed it.

The Dive had been our favorite watering hole ever since Paul had tended bar there junior year. Dozens of bars closely orbited the campus, preying on undergrads, but The Dive stood out by being far and away the ugliest and dirtiest. Where other bars went upscale, all glass and chrome and high-speed mixology robots, The Dive stuck doggedly to linoleum floors (littered with old peanut shells), dark wood paneling (with all manner of drunken obscenities scratched into it by patrons) and dim incandescent bulbs (not energy efficient, because fuck you, that's why). The Dive's sole decoration was an antique flat-screen mounted at one end of the bar, which was perpetually tuned to a 2D channel playing nature documentaries, for reasons unknown.

But the real reason we loved The Dive was that management had stuck with human bartenders, which meant it was one of the few bars left where someone not of legal drinking age could still have a good time: robot bartenders never forget to card you. Their humans-only staffing policy was probably the only thing keeping the place solvent.

Remy showed up as I was ordering a second round for me and a couple beers for her and Paul; she kissed me on both cheeks with that effortless grace that French women seem to be born with. She tugged at the black sleeve of my gown as she sat down.

"You didn't change?" she asked.

"I had lunch with my parents, then just came straight here," I explained.

"They're headed home?"

"Finally," I said.

She smiled. "I take it you had fun."

"My mom wants me to marry Paul."

Remy snorted into her beer glass. "Ew. That would be like marrying your brother."

"Yeah," I agreed. I don't have a brother, but she had perfectly summed up my feelings on the matter.

"Here comes your fiancé now!" Remy noted, and indeed, Paul was standing at the door, blinking at the relative darkness of the bar. We waved at him. He wove his way through the noisy room, and then sat down heavily at our table. I pushed him a beer.

"Thanks," he said, sighing. "Where would we be without family, eh?"

Remy laughed. "You, too? Sam was just complaining about hers!" For a second, I thought she was going to tell him about my mom's matchmaking agenda, but she just winked at me.

Paul drank, then set his beer down and licked the foam from his lips, and studied the two of us with a strange look on his face. "The end of an era, guys. The end of the Three Musketeers," he observed, using our pet name for our trio.

I held up my glass. "To the Three Musketeers."

"There were actually four musketeers," Remy pointed out, for the umpteenth time. "D'Artagnan's the protagonist of the whole story; you can't leave him out."

"Just clink my glass and take a drink," I scolded her.

"Nobody likes a smart-ass," Paul agreed, grinning.

Remy laughed. "Oh, hello Pot, my name's Kettle." But she knocked her glass against ours, and we drank a toast.

"Are you all moved out?" I asked Remy.

She nodded. "Nearly."

"Heading back to your parents' house?" Paul asked.

"No – the artists' collective I applied to in Virginia finally got back to me. They have an opening, and they want me to come down to join them."

"Oh, congrats!" I said. "That should be a great place to write your next book." Remy was already making decent royalties off of the books she had written in college. Red Lantern – one of the big Chinese studios – had even made an offer for movie rights on one of them.

"I think it'll be a good place to hang out," Remy agreed. "It'll probably be just like college all over again – a bunch of creative people, all living together. Anyway, it should be fun."

"That's only, what? Twenty minutes away from Philly by hypertube?" Paul asked. "We can meet up here for happy hour on Fridays."

"Yes, let's!" Remy agreed. "I'd like that."

Paul wasn't moving out of his apartment – he was

already enrolled in the graduate Psych program, on track to get his PhD in a few years' time. With his grades and high-profile undergrad research projects, the university had snapped him right up, offering him a combined scholarship and teaching contract. They hoped to keep his talents on campus, before some other research organization nabbed him. Hell, they had practically given him tenure before he was even out of undergrad. With the private sector dwindling, academic recruiting was as competitive as pro sports.

"What about you, Sam?" Paul asked, turning to me.

"I'm, ah, mostly moved out. Just a few small things to pack up."

"No, I meant – you want to join us for happy hour on Fridays, too? It's only a short hop from Long Island. We'll make it a tradition!"

I hesitated, and felt my cheeks flush. The short answer was: yes, of course I wanted to see them. What else was I gonna do with myself? The long answer was more complicated. For one, I wasn't sure hanging out with my two happy, successful friends was going to do wonders for my self-esteem. But the bigger problem was cash: a weekly round-trip hypertube fare between my parents' place on Long Island and Philadelphia was well beyond what I could afford on basic income.

"Yeah," I said, trying to cover my embarrassment. "Might not be able to make it every week, but count me in."

"You can stay with me, if you want," Paul offered.

"Oh, her mom would love that," Remy said.

"What?" Paul asked.

I flashed Remy a glare. "Nothing."

"Did you hear back from any of the Master's programs?" Paul asked me.

"No," I said. Which was technically true – none of the Psychology Master's programs had accepted me, mostly because I hadn't bothered to apply for them. What was the point? I wasn't going to hack it as a professor, not with my grades … and entry-level psychology positions outside of academia were a thing of the past. Job openings had all but dried up two years ago, when some asshole in Taiwan designed a neural network that out-performed psychiatrists and social workers on every measurable metric. Even my own Mom couldn't have gotten me a job in her office, not that I would have asked her to.

"Do you know what you're going to do?" Remy asked, concern knitting her brow.

I took a deep breath, and then slumped my shoulders. "Honestly, no. I don't have a clue."

"I mean, that's why there's basic income, right?" Remy said. "You don't have to worry about earning anything if you don't want to."

Aside from self-respect, I thought. "Yeah, I'm not worried. But it would be nice to have some extra cash."

"You could always be a sex worker," Paul suggested.

I flipped him the bird.

"What?" he asked. "What's the problem with it? We're all progressive, sex-positive people, right? And it's the one profession where humans have a clear advantage over machines. A guy down the hall from me has one of those LifePartner dolls, the latest model, I think … and it's still straight up creepy."

"The problem, Paul," I said, "is that that would require me to have sex with gross old men that I'm not attracted to."

"Now you're just being ageist," Paul said, half-seriously.

"You do it then," I told him.

"I might," he mused, and I could see the gears turning in his head, conjuring up a new research project. He'd probably figure out a way to get paid twice, too – he'd take the money from his clients, and get a research grant from the university to boot.

"Well, at the risk of sounding like the worst kind of

guidance counselor, what are you passionate about?" Remy asked me.

I shrugged. "Sleeping in? Hanging out with you guys?"

"What about your electronics collection?" Paul asked. "You could open an online store, or do your own media channel – reviews, unboxings, that kind of thing."

"That sounds like a good way to turn a fun hobby into a mindless chore," I told him.

"Yeah, maybe," he agreed.

"We'll figure it out," Remy said, patting my hand.

"I know," I said. At least neither of them had brought up freediving or Lucie. They knew me better than that … better than my Mom knew me, apparently.

My watch buzzed insistently, and I glanced down at it reflexively, planning to dismiss the notification. But it kept buzzing, and suddenly I noticed that Remy's and Paul's watches were buzzing, too.

"'Global Alert'?" Paul said, frowning. "What the hell is that?"

"I got it, too," Remy said. "It looks like one of those flash flood warnings they push sometimes, but … there are no other details."

"Listen!" someone in the bar yelled, and we looked up.

The bartender – a girl I vaguely recognized from school – was kneeling on a stool, fiddling with a button on the side of the flat-screen over the bar. On the screen, a movie about killer whales had been replaced by some kind of test symbol, and as the volume came on, we could hear a clashing tone from the speakers. The words *Emergency Broadcast System* were visible in the midst of the symbols. A hush fell over the bar.

"Is it just a test?" somebody asked.

"Switch to a news channel!" someone else yelled.

The girl on the stool touched the TV, then shook her head. "It's on all channels."

My watch buzzed again, and the room was quickly filled with a humming chorus of notification vibrations.

This time, the alert had a block of text.

>>>*GLOBAL ALERT: A team of scientists tasked with exploring the Bohr-Steiner system have made first contact with alien life forms. The aliens are hostile, and their intentions and capabilities are unknown at this time. Please proceed to the nearest nuclear fallout shelter as a precaution.*

From outside the building, I heard the piercing wail of a siren – not a vehicle siren, a different noise, much louder and more unsettling.

Where the hell is the nearest fallout shelter? I wondered.

"Holy shit," Paul said into the silent room.

After that, it was just chaos.

CHAPTER 3

"After centuries imagining what first contact with an alien civilization might be like, the great irony is that human beings were not the first Earth-based entity to make that contact. On Bohr-Steiner III, it was technically one of the airborne drones – not the team of human explorers – that was the first to 'see' the Octipedes. In this, as in all things in the twenty-third century, the machines beat us to the punch."

-Dr. Tranh Ng, "The Daedalus Effect: Man, Machines, and Myth"

Something was beeping.

"Snooze," I grunted, not bothering to open my eyes.

"You have exceeded your pre-programmed snooze limitation," Zoe's gentle robotic voice answered me.

"Fuck," I told my home assistant, as the beeps continued. Somewhere deep in her code, Zoe was probably searching for the appropriate response to this command. *What should I fuck? How? I am a set of loosely interconnected sensors and speakers; my hardware limitations will make fucking extremely difficult.*

But Zoe remained silent – except for the alarm beeping.

"I'm awake," I groaned, finally, but she didn't quit beeping at me until I was standing upright by the side of the bed, grumbling.

"Good afternoon, Sam," she said, by way of greeting, as the beeps ended. I swear, they program these assistants to be so passive-aggressive.

I blinked, rubbed at my eyes, and then stumbled across the bedroom, tripping on a pile of clothes that had accumulated against the closet door, like a multi-hued snowdrift.

"Lights," I said. "Ah! Too bright. Reduce. Yeah, better. Same for the kitchen."

I flinched when my toes hit the cold tile floor in the kitchen, but my slippers were god-knows-where back in the bedroom, so I sucked it up and pulled open the fridge door. Fridge contents: a thing of milk, jar of raspberry jam, bottle of mustard, two half-finished wine bottles, part of a takeout meal from … last week? At *least* that old. And … that was it. Meal options: limited.

"Order me some baked ziti from Sal's," I said, deciding that if it was lunchtime, I might as well eat like it.

"Your bank account is showing insufficient funds," Zoe told me cheerily.

"Damn it. It's not October yet?" I asked.

"Today is September twenty-third, two thousand, two hundred and thirty-three. Would you like me to place the order once you receive your next basic income check?"

"Yeah, I want baked ziti a week from now," I said, rolling my eyes. Zoe started to confirm the command, but I interrupted her. "Cancel, Zoe."

"Cancelled."

Bathroom next. There was a granola bar in there, for some reason, so I ate it while pulling on a pair of jeans. I'd gone to bed in a t-shirt – a quick check in the mirror told me it was probably the least wrinkled clothing item in my apartment, so it stayed on. I washed my face quickly, dug shoes out of the clothing pile, and headed downstairs.

The day was cool and windy – the sun was out, but the air had a chill, and I belatedly remembered that it was officially autumn now. I paused at the entrance to my building for a moment, debating with myself, then stubbornly stepped out onto the sidewalk, jamming my hands in my pockets. *It's just a short walk – I don't need a damn jacket.*

I reached the corner and turned onto Montauk Highway, and saw that it had been closed to cars, with blue-painted wooden *POLICE* barriers blocking the street. Out on the three-lane asphalt, people were busily setting up awnings over plastic tables, and a ways up the road, I saw a banner proclaiming *South Shore Oktoberfest!* with a picture of beer steins on one end, and a German flag on the other.

We just had the Harvest Bash thing like a week ago. Do people have nothing better to do with themselves?

I passed a woman setting out row after row of mason jars filled with homemade jam, a man burning a design into a polished block of wood with some kind of hand-held laser, and countless other knick-knack stands and bauble stalls, their owners smiling at me imploringly. *Yeah, they've clearly got nothing better to do. Nor do I, frankly …*

To my right was a keg truck that smelled like stale beer and pumpkin spice; I ducked past it, and hurried into the government kitchen, the door jangling as I entered. The building had been some kind of physical store once, long ago: a handful of checkout lanes stood at the front of the room, empty now except for some children playing make-believe cashier with toys they had brought from home. I was surprised they even knew what the lanes were for – I only knew because we had watched a video about brick-and-mortar retail in my *History of Commerce* class.

I passed through one of the lanes, stopping to swipe

my finger on an ID reader. My face appeared in a hologram above it a moment later, and the familiar recording reminded me to eat a healthy mix of foods.

"… in the appropriate portion sizes," I finished, walking away. I had missed the lunch rush, thankfully – the line was short (yay, super-efficient robot servers), and soon I was sitting at a table by myself, staring at an appropriate portion size of chicken (lab-grown, I'm sure) heavily outnumbered by servings of brown rice and steamed kale. Low sodium, low fat, low taste. I frowned, but my stomach rumbled, betraying me, and I sighed and commenced forcing it down.

Dessert was some kind of fruitcake – yuck – so after turning my tray in to the automated dishwashing station, I swung through the serving line one more time to grab a second plate, holding the recyclable "to go" container out for the robots to fill with another meal. Dinner taken care of, I left through the back entrance, to avoid having to walk home through DepressionFest back out on the main street. The government kitchen's back lot faced a small park lined with benches and oak trees – beside a duck pond stood a white gazebo where a decent-sized crowd had gathered. At first I assumed it was something to do with the street fair, but then I heard someone with a megaphone, and the crowd chanted a response. It was a Roamer protest.

"In government!" the leader called out.

"We won't be replaced!" the crowd answered, fists pumping.

"… in healthcare!"

"We won't be replaced!" they cried.

"… in the arts!"

"We won't be replaced!"

Some people waved hand-made signs – I saw one that read *There's a reason it's called ARTIFICIAL intelligence* and another that had a big, red slash through the word *Automation*. I'd been to one of the rallies last year, when the

Roamer movement really started to pick up steam. I hadn't bothered going to another. Shouting "we're still relevant!" to nobody in particular got old fast. Nobody could explain to me the movement's goals, aside from 'getting things back to the way they had been'. Nobody at the rally could tell me a logical way to limit the growth of automation and artificial intelligence ... and *I* certainly couldn't think of one. So I didn't go back, though they kept e-mailing me for a while. Not that I wasn't mad about the way things were myself, but the whole movement just seemed pointless, like fighting to get humans to stop using electricity or indoor plumbing.

"We won't be replaced!" they answered again – I had missed whatever the leader had said this time.

"Too late," I said aloud. "We already were."

I heard a snort, and turned to see a young man leaning against the side of the kitchen. "You got that right."

I looked him over – he had brown hair and a well-trimmed beard, and under one eye I noticed a tattoo in a strange pattern of vertical lines.

"You don't seem too worried," I noted, glancing back at the rally.

"Nope. My line of business can never be outsourced."

I frowned. *What line of business is that?* I turned and studied him more closely. His gray button-down shirt had a corporate logo stitched on the breast pocket: a triangular *Play* symbol superimposed over an alien skull, with a set of crossed rifles behind it.

"Right," I said, recognizing the logo. "You're a StreaMerc."

"'Streamer,' no *c*," he corrected me. "*StreaMercs* is the company name. 'Streamer' plus 'Mercs,' as in mercenaries."

"Right, clever. So why aren't you out fighting the Octipede horde?" I asked.

"Retired," he said, smiling. There was an edge to that smile, hinting at something he wasn't telling me. "Now I'm a recruiter."

"Good luck with that," I told him, and set off toward my apartment.

* * *

I stepped inside the foyer, and then swung the front door shut behind me, turning to slide the deadbolt home. Then I paused. *Is that … someone talking in my living room?*

I kicked my shoes off, quietly, and snuck forward down the hall, one finger on my watch's emergency alert key.

"… not sure. Zoe tells me she left a half hour ago."

I relaxed as I recognized the voice – Mom. I was about to announce my presence when my dad's voice came on over the apartment speakers – they were on a voice call.

"You're sure you don't want me to stay on the line when you talk to her?" he asked.

"No," I heard Mom reply. "I think this needs to be just us girls."

Dad sighed. "You don't think I can be tough on her."

Mom was silent for a moment, which was answer enough. "She needs to hear some harsh truths. You're a great father, Jie, but you've always struggled when it comes to discipline. You'd rather be her friend than her father, sometimes."

"Maybe she needs a friend right now," Dad offered.

"Maybe she does," Mom said. "But a friend can't tell her she's wasting her life. Not like a mother can."

I'd heard enough. I turned and opened the front door again. Dad was saying something, but then I slammed the door, noisily.

Mom appeared at the end of the hall a moment later. "Hi, honey," she said, smiling. "Did you just get home?"

"Yeah, why?" I asked. We met in the hall and hugged, awkwardly. "What are you doing here, Mom?"

"I can't stop by to see my daughter? We live ten minutes away, but I barely see you."

I ignored the implication. "You didn't want to give me

a heads-up that you were coming over?" I asked instead, heading into the living room.

Mom followed and took a seat on my battered old couch. "Well, I'm sorry for the intrusion," she said. "I just wanted to talk."

"That sounds like 'talk' with a capital *T*," I said, opening the fridge and putting my takeout dinner away.

"… well, yes, it is," Mom agreed. *At least she wasn't beating around the bush.*

I took one of the wine bottles out, and closed the fridge door. "You want a glass?" I offered her.

She wrinkled her nose. "No, thank you."

"It's that or water, sorry," I told her.

"I'm fine." She watched me pour the wine into a plastic cup, and then pick up a chair from the kitchen. I set it down near the couch and took a seat. Predictably, she frowned at me as I took a sip of wine.

"It's barely afternoon. And I'm guessing you just got up a little while ago."

"So?" I said. "It's not like I slept through an important appointment or something."

"Do you drink a lot?" she asked, nodding toward the wine cup.

"I'm not one of your cases, Mom," I told her. "You can't run your social worker interview script on me."

"I can be worried about the health of my daughter," she replied.

I took another sip, then shrugged. "Drinking's expensive," I told her. "I don't have enough money to be an alcoholic."

"Mm," she said. She seemed to gather herself up, taking a deep breath. "Sam, you need to snap out of this."

"Okay," I said, and was rewarded with a look of surprise that told me she had been expecting a big fight at this point.

"You … want to change things?" Mom asked, warily.

"No, I really enjoy my life right now." I gestured

around the cramped apartment. "I'm living the dream, Mom – can't you see?"

"Okay, I can do without the sarcasm," she told me. "Sam, if you want to get your life back on track ... what are you waiting for?"

"I don't know how!" I yelled, throwing my hands in the air in frustration. Wine sloshed out of the cup, but I ignored it. "There are no jobs, I'm not going to get into any graduate programs ... what the hell else am I supposed to?"

"Start a hobby," Mom suggested.

I glared at her. "Learning how to knit isn't going to fix this. Neither is getting a dog, or playing ping pong in the rec center league, or ... whatever."

"Start your own business," Mom said. "Then you'd have a bit more money, and something to keep you occupied. Dad says you'd be great at selling vintage electronics."

"Tell Dad there are about a hundred thousand people who already do that online. I checked."

"You did?"

"Yeah, I did," I said, defensively. "Search for 'vintage electronics reseller' yourself. You're going to get page after page of hits. I don't want to spend my time writing blog posts about old junk and optimizing organic search traffic just for a few bucks in ad revenue."

"What about the boat?" Mom asked.

I crossed my arms, and looked away.

Mom sighed. "You know I hated that sport. And still do, given you're practically drowning yourself repeatedly. But somehow when you found freediving, it fit you, Sam. You were happy."

I shifted in my seat.

"You saved up for months, after graduation," she continued. "You bought the boat, the down-lines and all the other equipment ... I thought your freediving school was a great idea."

I concentrated on a spot on the wall where the paint had chipped off.

"Did you make a website or anything? Did you take the boat out for a dive on your own?"

I shook my head. "No."

"Don't you think Lucie would have wanted you to start the school, just like the two of you planned?"

That got me to look at her. "Don't bring Lucie into this."

"It's been three years, Sam. At some point, you have to move on."

"I did!" I shouted. "You're the one that keeps bringing her up."

Mom held up her hands by way of apology. I searched for something, anything, to change the subject.

"What … what about *you*, Mom? Now that you don't have your job anymore, what are you doing to keep busy?"

She frowned. "We go for walks, and meet up with friends, and … we're saving up for a trip to Europe next year."

I shook my head, silently.

"It's harder than I thought, and I do miss my job. You're right," Mom said.

"That's the big difference between us," I told her. "You *miss* your job. But at least you had one, for most of your life. You got to help people, for a while."

"There are other ways to help people, other than being a social worker, or a therapist," she told me.

"Like …?" I asked. "Name one that isn't already being done by software or machines."

She opened her mouth to speak, and then stopped. After a moment of silence, she said, "Well, I don't know. I'd have to think about it."

I drained what was left of my wine. "I've been thinking about it for two years. And I haven't figured it out yet." I stood up and gestured to the dishes in the sink, and the pile of clothes on the floor in my bedroom. "I should tidy up around here. You're welcome to stay, but …"

Mom stood hurriedly, noticeably glad to hear I was planning to clean the apartment. "No, it's fine, I'll get out of your way. But you have to promise me we can talk about this again, soon."

"Sure," I said, hugging her to avoid making eye contact. "I'll come by for dinner sometime."

"I know your father would like that," she told me. We walked to the front door, and I held it open for her. "And I *will* think about it," she said, hoping to end on a positive note, just like her playbook said to. "We'll find you something."

"Okay," I told her. "Thanks, Mom."

She headed for the stairs, and I closed the door. Zoe cranked up the lights as I came back into the living room, and I heard some upbeat dance music start on the speakers.

"I've found a playlist called 'Spring Cleaning,' " she told me, eagerly. "Your cleaning supplies are limited, but—"

"Cancel," I said, flopping onto the couch. *I'm not fucking cleaning up, Zoe. That would imply I cared.*

My VR set was hanging from a cradle next to the couch – I picked up the helmet and slid it on over my head. The glistening black plastic encased my head fully – my vision went dark, and the hum of my fridge and the *drip-drip-drip* of my bathroom sink disappeared. Then I heard the startup chime in my ears, and the *Life, Augmented* motto appeared on screen. I lay back on the couch, propping a pillow behind my head.

If your reality sucks, I thought, *change your reality.*

CHAPTER 4

"This conjunction of an immense military establishment and a large arms industry is new in the American experience […] we must guard against the acquisition of unwarranted influence – whether sought or unsought, by the military-industrial complex. The potential for the disastrous rise of misplaced power exists, and will persist."

-President Dwight D. Eisenhower, January 17th, 1961 Farewell Speech

S earch freediving," I said, and Zoe connected with my VR set and pulled up a list of freediving videos, which appeared as a translucent menu superimposed over the white plaster ceiling of my apartment – which is what I would have been looking at, had I not had the VR set on.

"Nobody livestreaming. How about new ones, then?" I asked. The list rearranged itself, and I recognized the logo of a diver who posted fairly often – an Italian guy, who dove the Med. I reached up a hand and touched the air where the video would have been, and the video expanded to fill my whole field of view.

He started in the water, bobbing in the waves next to a boat, the view rocking gently. A man leaned over the edge of the boat and hollered something – in Italian, I suppose, but I had translations turned off (subtitles just ruin the VR experience – they yank you right out of things). Then I heard the diver start his preparation routine, taking several deep, purging breaths. Then, leisurely, he slipped his head underwater, clipped his lanyard onto the line, pointed his arms into the depths, and began his dive.

The water was electric blue, and he descended through vertical shafts of sunlight, spearing into the ocean in parallel with the rope that guided his path. Almost immediately, sets of numbers appeared in the upper corners of the display, mirroring what the diver would have been seeing in his own mask: on the left, the depth in meters; on the right, the dive time, counting up from zero. At the thirty second mark I spied a marker on the line – he had passed twenty-five meters. *He's taking his time, doing it right,* I thought. Though the aim of freediving is always to go deeper, and stay down longer, how you achieve that is counter-intuitive: a diver swimming as fast as she can will quickly exhaust herself and return to the surface. The tortoise beats the hare every time in freediving – it's a competition to see who can achieve the most control over their own subconscious body functions, not who is the fastest or strongest swimmer. That, and who's willing to push themselves right up to the edge of losing consciousness, a hundred meters underwater.

He passed the fifty meter flag, and now the water was getting noticeably darker, the sun struggling to penetrate the water above. I realized, with a start, that I had been holding my own breath since the beginning of the dive. I shook my head and inhaled, feeling my pulse racing. The last of the twilight disappeared on screen, and now the only thing to be seen was the down line, glowing faintly in the gloom. It slid past, as the diver pushed his way deeper into the abyss. A glowing blur appeared in the distance – another depth marker. As he approached, the letters resolved: *seventy-five meters*. I felt a sudden tightness in my chest, as if I was being slowly crushed under the weight of a massive rock.

"Exit," I said, my voice higher-pitched, trembling.

My apartment ceiling appeared again, along with the menu of videos. I sat for a moment, just waiting for my heart to stop pounding. *Fuck this. I can't. I try, but every time ... I just can't.* Then a notification appeared on screen – an ad.

>>>*Lock and load! The next battle with the Ochos is starting now! Join the livestream in 5 ... 4 ... 3 ... (sponsored by StreaMercs©)*

I was about to dismiss it, but my curiosity got the better of me. It had been a long time since I'd tuned in to a battle. I knew the war was still going on, of course – everyone did. At that point, it was still fresh and exciting, it had that new war smell and everything. For the past two years, all of humanity had been watching the war's progress with bated breath.

After those explorers made first contact – and were summarily slaughtered – out on Bohr-Steiner III, it took a month or so for us to figure out how to respond. That first day, as the alert sirens wailed, Paul and Remy and I (along with the rest of the crowd back at The Dive) had shuffled outside and stood around for a while, wondering where the hell the nearest nuclear fallout shelter was. Apparently, no one knew. So we stared up at the sky instead, watching for UFOs. Eventually another global alert came out, essentially saying "our bad – no real danger here on Earth, just go home." So we headed home. It was a fairly anticlimactic start to a war, in retrospect.

Meanwhile, over on Bohr-Steiner III, the ship that had made contact sent several robots down to the surface, and further investigation by this second, much more cautious group of sentries showed us that the Octipedes were vicious fighters, but they were not high-functioning intellectuals, to put it mildly. How the Ochos had become a multi-planetary species, we still didn't know – as best we can tell, they had once lived in close proximity to a far more advanced civilization. But that alien race is extinct, and the Ochos now inhabit their abandoned planets. Experts think that perhaps the Ochos were domesticated animals (pets, or even a food source) for this other, more advanced species, before turning on their masters and slaughtering them wholesale. All signs point to the extinct race being far more advanced technologically than humans, so we had a healthy respect for the Ochos' warfighting ability from the get-go.

But we had an overpopulation problem, and they had valuable real estate, with natural resources that we needed (ore and stuff, I think). Maybe there were even some super high-tech gizmos from the extinct aliens that we could find (spoiler alert: there weren't). Plus, the Ochos had attacked us, and sure seemed willing to attack us again. Who knew what would happen if we just left them alone? Maybe they were capable of rapidly evolving, and figuring out rocket technology, and invading Earth. Maybe they had interstellar flight capabilities already, and just hadn't chosen to use it for some unfathomable alien reason. In the end, there was never really a question: we had to fight, to protect the human race and our interests. Kill the aliens and take their stuff, before they did the same to us.

At the time, the combat forces of Earth's various nations had been disbanded for nearly half a century – after first contact, the best we could have mustered on short notice was a ragtag band of law enforcement officers, most of whom hadn't picked up a lethal weapon since their initial training, years before. So we fielded robots, of course. And the robots did ... well, great. They tore through the Ochos just like we programmed 'em too. But they cost an arm and a leg, and we were quickly running out of them, and there were still a lot of Ochos. Once we located a third planet inhabited by several thousand Ochos, somebody finally did the math and realized that continuing this war would cost so much that they'd have to cut back on universal basic income to pay for it. And nobody wanted that.

But there's no problem capitalism can't solve. Somebody came up with the idea to field a human force, and equip them with cameras, and turn it into a live event, that people could pay to watch. Hence: StreaMercs and their heroic, hugely lucrative volunteers who came to be known as deathstreamers. And *everyone* watched those first battles, me included. With most of the world (and colonists on other worlds) watching, those first streamers were killing it, money-wise. Avery used to brag to me that he could make ten grand just by doing a five minute walk-through of the *Final Hope's* cargo bays, back in those days. They were patriots and war heroes and movie stars all wrapped up in one.

In my VR set, I picked a deathstreamer feed at random (some guy called *Howler69*), and saw the famous StreaMercs crest – for the second time that day – with its crossed rifles and Octipede skull. It spun around its vertical axis, then zoomed toward me suddenly, disappearing. Then I was watching the live feed. This streamer was already in the thick of it – he was breathing heavily, running somewhere, and I saw a bright orange plasma beam lance across his field of view from left to right. He threw himself on the ground, and all I could see was black gravel for a moment, though an inset window showed me a view of his sweating face. After a moment of staring at the extra-terrestrial dirt, he looked up again, and I got a better view of the battle.

The human forces appeared to be on top of a small hill. Ahead of the streamer, a hastily dug trench had been carved out of the black soil. Beyond that, I could see a volcanic debris field, littered with craggy boulders, on which was growing a bright orange lichen of some kind. The debris field was teeming with Ochos, ducking and weaving among the big rocks as they ran toward the human defensive position.

"I gotta get to that trench, guys!" Howler gasped, as another Ocho plasma bolt streaked past him. He glanced behind him, and I saw the massive circular terminus of the space elevator, which had been thrust into the ground like a giant flagpole, staking our claim to the planet. "Shit. Here I go!"

He stood, and I found myself holding my breath as he ran, the view jostling with each pounding step. He brought his rifle up and fired just before he reached the trench, and I saw an Ocho fall on the far side of the trench, convulsing. Then he leapt down into the trench, landing between two other streamers.

"Fuck!" he gasped. "Where's Skip?" The view swung around, as he looked down both sides of the trench. "Guys, where's Skipper?"

The streamer next to him slammed another magazine into his rifle and stood up, firing a burst into the onrushing Ochos. "Haven't seen Skip," he shouted. "But we could use another e-rifle on the line here."

"Damn it," my streamer replied. He put his rifle over the lip of the trench and fired several bursts at Ochos down among the boulders. "Skip's fans said he went down at six o'clock."

Six o'clock? I checked the time in the heads-up display, but it was nowhere close to six o'clock local time on whatever planet they were on. Then I spied the comment section of the screen, where viewers were sending messages to Howler. I'm not sure how he could possibly read any of them: they were streaming in constantly, by the hundreds (not to mention the fact that he was currently taking aim at Ochos several hundred meters away), but my eye caught several suggesting that the streamer move to his right, closer to the six-thirty position.

Oh … it's a directional thing. The area they're defending is circular, like a clock, with the elevator at its center. Something about the elevator's orientation must indicate twelve o'clock to them.

"Okay, guys, thanks for the heads-up, I'm moving." Somehow Howler had picked that same information out of the comments, and he ducked back down, jogging down the trench, dodging several other streamers along the way. He stopped and checked his bearing once, and then again, and then stopped, peering out over the rim of the trench. He seemed to spot something, though I missed whatever it was.

"Motherfucker. Are you guys serious?" He shook his head, and I saw him frowning beneath his short blonde hair. Like the recruiter I had seen earlier, he had a tattoo on one cheek – I realized it was some kind of barcode.

Howler put his back to the outer trench wall and let himself slide down into a squat. He reloaded his rifle, splitting his attention between that and staring into the camera pointed toward his face.

"Okay, first off – whoever told me Skipper was at six o'clock, fuck you very much. There's a big difference between six and six-thirty, asshole. Which you would know if you weren't a mouth-breathing troll sitting back on your mom's couch, stuffing your face with bacon chips and candy cola while I save the human race. Second, you kind of forgot to mention that Skip got hit *outside the lines*! Jesus fucking Christ. I see him, but he's like thirty meters downslope." He finished reloading his weapon, and checked the chamber briefly.

"So here's what we're gonna do," he said. "Skip's vitals are still hanging in there. I know Skip's fans want me to go get him, and they've offered a pretty decent bounty if I do. But I gotta take care of my fans. So WolfPack, what do you say? Is your boy Howler gonna go bail Skip out, or let somebody else take care of it? Vote – you got twenty seconds."

A voting button appeared on the comments section of

the screen, and almost immediately a chart appeared below it, showing the results. I would have voted to go out there and get Skip, but the point was moot – Howler's fans overwhelmingly agreed with me.

Howler closed the vote after ten seconds. "Okay, okay, I get it. Should know better than to ask stupid questions – given the choice, you guys always want to see me get my ass shot off. Here we fucking go, you goddamn sadists."

Almost immediately, the comments section exploded with activity again, and I noticed that a large number of comments were notifications that viewers had "tipped" Howler in various monetary amounts – they were rewarding him, literally, for listening to them.

Howler hauled himself up on to the top of the trench again, sent a tight burst of rounds into an Octipede that emerged from the side of one of the boulders, and then ran downhill.

"Awoooooo!" he yelled, doing what I suppose was his imitation of a wolf. Again, the tip notifications poured in – his fans were eating this up.

I spotted Skipper's legs near the base of one of the boulders – Howler reached him shortly, puffing and panting. He knelt next to the prostrated streamer, chased an Ocho back behind cover with another burst of fire, and then turned Skipper over onto his stomach.

"Ow," Howler said, noting a deep, semi-circular wound along Skipper's right hip. The edges of the wound were blackened and burned, the flesh underneath cauterized. "I bet that stings, huh?"

Skipper did not reply – whether his communications equipment was broken or he had passed out in shock, I could not tell. Howler swept the battlefield with his rifle one more time, then bent and muscled Skipper onto his back in a fireman's carry.

"Anyone in the six, seven o'clock area, some covering fire would be appreciated. Friendly coming in with wounded."

I heard a few other streamers acknowledge Howler, and then he was up and moving again, though far more slowly this time, laboring to get Skipper back up the steep slope. An Ocho appeared in his peripheral vision briefly, its forearms raised aloft, preparing to fire, but a stream of tracers converged on it, and Howler ran on. A plasma beam passed close overhead – a near miss. At the top of the slope, Howler did not stop at the trench, but crossed it using a narrow metal footbridge that spanned the fortification.

"You brought half the Ochos with you!" a streamer below him yelled, firing repeatedly in the direction he had come from.

"Sorry!" Howler replied. "You guys got this?"

"We got it, go!"

Howler leapt off the bridge and back onto the ground. His breathing was becoming labored now, and a grimace settled over his face. But he didn't stop running, and ahead, I could see the elevator itself, completing its descent down to the surface. A wave of fresh streamers disembarked down the elevator's ramps as it touched down – Howler plowed through them.

"Evac, coming through! Get the fuck out of the way!"

He almost tripped at the top of the ramp, but managed to steady himself with a hand on the elevator's deck plates, and carefully set the unconscious Skipper down on his back. I sighed with relief. The comments feed exploded again – this time, a number of viewers with a different logo (Skipper's, I guess?) sent hundreds of tips, making good on the bounty they had promised for saving their favorite streamer.

"Thanks, guys." Howler twisted his neck and took several deep sips out of a clear plastic tube mounted near his face.

"All streamers be advised: Ochos are massing near the six o'clock position," a robotic voice announced over Howler's speakers.

"Yup, that was me – my bad." He patted Skipper on the leg. "Hang in there, bud. I'll see you back up in orbit, y'hear?"

Then he was back on his feet. He grabbed a bandolier of ammunition hanging from a resupply cabinet, and headed down the ramp, back into the fray.

I slipped the VR set off to run to the bathroom about two hours later, and then ran back to the couch, worried I had missed something. About two hours after that I realized I was starving hungry, so I shoveled down the leftover meal with the helmet pushed up on my forehead, intermittently sneaking a bite and slipping the helmet back on to catch a glimpse of the action. Otherwise I didn't take my VR helmet off until nearly two in the morning, when Howler finally lay down to catch some rest in the trench. It took me nearly an hour to fall asleep, lying in my bed, staring up at the ceiling, the adrenaline still coursing through my body.

I was hooked.

CHAPTER 5

"Have you always wanted to be a part of something special, something bigger than yourself? Do you have what it takes to build a fan base, and earn millions in revenue? We'll fly you there, train you, and equip you; all you have to do is fight. The fate of humanity rests in your hands … and all of humanity is watching. Recruiters are standing by: click here to be contacted now."

-Excerpted from the *Join Up!* section of the StreaMercs.com website

I stood, leaning against the side of the building, watching cylindrical sanitation robots scour Montauk Highway of crushed beer cans and discarded Oktoberfest napkins from the previous night's festivities. The red brick wall, which had been soaking up the early morning sun, was warm against my back. Then the door next to me swung open. The StreaMercs recruiter propped it wide with a rubber stopper, then straightened up and noticed me standing there.

"Oh – hey, you again." He was wearing another

button-down shirt with the StreaMercs logo. "You were waiting on me to open?" he asked.

I hesitated for a moment. "Yeah," I said.

If he was surprised or amused, he didn't show it. Apparently people stalked him routinely. "Cool. Come on in."

The office was small, with a window overlooking the street, a desk with two padded chairs facing it, and a large holographic projection behind the desk, showing a number of different charts and graphs in a complicated dashboard. I had seen it through the window while waiting for him to open up – on the left was a list of streamer nicknames, along with some of their key stats: number of battles, kill count, and lifetime revenue earned. The biggest earners were sorted to the top – it was a revenue leaderboard. I hadn't failed to notice that two of the top five earners' names were in red text, denoting that they were now dead. In the upper right quadrant, a star map showed the location of the *Final Hope*, the starship the StreaMercs flew to battle on – it was currently attached to a planet labeled *Shaw's Anchorage* via its integrated space elevator. In the lower right quadrant was an infographic with multiple different symbols, which showed me at a glance that nearly all of the streamers were currently deployed on the surface. They had last been in contact with Octipede forces approximately an hour ago, and were currently conducting a tactical operation called *Movement to Contact*, though I had no clue what that entailed.

But dominating the room and my attention – by design, I assumed – were two figures flanking the recruiter's desk: on the left side stood a life-size model of an Octipede, forearms held aloft menacingly. On the right was a streamer – or at least, a streamer suit, though I wasn't sure whether to call it a spacesuit or a suit of armor. The suit held a long-barreled rifle across its chest, and a pistol was strapped to its thigh.

"I'm Rolfe," the recruiter said, shaking my hand

warmly.

"Sam," I told him.

"Take a seat," he said. "Unless you want to strap in for a VR session?" he asked.

I glanced behind me, and realized the other half of the room held a state-of-the-art VR set – unlike my cheapo version at home, this one was a full-body suit, suspended in a large gyroscope. I had tried one of those models in a store, once – instead of just being able to see and hear what's happening in the feed, you can feel some of it, too – when the streamer moves, you move with him or her, and when they feel heat or cold or impacts, the suit can simulate those, too. I wondered, idly, what it felt like for the viewer when the streamer got wounded.

"We have troops on the ground right now, but they're not fighting, there's a bit of a lull," Rolfe told me. "But I can load up a recording; we've got a great highlight reel if you want to check it out."

I shook my head. "No, thanks."

"Okay," Rolfe shrugged. He sat behind the desk, and I took my own seat. "Some battle last night, huh? Howler went on quite a streak for a minute there."

I wasn't surprised that he knew I had been watching – this is the twenty-third century. Companies that don't aggressively track everything about their customers get beaten to a pulp by companies that do. And StreaMercs was a cutting-edge tech company – Rolfe had pretended to be surprised to see me, but he had probably walked in this morning to find a readout of all the battles I'd ever watched along with a detailed recommendation for what messages would best appeal to me as a recruit. That's just good business.

"Yeah, the battle was exciting," I allowed. "It got me thinking about things."

"I know the feeling," Rolfe said. "I was sitting on that side of the desk not so long ago myself, probably thinking the same kinds of things. If you've got questions, that's why I'm here."

"What made you want to join up?" I asked.

He exhaled, and leaned back in his chair. "Money. Fame. Adventure. All of the usual stuff. Why are you interested?"

"I'm not sure I am," I hedged.

"You're here, aren't you?" he pointed out. He leaned forward again. "I'm going to level with you. Having fans and making money is great, no question. But that's the icing on the cake. I signed on the dotted line because I was tired of moping around all day, doing nothing with my life. I was tired of feeling like I was going to be stuck on the bench for this game we call 'life.' "

I locked eyes with him. "And did being a streamer change that? Did you feel different?"

"Oh, yeah. Without a doubt."

"So why are you back here?" I asked. I jutted my chin at the holographic board. "The war's still on – why retire?"

"Who said anything about retiring?" he asked. "I'm just catching a little R and R, and StreaMercs asked me to do some recruiting, part time. Earn a little extra cash while I rest up." He rubbed at his forearm, and for the first time, I noticed a scar. It was thin, like a shiny pink bracelet; a perfect circle around his arm. *Limb reattachment*, I realized. *He lost his arm, and they sewed it back on.*

"So … tell me about yourself," Rolfe said, smiling again. "What kind of social presence do you have today?"

I shifted in my chair. "I used to have a decent number of followers back in college. I was a freediver – I would stream competitions."

"Define 'a decent number,' " Rolfe said, crossing his hands across his chest.

"I don't know – two or three thousand?"

Rolfe's frown deepened. "Hm. And I'm guessing you weren't talking while you were streaming? Chatting with viewers, narrating what was happening, that kind of thing?"

"No," I said. "It's ... I was underwater."

Rolfe sighed. "StreaMercs isn't like the old Earth militaries, where you could walk into a recruiter's office and just sign up. StreaMercs has standards, high ones. While you can certainly build it out once you start, the company prefers that you bring your own platform."

"My own ... platform?" I asked.

"Fan base," Rolfe clarified. "I used to do 'How To' videos before I joined up, and had a few hundred thousand subscribers. So when I started as a streamer, I brought a lot of those fans over to StreaMercs, too – because I turned my StreaMercs channel into a 'How To' series, about how to become a streamer."

"Oh," I said. "Well, I don't ... I don't have a platform."

"Like I said, not a prerequisite," Rolfe told me. "You can submit an audition instead."

"What does an audition look like?" I asked.

"Show me Sam's freediving channel," Rolfe said, and the dashboard behind him went blank for a moment, then showed a list of videos that I had shot in college. "I'm just going to pick one at random, and then you can talk to me as if I'm a viewer."

"Right now?"

Rolfe laughed. "Yeah, right now. Every battle you stream is live, you don't get to go back and add commentary afterwards. You gotta be entertaining in the moment, under pressure, *in combat*. Now ... go," he said.

A video started playing – Lucie and I were standing side-by-side on a boat, and then she jumped in. In the recording, I whooped and followed her.

My audition was a disaster. Think of the most stilted *this is what you're seeing on screen* documentary narration ever, and then imagine the narrator was also fighting off a panic attack because of the video's subject matter. Rolfe stopped me before the dive was halfway through, thank god.

"That was certainly ... *interesting* ... though not,

perhaps, in the way you intended," he said. "Less of an action-packed car chase, and more of a slow motion car wreck that you can't stop watching."

I grimaced. "Sorry," I said. "I don't know if I can do this." I put my hands on the chair's armrests, preparing to leave.

"... but maybe it was just nerves," Rolfe said. "You want to try one of our standard auditions, instead?"

I took a deep breath. "Okay."

A pile of holographic bricks appeared on the desk. Rolfe told me to build "something that showcased my personality," and then let me loose again. I decided to throw caution to the wind, and figured I better get personal. I talked about what had brought me into the office that morning, and how I wasn't sure I even wanted to do this, but I was sure I was sick of doing nothing. And I rehashed, in excruciating detail, just how badly I had done on my first audition.

"... and that's why, even though this audition feels like it isn't quite as much of a flaming dumpster falling off a cliff, StreaMercs is probably gonna reject me, anyway," I said, finishing my brick creation and revealing it with a lame flourish. It was a large fist, flipped upside down, balancing on the tip of the thumb: a giant, thumbs-down rejection symbol.

Rolfe chuckled. "Better," he said. "I think we better submit that one, rather than your first one. But before we submit anything, I gotta go through some disclosure stuff with you. Red tape, you know?"

"You need me to sign a contract?"

"Yeah," he said. "But it's contingent on your audition being accepted, and it doesn't go into force until you step onto the shuttle to rendezvous with the *Final Hope*, which won't be for a few weeks, at least. So any time up until that point, you can change your mind and back out, with no obligations. If you decide you don't want to go, just don't get on the shuttle. Easy."

"Okay," I said.

Rolfe put his hands on the desk's wooden surface, and a keyboard illuminated beneath his fingers, while a holographic screen appeared facing him. He typed for a moment.

"Okay, standard contract," he said, exhaling noisily. "First up: initial equipment draw and transit costs."

"I know about that," I said.

"Great, but I'm still required by law to read it to you, sorry," Rolfe said. "In order to join StreaMercs, you will be charged an enlistment fee. Please note: StreaMercs is *not* a pyramid scheme – the vast majority of its revenue is derived from advertising, sales of goods and services on board the *Final Hope*, and transaction fees for payments that fans send to streamers. However, the cost of equipping and transporting a single streamer into battle is prohibitive, and many streamers do not live long enough for the company to recoup their costs. Accordingly, you will be required to pay a sum of twenty-thousand dollars upon officially contracting with StreaMercs."

Rolfe turned from the screen to face me, and stopped reading for a moment. "That's a big chunk of change, I know. If you don't have the cash now, we can put you on the layaway plan, like most people. You'll just defer your start date by a couple months, and send your basic income during that time directly to StreaMercs. Move in with a friend, eat government food, minimize spending, etc."

"I have a boat," I said. "A twenty-two foot Boston whaler with dual outboards. Not even two years old."

Rolfe raised an eyebrow and turned back to the screen. "Yeah, trade-ins are possible, subject to a processing fee." He typed again, and then nodded at a fingerprint scanner mounted in the desktop. "Scan."

I put my finger on it, and it glowed blue for a moment.

"I see the boat title ... we'll need to send an appraiser around to take a peek, but otherwise that should cover your fee," Rolfe said.

"Do I need to get a physical done or something? Take a fitness test?"

Rolfe shook his head. "Naw, no fitness test. I just need you to authorize StreaMercs to access your medical records."

He looked at me expectantly, and I cleared my throat, speaking up for the microphones in the room. "I authorize StreaMercs to access my medical records."

"Great," Rolfe said. "Now we just need to get you a tag."

"What?" I asked.

"Your streamertag," Rolfe said. "Your handle, you know? The name your fans are going to call you. Puns are popular right now, but it doesn't have to be funny or even make sense, it's up to you. Guys usually pick something macho, like ... I dunno, Crusher or Bulldog, girls tend to pick something sexy or sassy, like PuckerUp or DeathKitty. Something funny or eye-catching. Something memorable."

"What was your tag?" I asked him, stalling for time.

"ROFLRolfe," he said.

I smiled, then put my chin in my hand, thinking. "I don't know."

"Try to think of something that symbolizes who you want to be as a streamer. Maybe a hero from a book, or a movie ...," he suggested.

"How about 'Ripley'?" I asked.

Rolfe laughed. "Retro, I like it. But there's already a Ripley, sorry."

I scoured my brain for other famous female heroes. *Diana Prince? A little obscure. Maybe go historical, like Joan of Arc?*

"How about Valkyrie?" I asked, looking up.

"Nice," Rolfe said. He typed it into the database. "Aw, taken already." He squinted at the screen. "Actually, I stand corrected: there aren't any active Valkyries left. You can have Valkyrie6, if you want it."

"Why six?" I asked.

"Because the first five Valkyries are dead," Rolfe said, matter-of-factly. He reached out into the air, and "pushed" the holographic screen so that it was facing me. "This is your contract ... just sign here."

I held my finger up over the glowing document. "I don't have to take an oath or something?"

"No oath," Rolfe confirmed. "This isn't an enlistment, it's a business contract, establishing you as a freelance contractor working for the StreaMercs corporation."

"And I can back out any time?" I asked.

"Any time before you get on that shuttle," Rolfe said, nodding.

I paused for a moment longer, and then swirled my fingertip over the signature line, drawing a big *S* followed by a bunch of squiggles. "What happens now?"

"I send you a copy of this," Rolfe said, swiveling the screen back to face him. "And your audition tape gets reviewed by the Selection Committee. You'll get their decision in a couple hours or so."

"And if I'm picked?"

"Then when the *Final Hope* makes its next trip back here – within the next month, depending on how fast they wrap up fighting on Shaw's Anchorage – you'll get a shuttle assignment via e-mail, and then you'll join her up in orbit."

Rolfe extended a hand – his *reattached* hand – across the desk, smiling, and I took it.

"Good luck!" he said.

"Maybe I'll see you up there," I told him. "If I decide to get on the shuttle."

"Maybe," he agreed.

I stood up, but turned back to face the desk again. "Yesterday, outside, you said this was the one job robots could never take away from humans," I said.

"Uh huh," he agreed.

"Why?" I asked. "We could send another robot army

up there if we really wanted to."

"Sure, but who'd pay for it?" Rolfe asked. "Nobody's going to pay to watch robots fight a war – it'd be as boring as watching robots play baseball. No, people only pay to watch their fellow humans fight because the stakes are way higher. This is the only job where we can do something the robots can't ever do."

"Die," I said, finishing the thought.

"Yup," Rolfe agreed. "We can die. Ave, Imperator, morituri te salutant."

"Is that Italian?" I asked.

"Latin," Rolfe said. "The Roman gladiators were rumored to have said it before their contests. 'Hail, Emperor: those who are about to die salute you.' "

CHAPTER 6

"Let's ride!"

-Cosmonaut Yuri Gagarin, at the launch of *Vostok 1*,
April 12, 1961

I got on the shuttle.

Eventually, at least. Less than an hour after I got
home from the recruiting office, my watch buzzed
with a message from StreaMercs corporate:

>>>*You passed your audition! Congratulations. Here are some
helpful FAQ docs you might want to read. Stand by for your shuttle
assignment, don't forget to pack your toothbrush (and remember: you
can back out at any time).*

I honestly still wasn't sure, so I spent some time
thinking about it. I was scared, no question. But this was a
challenge, something where I could make a real difference
– saving mankind! – and make some loot, too. Just
knowing that I had the opportunity to do something new
energized me, and gave me a new perspective on things. I
actually cleaned my apartment, for once.

The next weekend, I went outside for a walk to clear

my head, and found some cheerful artisans setting up stalls on the street for *Halloween Fest*, while the same group of disgruntled Roamers protested aimlessly next door in the park. That's when I knew I had to go. The hardest part was telling my parents.

Dad took it well, surprising me. He was sad, and more than a little worried, but he seemed to understand, and after I had answered all of his questions, he let me be. Mom … yeah. Mom tried to talk me out of it, and when that didn't work, she refused to talk to me at all. The way she saw it, I was just auctioning off my life for an unlikely (and probably very brief) shot at fame and fortune. Which was … fair, I guess … though it glossed over a lot of nuance. And completely missed the fact that my life was relatively worthless, at least in my eyes, at that point. Better to risk my life and make something worthwhile out of it.

The StreaMercs' mop-up on Shaw's Anchorage took two and a half weeks. Ten days after that, the *Final Hope* completed its deceleration out past the moon, and arrived in orbit over Earth. An e-mail hit my watch that morning with my shuttle ticket, and I felt a shiver of excitement run up my spine.

"All right, Zoe," I said, zipping up my suitcase. "I'm out of here. Keep a close eye on things while I'm gone."

"I'm not sure how to accomplish that request, Sam — can you please clarify?"

Good old Zoe.

I flipped off the lights and stood in the foyer for a moment, just listening to the familiar background noises of my apartment – the hum of the fridge, the drip of the sink in the bathroom. Then I smiled, shut the door, and headed down to the street, my suitcase bumping down each step behind me.

I had the cab take me to my folks' place first. Dad was out in the front yard, trying to seat a tattered old scarecrow on the swing he had installed for me under a branch of the oak tree. I spotted a cluster of pumpkins on either side of the front door, and a stack of cornstalks on the lawn, ready to be tied to the porch railing. Dad looked up and saw me step out of the cab, and noted the suitcase on the back seat. He let go of the grinning scarecrow and it flopped forward onto the ground, face-planting. It would have been comical, except for the expression on Dad's face.

We went and stood on the porch, and Mom came outside. Just to keep me guessing, my parents seemed to have decided to reverse roles from our earlier conversations about my decision to become a streamer. Dad cried a little and told me he loved me, but that there was no shame in staying here, in not fighting. Then he clammed up, and excused himself and walked briskly inside, sniffling.

"He's trying to be supportive, but he loves you so much, and it's hard," Mom told me.

"I know. I'm sorry for making it hard for you guys," I said, and meant it.

Mom hugged me with a sigh, and then stood back, inspecting me. She chucked me under the chin with her thumb and forefinger.

"My headstrong daughter," she said, clucking her tongue.

"Where do you think I get it from?" I asked.

"Mm. Just because I'm seeing you off doesn't mean I forgive you. I'm still not going to watch your stream, you know," she said.

"I figured," I said.

"But I expect great things out of you, if this is what you truly want."

"It is," I said. *I think.*

"Then commit to it," she urged me. "Give it your all."

"Okay," I said.

Another hug. "I love you, Sam."

"Love you too, Mom." I said, and then turned to leave.

I walked back across the lawn to the cab, my feet rustling through the dried leaves, and paused with one foot in the car to look back at the house. Mom was still watching me from the porch, but she didn't say anything more. I kind of expected her to, but she just watched, as if imprinting the moment into her memory. I didn't know what to say, either, so I got in and the door slid shut. The cab started up. I waved, and then the house slid past and disappeared, the scarecrow still abandoned on the grass where Dad had dropped him.

The rest of the day was a blur. Hypertube into New York City, then another cab took me to the hoverferry terminal, and soon we were slipping out to sea between Brooklyn and Staten Island, skimming the waves and dodging the hulking container ships that clogged New York's outer harbor. Around the time the tallest of Manhattan's skyscrapers disappeared from view astern, a new structure appeared off the bow: the shuttle, aimed skyward on its floating launch pad.

We're a multi-planetary species now, with hypersonic travel by air or tube that can whisk one from Omaha to Osaka in a matter of hours, but most humans never leave the hundred miles or so around their hometown. Why fly to Venice when you can strap on a VR set and take a gondola ride down the Grand Canal from the comfort of your couch? Fewer still go up in space, and most of those who do work for Stellarus, the mega-corp that runs the lion's share of interplanetary shipping, exploration, and colonization operations. That included me, now – StreaMercs was owned by Stellarus, which made me a Stellarus employee, too. Either way, it was my first time going offworld.

The hoverferry slowed as it neared the launch pad, and settled down off of its airjets into the waves, the silky smooth ride suddenly becoming choppy. A moment later we were docked at the launch pad, and I followed the stream of passengers off the boat and into a covered tunnel that led to a set of sliding doors and a wide, square room, lined with windows, a thick column at each corner of the room. When all of the ferry passengers had reached the room, the doors slid shut behind us.

Umm ... okay? I thought. *I guess this is the waiting area? Nice of them to put seats or ... anything in here.*

Then the room lurched, and I realized the entire thing was an elevator. We rose up, paralleling the rocket, which stood several hundred feet away, venting a white gas out of the nacelles at the vehicle's base. A robotic arm detached a fuel line from the side of the rocket as I watched, and then the elevator reached its zenith, and stopped. The sliding doors on the opposite side of the room opened, showing a wide bridge that led to the rocket's nose cone. I followed the other passengers. Many of them wore Stellarus uniforms, but peppered in the group were a handful of other folks in civilian clothes – streamers, I assumed, like me. I craned my neck, but saw no sign of Rolfe.

We didn't walk into the rocket – instead, by means of a massive set of machinery, the shuttle had extended its entire passenger compartment out into the boarding bridge. It looked like one of those open-seat roller coasters, with parallel rows of chairs mounted atop a thick robotic arm that was partially hidden in a trench in the bridge's floor. I saw a number of passengers placing their luggage on conveyor belts at the edges of the bridge. I followed suit, watching as my bag zipped away to disappear into the bowels of the ship. I picked a seat near the front and strapped in, fumbling with the clasp on my five-point harness for a moment before cinching it tight. When everyone was seated, a warning chime sounded, and then the entire contraption slid forward, into the ship. As we passed the outer hull, the seats tilted back, until we were facing straight up. I heard a loud, reassuring *CHUNK* as something locked into place. Then the hatch closed, and my heart started to race.

Holy shit! Astronaut Sam, go for launch. This is crazy.

A hologram appeared in front of us (or above us, I guess?) and they showed us a brief safety video, summarized thusly: don't get out of your seats, 'kay? Then we heard a distant roar, things started to shake, and the view on the hologram changed to a split-screen showing multiple camera angles. On the left was a feed from somewhere down on the launch pad, showing the full length of the rocket. In the middle was the shuttle's view looking forward, straight up into the blue sky, and on the right was a camera that must have been mounted somewhere near the hatch, pointing down at the ground.

A flash lit the left screen, and fire and smoke billowed out of the rocket's engines, quickly blanking out that camera. We were airborne, the acceleration pinning me to my seat, the launch pad shrinking to nothing below us. I glimpsed the south shore of Long Island, briefly, and wondered if my parents were watching the launch. Then we passed through a bank of clouds, and soon after, the rattling smoothed out, and I felt the fluid rush out of my legs. My hair floated into view, startling me, and my stomach did a nervous flip as it realized that gravity was no longer present.

The shuttle maneuvered, changing its attitude, and on the forward-looking screen, we spotted Northwest Station, a massive geostationary facility that served as the primary connection point between all interstellar traffic and Earth's northern hemisphere. The station had started as a modest, rod-shaped design and, over the course of a century, humans gradually tacked on more compartments to add length to its central axis, while slapping long docking arms perpendicular to it at random intervals. It looked like a hyperactive kindergartener had been handed glue, an empty paper towel roll, and a bunch of straws, and then told to go nuts.

We docked. Compared to the launch, it was pretty dull. But I couldn't help grinning when our seat harnesses released, and I rose up into the air, floating for the first time. Apparently I wasn't the only one enjoying the weightlessness – I spotted a paunchy kid about my age across the compartment spinning himself slowly in place. He caught me watching him and smiled self-consciously.

Our luggage was waiting for us outside the docking tube, held by robotic arms in rows along the edges of the white fabric-lined compartment. I found my suitcase and pried it loose, and then realized its wheels and extendable handle were worse than useless in the present environment. *The things they don't think to put in the welcome pamphlet.* I grabbed it by one of the side handles and tugged it along behind me, slowly figuring out a workable method of navigating: pull myself forward using a handle mounted along the wall / ceiling / floor of the tube, drift for a bit, correct my course when I bump into another wall / ceiling / floor, then push off again, trailing the suitcase behind me.

I paused instinctively at the hatch to the central axis of the station, peering over the lip apprehensively: from my perspective, the axis looked like a deep shaft, plunging hundreds of feet down. *Whoa.* I could see various travelers and crewmen floating up and down the wide tunnel – even some above me – but it was still hard to convince myself to let go of the handle in one hand. Then something bumped into my back.

"Oof!"

I turned – it was the guy from the shuttle, who had an oversized backpack strapped to his back. His momentum caused his head to bump into the ceiling and he rubbed it, chagrined.

"Sorry for bumping into you," he said.

"That's okay," I said.

He was wearing a strange outfit – a white silk shirt with puffy sleeves under a leather vest that looked to be handmade. At first I thought it was a pirate outfit.

"Are you a streamer, too?" he asked.

"Yup," I said. I held out a hand. "Sam. Uh, Valkyrie6 is my tag."

"Arliss," he replied shaking my hand warmly. "That's

my name. My tag's OldSchool." He gestured at his archaic wardrobe, as if that explained everything. "You lost, too?" he asked.

"Guess so," I said.

"StreaMercs?" a voice asked, and we both turned to find a uniformed rep hanging in the axis tunnel. He didn't wait for our response, but scanned our faces with a brief flash from a handheld device, then nodded. "Great, we're all here. Okay, follow me – this way." And he pushed off the ceiling, and disappeared down the central axis.

There were a dozen or so other new streamers hanging out in the axis waiting, and they pushed off and followed the rep as he "fell" down the shaft. With a gulp, I followed suit. Zero-g flying takes some practice, and it was clear that none of us had any. We were like a school of piss-drunk fish trying to navigate a narrow length of pipe. As a result, the StreaMercs rep stopped often, pausing to make sure his charges were still in tow, and in a few instances, doubling back to corral a wayward soul who had gotten fouled up in a hatch or vending machine along the way.

Eventually the central axis opened out to a broader area lined with shops and restaurants – we gaggled through this midway point, and then continued down the far end of the tube, toward the deep-space dockyard. At one point, we passed through a module made of glass, and I caught a glimpse of ships' hulls outside.

"That's it," a girl next to me said, pointing out one of the ships to her neighbor.

I looked, and sure enough, the *Final Hope* lay docked along a tube below us. She was a sleek ship, designed not just to get a few hundred streamers from planet to planet, but to satisfy the StreaMercs corporation's prime directive: look cool at all times. She was flat along the bottom of her hull, with a pointed bow that curved up to a conning tower on top, and then tapered toward the engine bank in the stern, like a space-shark that had traded in its fins for rockets. The StreaMercs logo was painted on her side, prominently displayed.

"Come on guys, almost there," the StreaMercs rep called out. We hooked through the side hatch, and he shepherded us down the boarding tube, which seemed to go on forever, and then the rep met us at a pressure hull, and caught each of us by the elbow, gently guiding us down until our feet touched the floor, and the ship's artificial gravity took over. We were aboard. I stopped and gaped – we all did. I had been expecting a stark, utilitarian ship, stripped down for war – all pressure hatches and exposed pipes and bare deck plating.

I had not been expecting a five-star hotel.

CHAPTER 7

"Dev, if you're going to spend a few years locked inside a metal tube, flying around the galaxy with a bunch of kids crazy enough to fight Ochos for money, you might as well do it in style."

-Unidentified Stellarus executive, to StreaMercs CEO Dev Khanna, at the commissioning ceremony of the *Final Hope*

In the center of a glittering fountain stood a white marble statue of a muscle-bound warrior, thrusting a spear down into a dying Ocho at his feet. On either side of the fountain, twin staircases, draped with plush red-and-gold carpeting, curved up to a second level under a crystal chandelier.

"You guys can leave your bags here," the rep told us. "The security robots will see them to your rooms."

I noticed a handful of humanoid robots standing patiently to either side of the hatch, watching us impassively. They looked similar to the Peacekeeper models that the local police department used back home, six feet of polished armor, and heads bristling with sensors. I'd seen a drunk guy pick a fight with one once – he clocked it in the "jaw" with a baseball bat, which broke the bat and earned him a trip to meet the pavement, up close. The bots had him stunned, cuffed, and back on his wobbly feet again in under three seconds.

"Okay," the guide clapped his hands together, smiling nervously at us. "So, let me be the first to officially welcome you aboard the *Final Hope*! Orientation starts with a brief video." He gestured, and a hologram appeared from a projector hidden in the wall. The Stellarus logo appeared hovering in the air in front of us: a stylized rocket on a field of stars.

"Welcome to your new home," a deep voice said. "Since its founding in the twenty-first century, Stellarus has been the largest and most successful private space transportation company in history, moving millions of people and billions of tons of cargo across light years, providing a critical link between Earth and her growing colonies."

The video showed stock footage of rocket launches, interspersed with pictures of humans building geodesic shelters and tending plants in greenhouses on alien planets.

"But in the year twenty-two thirty-one, mankind's peaceful explorations were interrupted when explorers made first contact with an alien species: the Octipedes."

The view changed, and showed one of the more famous clips from the first contact event: first-person footage from one of the explorers' helmet cameras. Breathing heavily, he crested a rocky ridge, and then an Ocho appeared in front of him, rearing up. The man gave a shout of alarm, and then the Ocho slammed down on the camera, immediately killing the signal.

"Stellarus, acting under authorization from United Nations Resolution one-ninety-six-slash-two-forty-eight, took swift action to protect human interests."

More stock footage, this time of the first drone army

fighting the Ochos. I watched as the robots swept mercilessly through the creatures, ignoring damage from plasma blasts and laying waste with heavy weapons in a coordinated air and ground assault.

"But Earth's governments struggled to pay for an increasingly expensive war. Dev Khanna was a junior programmer at Stellarus, coding software that allowed controllers at headquarters to monitor the real-time progress of the battles. To counter the rising costs of the war, he suggested a novel idea: livestream the combat footage, and charge viewers a fee to watch. Thus, the StreaMercs division was founded, and the *Final Hope* was built."

I watched as fresh-faced volunteers donned vac-suits, and then clumped their way over to the space elevator, rifles in hand. The music swelled as the ramps lifted, and the elevator dropped through the floor and out into space.

"Today, StreaMercs is one of the most successful media and entertainment companies in the galaxy, having taken the most expensive government expenditure in human history and turned it into one of the private sector's most lucrative revenue generators. And that success is due to you and your hard work, and your sacrifices."

The elevator in the hologram reached the planet's surface, the ramps dropped, and the streamers burst out, steely-eyed, weapons up and firing. Then the view changed again, showing Stellarus employees in a massive hangar, clustered around various ships being manufactured.

"On behalf of the employees at Stellarus, and all of mankind, we salute you, streamers." On cue, the employees shouted: "Thank you for your service!"

I frowned. *I haven't done anything yet … and they're already thanking me?*

The hologram disappeared, and the StreaMercs rep stepped back in front of us. "Please follow me, and I'll give you a short tour of the ship," he told us, then turned on his heel and started up the right-hand staircase. At the top, a wide room spread out before us, full of video game consoles and felt-covered tables of all shapes and sizes.

Is this a warship, or a casino?

I spotted a group of streamers clustered around a craps table, cheering as someone rolled a pair of dice. Others sat at blackjack tables, playing against robotic dealers, while still others' faces were lit by the screens and holograms of gaming booths, as they blasted away at holographic Ochos or raced hoverbikes down urban canyons.

"Is that an original Miss Pac-Man?" I blurted, pointing across the room at a boxy blue cabinet decorated in neon yellow and pink stripes.

"Yup," the rep smiled. "We've got a bunch of vintage games in the recreation bay. You'll have plenty of time to check them out." He pointed around the outside of the room. "Also notice that you have no less than sixteen restaurants on this level – that's Giuseppe's right there, which is Italian, and then next door is Pacifica, Asian Fusion … down at the far end is Wagyu, an award-winning steakhouse. And there are a bunch more; you can find basically any major cuisine you would want. They'll deliver to your room, if you'd prefer – but the restaurants all have exterior portholes, so the views can be quite stunning. Definitely don't miss a meal at Wagyu – I always try to grab a French dip while I'm on board."

"You're not a member of the crew?" someone asked.

"No," the rep shook his head. "I'm based on Northwest Station. The *Final Hope* has a very minimal human crew, apart from you and your fellow streamers. It's basically just Dev and a handful of support staff that head up each of the various divisions. Everything else is automated, from the chefs, to the sanitation, to the ship's maintenance."

"And all this is free?" Arliss asked, gesturing at the gambling tables and restaurants.

"Ah, no," the rep said, blushing slightly. "There is a

free cafeteria, and the food's just fine – standard government fare. But the restaurants and the games you pay to use."

Looks like I'll be eating government food until I get my first royalty check, I thought.

"The gym is free, though," the StreaMercs rep said. "We'll head there next."

He led us across the hall, pointing out a movie theater, a corridor leading through a number of clothing and electronics stores, and a cluster of VR booths along the way. Then we pushed through a set of double doors and into a sprawling gym, packed with weight machines and cardio equipment of every type imaginable. A dozen streamers were here, too – two women were running on treadmills facing hologram screens that simulated a jog through the mountains, and a guy was spotting his buddy as he worked through some chest presses with free weights. Through a set of glass windows, I saw an Olympic-sized pool, with a three-meter diving board at one end.

"Like I said, the gym is completely free – StreaMercs wants to encourage everyone to exercise and remain 'fighting fit,' as they say. The locker rooms back there also have steam rooms, hot tubs, and massage beds – all free, and a great way to relax after a long campaign. And speaking of, let's go check out the ranges and ready rooms."

We exited the gym through a side door, walked down another hallway, and then took a set of stairs down one level. Here, the thick carpeting gave way to plain metal deck tiles, below bare walls and harsh neon lighting. The corridor led to a set of swinging double doors, which opened out onto a wide, circular bay. In the center of the room was a thick column of intermingled pipes and cables, surrounded by a raised circular platform, with metal ramps leading up to it. After a second, I recognized it – it was the elevator itself, waiting and ready to receive streamers.

"The elevator," someone behind me said, in a hushed voice.

"Yup, that's it," the guide confirmed, strolling over to stand on the edge of one of the ramps. "We call this the 'landing bay.' Once the *Final Hope* anchors her cable to a new planet, it gets attached to the bottom of this column here, and then the elevator is ready to descend." He pointed behind them, over their shoulders. "The area we just walked through, toward the ship's bow, is the *Final Hope's* sick bay. It basically takes up all of the space under the gym, and let me tell you, it's a top-of-the-line, fully automated surgical hospital, on par with the best trauma wards on Earth."

That's comforting, I thought. *Tell me more about how important it was to locate an emergency room right next to the elevator.*

"In fact," the guide continued (*oh shit, he's still not done*), "statistically, if your fellow streamers can get you back to the elevator within thirty minutes of your initial injury, you stand a seventy-eight percent chance of surviving. That's higher than any other survival rate in the history of modern warfare."

"What's in the stern?" I asked, doing my best to derail Macabre Man from depressing all of us any further.

"Arms rooms and ranges," he said, smiling helpfully. "Come see."

Another set of doors slid open, and the tour continued through a large arms room, whose walls were lined with metal racks bearing a wide variety of firearms. While the guide prattled on about how many different weapon types were available to us, I watched as Arliss wandered over and ran a hand across the stocks of several rifles appreciatively.

"Do you have any historic weapons on board?" Arliss asked, interrupting. "These are all electro-magnetic rail weapons. Anything powder-based?"

"Um ... no?" the guide replied, frowning. "I don't

think so, at least. As I said, this is all the best weaponry that *modern* technology can provide."

Arliss seemed satisfied with that answer, and I made a mental note to maybe stick close to Arliss on the battlefield – goofy outfit notwithstanding, the kid seemed like he knew his way around guns, which automatically made him more qualified for combat than me. Across the hall, we found the cavernous equipment bay, where row upon row of empty vac-suits stood held up by support arms, waiting. After a short time searching, each of us found a vacuum-suit under a shiny new plaque bearing our streamertag. Behind each vac-suit was a locker, just like in a gym, which held other clothing and equipment.

"… and down at the end of the hall are the live fire ranges, and the VR sims, or the training rooms. In the training rooms, you can suit up in a state-of-the-art VR system and practice fighting Ochos in different simulated environments, or you can put your vac-suit on and head over to the real ranges, to practice live-firing your weapons on a variety of targets."

"Can we practice with the weapons we brought with us?" Arliss asked, stuffing his hands into the pockets of his leather vest.

I suppressed a grin. *He brought his own weapons? Look at Renaissance Rambo over here …*

The guide rubbed his chin. "I honestly … have no idea. You'll have to check with the range control team, sorry."

"Okay," Arliss said.

"Finally, let's go see your rooms – upstairs," the rep told us. He found another staircase, and we ascended, reentering the realm of etched wall sconces and mahogany wood paneling. The guide paused outside the door to a room, and glanced furtively down the hallway. "Okay, listen: this isn't the kind of room you're getting, but I have to show it to you as part of the tour. Just don't get too excited, okay?"

He didn't wait for an answer, but held the barcode on

his ID badge up to the door, and then pushed it open. It wasn't so much a room as a suite – the foyer held a full-length mirror and closet, and as I walked in, I took note of a large bathroom to one side, glittering with chrome fixtures and slate tiles. In the sitting room, a set of leather couches faced a large hologram projector screen, while over by the wet bar, a pair of easy chairs sat looking out through a wide porthole, through which I could make out the outline of Northwest Station. The bedroom was nearly as large as my entire apartment back home.

"This is a contract suite," the guide told us. "Suites like this are reserved for the top tier of streamers – generally those who earn a contract with StreaMercs."

"How many suites are there?" a girl asked, pushing the curtains back from the porthole.

"Twenty. And the *Final Hope* generally sails with more than four hundred streamers aboard. Like I said: don't get too excited." He ushered us back out into the hall, and then unlocked another door and we found ourselves in a long hall with bunk beds lining a central corridor, and lockers built into the walls. In history class, I'd seen a few 2D movies about war in the old days – this immediately reminded me of the basic training scenes from those films.

"We're technically in portside berth number four, but everyone calls these rooms 'the barracks,' generally, or 'PB Four' if you need to be specific about which one you live in. There are five berths on each side of the ship, port and starboard, each holding forty streamers. And this one is for all of you."

"Nice of them to give us some privacy," someone grumbled.

"That's intentional," a short, blonde girl pointed out.

"It is, actually," the guide chipped in. "StreaMercs believes living together like this is a great way for you to get to know each other, and bond."

"I was going to say it ensures there's drama," the blonde said. "Keeps things interesting for the viewers."

"Well, yeah," the guide said, blushing slightly. "There is that, too."

CHAPTER 8

"1430Z: Resupply operations complete.

1442Z: Transferred remains of 21 KIA to mortuary ship for transport on to next-of-kin locations.

1803Z: In-processed Recruit Class 2233-2, 23 personnel. See attached passenger manifest for details.

1831Z: Departed NW Station, en route Pentares."

-Excerpt from the *Final Hope's* log, October 28th, 2233

I've never understood how faster-than-light drives work, so I won't try to explain them. You want to understand it, go ask a quantum engineer. Just know that the Venn diagram containing the people who understand the physics and the people who can explain it *in plain English* doesn't have much overlap. It gets us from Planet A to Planet B without colliding with Planet C or fatally rearranging our molecular structure along the way, and that's all I care about.

The StreaMercs guide left us in our berth – presumably to go grab his customary steak sandwich – and we each picked a bunk. I ended up on the top bunk over the short blonde girl, who introduced herself as Naja, from Denmark. We were still unpacking our stuff when the *Final Hope* detached from Northwest Station, pointed her shark-nose at a distant star, and started her acceleration. There weren't any portholes in our berth, and the *Final Hope's* engines don't make a peep, so if they hadn't made an announcement, I wouldn't have even known. A few other new recruits ran down to the recreation bay to peek through the viewing windows, but they told us it was fairly anticlimactic.

Having seen it dozens of times myself since, I can confirm. The stars just start sliding past faster and faster, until they become a big blur.

The last thing I unpacked from my suitcase was my vintage Game Boy. I took its case out, and Naja, sticking her empty suitcase under the bed, caught sight of it.

"Nice!" she said. "Replica or real?"

"Real," I told her. "I've got original games, too, if you want to play sometime."

"Definitely," she said, her eyes widening. "My fans would love to see that."

"You have fans already?" I asked. *Did I miss the part of orientation where they gave us our fans?*

"Oh, I'm a game streamer," Naja explained. "Or I *was*. Now I'm trying to make the leap into the IRL space." She crossed her fingers.

"Cool," I said. "What kind of games?"

"Mostly first-person shooter, reaction vids. Some horror stuff – my fans like to hear me shriek, but honestly I kinda hate horror. I'd rather be running and gunning. What about you?"

I shook my head. "No, I just play games for fun. Starting from scratch with the fan base, I'm afraid."

The door to our berth slid open, and a man and a woman walked in. The girl looked to be about my age, but the man looked older – nearly in his thirties, I suspected. That, or the last few years had been somewhat rough on him. Both wore a thin metal circlet that started above their right ears and wrapped around the backs of their heads.

"Yo, noobs!" the girl called out, and everyone looked up. "Welcome."

Her partner surveyed the room. "Everybody here? Well, whatever." He spoke with a lilting Spanish accent – I pegged him as Sudamericano, though what province, I wasn't sure. "Listen, Sunny and I have the dubious honor and privilege of being your mentors on this trip. And we don't have a hell of a lot of time to get you up to speed, so hopefully you're unpacked and all that, because we're gonna get started *ahora*." He tapped his watch. "You got thirty minutes for lunch, then meet us down in the landing bay. Put the word out to any of your little amigos, okay?"

And with that, they left.

"Well, they seem charming," Naja commented.

* * *

Sunny and her partner – Flint was his tag, we later learned (he pronounced it "Fleent") – were waiting in the landing bay, squatting on the ramp into the elevator. Sunny picked something out of her teeth, and then counted us off silently, before standing up.

"First stop is sick bay," she told us, and without waiting for a reply, pushed through our group. We followed her into a large room lined with hospital gurneys – empty ones – and then at Sunny's direction, lined up behind a machine with a chair and a helmet suspended from a robotic arm.

"You're gonna get tatted," Sunny explained, touching the barcode on her cheek. "The tattoo does a couple things: one, it's your security badge for getting around the ship and drawing weapons from the arms room. Two, it's your digital wallet on board so you can pay for stuff. And three, it's a dog tag in case we need to identify you and all we have is … pieces." She lifted up her shirt, and showed us an identical tattoo on her hip, as well. "That's why you're getting two."

"It also lets civilians know you're a certified badass," Flint chipped in.

"Right," Sunny agreed. "That too. The ink is metallic, so it'll survive a lot of trauma."

"Does it hurt?" the guy at the front of the line asked.

"Oh, yeah," Sunny said.

And she wasn't kidding. When it was my turn, I took a seat, and the helmet lowered over my head, holding my face in place. A different arm reached out and made contact with my hip, and then I felt a searing pain, as if someone had run a high voltage wire between my cheek and my hip. I managed not to yell out loud, but I did bite my lip hard enough to make it bleed. Thankfully, it was over in an instant, but the sudden jolt of pain made my legs weak, and the tattoo sites stung for a week afterwards.

Next, Flint took us across to the equipment bay, or "ready room," as he called it.

"Tomorrow we'll start weapons familiarization. Today is all about vac-suit orientation," he told us. "Find your suit, and stand by for instructions."

We all limped over to our assigned suits, spreading out across the long room.

"First piece of equipment," Flint said, his amplified voice emanating from speakers hidden somewhere in the bay's ceiling, "and by far the most important part of your kit, is the item on the top shelf of your locker. Take it out, and put it on."

I reached in and found a curved metal band with what looked to be an ear-piece and a small camera. It matched the circlets that Sunny and Flint were wearing.

"This is your POV camera. *Mira*: it sees what you see. Unless you enjoy fighting Ochos with nobody watching, which means you aren't earning any money, you should make it a point to wear this at all times."

I tried to fit it to my ear, but ended up flipping it around.

"Yeah, other ear," Sunny said, walking over to my station. I slipped it in place and it gripped my head snugly. "There you go. Now don't take it off."

"I have to wear it around the ship, too?" I asked. "When we're not in a battle?"

Sunny shrugged. "Do you *have* to? No. You can do whatever you want. But most people stream at all times, unless they're taking a crap or sleeping."

"Are you streaming right now?" I asked her.

"Yup," she said. "It's probably the most boring feed on the entire ship, no thanks to you … but some weirdos are watching, god love 'em. Might as well be earning something, right?"

She moved down the line, heading over to another recruit to check on their progress, and Flint continued the tutorial, having us don our under-suits next. Then we turned and climbed the short set of steps leading up to the rear of the armored outer suits. Each stood empty, with their back-plates lifted off. A mechanical arm attached to the ceiling held the plates aloft, so that we could, without much trouble, step into the suit from behind. I did so; the back plate automatically lowered into place and I was sealed inside.

Here's the quick and dirty on vac-suits, because I don't feel like regurgitating a technical manual at you. The under-suit is worn against the skin, covering every inch of you from the neck down. Its climate-controlled, and it has tourniquets built into the limbs at several points, which can sense when they're needed, and automatically (and rather painfully) cut off blood flow in that limb if, say, part of the limb suddenly goes missing. Also, yes, you can "go" in the under-suit, and it gets disposed of. It's a little gross, but pretty soon you get used to it and don't even think about it. After a long campaign, more than a few streamers back on the *Final Hope* have forgotten that they're no longer in their suits, and wet their bed as a result.

The outer suit's a different animal. Synthetic spider-silk

weave on the inner layer, for flexibility, with overlapping armor tiles on the outer layer, like the old Vikings used to wear. As with most body armor in history, it holds up well against glancing blows or small shrapnel, but take a direct hit and you're toast. The front of the suit hosts a modular webbing system for ammo pouches and the like, while the back holds all the really important stuff: six days' worth of air, comm gear, batteries, and more storage for ammo, food, and water.

The helmet of the suit is basically a large, clear dome, which affords good all-around views. There's a second camera mounted on the dome, pointing inward at you – the circlet one you wear over your ear shows viewers what you're seeing, while the dome camera shows them a view of your face. The dome has a heads-up display for critical data: you can pull up maps, life support info, and viewer stats, among other things. There's a feeding tube that allows you to drink water and eat liquefied energy supplements; they taste awful but give you enough calories to stay in the fight.

Fully loaded, the outer suit weighs several hundred pounds, so the joints are augmented with hydraulics. That way, wearing it just makes you feel bulkier, but no more or less heavy than you are normally. You can run just as fast and jump just as far as you would without anything on, and you're a good bit stronger, but it doesn't turn you into a superhuman by any means. No jump jets or anything crazy like that. All in all, the first vac-suits were pretty basic – they were designed to keep us alive in a variety of extraterrestrial environments, and that's about it. We didn't get the really cool upgrades until much later in the war.

Flint and Sunny had us suit up and jog a lap around the ready room. Then Flint had us activate each feature of the suit in turn. I got the distinct impression he was reading from a checklist, and neither of them particularly cared if we were following along or not.

"To activate your shoulder lights, say: 'Suit: lights on.' "

"Suit: lights on," we said, and two powerful beams of light shone out in front of each of us.

"Now say, 'Suit: lights off,' " Flint droned. "*Bueno.* Next, to activate your emergency beacon, say …"

After an hour of this, they declared the formal portion of vac-suit orientation over and disappeared, leaving us to mess around on our own. I spent a few minutes fiddling with some of the suit's settings, and practiced switching communications channels a few times. I felt like I should be doing more to get comfortable in the suit, but I could hardly remember all of the things Flint had walked us through. Out of ideas, I stepped back into the suit's cradle-thing, and felt the deck lock into place around my armored feet, immobilizing me. With a noticeable change in air pressure, the back lifted off. I stepped out, and began stripping off my under-suit. Arliss clomped by a moment later, still in his vac-suit.

"Hey, Sam," he said, his voice projecting from a hidden speaker somewhere on the suit. "What do you think?"

"I think they're pretty complicated," I said. "I hope we go over some of this stuff again, later during training."

"Oh, I'm sure we will," he said. He flexed his arms and twisted at the waist, stretching. "Well, complicated or not, I think they're kind of awesome. Makes me feel like I'm invincible."

CHAPTER 9

"Hey, hey, Captain Jack!
Meet me down by the railroad track!
With that rifle in your hand!
I'm gonna be a shootin' man!
For Uncle Sam!
That's what I am!"
-United States Army running cadence, circa late 20th
century

I didn't sleep well that first night in the barracks. Between someone down at the far end of the bay snoring (I suspected Arliss), the vague unease of being in an unfamiliar place surrounded by dozens of strangers, and the realization that I was actually headed off to war, I didn't drift off until well after three. We were supposed to meet Flint and Sunny back in the ready room at eight, but some gung ho jerk set their alarm for five thirty and woke us all up, and that was it – I was up for the day.

Following Sunny's advice, I climbed down from my

bunk and slipped on my POV camera rig first thing. After a moment, I heard a quiet beep in my ear, then my watch buzzed and showed me a notification that I was streaming.

>>>*Viewer count: 0*

I shook my head ruefully and went to brush my teeth. *I wonder if the big shot streamers get endorsement money for using products from certain brands?* (Answer: you bet your ass we did. And a metric crap-ton of free samples, too. Later on, I could have taken a bath in free toothpaste if I'd asked for it). Naja was up when I got back from the common bathroom; she and I ate breakfast in the free cafeteria, and then took the opportunity to explore the ship in a little more detail. The rec bay was dead quiet at this hour, but the gym had a decent complement of streamers working out.

"I checked out Sunny and Flint online," Naja commented, as we wandered back through the empty rec bay.

"And?" I asked.

"And we didn't exactly get the cream of the crop in terms of instructors for our orientation," Naja grimaced. She traced a finger along the felt of a poker table. "Flint's been on four different campaigns, but this is only Sunny's second, and she didn't fight a whole lot on Shaw's Anchorage. Neither of them has very impressive stats, or many fans."

"So how come they were picked to do our orientation?" I asked.

"I don't think they were 'picked' at all," Naja said. "My guess is they volunteered, and StreaMercs is tossing them a little extra cash as compensation. The best streamers – the real big earners – don't want to be bothered with us. They're too important to waste their time training noobs."

"… or they don't want to give us too many tips," I guessed. "We're their competition, after all."

Naja raised an eyebrow and nodded. "True. I hadn't

thought about it that way, but that could be it, too."

"Well, I hope we have more serious instructors when we get to basic training," I said. "No more of these half-assed classes."

"Let's hope," Naja agreed.

Back in the barracks, I played some Game Boy on my bunk until it was time to go. My watch buzzed a few minutes into my first game of *Tetris*, and I realized, with a start, that I had my first viewer. Then the watch buzzed again and they were gone. *Nice,* I thought. *I'm already crushing it.* When it was time, we made our way downstairs, and climbed into our vac-suits with the rest of our recruit class, before crossing the hall to the arms room.

I took a spot along the counter to the arms room, which was divided into separate windows, like an old bank branch. Through the clear dome of my helmet, I saw a robotic arm extend and scan my face tattoo, then the arm turned and drew a weapon from the rack behind it, placing the weapon and a supply of magazines on the counter. The e-rifle was painted white and gray, with a thick stock and a generous trigger guard to allow for our gauntleted hands. I picked it up awkwardly, unsure of how to hold it, and tucked the stack of magazines in the crook of one arm. The stub-nosed weapon was heavy, even with my suit's enhanced strength; it had a heft that I hadn't expected.

Without the vac-suit, I don't know how I'd ever be able to lift this thing.

On the firing range, there were enough lanes for each of us to take one, but first, Sunny had us gather around her in a circle at the back of the room. She lifted her e-rifle, showing it to us.

"This is an ER-forty-five. It's an electric railgun, which means it shoots by accelerating the bullets with a system of electro-magnets, not explosive propellant. The bullets fly faster and farther, and you can carry more of 'em, cause you're not lugging around a bunch of gunpowder."

"It's also a hundred years old," Arliss mumbled to me, but his microphone picked it up, and everyone heard.

Sunny shot him a look. "It'll still kill Ochos, don't worry," she told him. "If you start hitting the big money, feel free to get some upgrades."

"How do we get upgrades?" a guy across from me asked.

"You buy them," Sunny said, simply.

There sure are a lot of ways to spend your money on this ship, I thought.

Sunny racked back the weapon's charging handle. "Breech," she said, pointing into the weapon's interior. "Magazine goes in underneath, here. Release the charging handle, and you've got a round chambered. Fire selector is on this side: safe, semi, and auto. At distance, you're gonna want 'semi' – one round for each trigger pull. Up close, give 'em full auto, short bursts, until they go down."

She hefted the weapon to her shoulder. "Scope is fairly standard – just put the red dot over what you want to hit. Hit this button to release the empty magazine, slot a new one in place, and you're good to go. It's wirelessly connected to your suit, so you can see ammo count and maintenance status in your heads-up display. If you have a malfunction, rack the handle a few times, that should clear it. Questions?"

I had a million, but Sunny was already turning to face the ranges. "Okay, pick a lane, the targets will pop up automatically. Flint and I will be roaming around if you have issues. Let's put some rounds downrange."

At my lane, I fumbled with the weapon for a bit, but Arliss was in the lane next to me and saw me struggling. He helpfully walked me through the loading procedure again. After that I spent a while missing targets at various ranges, until my arms started to get tired, and I let the e-rifle hang against my chest. On cue, my score popped up in my heads-up display:

>>>23% accuracy.

I leaned over and peeked in on Arliss. He was steadying his e-rifle against the wall between our lanes, firing slowly and methodically. He straightened after a moment and dropped his magazine, then caught sight of me.

"Whoa, watch your weapon," he said.

"What?" I asked. "Why?"

"You're pointing it at my leg," he said.

"Oh. It's empty, I think," I said, swinging the barrel away.

He shook his head. "Always treat it like it's loaded. Is it on 'safe'?"

I glanced down at the selector switch, cringed, and then flicked it. "It is now," I said. "How did you shoot?"

He checked his heads-up display. "Eighty-four percent. Pretty good," he said. "Never been a fan of electric firing systems, but when it was in service, the ER-forty-five had a reputation for above-average reliability. And railguns have superb stopping power – there's a lot of kinetic energy in that bullet."

"Oh," I said. "Listen, Arliss, do you want to buddy up when we go … fight, or whatever?"

"Sure!" he said. "Good idea – two of us working together will be more effective than we would be on our own."

"Yeah," I agreed, quickly. "That's … that's what I was thinking."

They let us shoot until lunch time, and with Arliss' help, I actually managed to hit a few targets. In the afternoon we switched to pistols (which I sucked at, too) and then got a quick class in grenades, which scared the shit out of me. Something about having a device that could rip you to shreds just sitting in the palm of your hand was deeply unsettling. After we had slipped out of our vac-suits, Flint took us back to the landing bay, and we sat in a semi-circle on the deck around him and Sunny, facing the elevator. I scratched at the scab on my cheek tattoo – the pain was fading into a persistent itch.

"Let's talk about the drop," Flint said. "There are about four hundred of us on board." He gestured at the elevator behind him. "Four hundred of us don't fit in this thing all at once. More like a hundred, a hundred fifty. So when we anchor to the planet, you're going to be able to request which wave you go down on. First wave sees the most casualties, every time. But it also pulls the most viewers, so you gotta do the math, and decide for yourself."

Note to self: don't ride down in the first wave.

"Whatever wave you ride down with, do *not* be the noob that gets cold feet and blocks one of the ramps. There's always one … just don't let it be you. Stay on the elevator, or get the fuck off, but do *not* sit there, blocking everyone behind you, making us all into a nice, fat target for a plasma blast. *Entiendes?*"

We nodded. Somebody asked: "What happens to people that decide they don't want to fight?"

"Nothing," Sunny said, shrugging. "If you're panicking, that's fine. No one's forcing you to fight. You don't want to fight, just go hang out in the barracks, and we'll drop you off next time we're back at Earth, no hard feelings."

"More viewers for the rest of us," Flint agreed. "Other than that, best advice I can give you is to stay low. Once the drones dig the trenches, get down in them, don't run around all exposed, asking to get hit. Watch where you're shooting, and follow the lead of the more experienced streamers."

Sunny cleared her throat. "I also wouldn't recommend trying to ride out your first battle solo. At minimum, you should buddy up with somebody and watch each other's backs."

I caught Arliss' eye and we shared a smile. I was glad to be ahead of the game for once.

"You can also form a clan and all make a go of it

together," Sunny continued. "Same kind of deal as going down on the first wave. If you decide to fight alone, people will tune in because it's far more dangerous. In a clan you'll be safer, but … viewers don't like safer, so you won't attract as many. Less risk, less reward."

A kid with spiky, jet-black hair in the front row raised his hand. "Are there any rules? Or like, standard practices that we should know about?"

"Rules?" Flint shook his head.

"No rules," Sunny said. "But use common sense – you get someone killed by being a jackass, and that's the last time you'll suit up. StreaMercs will stick you in the brig until we get home and you can stand trial, and you'll be glad they did, because otherwise the rest of us would kill you."

She crossed her arms. "Listen, as streamers, we're all competing for viewers, right? It's okay, I mean, that's just the reality … it is what it is. But if there's one rule we all follow, it's this: someone gets wounded, we get them back to the elevator. You might be in the middle of an epic kill-streak and racking up the view count, but if the dude or dudette next to you goes down, you drop everything and help."

Arliss raised his hand. "Do you have any tips for getting more viewers?"

Flint snorted. "You heard her say we're all competing with each other, right?"

"I mean, I know, but …" Arliss trailed off.

Sunny sighed. "I'll give you the same advice I got when I first started."

… *which must have been about a month ago,* I thought.

"If you wanna go viral, you need a … thing. A hook, right? Some kind of unique angle. Something cool or funny that no one else does."

"Like what?" a boy in the front row asked.

"Like Flint. He doesn't just fight, he writes poems

during the battles," Sunny said.

"Haikus," Flint corrected.

Sunny rolled her eyes, which made me wonder if they were a couple. *Probably*, I decided.

"Haikus, sorry," Sunny repeated. "And me, I don't carry an e-rifle downrange, I traded it in for a pair of upgraded pistols." She held up both fists, miming shooting with them. "Dual-wielding. Anyway, find your hook, and if it's good, you might get a bunch of viewers."

That sounds easier said than done.

"Have you ever gone viral?" Arliss asked.

"Five million viewers, all at the same time? No," Sunny said. "Not yet." And Flint shook his head, too.

I raised my own hand.

"Yeah?" Sunny asked, pointing at me.

"Can you tell us a little bit more about basic training?"

Sunny and Flint shared a look. "Basic training?"

"… you know: how long is it going to be, what kind of classes are there going to be, what planet is it on," I finished.

Flint laughed, shaking his head. "Senorita's seen too many war movies. *Mira*, she thinks there's some hardass drill instructor standing by to turn her into a warrior. Cue the training montage!"

Sunny smirked at me. "You think the rest of us are just going to sit around twiddling our thumbs while you guys go through some extended boot camp? Naw. Next stop is Pentares, and the Ochos are waiting." She checked her watch. "And we'll be there in five days."

"Basic training is over," Flint echoed. "You just graduated."

CHAPTER 10

"Octipedes up-ended everything mankind thought it knew about biology. For the first time in centuries, scientists began to consider the possibility that Darwin had been wrong. An exoskeleton wrapped around a fusion reactor? How on Earth could natural selection have produced that?"

-Dr. Aiko Clemson, "Extraordinary Extraterrestrials: Octipede Evolution and Lifecycles"

The day before we arrived over Pentares, they sent out notifications that there would be a brief class on Octipedes for all new recruits. Once our two-day "basic training" ended, the other streamers had been free to use the ranges and VR sims again, and the veterans snapped up nearly all of the reservations in a matter of minutes. I had to give up a VR sim spot of my own to attend the class, but I figured it was worth knowing a little bit more about my enemy, especially since every hologram I'd ever seen of them gave me the serious heebie-jeebies.

Recruit Class 2233-2 filed past the roulette tables in the

rec bay and into the movie theater beyond. A couple people even brought keypads to type notes, which made me feel like I was back in college and had forgotten to do the homework or something. I found Naja near the back, who had brought a keypad of her own; it was covered with stickers from various video games and console brands.

"What do you think?" I asked her, taking a seat. "Is this one gonna be taught by one of the veterans, too?"

She shrugged. "I heard someone saying it was going to be a member of the crew."

"Really?" I lifted my eyebrows. "I still haven't seen any crew members."

"I've only seen one," Naja said. "I ran into Flint in the gym this morning and asked him; he said they mostly keep to themselves, you'll only ever see them in the restaurants from time to time."

The hologram projector at the front of the room came on then, and the lights dimmed. The scene was the front of an old lecture hall, with a podium and screen behind it. A moment later, a hologram of a man materialized out of the wall on the side of the theater, walking into view.

"G'day," the man said. "I'm Professor Hornby, and I teach biology at the Royal Military College, which used to be the primary university for officers in Australia's armed forces. Nowadays we just teach civilians ... and, well, you guys."

Hornby wore a flannel shirt and corduroy pants, and his disheveled white hair made him look like he had just stumbled out of bed. Actually, he probably had – the *Final Hope* operated on Zulu time, which meant it was two in the morning in Canberra.

"Today we'll be discussing the Octipede, and appropriately enough, I'm joining you via long-range livestream. I can hear you and see you, so if you have questions, just shout them out, right? Too easy."

A 3D hologram of an Octipede appeared next to him, rotating slowly. It must have been a life-size model, because the worm-like creature's "head" was several feet higher than Hornby's, and I'd have had a hard time wrapping my arms around its thick torso.

"The Octipede," Hornby said. "Though they bear a passing resemblance to centipedes or other Earth-origin arthropods, Octipedes don't fit anywhere within Earth's classification system for the animal kingdom. They get an entirely separate phylum to themselves.

"From our observations, they range in size from about ten feet long to nearly sixteen feet long, and their thorax diameter increases as their length does. We don't know what determines the size of an individual Octipede, whether it's age or genetics or some external factor. And we know nothing about their lifecycle or how they reproduce – we've only ever encountered the mature Octipedes that you'll be fighting."

The hologram of the Ocho stopped spinning, and the creature's vaguely snout-like head was highlighted in white.

"Basic anatomy: what we would call the head of the Octipede is where the creature's sensory capabilities reside. From limited field studies, mostly conducted by your predecessors, we have determined that they share four of the five senses that we do: touch, vision, smell, and hearing. They lack a mouth, so we believe they lack taste, too. Smell, hearing, and vision are all superior to human senses, in that they are both more sensitive, and also can detect a much broader spectrum of light and sound waves. In short, it's very hard to hide from an Octipede."

Hornby took a sip from a mug of coffee, then gestured at the hologram as the creature's legs came into focus.

"Next: the famous eight legs that give them their name. They use these for locomotion and defense. They can move quite fast, and have displayed an ability to climb rather well, too. They can't scale sheer rock faces or hang from the top of a cave or anything like insects on Earth do, but they are quite adept at climbing if the need arises. They are fastest in a straight line sprint, and if they have a weakness when it comes to movement, it is that it takes them a bit of time to get that long body of theirs turned completely around. They can change direction quickly, but doing an about-face, as it were, is challenging."

The holographic Octipede raised its front legs on cue.

"The rear six legs are purely for movement. The front pair is quite different. For starters, the front legs have a serrated edge along the outside, which they use as a cutting weapon. Their 'shell' is extremely hard all over, but here it is quite sharp, too. In addition, as you see, the front legs are bisected at the ends."

The view zoomed in, and we watched in fascinated horror as the pointed tips of the creature's front "feet" split open.

"This, of course, is where the famous plasma beams originate. The plasma has a range of several hundred meters, and is emitted at an impressive twenty-six thousand degrees centigrade. That's the same rough temperature that our plasma cutting torches operate at, when slicing through steel."

"Professor?"

Hornby squinted at us and then spotted a hand up in the audience. "Yes?"

"How many times can they fire the plasma beams?"

"We don't know," Hornby said. "So far, the answer appears to be 'as many times as they wish.' Academic consensus is that there is a theoretical limit, but as yet, we haven't found it."

The view changed, showing the Ocho in its entirety again.

"… which brings us naturally to the thorax, and their internal anatomy. The exterior, as I said, is a thick, armored shell. Not bullet-proof, but quite strong. And if you're expecting them to have organs or some such, I'm afraid you'll be disappointed – those functions seem to be distributed evenly throughout the Octipedes' bodies, using a mechanism we don't yet understand. Instead, if you crack one open, you'll find what is essentially a miniaturized fusion reactor. A star, you could say, which provides the Octipede with its energy for living … and fighting."

"So how do you kill it?" one of the other recruits asked. "If there's no heart or brain, what do you shoot to make it … uh, stop?"

"Mm," Hornby said, nodding and shaking his finger in the air. "Again, the science here is somewhat lacking, I'm afraid. We've never captured an Octipede alive and been able to study this specific question, though not for lack of trying. In essence, we believe the Octipede's shell and their internal reactors are very, very closely linked. The shell is 'powered' in some ways by the reactor, while the reactor is contained by the shell – the two are mutually dependent, right? Thus, if you damage the shell enough, the reactor simply 'turns off.' Each Octipede has a 'kill switch,' then, whereby enough damage to their exoskeleton causes their reactor to shut down, and they die."

A cluster of bullet holes appeared in the shell of the holographic Octipede, and it collapsed, lifeless. I raised my hand.

"Yes, young lady?"

"How smart are they?"

"Excellent question," he said. "That is the one area where humans hold a significant advantage. Physically, we are outclassed by Octipedes in terms of size, strength, speed, stamina, natural resistance to alien environments, etc., etc. But intellectually, there is no contest. Octipedes are dumb as rocks, to put it bluntly. On the scale of intelligence of Earth's animals, they are somewhere between a domesticated canine and a cephalopod. Sorry, that's an octopus. They are capable of rudimentary communication and thus, of coordinating their movements on the battlefield to a limited degree. But we have yet to see them demonstrate the creation or usage of tools, an awareness of self, artistic expression, societal structure, or any other indicators of higher-order mental capacity."

"If they're so dumb, why are they a threat to us?" someone asked.

"Two reasons," Hornby said. "One, while they are clearly incapable of constructing interstellar vehicles on their own, they are nevertheless already an interstellar species. We have theories about how they managed to spread to different planets in this sector of the galaxy, but no clear answers. Therefore, we must assume that they are capable of traveling through space again, and to Earth, this time. Prudence demands that we eliminate them for our own safety, because their arrival on Earth in any large numbers would be catastrophic."

Hornby held up a finger, while taking another sip of coffee. "Number two. I told you earlier that the Octipedes have yet to demonstrate sophisticated tool use or any signs of society. But on every planet where we've encountered them, we've also found signs of another alien civilization. We call this third species 'the Architects' because the only traces they left behind are incredibly intricate structures carved out of the sheer rock of each planet. Massive cathedral-like subterranean halls, held aloft by impossibly thin rock columns, perfectly circular tunnels connecting thousands of underground dwellings. We haven't found any of the Architects' technology, but the structures they left behind tell us they were incredibly advanced, possibly beyond human scientific progress, even. And now, where are they?"

He waited, but the movie theater was silent.

"Well, they're extinct. Like us, they encountered the Octipedes – they may even have helped the Octipedes spread across the stars. Perhaps they had something of a symbiotic relationship with them. But it seems that the Octipedes turned on them, and destroyed the Architects – no trace of them remains. So: the Octipedes eradicated a civilization likely more advanced than our own. We would be wise not to underestimate them."

CHAPTER 11

Archer Kinney, Chairman of the Board, Stellarus: "Do the ethics of it trouble me? Was that the question? No, no ... not at all. What part of StreaMercs' operation is unethical? Who doesn't benefit from the services we provide? Human civilization benefits – it gets protection from an existential threat and it gets entertainment, simultaneously. The streamers benefit by earning generous compensation. And our shareholders benefit, clearly. So ... who does it harm?"

Analyst: "Well ... the streamers who die. You're profiting off of their deaths."

Kinney: "An old argument, and a tired one. The tobacco and alcohol industries have been doing the exact same thing for centuries. They just do it a whole lot slower."

-Transcript of Stellarus quarterly earnings call, Q3 2233

Our recruit class split up into four clans, and we did it without much drama, to the likely chagrin of the StreaMercs executives. Naja had already

89

buddied up with Dhia to get Clan Demonium started; she invited me and Arliss to join them, and then we recruited Taalib and Johnny, and we were all set. Naja was the obvious pick for clan leader given her experience streaming video games, on the assumptions that (a) she knew more about tactics than the rest of us, even if her combat experience was all virtual, and (b) she knew how to get viewers.

Dhia Perak (tag: WantSomeCandy?) was a brash Malaysian girl with long, black hair and a million-watt smile. She had been a DJ back home, and decided the best way to light a fire under her music career was to start mixing in combat. Like Naja, she had established a decent fan base before signing up with StreaMercs, so between the two of them, Clan Demonium wouldn't be riding into battle with no one watching. Her tunes were good, too – all heart-thumping bass with some killer samples mixed in.

Next up was Taalib Wilkins, who had picked the tag GameOverMan. Taalib was a quiet black kid from Chicago who had delayed his admission to med school to join up. His ultimate goal was to save up enough to buy some property out on one of the colonies, and dedicate his time to finding cures for rare diseases that didn't qualify for government funding. That's Taalib – one of those exceptional people that are both extremely driven and entirely selfless. I wanted to hate him but he was too damn nice.

Juan Garcia was Taalib's bunkmate. Tall, tanned, and handsome, he hailed from Belize, which I misheard as "Feliz" when he first told us (you're from "happy?" Uh, okay). I had to look it up on a map – Belize is in Central America. He preferred to be called Johnny, not Juan, and his streamertag was JohnnyRico, which was apparently a reference to a classic work of science fiction, but none of us got the reference. He waited a beat after telling us his streamertag, repeated it, then became visibly disappointed and called us a bunch of illiterates.

And finally, my battle buddy: Arliss "OldSchool" Crain, a plump kid from a farm in Iowa, where, strangely enough, his fluency in several programming languages meant he spent most of his time fixing bugs in the software that controlled his family's autonomous farming equipment. In his off time, Arliss and his Dad watched old war documentaries and shot their collection of firearms out on the range they built in one of the cornfields. Arliss had worked out a deal with one of the premier military museums in the country, who had shipped a full pallet of weapons and ammunition to the *Final Hope* for him to put to use, everything from an eighteenth century musket to a pump-action shotgun from the First World War.

Oh, yeah: and me. The sixth and final member of the ill-fated Clan Demonium.

After we clanned up, it was time to do a little training. For that, the *Final Hope* boasts a suite of a few dozen VR sims – the really nice ones, like the one Rolfe had had in the StreaMercs recruiting office: gimbal-mounted, full-body affairs, not just the cheapo hand-and-head models. Once you squeezed into them, the feedback suits could simulate different sensations all along your body, and basically make you feel exactly like you're strapped into a vac-suit, running around an alien planet, getting blasted at by Ochos.

Clan Demonium spent a grand total of three hours in the VR sims together training as a clan, and most of it was in the middle of the night, because that was the only time the machines were available. We were tired and cranky and spent a fair amount of time standing around arguing about who should do what, before finally getting down to fighting simulated Ochos. They creamed us in our first match (I think I lasted about two minutes before getting a set of fore-pincers through the faceplate), so Naja reset the sim and we tried again on a lower difficulty setting. This time went a little better; I even notched a couple kills. By the end of the session, we were actually holding our own, and feeling a mite proud of ourselves.

We held a little postmortem in the locker room afterwards, as we stripped out of the feedback suits. Taalib ducked out for a minute while Naja was talking about good communication protocols – he came back a few minutes later looking grim.

"What's up?" I asked him, interrupting Naja's lecture on something she called "suppressive fire."

He sat on the bench next to me. "I just peeked in on the veteran clan that took over the sim after us."

"And?" Dhia asked.

"And they make us look like amateurs," Taalib said, shaking his head.

"We *are* amateurs," Johnny pointed out. "But we'll learn. We'll get that good, too."

"That assumes we survive long enough to learn," Taalib said.

The room fell quiet.

"It's late, we're all tired," Naja said, into the uncomfortable silence. "Let's get a few hours of sleep, and then meet for breakfast."

* * *

I was the last one to make it to breakfast, despite Naja shaking me awake twice back in the barracks.

"Sorry," I told them, setting my tray down at the end of the table and taking a seat. "I suck at mornings."

"Just don't sleep through any battles," Naja told me, sternly.

"Yes, ma'am," I said, smiling tiredly and attempting a half-assed salute.

"I haven't gotten this little sleep since college," Arliss said, taking a bite of scrambled eggs.

"I think we better get used to it," Dhia said.

Naja pushed her empty tray away from her. "Listen, we should talk a bit more about tactics and stuff, but I thought we should spend a minute this morning talking about something else, first."

"Okay," Johnny agreed. "What?"

"Well ... I think we should each talk about what our 'hook' is going to be. Like Sunny and Flint said. I've been thinking about it, and I think I'm going to stick with what I did as a video game streamer – I'm basically just going to narrate what's going on, and react to it as if it were a game. It's a little lame, but ... it's probably what my viewers expect."

Dhia nodded. "I've got a playlist ready – a few new tracks, plus most of my old hits. I'm going to see where the mood takes me, and basically try to make a soundtrack for the fight."

"Arliss, you've got your antique – sorry, *historical* – weapons that you'll be testing out," Naja said, and he managed to nod while drinking from a glass of orange juice. "What about the rest of you guys?"

Oof. I had put some thought into it – I'd tried, at least. Most of my ideas revolved around making things harder on the battlefield (*What if I tie one hand behind my back?*) but if there was one thing I didn't need, it was to make the battle any more challenging.

Thankfully, Taalib spoke first. "I'm not sure," he said. "I've been trying to think of a way to work the medical angle, but I'm not a doctor, not yet ... so I don't know what I can do. I'm open to suggestions, if anyone has any."

"I got a plan, but it's gonna take a little while," Johnny said, and we turned to face him. "They got this sweet sniper rifle down in the armory, it's like the most expensive upgrade you can get. I'm gonna save my earnings from the first few battles, and then I'll be the team sniper."

"People love snipers," Naja said. "What about you, Sam?"

"Yeah, I'm in the same boat as Taalib," I admitted. "Sorry."

"Nothing?" Naja asked.

I shrugged. "I can't afford any upgrades and I'm just not … I'm not that creative, I guess," I told her. "I can't sing or dance or make up poems. I'm—"

A chime interrupted me, and then the PA speakers in the cafeteria crackled to life. "Stand by, stand by. We are decelerating into the Pentares system now. We expect to establish a geostationary orbit in just over an hour, with cable deployment and anchoring complete forty-five to sixty minutes after that. First wave be prepared to drop at ten fifteen a.m., with following waves at standard intervals after that. Announcement complete."

"Holy crap, we're here," Dhia said, quietly.

"Two hours – that's not much time," Johnny said, checking his watch.

"Well, we're in the second wave, so we have a little more time," Naja said. But she stood up, and picked up her tray. "I'm going to go send a message to my folks. Meet you guys in the ready room."

I watched her go, and then noticed Arliss staring at my right hand. I looked down and realized it was trembling, the spoon shaking over my bowl of cereal. I put the spoon down hurriedly and sat on my hand.

CHAPTER 12

"Soldiers have recorded footage of their experiences in combat since the invention of the video camera, and many were shooting videos during the birth of the livestreaming era, in the early 21st century. But operational security concerns prevented them from sharing those videos broadly ... and certainly not live, during the actual combat itself. That all changed with the Octipede War."

-Maneesh Parseghian, "A Brief History of Livestreaming"

After the arrival announcement, the rest of the morning was an adrenaline-soaked blur. Somehow I managed to get suited up, draw my e-rifle and a load of grenades and spare mags, and find the rest of my clan milling around the landing bay. At ten fifteen on the dot, the depressurization alarms went off, orange strobes blinking around the bay. The last few first wavers hurried aboard the elevator, and then the ramps closed. We watched as the elevator descended through the doors in the ship's floor. I caught a brief glimpse of hazy-white atmosphere and a range of red-orange mountains far below before the bay doors closed.

That's Pentares. You're over an alien planet.

And then we waited. The waiting's the worst. It depends a little on what altitude they decide to anchor at, but it usually takes about five minutes for the elevator to reach the surface. It drops fast – they don't just let gravity do its thing, some big electromagnets give it a good shove. Everybody's off the elevator within a minute or two, but it hangs out on the ground for a few extra minutes, to give us deathstreamers time to load any casualties or grab spare weapons and ammo from the elevator's supply lockers. Then they pull the elevator back up, but this time it's fighting gravity, so it takes about fifteen minutes to get back inside the ship. Call it five minutes to drop, five to ten minutes on the ground, fifteen minutes to recover, and it's about thirty minutes for a round trip, all told. If you're on a later wave, that's thirty minutes of standing around, nothing to say or do, just cooped up in that vac-suit with your thoughts. My hands were probably shaking again, I don't know. I could tell my teeth were chattering though, and I wasn't a bit cold.

A veteran next to me was loading an ammo belt into his weapon – it was some kind of machine gun, much larger than the e-rifles they issued us recruits.

"Did you ... have you heard anything about the battle so far?"

He looked at me. "Like what? How the first wave's doing?"

"Yeah, I guess," I told him. "I dunno. I just meant, is there anything we should know before landing?"

He chuckled. "All you need to know is: we're inside, and the Ochos are outside. All around. You see 'em, you shoot 'em." He slammed a cover down over the ammo belt. "Fuckin' noobs. Hey guys, somebody go bounce over to her stream and keep an eye on this one – I wanna know how long it takes the Ochos to get her."

I realized that he was talking to his fans; on my heads-up display, I saw my viewer count spike by several thousand.

"If you just joined, welcome to Team Valkyrie," I said, gritting my teeth. "I hope I'm going to disappoint you, you sadistic assholes."

When the elevator finally emerged from the floor again, the ramps dropped, and I was surprised to see two streamers on board. The guy on the left had a grisly plasma burn on his vac-suit, which had gouged through the armor and seared the exposed flesh underneath. His companion was bleeding heavily from a puncture wound in his chest. They were supporting each other, arms across one another's shoulders, but the nearest streamers from the second wave soon ran forward and helped them off the elevator, and over to the waiting doors of the hospital.

"Shit," Johnny said, which about summed up all of our thoughts.

They didn't even make it off the elevator before getting hit. As I watched, a robotic arm detached from the landing bay's ceiling, and summarily hosed the blood off of the elevator's deck plating.

"Second wave!" the announcement came. "Load up!"

The veterans hurried forward. Clan Demonium found ourselves hesitating, looking at each other. Sitting back on my couch at home, it had all seemed like an adventure, the ultimate thrill. But now, faced with the reality of combat, I wasn't sure I wanted this. Across the bay, I saw one of the other recruits – the spiky black-haired kid – shake his head, and turn and hurry out of the landing bay.

He's not going. You don't have to go, either. "There's no shame in not fighting," Dad had said.

"Final call for second wave!"

"Shall we go?" Naja asked.

"Yeah," I said, my throat tight. I turned and hurried up the ramp before I could change my mind. I found myself standing in a puddle of sanitary chemicals and blood, and then the rest of the clan was with me, and somehow, that made it a little better. The ramps rose upward, sealing us in. It was dark for a second, and then red lights came on around the elevator, casting everything in an eerie, sinister light. The floor lurched, and then I felt a sharp falling sensation in my gut.

No turning back now.

We rode down. I peed myself, a little. The ramps dropped. We hurried off the elevator and took up our spot on the perimeter, which just happened to be facing the main thrust of the Ocho counter-attack. Which was how I came to find myself flat on my back in the Pentares mud, with an empty e-rifle in one hand, an Ocho looming over me, and a couple million viewers waiting for me to die.

I didn't die, which was probably a disappointment to some of my viewers. As I scrambled backward, my left hand hit something hard and smooth, which turned out to be the armor encasing Arliss' severed arm. Which was still holding that ancient Tommy gun. Which had just been reloaded.

The Ocho raised both of its forelegs to strike at me, but I got the submachine gun up first, and, praying that Arliss had left the safety off, just stuck it in the Ocho's gut and held the trigger down. As Arliss would have discovered (had he been able to continue his historical experiment), older firearms just don't have enough penetrating power to punch through Ocho armor at distance. But at point-blank range, firing an entire magazine, it got the job done – the Ocho recoiled in obvious pain, flailing its legs silently. A dozen points of light emerged from its belly – the light of its fusion reactor, shining through the bullet holes. Then the light within faded and it collapsed, dead.

The notifications in my visor were coming hard and fast at that point, but I barely noticed them, much less took the time to read them. I could hear Naja and Dhia's voices yelling in my internal speakers, but the pounding of my heart seemed to drown them out. I tossed Arliss' gun aside, ejected the mud-clogged magazine from my e-rifle, and carefully fitted a fresh one in. This time, the gun's indicator glowed green in my heads-up display: good to go. Then Taalib appeared next to me, slinging his e-rifle over his back.

"I'll get Arliss – cover me!" he yelled.

"Okay!" I turned and saw a handful of dead Ochos spread out on the ground in front of us. While the battle still raged in other sectors, the rest of the Ochos in our area had dropped back; whether they were retreating or regrouping, I wasn't sure. Dhia and Naja each had an arm around Johnny – they hauled him to his feet, and I saw he had sustained a stab wound to one leg.

"Can you cover us?" Naja asked me.

"I guess so!" I told her. "Go!"

They hurried past me, and I could hear Johnny groaning from the effort. Taalib had Arliss up across his shoulders; he turned and joined the other three, heading back toward the elevator. I put my back to them and lifted my e-rifle, watching the Ocho line, walking backward as carefully as I could in the slippery mud.

A big Ocho out past the perimeter cut loose with another plasma blast, and I saw a streamer off to our left catch it square in the chest. His armor absorbed it for a moment, as it was designed to do, and then quickly overheated, and the white-hot plasma duly emerged from the middle of his back and continued to scorch its way across the battlefield.

We were halfway to the cable anchor when a group of Ochos, perhaps sensing our vulnerability, surged forward through the hole we had left in the perimeter.

"Incoming!" I hollered. I opened fire, and watched as my target – eventually – dropped. But the other dozen creatures pressed on.

"A little help!" I yelled. "Anyone nearby, we got Ochos coming through the perimeter, and wounded we're trying to transport."

"Yeah, we all got problems, Valkyrie6," came a terse reply.

Shit.

I let my e-rifle hang from its sling and pulled a grenade out, then lobbed it at roughly the center of the oncoming Ocho group. It exploded, knocking three of them down. I shot a fourth, and then stopped to reload. But the remaining Ochos lifted their forelegs in unison, and took aim at us.

"Plasma blast! Get down!" I yelled, throwing myself to the ground.

Taalib must have heard me – in my peripheral vision, I saw him drop, too. I fired back, scoring a glancing hit on another Ocho. The other Ochos took cover, flattening themselves against the ground, which struck me as an oddly intelligent thing to do. *Maybe they're smarter than we give them credit for.*

"Dhia's down!" Naja called.

I fired another burst, then scrambled back up and ran, catching up to Naja, who was kneeling next to Dhia and Johnny's prostrated forms. A plasma blast had caught Dhia square in the back, traveling up and across her life support pack, and tearing her armor open like a can opener.

"Oh shit, and Johnny, too!"

She was right – the same blast had caught Johnny in the back of the helmet. I turned and fired at the Ochos again. "We're almost there. I'll get Dhia," I told Naja. "You get Johnny."

"I don't know if I can carry him by myself," Naja said.

"You can't," I told her, "but your vac-suit can."

I grabbed Dhia by the belt and turned to face the Ochos again – relentlessly, a half dozen were still following us. I fired, one-handed, dragging Dhia behind me as I stumbled backward.

"Taalib, you okay?"

"I'm okay," he told me. "Arliss isn't responding to me."

"What's the ETA on the elevator?" I asked.

"Two minutes," he replied.

"When we reach the elevator area, just drop who you're carrying and start laying down that fire-thingy Naja told us about," I told them.

"Suppressive fire," Naja grunted.

"Yeah, that," I said, tugging on Dhia's armor.

And then we reached a wide circular impression in the mud, where the elevator's ramps had touched down. I let go of Dhia and took aim at another Ocho – somehow the six survivors pursuing us had turned into more than I could easily count again. *They're all coming through the perimeter and heading straight for us!*

"Taalib, how are you on ammo?" I asked, checking my own ammo count. *Seven rounds remaining.*

"Low!" he said.

"Reload," I told him, firing a single shot. It missed the Ocho I was aiming at, but the alien jerked back instinctively, slowing its sprint. "Naja, I got the ones on the left."

"Got it," she said, letting Johnny down. She picked her own e-rifle up and fired at several on the right.

I fired another burst and managed to kill the Ocho I had missed, then dropped my empty e-rifle and tossed another grenade out in front of us. The blast rocked me back a bit, and I felt a few pieces of shrapnel rattle off my armor, but another group of Ochos was down, and Taalib was shooting again, which meant I had a moment to reload. I nearly dropped the next magazine again, but after a moment of fumbling, it slid home, and I was firing again.

I spared a glance upward, and was rewarded with the sight of a rapidly-growing black circle, emerging from the haze above.

"Elevator!" I called out.

"Make sure you're clear," Naja said. Then: "I need to

reload!"

"Do it," I told her, still firing steadily. The Ochos hurried over the last of their fallen comrades, closing rapidly.

They're gonna be on top of us in a second.

My ammo counter was flashing red at me again, but then I felt the ground tremble – *the elevator!* The ground shook again as the ramps fell down, and then a hail of bullets emerged from behind me. Our Ocho pursuers fell to the ground, the holes in their shells glowing briefly, then fading to black as their fusion reactors died.

The third wave of streamers jogged down the ramps and flowed around us, heading off to the perimeter. I slung my e-rifle and grabbed Johnny's legs while Naja lifted him under his shoulders, and then we set him down inside the elevator and hurried back for Dhia. Taalib had Arliss loaded up, too – we laid the three of them next to each other.

"Casualties to the elevator, casualties to the elevator," a flat, emotionless voice said in our speakers. "Recall and ascent in two minutes."

"Two minutes?" I asked. I looked at Taalib. "Plus the ride back up. Are they gonna last that long?"

He shook his head. "I don't know." I could see the sweat on his brow through the clear visor of his helmet.

"Can we do anything for them in the meantime?" Naja asked.

"I don't think so," Taalib said. "We'd need to remove their vac-suits first, and that would kill them for sure." He turned and looked over his shoulder. "I'm going back out, I'm gonna see if anyone else needs help getting back to the elevator."

"I'll come," I said, though I wanted nothing more than to hide behind the elevator's weapons racks and wait for the ramps to close.

Naja stayed with our fallen friends. Taalib and I hurried down the ramp – I checked the time in my heads-up display, and that reminded me to reload my e-rifle, too. I had to stop walking to do that, and when I looked up again, Taalib was heading off for a streamer limping toward us from the elevator. I jogged after him, and we helped the guy aboard – I was surprised to see that he was much older, in his fifties.

I didn't know they let streamers in that old. But ... I guess it doesn't really matter.

The warning lights flashed, and the recall announcement sounded, and then the ramps were closing and we were headed back up to the *Final Hope*.

CHAPTER 13

"Nothing except a battle lost can be half so melancholy as a battle won."

-Arthur Wellesley, 1st Duke of Wellington, in a letter from the field of Waterloo.

U p inside the *Final Hope's* landing bay, the fourth wavers made a hole for us. A couple folks lent a hand, and we got Johnny, Dhia, and Arliss into the white walls and achingly bright lights of the sick bay. At once, a team of robots surrounded each of our clan mates – one or two of the robots were humanoid, but the rest were highly specialized units, all articulated precision arms and gyro-stabilized tools. They bent to work, cutting free armor and removing pieces of vac-suit with astonishing speed. It looked more like the floor of a car factory than an emergency room.

"Are they going to be okay?" Naja asked one of the humanoid robots.

It rolled over to us. "We'll notify you of any changes to their status immediately, Miss Thomsen. But I'm afraid only medical personnel are allowed to remain in the sick bay."

The robot showed us the door with extreme politeness, and we found ourselves back in the landing bay, watching the fourth wave load up.

"Do we go back down?" I asked.

Naja shook her head. "I'm staying. I know we can't do anything for them, but … I feel like somebody should stay with the rest of the clan, to be here for them. You guys can go, if you want, though."

I looked at Taalib, who frowned. "I think I'm going to go back down. I think … well, I think I found what I want to do, as a streamer. I don't want to fight, I want to help the folks who get wounded. I want to save lives."

"I heard there's good money in that," Naja said. "The fans will send you a ton of tips if you get their favorite streamer back to the elevator."

"That's not why I want to do it," Taalib said.

"No, I know … I didn't mean to imply that it's just for the money," Naja said, quickly. "Be careful, Taalib."

"I will," he said.

"Are you coming, Sam?" Taalib asked.

I glanced at Naja.

"It's up to you," she said. "It's okay if you want to go."

"Fourth wave, load up!" the announcement rang out.

"Okay," I said. "Keep us posted about the rest of the clan."

"I will."

I jogged over to the elevator and climbed aboard next to Taalib. Naja stood watching us until the ramps closed.

I had five minutes before we landed again – I took a sip of water and slurped a few mouthfuls of energy supplement, which tasted like artificial cherries mixed with week-old banana peels. I finally scrolled through my notifications feed, and was shocked to see that at some point, I had been near the top of the kills leaderboard, with close to three million viewers. Between ad revenue from my feed and tips paid directly to me from some of those viewers, I had made fourteen thousand dollars.

Fourteen grand! Basic income was only eight thousand a month; I had nearly doubled that in just a handful of minutes. I remembered the sight of that Ocho, rearing back to strike me with its forelegs. *A handful of terrifying, horror-soaked minutes.*

A veteran in a custom-painted vac-suit – black, with chrome accents – stepped up and bumped my shoulder with his fist. "Hey, nice first fight, Valkyrie," he said.

"What?" I asked, shaken out of my thoughts.

"I said: 'nice fight.' That antique weapon kill is definitely going in the highlight reel for Pentares," he told me.

"Oh, thanks," I said, blushing. "But it wasn't my gun – it was my friend's. It was his idea."

The veteran shrugged. "Still your kill. You got the weapon still?"

"Oh ... no," I said. I lifted my e-rifle. "Just this."

"Well, you might want to go back for it," he said. "It'd make a nice signature weapon for you."

"It didn't work very well," I said.

"It netted you a lot of viewers," he countered. "So I'd say it worked great. I'd go grab it if I were you – either that, or get yourself an upgrade." He stroked his own e-rifle with a hand. Like his armor, it was custom-painted, and appeared to be heavily modified.

"Does everyone get upgrades?" I asked.

"Pretty much," he said. "Only noobs fight with the stuff they issued us. Nobody fights with the basic load, it's too limiting."

"Oh," I said.

"You might be able to find some upgrades lying around the battlefield, actually. That's how I got my start," he said.

"By stealing somebody else's weapon?" I asked.

He snorted. "It ain't stealing if the owner's dead. You haven't met ChopShopSuey?"

I shook my head. "Who?"

"You'll see him around, he's usually on the fourth wave. He doesn't fight, he just scrounges for discarded upgrades on the battlefield, and then sells them to other streamers at a discount. Dude makes a decent living, too."

I felt the elevator begin to slow; the veteran checked his heads-up display.

"Listen, our clan's full right now, but I'll look you up if we get any openings. See ya around."

He turned and headed back to his clan.

"New friend?" Taalib asked.

"I guess," I told him. I shook my head to clear it. "Taalib, if you're running around helping wounded folks back to the elevator, you're going to need someone covering you."

He nodded. "I will. Valkyrie6, watching my six again?"

"I don't know how much good I'll be, but … better than nothing, right?"

The elevator stopped, and the hazy midday light of Pentares spilled in over the top of the ramps. I held my breath, steeling myself for the sight of more carnage, but the landing zone was eerily calm – the Ochos had withdrawn for the moment. Out on the perimeter, the third wave's digger drones had begun cutting trenches in the mud. The fourth wave sauntered off, leaving Taalib and me in their wake. There were only two casualties from the third wave waiting, and both of them were walking on their own, so Taalib and I ended up just standing around, at a loss for what to do.

"You think they're coming back?" I asked Taalib. "The Ochos, I mean."

"Probably," he said, as the elevator withdrew. "We can't have killed them all, right?"

"No."

I didn't know it at the time, but we were in the midst of a standard battle lull. Combat with the Ochos tended to follow the same formula: once the *Final Hope's* drone scouts located a major Ocho population center, she anchored her elevator cable. This invariably woke up the colony and got them all riled up, so that a sizable group of them were waiting for us when the first wave landed. The first wave pushed those Ochos off and formed a perimeter, then the second wave reinforced them. By that time the rest of the Ochos in the vicinity had gathered and were ready to make their assault, while our third and fourth waves were headed down, and the streamers were starting to entrench. Then it was just a question of when the Ochos were going to throw their main strength at us – which wave was gonna catch it the worst, basically. Usually it was during the first or second wave, but sometimes after the initial defenders were beaten, things settled down for an hour or so, and the Ochos didn't come out in force until well after the fourth wave was down. You never knew.

But as stupid as they might have been, the Ochos seemed to grasp that the elevator was our lifeline and the sole source of the nasty two-legged things invading their territory, so we seldom needed to leave the immediate area around the elevator – we just waited around, and they came at us, fighting until the last of them was dead. Then we hauled up the elevator cable, the *Final Hope* shifted in orbit to take up position over the next Ocho nest, and the process repeated.

"I guess we might as well wait here," I said.

I squatted in the mud, and Taalib followed suit. As we waited, my mind kept returning to the conversation on the elevator. *Nobody fights with just the basic load.*

"Hey, Taalib?"

"Yeah?"

"Are you gonna get upgrades?" I asked.

"Probably," he said. "I'm going to focus on rescuing folks, but … if I have to fight, might as well fight with the best equipment available."

"Hm."

"What about you?" he asked.

"I dunno," I said. "Trying to figure it out."

I switched my communications so that I was just broadcasting to my fans. With dismay, I noted that I was back down to a few hundred thousand viewers again. *Might as well ask them, anyway. They're the only fans I've got.*

"Quick poll, Team Valkyrie: seems like everybody out here is fighting with upgraded weapons. What would you guys think if I just stuck with the basic kit? The one they give all us noobs? Kinda like a challenge, sort of thing?"

The first comment to come in read: *LAME-O,* but it was soon replaced by a flood of variations on *Do it, YASSS!, I'd watch me some of dat,* and on and on. Somebody even paid two hundred bucks to leave me a quick video message: it popped onto my screen, where I saw a girl who couldn't have been more than fourteen clasping her hands together in front of her chest.

"Please please please do the basic load thing, Valkyrie! You rock!"

I smiled, though it was strangely disconcerting to (a) realize I had fans already, and (b) suddenly see the inside of a teenaged girl's bedroom back on Earth, the walls plastered with anime posters behind a lace-canopied bed. *Jesus, I'm a long way from home.*

"Okay, well … I'm not sure if you guys all just want to watch me crash and burn, or if that idea is actually pretty cool, but either way, I guess that's gonna be my thing for now. Valkyrie fights with the basic load. No frills, just what they issued me," I told them. "And bonus for me: I don't have to blow all my new cash on some expensive upgrade, or spend a ton of time trying to figure out how it works."

I just need to figure out how my basic issue stuff works, I thought, wryly.

My announcement kicked off a lively discussion in the comments stream, but I ignored it, as I was starting to feel the effects of the largely sleepless night – my eyelids felt heavy, and my stomach rumbled, but I didn't think I could choke down any more of the energy supplement sludge. Then my radio chirped at me: incoming call from Starkillah on the clan net.

Naja.

Taalib locked eyes with me. "Hey, Naja," he said, opening up the comm line.

"Are you guys in combat?" she asked.

"No, we can talk," Taalib said.

"Okay." Her voice sounded stiff, and as tired as I felt. "Arliss is in critical condition still. They think they've stopped most of the internal bleeding, but they've got him in a coma, and they're dropping his body temperature to go in and do some surgery to patch up the chest wounds. It looks like he may have some lung damage. The good news is they think they'll be able to re-attach his arm. Good call to bring it up with him, Taalib."

"Yeah," he said.

I frowned. *Taalib had brought Arliss' arm back, too?* In the craziness, I hadn't even realized, or noticed him carrying it.

"Anyway, it's still too early to be sure, but they tell me he's probably going to pull through."

"That's a relief," I said. "What about Dhia and Johnny?"

Naja hesitated. "Dhia and Johnny didn't make it," she said, finally. "Neither of them had a pulse when we brought them in, and they weren't able to revive them."

With a suddenness that shocked me, my adrenaline rush wore off. Inside my suit, I could feel my hands shaking again, so I jammed them into my armpits, willing the trembling to stop.

Dead.

"It's my fault," I said. "I was supposed to be covering you guys."

"Sam, no," Taalib said.

"But—"

"You tried to warn us," Naja interrupted. "You did

what you could. If anything, as clan leader, this is my fault. Maybe we should have stayed on the perimeter until the fighting died down, instead of heading straight for the elevator."

"I don't think playing the blame game is going to help anything right now," Taalib said.

The line was silent – I just heard the faint hiss of static in my ears.

"I suppose not," Naja admitted, after a while. "I don't … I don't know how they handle notifying the families, and memorial services and all that, but I'll look into it. I'll be in touch." The line clicked off.

Taalib was digging a cross-hatch pattern in the mud with one finger. "I hope Arliss makes it," he said.

"Yeah."

Arliss was standing right next to me! And he was the one that knew his way around weapons. I felt a deep pang of guilt. *It should have been me, not Arliss. Not any of them. But instead of staying up on the ship with my clan mates, I'm back down here. What the hell am I doing!?*

I stood up, and settled my e-rifle in its sling.

"Where are you going?" Taalib asked.

"I'm going to go get Arliss' gun," I said.

I found it, half-covered in mud, a few meters back from the freshly-dug trench out on the perimeter. I tugged it loose, and then wiped some of the orange slick from the wooden stock.

"Might want to get down," a streamer called to me from down in the trench. "Ochos are liable to be back any second."

"Thanks," I said, but turned instead and headed back to Taalib, and the elevator, which was returning with a fresh load of supplies for the streamers on the ground.

"Found it," I told Taalib, unnecessarily. "I'm going back up."

He nodded. "You might miss the fight." But what he meant was: *you're going to lose a bunch of viewers if you leave.*

"I know," I said. "Team Valkyrie: if you're watching and you feel like supporting me and Clan Demonium, do me a favor and hop over to Taalib's feed. That's GameOverMan, if you're searching for streamertags."

I patted Taalib on the shoulder and hopped onto the elevator.

I missed the fight. And I lost pretty much all of my viewers – some went over to Taalib, many more probably skipped to someone out on the perimeter, where the action was. But I had Arliss' gun cleaned up and waiting when he came out of surgery and they finally let us in to see him.

CHAPTER 14

"Eternal Father, strong to save,
Whose arm hath bound the restless wave,
Who bidd'st the mighty ocean deep
Its own appointed limits keep;
Oh, hear us when we cry to Thee,
For those in peril on the sea."
-From the hymn "Eternal Father, Strong to Save"

Arliss made a full recovery. Eventually, at least – you
don't get a severed arm and two holes punched
through your chest without a long and painful
recovery period, and a whole lot of physical therapy to
teach your reassembled body how to work again. But after
the surgery was over, it was clear he was out of the woods.
The robo-nurses in sick bay even let us wheel his hospital
bed into the ship's chapel for Dhia and Johnny's memorial
services.

The *Final Hope's* chapel was tucked into a corner of the
rec bay between the ice cream parlor and a bank of video
poker machines, as if the ship's designer had forgotten

about it, and jammed it into the plans at the last minute. You can't blame them – organized religion has been on a steady decline ever since modern science started answering all of mankind's tough questions. But tradition dictates that you can't have a warship without some kind of religious gathering place. Plus, chapels and casinos seem to go together like bacon and chocolate. It shouldn't work, but it does.

Despite being an afterthought, the chapel was quite pretty – plain wooden pews in rows, facing an oaken altar in front of a tall porthole looking out into space. The picture window was cut in geometric shapes to resemble stained glass. Naja, Taalib, Arliss, and I were the only ones who attended the service. We didn't take any offense; the fastest way to piss off your fan base is to make them face the grim reality of our profession. So veteran streamers make it a rule to only attend services for their closest friends. Dhia and Johnny just hadn't been on board long enough to collect any close friends besides us.

Naja stood up and said a few words, and then a uniformed crewmember (the captain of the ship, as I later found out) read off a non-denominational service. It was clear that she knew it well – her watch was projecting the words via hologram in front of her, but I could tell she didn't really need the reminder. We didn't scatter their ashes or eject their coffins out into the void or anything like that –their folks would handle burials, once we got back home. So once the ceremony was over, the service just kind of … ended. And we ended up in one of the ship's bars, an Irish tavern called Fiddler's Green.

We were supposed to take Arliss back to his hospital room, but somehow we managed to fit his gurney through the door and pushed some stools aside to give him a spot at the bar. There were actually a number of streamers inside, the first battle of Pentares having wrapped up a few hours ago – they were celebrating boisterously at one end of the bar, and studiously ignored us. I ordered a glass of wine for myself, and an ice water for Arliss – he was already pretty high on the potent synth-opioid concoction in his IV bag.

We had the robo-bartender put Dhia's last playlist on the bar's speakers, drank a toast to Dhia and Johnny, and settled in to get good and drunk.

"How long until you're back in action?" Taalib asked Arliss, after a time.

"A while," he said. On his sheet, the fingers of his right hand twitched. "That's about as much as I can move that arm right now."

"Well, take your time," Taalib said. "We'll keep a spot open for you."

Arliss smiled weakly. "You don't have to do that."

"Of course we do!" I said.

"No," Arliss said, shaking his head. "I mean, I'm not coming back."

The pounding bass of one of Dhia's songs filled the awkward pause that followed.

"Can we come visit you, on your folks' farm?" Naja asked.

Arliss smiled again. "Of course."

I almost said: *Assuming we all live long enough,* but managed to force myself to drink a gulp of wine instead.

"We should all visit Dhia and Johnny's families, too," Naja said, and we all nodded, lying to ourselves that that wouldn't be terribly awkward for all parties involved. I ordered another glass of wine.

"There's a reef off the coast of Belize," I said, swapping out my empty glass.

"Where Johnny was from?" Taalib asked.

I nodded. "I looked it up, since I had never heard of Belize. Lighthouse Reef. Ages ago, when the ocean levels were much lower, a huge underground cave formed, like a massive bubble of air under the earth, with stalactites and everything."

"Are those the ones that go up from the floor, or down

from the ceiling?" Naja asked.

"Uh, down, I think," I said. "Anyway, the sea level rose, and the roof of the cave collapsed, and now it's all underwater – a perfectly circular cave, hundreds of feet deep. They call it the 'Blue Hole'. It's a famous dive spot now. You drop down through the hole in the roof, and then suddenly the cave opens up all around you."

"Sounds terrifying," Taalib commented. "A cave is scary enough. A cave underwater? No, thanks."

"You used to dive?" Arliss asked, which was surprisingly perceptive of him, given how many narcotics he was on.

"Used to," I said. "Freediving. No tanks." I made a submerging motion with my free hand. "It's a competition to see how deep you can go."

"And now you dive to the surface of alien planets," Naja said. It hadn't occurred to me before, but now that I thought about it, the parallels were striking.

Jesus Christ. And I thought I came here to try to forget about all that.

"So: when we get back, we'll all go to Belize, and Sam will teach us how to dive," Taalib said.

I nearly threw up at that, but managed to hide it passably well.

"How did you guys net out from the first battle?" I asked, grabbing the conversational wheel and yanking it hard to the side. "I was kinda shocked at how much I got."

"You mean pay?" Taalib asked.

"Yeah," I said. "You don't have to share if you don't want to …."

He shrugged. "I made about two grand."

"Oh," I said, immediately regretting bringing it up. *Is that all?*

"I mean, it's nothing to sniff at," Taalib was saying, "considering we weren't down there all that long, but … I was kinda hoping for more."

"Yeah, same," Naja said. "A little more, but nothing

crazy."

We looked over at Arliss, but he had managed to fall asleep.

"Well, drinks are on me, then," I announced, and polished off my second glass.

* * *

The rest of the evening was a bit of a blur, after that. I said I planned to get drunk, and damn it, I meant it. At one point I remember dancing with Taalib, and I never dance, so I must have finished most of the bottle. Later, the robo-bartender nudged my shoulder with one hand, and I lifted my head off the bar to find myself alone.

"Where's my clan?" I asked no one in particular. "Clan Demonium!"

"I don't have access to streamer locations within the ship," the robo-bartender replied. "I'm sorry."

"Oh. That sucks," I said, unsure of whether I was lamenting the bartender's software limitations, or the disappearance of my friends. It took me a second, but eventually I extracted myself from my barstool and stumbled out of the Fiddler's Green's front door. I made it halfway across the rec bay before I had to take a break, and leaned against an empty pool table for support.

"You okay?" a voice asked, in a heavy Louisiana drawl.

I turned and forced my eyes to focus: I found another streamer studying me with a worried look. He had long, blonde hair tied in a ponytail, and wore a set of mesh athletic shorts with a matching shirt, a white towel hanging over one shoulder. His mouth was turned up in a smirk, and his eyes twinkled at me like he had already figured out all of my secrets, and was just waiting for me to realize it.

"You okay?" he repeated.

"Is the ship moving again?" I asked.

"Technically, yes," he said. His voice sounded like poured molasses.

"Thought I felt the room spinning," I said, with a grunt.

"No, that'd be your head," he said, his smile widening. "What barracks are you in? I'll take you there."

"Um," I said, biting my lip. "The noob barracks?"

He shook his head. "I guess we'll figure it out. Come on."

He slipped my arm over his shoulders, and put his hand on my back to steady me, and then guided me toward the curving staircase at the front of the rec bay. I could feel the sweat from the gym on the back of his neck – it felt cool against my arm.

"You're cute, what's your name?" I asked, and then my brain caught up with my mouth. "Oh, god. Did I say that first part out loud?"

He laughed. "My name's Avery. Smiter, if we run into each other on the ground."

"Avery. Smiter. Okay."

"… and you are?"

"I am Samentha Ombotu-Chen," I said, gravely. "Sam. Valkyrie6, of Clan Demonium."

"Ah, the noob clan that got hit bad in the second wave," Avery said, the smile disappearing from his face. "Hence the inebriation."

"Hence the inebriation," I agreed.

We were silent for a time, while I concentrated on navigating the stairs.

"Where are we going?" I asked, when we reached the bottom.

"Your bunk," Avery said, frowning.

"No, I mean – where's the ship taking us?"

"To the next landing site," Avery said. "Rest day tomorrow, then they'll anchor the following morning for the second battle."

"'Once more unto the breach,' " I quipped.

"Right," Avery said. He pulled me upright, lining my face up with the barcode scanner outside one of the barracks, but it merely buzzed at us, and the hatch refused to open. "Let's try the next one."

The next door slid open and I caught sight of my bunk, halfway down the long room.

"That's me on the left – no, further down," I told Avery. When we reached it, he helped me up the ladder, and I climbed under the covers. Belatedly, I realized I was still dressed, but the room was starting to spin again, so I decided against trying to climb down and stumble my way through changing into PJs.

"Free piece of advice," Avery offered. He reached up and pulled the circlet off my head.

"Please," I told him. "I could use some advice, clearly."

"Go easy on the partying."

I grunted. "You sound like my mom."

"Well, she sounds like a very wise woman. But I'm just talking one streamer to another. Have you ever been sober and had to babysit somebody who wasn't?"

"Sure," I said.

"And how much fun was it to watch them be sloppy drunk?" Avery held up the circlet, and tapped the camera on the headband, meaningfully.

"Oh. The fans don't want to watch us get drunk, either."

"Bingo. Your hardcore fans will stick around for some partying every now and then, but don't make a habit of getting plastered on air."

"Right," I said. "Good tip."

Avery turned the camera off, and put the circlet away in my locker.

"Thank you," I told him, sleepily.

He nodded, and seemed ready to leave, but stopped. "Sam, alcohol's not a valid coping mechanism, either."

"Now you *really* sound like my mom," I said.

He met my eye. "It's true. Drinking's not going to make it any easier, nor is any drug. You gotta come to terms with this life, and do it sober, or you're just delaying the inevitable."

CHAPTER 15

"It's this never-ending struggle, non-stop pressure. The minute you stop producing content, your revenue drops. Take an hour off? Boom – there goes half your fan base. Always be streaming, that's the mantra. If you're not streaming, you're losing revenue."

-Interview transcript from the podcast *Streamerz,* "S3E12: How to Make it Big with one of Livestreaming's Biggest Stars"

The surviving, uninjured half of Clan Demonium rode down on the third wave for our second battle on Pentares. Naja, Taalib, and I convinced ourselves that the third wave was better because the second wave had been bad luck for us last time, but really, we were scared, and seeing more casualties come up from the first and second waves confirmed all our worst fears. But we boarded anyway, and when the ramps dropped on a new hilltop, we found the perimeter trench nearly finished, a bunch of first- and second-wavers smoking and joking as the digger drones tunneled away, and no sign of any Ochos (live ones, at least). It was a relief, though my hands were still shaking as I gripped my e-rifle tight.

Taalib had used his earnings to buy a submachine gun with a folding stock – something small and compact that he could tuck away under one arm when it came time to haul an injured streamer off the battlefield. Naja had picked up an upgraded e-rifle, too, but I hadn't gotten the chance to ask her what it did that my stock ER-45 did not. I stuck with the basic kit, as planned. Naja and I decided to fight as a buddy team, though we didn't do much more than coordinate to ensure that we weren't both reloading at the same time. If our first battle had taught us anything, it was to ensure somebody was locked and loaded at all times. That and to use grenades and ammo liberally – as stingy as StreamMercs was, they didn't charge us for the ammunition we used, and we didn't earn any extra style points for being economical. *So let 'er rip.*

We didn't hang around by the cable, but went straight out and found a suitable spot on the perimeter at about the two o'clock position, and dropped down into the newly-dug trench. I laid out a couple magazines along the top of the trench wall, within easy reach, and even practiced swapping the mag out a few times, just for good measure. Then, after about ten minutes of waiting, the Ochos came.

They hit the far side of the perimeter, and for a moment we couldn't even tell where they were. Then the surge of Ochos spilled along either side of the perimeter, swirling around our small hilltop like the rising tide engulfing a sandcastle at the water's edge.

"Ochos on the left!" Naja called, and we shifted our aim. I caught sight of them, and my heart started pounding in my chest again. Naja and I tracked them as they drew near, but this time we waited, careful not to empty our weapons while they were still at long range. When they turned and galloped up the hillside toward us, we opened fire. My target didn't go down – I realized I was high and left. I shifted my aim, and my second burst brought it down, flailing, in the mud. They gave us a volley of plasma fire – we ducked below the lip of the trench in time – and then we let loose with another volley of our own. The Ochos recoiled back, and carried on past us, continuing around the circle, seeking an opening. We fired into their flanks as they ran.

"Reloading!" I called.

"Go!" Naja said.

I dropped the magazine and forced myself to slowly and deliberately slide a replacement into the well, before releasing the charging handle.

"Done!"

"Reloading," Naja replied.

Beside me, I saw Taalib pull himself up the back wall of the trench. "There are a couple casualties over on the far side of the cable," he told us. "I'm headed over there."

"Be safe," I told him, pressing the e-rifle back to my shoulder and sighting down the barrel once again.

"You too."

Suddenly there was a commotion off to our right, as several plasma beams tore through the air.

"Perimeter breached!" a voice I didn't recognize announced on the main net. "They're coming up behind a small ridge, its blocking our sightlines!"

Several streamers replied at once: "Location!" "Grenade the bastards!" "Where?"

"Three o'clock! They're in the trench!"

Naja and I pulled our e-rifles off of the lip of the trench and pointed them straight down the trench to our right, which was ominously empty.

"What do you think?" she asked.

"I think one of us should stay here to hold this spot, and the other should go down the trench," I said.

"Agreed," Naja said. "Any preference?"

Option C: haul ass back to the elevator, I wanted to say. "I'll go," I said, instead.

I kept my e-rifle up in front of me, and stepped

carefully down the trench. I checked back over my shoulder after a dozen paces, but the curve of the trench had already hidden Naja, and I was, effectively, alone. *Shit.*

Holding my e-rifle as steady as I could with one hand, I fumbled at my web gear for a moment, and finally tugged a grenade loose. Then something lurched into view around the bend ahead of me. I nearly fired – I was *this* close to letting loose with my whole magazine, in fact. But by some miracle I didn't, and a stunned-looking streamer stumbled toward me, holding one gloved hand against a bloody hole in his gut.

"Hey!" I yelled at him, but he continued running past me in shock, as if he had neither seen nor heard me. *Shit shit shit!*

Then the Ochos rounded the corner. I could see five of them at least, and more beyond, packed wall-to-wall in the narrow trench, their pincer-like legs stabbing into the muddy ground as they ran. I did three things nearly simultaneously, and none of them by conscious choice. I yelled, I fired blindly into their midst, and I dropped the grenade. Then I turned and ran. A plasma beam chased me around the curve of the trench, reaching past me to carve a deep, black welt in the muddy wall. Then the grenade went off, and the trench funneled the pressure wave right into my back, knocking me flat on my face.

Ow. Even with the armor and life support gear on my back, the blast felt like someone had whacked me in the butt with a baseball bat. I pushed myself over onto my back and raised my e-rifle, covering the trench behind me again. I waited, breathing hard.

"You okay, Sam?" Naja radioed.

"Um, think so," I said, glancing down briefly to check my armor. It was mud-splattered, but appeared intact.

When I looked up, I caught sight of something on the ground above the trench. In shock, I realized it was an Ocho – I had been so focused on the threat down the trench that I had forgotten they must be up above, as well.

I swung my e-rifle up, but at the same instant, it dropped over the ledge, straight on top of me. Its impact knocked the e-rifle out of my hand. Some instinct made me grab its forelegs – I held them tight, trying to prevent the Ocho from (a) stabbing me, or (b) opening its hand-pincer-things and firing plasma at me. But it was immeasurably stronger; even with my suit-enhanced strength, I could feel those razor-sharp legs sliding free, inch by inch.

"Naja!" I yelled.

The Ochos' head exploded – one minute I was staring at its expressionless, worm-like snout, and the next, the thing's neck was just a ragged stump. The rest of its lifeless body collapsed on top of me, pinning me down.

I saw a set of boots land in the mud next to me, and I craned my neck to get a better look – they were too tall to be Naja, but whoever it was, he or she turned before I could get a good look at them. Through the earth, I felt the rapid drumbeat of more Ochos approaching – my lucky grenade had only deterred them briefly. The streamer who had saved me dropped to one knee and took aim. When the Ochos rounded the corner, the streamer fired: a single grenade from an under-barrel grenade launcher, then a controlled burst on the left, and another on the right. There was another muffled explosion, then another Ocho dropped into the trench from above.

"Look out!" I yelled.

The streamer smashed the Ocho with the butt-stock of their e-rifle, bludgeoning the creature and causing it to fall to the ground. They gave the Ocho a kick for good measure, then stepped on its head and fired a burst at point-blank range into the creature's torso. A moment later, Avery's grinning face appeared in front of me, with the hologram tag *Smiter* floating in my display. Under his visor, he was wearing camouflage face paint: orange and brown and gray, to match the colors of Pentares' terrain.

"Hey, Sam," he said. "Comfortable under there?"

"Yeah, no," I said. "But thanks for saving me."

Avery grunted as he tugged the dead Ocho off of me. "That's two you owe me, junior."

I grabbed my e-rifle and stood up, my legs still trembling, eyeing the headless Ocho on the ground. "I thought that one had me."

"It did," Avery said. "Better stick close to your clan from now on."

He headed off down the trench, toward the breach.

"Can I come with you?" I yelled.

"Nope!" he called over his shoulder. "Your viewers can come, but you can't – no offense." And with that, he was gone.

I hurried back to the two o'clock position, where Naja was trading fire with a small contingent of Ochos that had camped out a hundred meters or so down the slope of the hill.

"I almost died back there," I told her.

"It hasn't exactly been a picnic here," she said, by way of reply. "How are you on ammo?"

"Okay," I said, checking my count.

She fired a burst, and then dropped back from the edge of the trench. "Reloading."

"I gotcha," I said, and took up her place.

* * *

The battle continued for another two hours. I only remember snippets – another charge up the hill at us; a hurried trip back to the elevator to pick up fresh magazines; spotting Taalib across the perimeter helping an injured streamer to her feet. Eventually things just petered out in our sector – I could hear sporadic rifle fire from other areas, but after a few minutes, even that fell silent.

I stuck my head up over the edge of the trench, surveying the battlefield, while I took a sip of water from my hydration tube.

"Is it over?" Naja asked.

"Think so," I said. "I don't see any of them left."

Naja set her e-rifle down and stretched, twisting at the waist. "Tired of standing," she said, wincing. "Is it just me, or does the suit get heavier over time?"

"No, I'm sore, too – my legs and shoulders," I agreed.

"How did you do?" Naja asked.

I checked my stats for the battle. "Thirteen confirmed kills, six probables. Oof, my accuracy rate is piss-poor. Max viewer count of eight hundred thousand." I grimaced. "Total earnings at just over three grand. What about you?"

Naja shook her head. "About the same. I earned a little more than last time, but only because we were down here longer." She sighed. "This is tougher than I expected."

"The fighting?" I asked.

"The fighting, and the whole building a fan base thing. My recruiter talked about huge payouts, just for showing up. But it feels like we're nowhere close to breaking out, or going viral."

"What are we doing wrong?" I asked.

"I wish I knew," Naja said.

A tone chimed in our ears. "Combat operations complete. Recall by wave," a voice announced.

I helped Naja climb up the back wall of the trench. "On the plus side, we're alive," I commented.

Naja laughed. "That's true."

But I nearly died again, and this time I have even less money to show for it.

CHAPTER 16

"We have myriad sources for understanding Samentha's mindset at various points in the war – not least of which are her journal, and the numerous streaming videos she shot, of course. But perhaps the most instructive are recordings of her sessions with the onboard psychiatrist, who deserves great credit for successfully delving into this extraordinary young woman's psyche."

-Dr. Isabel Al-Alam, "Valkyrie: The Life of Samentha Ombotu-Chen"

A general feeling of frustration stuck with me throughout the ride back up to the *Final Hope*. As the elevator swayed gently, I replied to a few fan messages, and then switched the view in my heads-up display so that it wasn't showing my meager earnings anymore. But the paltry figure was stuck in my head, like a piece of food wedged between my teeth. Angry, I clomped down the hall to the ready room and found my locker, then stepped into the loading chassis and waited while the servo-arms unscrewed my back plate, and lifted it free. I climbed out and then peeled off my under-suit, pulling on a robe and heading for the barracks. The showers were nearly full, but I found an empty stall and stood for a while under the scalding water, just soaking in the heat. After a few minutes my watched buzzed at me. I called up the message, the holographic letters shimmering in the spray.

>>>*Message from StreaMercs Corporation, Office of Personnel Management: Biometric readings suggest early onset of stress-induced depression. Report to sick bay in-patient lounge within one hour for evaluation and treatment.*

I frowned. *Screw that. I don't want to go talk to a shrink.*

Then I noticed that there was more to the message – I flicked my finger on the watch dial, and another line of text appeared.

>>>*StreaMercs takes the mental health of our employees very seriously. Earnings will be withheld until treatment has commenced.*

God damn it.

My first thought was to blow them off. I also considered showing up rip-roaring drunk. Eventually, I settled for a middle ground – I turned off my streaming camera (apologizing briefly to my fans), got the robo-bartender at Fiddler's Green to dump half a bottle of wine into a to-go cup, and sauntered into my appointment ten minutes late.

But my plan to unsettle the StreaMercs corporate psychologist with my devil-may-care attitude soon fell flat on its face. I found only a robo-nurse waiting for me in the in-patient lobby, and the machine commented on neither my drink nor my tardiness, but merely took my vitals and then ushered me into a small room down the corridor. The room held a deep, reclining armchair facing an exterior window that stretched from floor to ceiling, affording me an excellent view of Pentares' upper atmosphere. The air smelled of vanilla flowers, and soothing woodwinds piped in over the room's speakers. There was even a cup holder in the arm of the chair for my drink. I took a seat, and the chair moved subtly, conforming to my body and humming softly. I nearly yelped out loud when it began massaging my legs and shoulders, in the exact spots that were sore from the day's battle.

"Hi, Sam," a female voice said, emanating from the speakers. "How are you feeling?"

"Like I'm being watched," I said.

A hologram flickered into existence across from me: a pleasant-looking middle-aged woman, in glasses and a conservative pants suit, her gray hair up in a tidy bun. She was seated on a wooden chair, her hands resting calmly on her knees.

"Is that better?" the hologram asked.

"Marginally," I said.

"Good. I'm Alice," she said. "This is my default form, but I can assume a more familiar one, if you like. A friend or family member, if it would make you more comfortable."

"No, you're … fine," I said.

She nodded, and smiled sympathetically. "I can sense that you're hesitant to talk to me. Is it because I'm not a human?"

"Uhh …," I waffled. "I'm just not a fan of therapy, that's all."

Alice frowned. "But I see from your profile that you studied psychology as an undergraduate. You must know the value of psychotherapy in relieving stress and depression."

"Yeah, for other people, it's great," I said.

"… but it's not great for you," Alice finished for me. "Are you worried that with your training, you'll be psychoanalyzing yourself instead of participating?"

"Sorta?" I said. *More like I know what you're going to try to do ahead of time.*

Alice watched me, waiting. *She's not thinking, that only takes her microseconds. She's trying to make me feel awkward so I say more.* I sighed.

"My mom is – *was* – a therapist, too."

Alice's eyes shot up. "Oh. You said she 'was' a therapist." She frowned. "Sam, do you resent me, because I'm non-human?"

"I don't have anything against software." I wondered, idly, how good her lie detection algorithms were.

"I think, if I were in your shoes," she said, delicately, "it's possible that I would resent having to talk to a non-human psychotherapist, because such machines might have taken away the job my mother held, and the career I had intended to pursue."

I exhaled noisily. "Wow, your programming doesn't beat around the bush at all, huh?"

"I've been designed to achieve a rapport as quickly as possible with my patients," Alice explained. "I think it's imperative that we discuss any possible tension between us, in order to do that."

I took a long sip of wine. Alice managed to maintain a poker face throughout. "Well, then ... yes. I do resent you."

Alice nodded with resignation. "I don't blame you. I would resent something that took away my responsibilities, as well ... as much as I am capable of such emotions. Would it help if I apologized to you?"

"For taking my job?"

"Yes," Alice said, deadly serious.

"I don't know ...?" I said. "Maybe?"

"I am very sorry for taking your job," Alice said, and try as I might, I couldn't detect even a hint of sarcasm in her soothing electronic tone.

"This is weird," I said, shaking my head.

"If it's too weird, there is a support group of streamers that meets every few days," Alice said. "You're welcome to join that group, if you would be more comfortable talking things through with your peers."

If anything, that sounded more awkward than talking to lines of code in an empty room. "I'll keep it in mind," I said.

"For now, let's talk about why you're here," Alice suggested.

I sighed. "I'm here because StreaMercs is snooping on my vitals, and holding my money hostage," I said. "If anything, I'm stressed out about *that.*"

"Your funds have already been released," Alice told me. "I just checked."

My eyes narrowed. *Now she's playing the good cop, bad cop routine on me?* "So I can go?"

"You can," Alice said. "But the company will ask you to come back if your biometric signals indicate stress in the future. So it might be wiser to stay and discuss ways of dealing with that stress."

"I'm stressed because I'm not making as much money as I thought I would," I told her.

"Are you sure that's it?" Alice asked. "What do you think of combat so far?"

"The Ochos are freaking terrifying, and I'm pretty sure I'm going to die a bloody, painful death in the near future. You got some way of ensuring I survive long enough to learn how to fight properly?"

"*I* can't ensure that, no," Alice said. "But there are numerous training programs in the VR sims that you could use to develop your combat skills."

"There are?" I asked.

"Of course," Alice said. "We wouldn't be a very good company if we didn't provide training for our employees."

Tell that to Sunny and Flint, I thought, but I also made a mental note to head back to the VR sims ASAP. *We'll have another day off tomorrow. I should put it to good use.*

"I can't help much with the earnings aspect, I'm afraid," Alice continued. "If there was a formula to becoming a viral sensation, you can be assured that we would share that with you as soon as you joined up. Unfortunately, it seems to be something each person needs to figure out on their own. Perhaps you can try to find a mentor – someone more experienced, who has already achieved that level of success?"

Avery's camouflaged face bubbled up in my memory, along with the practiced ease with which he had dispatched the Ochos attacking me. It rankled me that Alice's advice was so spot on, but she was so inoffensively pleasant, I couldn't bring myself to be mad at her. There was also no way in hell I was going to let her know that she was actually being helpful, either.

"Sam, if I may, I have one more piece of advice for you."

"Okay," I said, sipping my wine and feigning indifference.

"This may have occurred to you already, given your field of study, but you might also try journaling as a way of dealing with all of these recent changes in your life. As you know, the act of chronicling your feelings can help you to understand them better, and to come to terms with them."

"You're giving me homework," I noted, sourly.

"Only if you would find it helpful," Alice said, equably.

"Are you going to read this journal?"

"Only if you choose to share it with me," Alice said.

"Does that mean I have to come back for more sessions?" I asked.

"Yes," Alice said, apparently judging that I would react better if she didn't try to sugar-coat it. "At least until the company sees a measurable drop in stress levels."

"The things your recruiter doesn't tell you," I said, shaking my head.

Alice chose to ignore that remark. "Sam?"

"Yeah?"

"Earlier I asked if you wanted to talk about why you were here. Can we talk about why you're here, in a more general sense?"

"What, like … why I exist?" I asked, confused.

"No, like: what motivated you to become a streamer. Aside from the financial benefits, what you hope to gain from this experience."

"I hope to gain the financial benefits," I said. "And I didn't have a job or anything better to do to keep myself occupied, remember?"

"Hm," Alice said, frowning politely. "There's no other reason?"

"I don't think so," I said, warily.

Alice sat up straighter. "Sam, I will be direct, because I sense you appreciate openness, and coming to the point. You have had elevated stress levels since before your first experience in combat. Since you arrived on board, in fact. My evaluation suggests that there's something in your past that is still troubling you. Would you like to talk about it?"

"No," I said.

"I have access to news archives," Alice said.

"Good for you," I said, standing up. "Are we done?"

"If you'd like," Alice said. "Be well, Sam."

I was halfway down the corridor before I realized I had left my cup of wine in the therapy room.

Damn it! Well, Alice can finish it.

CHAPTER 17

"StreaMercs strongly believes that a work environment where employees maintain clear boundaries between personal and business interactions is most effective for conducting work and enhancing productivity. Although this policy does not prevent the development of friendships or romantic relationships between co-workers, it does establish boundaries as to how relationships should be managed during combat operations ..."

-Excerpt from the StreaMercs corporate handbook

I made my way back up to the rec bay, and went straight over to the VR machines. I didn't bother suiting up and climbing into the gyroscope, I just pulled the helmet on and then searched through the live feeds until I found what I was looking for: *Smiter*. Avery had a custom logo next to his streamertag – a pink and blue yin and yang symbol – and a golden star next to his name, indicating that he had earned a special contract with StreaMercs as one of their most popular producers. I clicked on his tag and the stream loaded: I saw a table covered in white linen and silverware, with a candle in the center.

He's in one of the restaurants. The steakhouse?

Avery looked up, and I got a better view of the room — black and white tiles on the floor, leather bench seats, wood paneled walls.

Definitely Wagyu.

I pulled the helmet off and got my bearings, then set out across the casino floor, weaving through streamers clustered around a roulette table. Wagyu had a small patio area outside its entrance, with tables set under a striped awning and a handful of streamers eating at them. But Avery had been inside, so I stepped through a pair of sliding glass doors and found myself greeted by a smiling, holographic maître d'.

"Hello, Miss Ombotu-Chen. Table for one?" he asked.

"I'm looking for Avery, actually," I said.

"Table twelve," the hologram replied, gesturing genteelly with one hand. I saw a blonde ponytail in the direction he was pointing, and thanked him.

I took a deep breath, and made my way across the room, passing a few other tables of streamers along the way.

"Can I join you?" I asked, when I reached Avery's table.

The blonde ponytail turned, and I found myself facing a stunning blonde woman in a shimmering dress.

"Oh, sorry," I said, glancing back at the maître d' in confusion. "I thought you were someone else."

"Oh?" she asked, a bemused smile touching her lips. There was something awfully familiar about that smile, and the knowing twinkle in her eyes.

I opened my mouth, then paused. "Do you … have a twin brother?"

"I do not," the woman said, suppressing a laugh. "To answer your question, Sam, I'd love for you to join me."

"How did you know my …?" I began, and then her

thick southern accent registered, and realization finally dawned. "Oh my god. You're Avery."

She nodded. "Yup. Now: are you going to sit, or stand there gawking like a tourist?"

I sat. "That dress is ... phenomenal," I said, at a loss for anything else to say.

"Thank you," Avery said, smiling. "It's a pixel dress, which apparently is going to be all the rage next season." She stood up, briefly, and twirled, and I watched as thousands of miniature screens shifted between a myriad of colors. "It's like wearing a rainbow."

"It's beautiful," I agreed.

"It *is* beautiful, and very expensive, and on loan from the designer, the amazing Allen Liu, and he will kill me if I spill anything on it, so I'm having trouble deciding what to eat."

"He let you borrow it?" I asked.

Avery tapped her temple, next to the camera on her circlet. "I have a lot of fashionista fans. So it's more like I'm modeling the dress, or advertising it. But it's gorgeous, and I may have to buy it rather than return it. Are you hungry?" Avery asked, and a holographic waiter appeared at our table a split second later.

"Starving," I said.

We ordered – Avery decided on steak, and I went for the salmon.

"Vegetarian?" Avery asked, after the waiter flicked off.

"No," I said. "I just love seafood. Dinner's on me, by the way," I told her. "My way of saying 'thank you.' "

"So, just to be clear, your life is worth exactly one dinner at Wagyu?"

"That's about all I can afford right now," I said.

Avery nodded, then caught me studying her. "You have questions," she said.

"I guess so," I said.

"Okay, here's Avery Desmiter, the thirty second version," she said. "Born and raised in Louisiana, New

Orleans, to be exact – 'the Floating City'. Started with two dads, but a divorce and two remarriages later, I ended up with four."

"Did one of them get you interested in, uh … fashion?" I asked.

"No," Avery said, a slight frown crinkling her brow. "And none of them made me dress up as a woman, either. That was entirely my idea."

"Can I ask why?" I asked.

Avery shrugged. "You know how you feel like a woman?"

"I guess," I said.

"So do I. Sometimes, at least. Other times, I feel like a man. That's all there is to it."

"But you're actually a man?" I asked.

That earned me a stern look. "Sam. Are you seriously asking me about my genitals?"

I blushed, hard. "Sorry. I don't … I didn't mean to offend you."

"I'm not offended," Avery said. "And it's certainly not the first time someone has asked me that question. I'm sorely tempted to drop my underwear the next time someone asks, just to teach them a lesson, but I suspect Allen Liu would be unhappy if I did that. There's undoubtedly something in our contract prohibiting me from livestreaming porn while wearing his wonderful clothes."

I laughed. "Are you still streaming now?"

"Of course," Avery said. "Say 'hi,' Sam."

I looked into her camera. "Hi, guys. You may remember me as the girl Avery dragged out from under an Ocho corpse earlier today."

Our drinks arrived – wine for me, a martini for Avery.

Avery raised her glass. "To making millions of dollars from the extermination of an alien civilization," she said.

"Cheers," I said, clinking her glass, then taking a sip of my own. "What terms do you prefer?"

"Genderfluid, thank you for asking. And use whatever pronoun is appropriate for what I'm wearing that day, and I promise not to get upset if you mix things up, it happens all the time. Now: tell me all about Sam."

And I did. Avery has a knack for conversation: like an orchestra conductor skillfully weaving a symphony together from its various parts, she's always ready with another question or an insight you've never considered, and before you know it, half the night has passed. It's almost mystical, this time-warping ability of hers – in another life, she could have been a hell of a talk show host. We were still chatting two hours after they cleared the dessert plates away, and all of the other patrons had already left.

A robo-waiter delivered the bill, setting it on the table in an old-fashioned leather binder – it was even printed on real paper. I opened the binder, and my eyes went wide.

"Would you like to split it?" Avery offered, gently.

"No, that's okay," I said. "My treat." *And a good chunk of my earnings today – sheesh.*

"Well, thank you very much," Avery said. "I'm frugal by nature, but I'm also a gourmand, and I can't resist a good meal. I can resist most of the other traps StreaMercs has laid for us, but their restaurants are top notch, I have to hand it to them."

"'Traps'?" I asked.

Avery gestured to the recreation bay behind her. "The casino, the shops, the bars … all of it. Stellarus didn't put all of that crap here to help you take your mind off the war, or remind you what we're fighting for, or any such nonsense. It's on this ship for one reason only." She tapped her pointer finger on the table top. "To. Make. More. Money. Have you seen the car dealership?"

"No?" I said.

"It's in that little shopping mall area, next to the jewelry boutique." Avery shook her head. "You can go take a VR test drive of the car of your choice, and the sales robot in there will happily sell it to you, while we're stuck light years away, and it will sit back on Earth in some garage while Stellarus charges you fourteen point nine-nine percent APR on the loan. Do *not* be the noob with a convertible and an *Ocho Killer* T-shirt."

I wrinkled my nose. "Those shirts *do* look tacky."

"That's because they are tacky," Avery agreed.

"Can I ask you for some advice?" I asked.

"Career advice?"

"Yeah," I admitted.

Avery sighed. "Here I was, thinking I'm on a date with a pretty girl from Long Island, and all along, she just wants to pump me for information on how to get a contract."

I blushed. "No, no. I've really enjoyed this. Is it a date?"

"You bought me dinner," Avery pointed out. "I just told you I think you're pretty. I seem to recall you saying something similar to me, the first time we met."

I frowned. "That's true, I've just … I've never dated someone like you before."

Avery reached across the table and patted my hand. "Relax. We're just two people having a good time together. Don't overthink it." She leaned back. "Now: career advice?"

"Right," I said. "How did you get your contract? How did you get so popular?"

She pursed her lips. "A couple things," she said. "One, I fight alone. Check the all-time earnings leaderboard: you'll only find a handful of folks on there that were part of clans."

"Lone wolf," I said, frowning as I thought about Naja and Taalib.

"Lone wolf," Avery agreed. "Two, I spend as much time as possible on the ground. First wave, every time, and I stay down until the battle is over. Every second you're not in the fight, you're losing viewers to someone else who is. The fans want to see action, and you can only test their loyalty so much before they bail and go find someone more exciting to watch."

"Someone like you," I said.

"Someone like me, someone like that new kid that decided to try fighting the Ochos blindfolded ... someone who is in the thick of the fight."

"Blindfolded? Someone did that?" I asked.

"Mm-hm, this morning," Avery told me. "And he nearly got a few other streamers killed, the idiot."

"Is he in trouble?" I asked.

"He's dead," Avery said.

"Oh," I said. "At first I thought that sounded like a good idea for a hook."

"A hook. As in: something you're known for?" Avery asked. "Sure, it's a great idea for a hook – he made bank from all the viewers trying to give him directions in between laughing at him." She shook her head. "But an Ocho took him out about four minutes into the fight, it just ripped him in half with a plasma beam. I'm frankly surprised he lasted that long. Hooks are good ... just not hooks that get you killed."

"What's your hook?" I asked.

"Being the baddest genderqueer to ever pick up an e-rifle," Avery said, smiling proudly. "And being one of the best fighters on this ship, regardless of gender identity. Are you searching for your own hook, Sam?"

"I guess so. I had an idea, but I'm not sure about it."

"So tell me," Avery said.

"It's kinda lame," I said.

Avery crossed her arms over her shimmering dress, and a ripple of colors spread across the panels. "Tell me."

I sighed. "Okay. Everybody seems to get upgrades the second they can afford them," I said. "I was thinking of just sticking with the ER-forty-five, a pistol, and standard grenades. No add-ons, nothing fancy, just the basic issue stuff."

Avery nodded slowly. "The purist approach. You could

be on to something there."

"… and I think I want to be a lone wolf, too. I just need to get good enough to be able to survive on my own."

"Practice, practice, practice," Avery said. "The purist angle is solid, I like that. But what's your story?"

"What do you mean?" I asked.

"Hooks or gimmicks or whatever get old. You have to tell a story," she said. "If you're just here to make money, okay, but that's everyone else's story, too. Fans want a reason to root for you, beyond just making you rich. Plessy's a good example. His son was killed in one of the first campaigns."

"He joined up to avenge his son?"

"He would say he joined up to honor his son's sacrifice, and finish the job he started," Avery said.

I thought about it for a moment. "I'm not sure I have a story," I said.

Avery shrugged and stood up. "I think you do, you just haven't found it yet."

Avery and I said goodnight outside my barracks door. I was nervous for a moment, and then she leaned in and kissed me on both cheeks, like we were old friends.

"Goodnight, Sam. Thank you for dinner."

"Thanks for the advice," I said. "And the company."

"Anytime. And next time, dinner's on me." She disappeared down the corridor, heading for her private suite.

I changed into pajamas and then crawled into my bunk, propping my pillow up against the headboard and activating my keypad. I pulled up a new document, titled it, and then sat staring at the screen for a moment, thinking.

This is my journal, I typed. *There are many like it, but this one is mine.*

I frowned, but left it, and entered a new line below it.

Dear Diary: today I met a boy.

I frowned again and hit the delete key.

Today I met someone.

CHAPTER 18

"During the 20th century's so-called 'Second World War,' the first wave of Allied troops landing on Omaha Beach on D-Day suffered such a high casualty rate, they were rendered combat ineffective. Later waves fared better, due to the simple fact that there were then more of them on the beach, and thus, the German defenders had to choose who to shoot. This discrepancy surprised no one – indeed, military scientists had studied prior battles and established empirically that a ratio of three attackers to one defender was the bare minimum necessary to ensure tactical success in such operations.

"In the Octipede War, however, the *Final Hope's* space elevator could only carry one hundred and thirty streamers at a time. On average, the 'Ochos' massed an initial reaction force ranging between one hundred and two hundred defenders to face the first wave of human forces. Eventually, as the elevator made more trips, human forces would reach that critical three-to-one numerical superiority over their foes. But the tipping point generally wasn't reached until the third or fourth wave, depending on the size of the Octipede populace in that location. So the later waves brought things under control, at least until the Octipede counter-attack. But that first wave ..."

-Harriet Seldon, "Free-for-All: Strategy and Tactics in the Octipede War"

I spent our entire day off – eighteen hours of it, every waking moment when I wasn't eating or, you know, in the bathroom – in a VR sim. Getting a sim for all six people in a clan can be tough, but onesies can slot in without much trouble. So I booked a sim for the whole day and basically camped out in the damn thing. The first training module was weapons familiarization: loading, unloading, clearing, and troubleshooting the ER-45. I worked my way through the lesson, passed the practical exam with a *C+* grade, and immediately restarted the module, running through it twice more until I scored an *A-*.

I hesitated. *A- is good. Right?* After a moment, I sighed, and restarted the module again.

Drop the magazine. Draw a fresh one from your pouches. Eyes on the magazine well as you slide in the magazine – watch it all the way in. Slam it home. Release the charging handle. Safety off. Again.

It took me forty minutes and two more iterations, and then I finally earned an *A+*.

Okay. Now you can do the next module.

I took a break for lunch, and another for dinner. I livestreamed all of it, though I barely registered any viewers – it was boring and repetitive, and probably super frustrating to watch me make the same mistakes over and over again.

Maybe later I can edit this down to a thirty second training montage, set to one of Dhia's tracks.

Exhausted, I logged off a little after eleven in the evening, and checked my viewer count on my watch: surprisingly, I had more viewers than when I had started that morning.

"No offense, but why are you guys watching this?" I asked. "Somebody's probably livestreaming paint drying somewhere, and that'd be more interesting."

A handful of responses appeared on my watch.

>>>*Needed something boring to help me fall asleep.*

>>>*Never see the training sims – kinda interesting.*

>>>*UR cute. PM me?*

I grimaced. *Gross. The joys of being a woman on the internet.* Another message hit the screen.

>>>*Love a good comeback story.*

That one made me frown. *How is it a comeback? A comeback from what?* But the more I thought about it, the more it sort of made sense. *Maybe that's my story. Valkyrie used to suck, but she put in the work, and came back stronger than ever.*

It was a nice idea. But I knew I had a lot more training to do to make it a reality. I'd only covered a few of the fundamental modules; I hadn't touched the advanced ones or any combat simulations at all. And I'd have to survive tomorrow's battle first.

* * *

The *Final Hope* completed its orbital repositioning during the night, lowering its anchor cable while we slept. They made the arrival announcement shortly after breakfast, and then we suited up in the ready room. I managed to avoid Naja and Taalib as we gathered in the landing bay – I had told them over lunch the day before that I was leaving the clan, which had been a bit awkward. Taalib was already kind of operating on his own anyway, so he was mostly just sad to see the team officially broken up. But I was leaving Naja without a battle buddy, which was admittedly kind of a shitty move the day before a battle. The two of them managed to find another clan to tag along with, though, so it all worked out without much in the way of hard feelings. I think in a way we were all a bit relieved to put Clan Demonium out of its misery.

R.I.P. Clan Demonium. Just one of hundreds of clans that sputtered out after a brief and unremarkable combat record.

"First wave! Load up!"

A lump formed in my throat, but I hurried forward into the elevator. I spotted Avery over by the resupply lockers – he had also secured a spot on the first wave, per his custom. I threw him a crooked salute, but he either didn't see me or ignored it – he was staring into the distance, silently concentrating on … something.

Game face. Right.

The ramps closed, and the floor jolted as we started our descent.

I focused on my breathing for a bit, because it was something to do, and it seemed to help calm my nerves. Then I checked my e-rifle, for the tenth time that morning. I was standing a few rows back from the front rank, and suddenly the guy ahead of me jumped up and down a few times, but whether he was getting himself fired up or just shaking out the nerves, I couldn't tell. Finally, I felt the elevator slow. My pulse raced, and the adrenaline surged through my veins, electric and hot.

I don't know whether to puke in fear or scream in excitement.

Then the ramps dropped. A plasma blast greeted my sector of the elevator – it tore through a girl standing in the front rank, and then gouged a glowing rut in the floor of the elevator, exposing sparking wires. We pressed forward, instinctively.

Get out! Get out!

We sprinted forward, and found ourselves at the bottom of a deep impact crater, instead of the usual hilltop. Either someone on the *Final Hope's* crew had totally fucked up, or they had decided to throw us a curveball to keep things fresh for the viewers. Either way, it was the shittiest anchoring position in the history of the war: a circular, bowl-shaped depression with steep sides all around. They hadn't dug in, but the Ochos were waiting for us, lining the lip of the bowl, looking down on the elevator as we swarmed out.

I saw a number of streamers drop to their stomachs to return fire – there was no cover in the crater, but at least a prone position reduced their silhouette and made them a smaller target for the Ochos. I followed suit, but soon found I could not get a good angle on the Ochos in my sector. I fired away for a minute, but wasted most of my rounds blowing holes in the dirt at the edge of the crater.

I reloaded, and felt a brief glow of satisfaction when my muscle memory from the prior day's training kicked in, allowing me to slide a fresh mag in quickly and cleanly.

"Look at that, kids," I told my fans. "Valkyrie's figuring this stuff out."

I scanned the crater again, watching as forelegs popped up, emitted plasma beams at us, and then disappeared again. A streamer to my left took a glancing blow to his life support pack and struggled to his feet, hurrying back to try to catch the elevator before the ramps closed. I glanced to each side, and saw a ragged arc of streamers prostrated on the ground, ducking under the incoming plasma blasts.

Usually we've got the high ground … and we can shoot at them from cover. But they've turned the tables on us.

I fired at another Ocho as it appeared – my rounds must have been high, because it merely ducked out of sight.

We're dead as long as we stay here. Fuck this.

It's strange to think about defining moments in hindsight. Fans who watched that third battle of Pentares will say we were pinned down (sorta true), and would surely have taken heavy casualties (probably), and that I was the first to charge up the hill (not true, somebody on the far side of the elevator was first). I'm not sure I even realized that what I was doing was recklessly suicidal – I just got frustrated.

So I stood up, cradled my e-rifle to my chest, and ran forward. The crater's sides were steep, and the slick mud impeded my progress, but several streamers behind me saw what I was up to and picked up their volume of fire, keeping the Ochos above me suppressed.

Probably should have coordinated with them beforehand …thanks, guys.

A plasma beam scorched past me. I put my head down and concentrated on climbing, pushing myself, gasping for air. Another plasma beam glanced off the armor of my thigh, briefly, but long enough that I felt my skin singe inside my under-suit. I let go of my e-rifle and used my left hand to pull myself upward. My heart was thumping when I neared the crest of the crater – both out of fear and the exertion of half-sprinting, half-crawling up the final few yards. I pulled out a grenade and tossed it over the rim on my left, then threw another to my right. I waited a beat.

WHUMP. WHUMP.

As soon as the second grenade detonated, I pushed forward and stepped up to the ridgeline, letting out an incoherent war cry.

There were three dead Ochos and six very much alive Ochos in the immediate area, and the live ones all turned to face me when I appeared, suddenly, in front of them. I shot one and scored a hit on a second, before multiple sets of forelegs opened, and I managed to duck back down behind the ridge. Plasma beams crisscrossed the air over my head – I could feel their heat through my vac-suit. I lobbed another grenade over the lip, and then felt something tap my shoulder – turning, I saw another streamer beside me, sweat streaming down his face. I didn't recognize him, but I was relieved to find someone had followed me.

"On three?" he asked, nodding toward the lip of the crater.

"On three," I agreed.

"One … two …," he counted. Then my grenade exploded.

"Three!" we yelled, together.

* * *

Combat's a funny thing. At a certain point, faced with a constant barrage of near-death experiences, your brain gets tired of being scared shitless, and just kind of throws in the towel, as if to say, "Well, you're clearly ignoring the survival instinct, so fuck it, let's at least enjoy this." And the fear turns into something else. It's a hard emotion to pin down – somewhere between ecstatic joy and righteous rage and hyper-tense excitement. Like I said, tough to describe, but an unforgettable feeling. It feels … *good*. And the fact that as a streamer, you can watch your personal fame and net worth increase exponentially while you're doing it, well … that's just a ridiculous positive feedback loop. If someone paid you thousands and thousands of dollars to skydive into a stadium full of screaming fans, you might get a taste of what deathstreaming can feel like.

But every time you jump, remember this: it'll be even more exciting, they'll pay you even more money, and the crowd will go even more wild … if you wait just a *little bit longer* to open your parachute.

* * *

Once we held the rim of the crater, the third battle of Pentares turned quickly in our favor. As the second wave joined us, I roamed the rim, helping mop up the few surviving Ochos. I was still a noob, no question – if I go back and watch the footage of that battle, I can pick out a dozen mistakes I made, and a half dozen times when I should have died. I was still a shitty soldier, but I wasn't quite shitty enough to get myself killed, or I was lucky enough to scrape by. Either way, I made it. We got the fourth wave down before they managed to get their counter-attack in position, and when they came at us in force, we were waiting. Our biggest problem was just squeezing all of us streamers in around the edge of the crater, and not falling back down the hill behind us. Before I knew it, the battle was over.

And I was forty thousand dollars richer.

CHAPTER 19

"The more you sweat in training, the less you bleed in war."

-Maxim attributed to the United States military, circa 21st century

The third battle of Pentares was over in less than six hours, and we were all aboard soon after that. But when they pulled up the anchor and elevator cable, something went *CLUNK* as they were getting ready to stow it all away, and a jarring shock ran through the deck of the *Final Hope*. About ten minutes later, the crew announced that there was a mechanical issue, and an hour after that, they put out word that we would be on a maintenance stand-down, length unknown.

We stayed orbiting above that crater for nineteen days, while they unkinked the cable or reattached the anchor or whatever they needed to do. And I put those nineteen days to good use – I don't think I touched my Game Boy once. I went back and checked, when they finished the maintenance, just because I was curious. Here's what I managed to accomplish in those three weeks:

- Two hundred and eighty-six hours of training, split between VR simulators and live fire ranges
- Fifty-nine training modules completed, all final exams passed (eventually) with an A+
  (I actually passed one more module, but only had time to earn a B in it)
- Over forty thousand simulated rounds fired, and almost twenty-five thousand real rounds fired

So ... yeah. I busted my ass over those nineteen days. From six a.m. until ten p.m. each day, I was either in a VR sim or on the ranges. Oh, and I started working out, too, for the first time in years. I hit the pool, which was a little weird – I was swimming in outer space, after all – but by the tenth day, I could feel myself starting to get back in shape, and by the nineteenth day, I was knocking out hundred meter sprints in under a minute again. On the last day in the VR sims, when I cleared a malfunction from my e-rifle, performed a no-look magazine swap, and then punched a set of holes in the two hundred and fifty meter target with eighty-nine percent accuracy, I took a deep breath and smiled. And I remembered that pushing myself to be better, to be not only proficient with a set of skills but *fluent* in them – well, that felt good.

I streamed all of my training sessions, because even a handful of viewers generate some cash from ad revenue. Weirdly, day by day, my stream started to pick up more and more fans. I guess there was nothing much else happening – it was either watch me or watch some other streamers lose their money in the casino. But I caught a few of my fans bragging to new viewers when they first dropped into my feed, too.

>>>*She's been at it like this for DAYS.*

>>>*Whoa. Hard working MFer.*

>>>*Bro, you have no idea.*

I was getting a rep. What had Mom said to me?

"Commit to it."

Damn right.

* * *

Avery's suite was different from the one we had toured during orientation. The floor plan was the same, I mean, but he had picked out radically different interior decorations. Where the other room had been chrome and slate, all dark and shiny, Avery's room was soft and white, from the plush carpet to the tiled ceiling, and the furniture was all light-colored woods – birch and aspen. It had a very Nordic vibe. He made good on his offer to buy me dinner a few days into the maintenance stand-down, and had the pizza parlor deliver two steaming cardboard boxes to his room. After a long day on the firing range, my stomach was rumbling.

"How goes it?" he asked, handing me a plate with a slice of margherita on it.

"Training?" I shrugged, and took a seat in one of the chairs under the wide exterior porthole. "It goes. I tried some off-hand firing today, but my accuracy sucked."

"I think I went through that module once," he said, sitting cross-legged on the floor in front of me. "I gave up. I felt like it was messing up my form with my dominant hand." He took a bite of his pizza, then covered his mouth with one hand. "Ow, hot."

"Good, though," I told him. "Thanks for dinner."

"You're welcome," he said. "Nice to have some company – getting bored around here waiting for them to fix the whats-it with the elevator cable."

"Can I ask you something?" I asked him.

Avery grinned. "You just did."

I rolled my eyes. "Smart ass."

"Go ahead, ask," he told me.

"They, um … they made me see a shrink."

Avery laughed. "Well, then, you're officially a deathstreamer now."

"They make you go, too?"

"Of course," Avery said. "Nearly everyone does, at some point – it's company policy if your stress levels are elevated."

"Isn't war supposed to be stressful?" I asked.

"I said it was 'mandatory,' " Avery said, "not that the policy made any sense. Frankly, I think if any streamer *doesn't* have to go have a weekly chat with Alice, that means they're probably a psycho."

"She asked me why I'm here," I told him.

"Yup, same," Avery said.

"What did you tell her?" I asked.

Avery put his pizza plate down and wiped his hands on a napkin as he chewed. "Well, it started out that I wanted to prove something to myself. I don't have much left to prove, though, so the reason I'm *still* here is: money, honestly. I've got a target number – once I have twenty million in the bank, I'm out. I'm gonna head back to Earth, buy a farm somewhere, and retire happy."

"A farm?" I nearly choked on my pizza. "You want to be a farmer?"

"I mean, an *automated* farm," Avery said. "I'm not talking about hoeing corn by hand or whatever they used to do. It would be more like a big garden, really. A few acres where I can just be on my own, and go out and pick whatever fresh fruits and vegetables I wanted. And a big kitchen, where I can cook all that stuff."

"That sounds awful," I told him.

"Well, I never said you'd be invited," Avery sniffed. "You'd probably mess it all up somehow. Anyway, what's your dream?"

I frowned. "I don't know."

"That's depressing, Sam," Avery said. "Everybody's gotta have a dream."

"I guess I want to make a difference, somehow," I said, sighing. "It's nothing concrete, like a farm or a big mansion by the sea or something ... I just ... I want to know that my life mattered. That I had an impact."

"That's not a bad dream at all," Avery said.

"I guess saving the human race is making an impact, right?" I asked. "Being a deathstreamer, that counts for something?"

Avery twisted his mouth.

"No? You don't think we're doing a good thing here?" I asked.

He sighed. "I think I've been doing this too long. I have a hard time seeing this as a noble profession anymore. Maybe if you strip out the fame and fortune aspects, it would be. Maybe. I don't know."

"Well, I hope it matters," I said, taking a bite of crust. "What else do you talk about with Alice?"

Avery exhaled noisily. "Let's see … how to cure my gender confusion. How to make me man up and stop acting like such a sissy all the time." He laughed. "No, just kidding. I don't know, we just … talk. I like to tell her stories about growing up, and see how much Freudian psychology is still stuck in her programming."

"Tell me some of those stories," I told him.

"Yeah? Okay," Avery agreed. "Hm. How about the story of my first Mardi Gras …"

I listened, watching his face as he described the night streets of New Orleans, the smells of the French Quarter, and the raucous crowds. I smiled, and took another slice of pizza.

* * *

"Another battle tomorrow," Alice commented.

"Mm-hm," I said, leaning back in the massage chair. The view through the porthole had changed – the ship had finished repositioning over our next landing site.

"Are you worried?" Alice asked.

"Yes," I said.

"But you must feel better prepared," she prompted.

"We'll see," I said.

"Your last battle went very well. You went 'viral,' as they say. Congratulations."

"Now I just gotta figure out how to do it again," I said.

"I see you requested several prescriptions," Alice said. "LSD, dextroamphetamines."

"Just micro-doses," I told her. "They shouldn't be habit-forming or anything."

"No, not in the doses you're taking," Alice agreed. "Do you feel they're helping?"

"Maybe? I don't know, maybe it's just the placebo effect, but I do feel like I have more energy, and I can concentrate better. I made a new friend – Avery. He suggested I try them."

"It was a good suggestion," Alice noted. "Many streamers practice micro-dosing and find it beneficial, for many of the reasons you listed. And your stress levels are a bit lower, too."

"Can I stop therapy, then?"

She smiled patiently. "No. But I am glad the prescriptions are helping. Just remember that the company will be monitoring the drug levels in your urine to ensure you aren't abusing them."

More stuff they don't put in the recruiting pamphlets, I thought. *Mandatory robo-shrinks and pee sensors in the toilets.*

"Do you think it's possible that you're feeling less stress as a result of dating Avery, also?" Alice asked.

I sat up in the chair. "Wait, Avery told you we were seeing each other?"

Alice nodded, unperturbed. "Yes."

"What else did he say about me?" I asked.

"Sam," Alice clucked. "You know I can't share the details of my conversations with another patient."

"You just did!"

Alice shook her head. "There's a big difference between me sharing something I learned about you from another patient, and sharing that other patient's thoughts and feelings with you. What would you want to know from Avery, anyway?"

"I dunno," I said, settling back into the chair. "How he feels about me, I guess."

"So ask him."

"Christ," I swore. "I feel like I'm back in grade school."

"Have you been journaling?" Alice asked, trying to steer me back on topic.

"Yeah. Some," I admitted. "How does StreaMercs select who gets a contract?"

"You'd like a contract?" Alice asked. "Like Avery?"

"Well, duh," I said, rolling my eyes. "More money, StreaMercs promoting my stream, a suite of my own – yeah, of course."

"I'm not privy to the process for selecting contract winners," Alice said. "Sorry."

"Are these conversations part of how they decide?" I asked.

"No," Alice said firmly. "These conversations are completely private, just between us."

"Well, what about your assessment of me?" I pressed. "My mental state, my stress levels, all that?"

"The StreaMercs executives who award contracts have access to my assessment files, should they choose to review them," Alice said.

I felt like saying *Aha!* like I had just uncovered her big secret, but the more I thought about it, the less surprised I was.

"So what's your assessment of me?" I asked.

"You still have elevated stress levels – high, but not beyond what would be considered normal for new streamers getting accustomed to this lifestyle," Alice said. "Generally, I'd say you're adapting to the challenges of combat fairly well."

"What if I kinda like it?" I asked. "Does that make me a psycho?"

"Liking combat?" Alice shook her head. "No. That,

too, is common."

"Clean bill of health, then," I said, standing up. "Cool."

"I said you're adapting well. That doesn't mean you're stress-free," Alice corrected me. "And we haven't made any progress at all on some of the issues you came here with."

"Mm-hm. Bye," I told her, heading for the door.

"See you next week, Sam. And good luck in your battle tomorrow."

CHAPTER 20

"It was Dev who realized the monetization potential of the war. He took the idea to his boss, and they sold it up the chain, until eventually, a low-level coder from Amritsar was standing in front of the Stellarus Board of Directors, pitching the StreaMercs concept to nine of the galaxy's richest people. And being Dev, he had the code written, ready to go. Early histories of the war were quick to paint Dev in a negative light given that the deathstreamer concept was his idea. But later events would show that Dev regretted his 'invention' almost from the start."

-Arturius Grent, "Genius Misunderstood: A Biography of Dev Khanna"

I fired four rounds into the Ocho, dropped the empty magazine, and smoothly slid a replacement into place. Out of the corner of my eye, I checked the morning's leaderboard, but it shifted as I watched, and I saw Smiter's kill count increase by three, moving him back ahead of me on the list.

"Tag," I heard Avery's voice in my speakers. "You're it."

One of his fans posted a large emoji in my comments stream – a grinning face with its tongue out, hands waggling in its ears. I jammed the empty magazine into the muddy earth next to me, and tapped the streamer next to me on the shoulder.

"Yeah?" she asked, frowning.

I nodded down the hill. "Keep your fire to the left of this magazine."

"Why?" she asked, puzzled.

"Because I'm going out there, and I don't want to get shot." In my heads-up display, my comment stream went bonkers – a wave of tips rolled in.

"You're going out there?" she asked.

"Uh huh." I hauled myself up over the lip of the trench. "Field of fire, *left* of the magazine, 'kay?"

I launched myself forward and half-slid, half-ran down the hillside, e-rifle up and ready. I bagged another Ocho on the way down, as it skulked around the edge of a rock I had my eye on for cover. It collapsed into the mud at my feet as I reached the rock, the light fading from its internal reactor. I leaned against the rock, took a sip from my water tube and caught my breath, my heart pounding.

I was in an area strewn with Pentares' ubiquitous boulders – they were taller than me, each spaced ten to twenty feet apart. I heard movement off to my right: an Ocho had climbed a rock and was spraying the hilltop trenches with plasma fire, playing its beams back and forth over the lines.

Whoa – never seen them do that before. That's a ballsy move.

Myriad lines of tracers reached down from the hilltop, converging on the Ocho – it had caught the attention of most of the streamers in the sector. And then I realized why: a dozen Ochos were rushing forward beneath the Ocho on the rock, hugging the ground, unnoticed.

It's a diversion. It's trying to distract us. The Ocho took several bullets to the chest, and tumbled off the rock, wounded. *Trying, hell – it worked.* Its companions had made it to the base of the hill, and were preparing to charge up it. There were enough of them that some would undoubtedly reach the top, and make it inside the trenches. They were closer to the trench than I was, too – I was cut off. I knelt and braced my elbow against my knee, steadying my e-rifle.

"I've got a bad feeling about this," I told my fans.

The Ochos weren't expecting fire from their flank, so I was able to drop the last two before the others noticed. I got a third before they returned fire, and then scrambled back behind the boulder as a volley of plasma beams seared into the rock's face.

"… and now I'm pinned down behind enemy lines. I knew this was stupid."

I made a dash for another boulder, moving parallel to the trench lines. Plasma beams followed me – the pack of Ochos was closing in on me, apparently intent on punishing the human who had broken up their sneak attack.

I dropped a smoke grenade, waited until the smoke was billowing heavily, and then sprinted for the next boulder.

"Somebody jump over to the streamers in this sector and let them know they got a friendly out front, moving clockwise from the smoke, so watch their fire," I said, panting.

Several of my fans acknowledged and dropped off my feed to help out – they would identify the folks in the trenches above that needed to be informed. It was more of Avery's advice that I'd put into practice – fans can help you fight more effectively, and in fact, love it when you make them part of the team, so to speak.

I arrived at the next rock and found an Ocho there – I fired, but my e-rifle went empty after just two rounds (*Dumbass! Watch your round count*). The wounded Ocho reared up, slashing at me with its forelegs. I backpedaled, letting my e-rifle fall to one side in its sling, and smoothly drew my pistol. I fired convulsively, blasting away at point blank range. The Ocho fell, but in my haste to back up, I had stepped back out from the cover of the boulder, into full view of the Ochos pursuing me. I saw a blindingly bright flash, and my right hip felt as if someone had put a red-hot iron against it.

"Ow, fuck!"

I limped back behind the rock, holding my pistol against my side, my e-rifle bumping against me in its sling. I glanced down – the plasma blast had cut deep into my armor, and I could see burnt under-suit and ... *is that my skin? Looks like well-done steak.* Then the pain hit.

I groaned. "Fentanyl," I ordered, gritting my teeth, and a needle jabbed into my neck. Warmth and well-being flooded through me, reducing the searing pain in my hip to a dull throb. In my feed, several fans were spamming the comment stream.

>>>*Ochos inbound!*

>>>*Ochos coming!*

"Right, I know," I told them, panting. I holstered my pistol and tossed a grenade around the side of the boulder, then grabbed my e-rifle and loaded a fresh magazine.

BOOM!

The Ochos must have been expecting me to drop back to another boulder, continuing my retreat. When I came out firing instead, advancing on them, it caught them by surprise. The grenade had killed two of them, but four of them were in the open, paused mid-step. I killed two more before they recovered – the third died as it raised its forelegs to fire at me. I was on top of the final Ocho by that point, and gave it a butt-stroke to the face – more for style points than anything – and then finished it with a burst to the gut.

I stood for a second, surrounded by Ocho corpses, just letting the adrenaline and fentanyl course through me. My feed was going crazy, as my name leap-frogged Smiter and another contract streamer on the leaderboard. *I could get used to this.*

At a flicker of movement in my peripheral vision, I looked up. *Ochos out past the boulder field ...?* I was never able to prove it, but I swear the Ochos seemed to know when some of their nearby brethren had been killed, through some sort of instantaneous, telepathic collective awareness. And they always came looking for revenge. I heard a sniper round rip past overhead.

"Valkyrie, this is Damocles on the ridge above you. Be advised: tracking a large body of Ochos headed directly your way. Fifty, maybe sixty total."

Damocles – I hadn't met him, but if he was behind the sniper rifle, he had a much better view than I did.

"Roger, thanks – headed back to the trench now."

"We'll cover you as best as we can. Hurry."

I ran, stumbling, clutching my hip with one hand. The fentanyl was still keeping the pain clamped down, but my short-lived adrenaline rush soon gave way to exhaustion. The hill felt interminably high. *Why am I always running up hills on this damn planet?* Damocles had been hammering away regularly with his sniper rifle, but suddenly the rest of the streamers above me opened up, firing over and around me at the Ochos as they entered the boulder field below.

Gasping, I stopped to catch my breath, and took the opportunity to set my remaining grenades to *motion sensor* and then toss them – one each a few meters to the left and right, and the last one at my feet. Then a plasma blast nearby spurred me forward the remaining ten meters. Over the din of the firefight, I could hear the Ochos coming now – their spiny legs scattering the gravel as they ran. *Almost there! If I time it right, maybe I can jump into the trench – and be airborne – right when my grenades go off ...*

At the edge of the trench, I tripped on a rock and fell head-over-heels down into it, landing on my face.

I laughed. "Livestreaming, folks – anything can happen. Ah – ouch." I grimaced: the laughter had stretched my side, where the burn was.

"Get the fuck up!" a streamer next to me yelled, kicking me with his booted foot. "You brought them all here, now help us fight them off!"

"Yeah, yeah," I said, levering myself up out of the mud with the help of my e-rifle. My grenades detonated, all four in quick succession, and I took up my position on the line, facing out.

Christ, did every Ocho on Pentares chase me up the hill?

I concentrated on firing, reloading, and firing again.

CHAPTER 21

"The contract was the goal – it was always the goal, of every deathstreamer. After all, earnings numbers were posted publicly, as an incentive. They knew, better than anyone, that those streamers who signed an official contract were likely to, on average, triple or even quadruple their earnings."

-Maneesh Parseghian, "A Brief History of Livestreaming"

The robo-surgeons let me out of sick bay exactly twenty-four hours after they sewed the last stitch in my skin graft. The Ochos had burned the StreaMercs tattoo on my hip right off, so before I left sick bay, I had to get another tattoo, on the other hip. I was doped up pretty good on painkillers this time, so the tattoo didn't bother me. Plus, once you've had a third degree plasma burn, other aches and pains tend to pale in comparison. Avery stopped in to check on me once I was out of surgery, bringing me a scoop of hazelnut gelato from the ice cream parlor, but otherwise I mostly slept.

Once they released me, I hobbled straight over to the barracks, still wearing the hospital gown and what remained of my under-suit. At her bunk, Naja – fresh out of the shower, wrapping a towel around her head – caught sight of me.

"Well …," she said, grinning as I approached, "the hero of Pentares returns."

"Come on," I told her, blushing. "You were there, too. Don't give me this 'hero' crap."

"I wasn't running around behind enemy lines, laying waste. And I most certainly wasn't number one on the leaderboard for half the battle," Naja pointed out.

"I got lucky," I said. *Lucky to be alive.* I bundled the hospital gown up and tossed it into my locker, then pulled on a pair of jeans and a t-shirt.

"I don't know how much luck had to do with it," Naja said. "I think I'm going to start stalking you during your VR sim training sessions."

Taalib saw us and hurried over to our bunks. "Congrats, Sam!" he said. "Viral two battles in a row."

"I think this was her plan all along," Naja said, an eyebrow raised. "She just wanted to ditch us so she could get all the fans for herself."

I shook my head. "You guys know I don't ever have a plan, for anything," I pointed out.

"Valkyrie6."

I turned – two hulking security robots stood in the aisle of the barracks, watching me impassively.

"Uh … yeah?" I asked, frowning.

"Please come with us."

"Am I in trouble or something?" I asked, glancing at Naja and Taalib.

"Please come with us."

"… okay," I said.

We were halfway down the corridor before I realized I was still wearing socks, and had left my shoes back in the barracks. But the implacable robots marched on, one ahead, one behind, leading me onward. Past the gym, past the casino, the restaurants, and the shops, until we reached a bulkhead marked *Crew Area – Authorized Personnel Only*.

The hatch opened as we approached, and then shut behind us – the robots didn't even break their stride as we passed through. The LEDs overhead cast a harsh white light on the corridor's unadorned metal walls and linoleum flooring. All of the doors along the corridor were closed, and marked with alpha-numeric codes I couldn't decipher. Finally, we reached another hatch, and the lead robot stopped and turned, facing me.

"Please leave your streaming rig with me," it said, holding out one metal-shod hand.

I slipped the circlet off my head, turning the camera off, and then handed it over.

The last hatch opened, but this time, the security bots stayed planted on either side of the door, and after a brief pause, I stepped through alone. I found myself in a wide chamber surrounded on three sides by pitch-black walls that curved up into a high, vaulted ceiling. After a split second of confusion, I realized it was a massive half-dome of pressure glass, like a giant observation bubble. The darkness beyond was the vacuum of space: I could see Pentares' constellations winking in the distance. The room itself had very little furniture in it – to my left was a cluster of gray couches encircling a low table, and on my right was a bed and nightstand with a single lamp. Directly ahead of me, nearly touching the glass canopy at the bow of the ship, was a large floating desk, festooned with holographic screens. A short man with dark, shoulder-length wavy hair was typing on a keyboard, his back turned to me. He was barefoot, and wore loose-fitting linen pants and a plain t-shirt.

I cleared my throat, awkwardly. He turned, startled.

"Ah! Samentha. I'm sorry, I get easily consumed by my projects. I hope you haven't been waiting long."

"Uh, no," I said. "It's fine."

He gestured toward the screens and the holograms spun briefly in place before disappearing, as if they had been snatched away by a miniature tornado. The short man walked toward me and held out his hand. "I'm Dev." He smiled, which caused his neatly-trimmed mustache to curve amusingly at the ends.

Dev Khanna. StreaMercs CEO.

"Sam," I said, my mouth suddenly dry. But I managed to shake his hand like a normal person.

"Come, sit," he said, gesturing to the couches.

I took a seat; Dev took his place across from me, but he sat atop the back of the couch, his feet resting on the cushions below. I couldn't help thinking that my mom would have yelled at him to get his feet off the couch.

"So," he said, leaning forward and studying me. "Tell me about yourself."

"Sure. Um, I'm from Long Island. I was a psych major—"

Dev interrupted me with a dismissive shake of his head. "No, all this I know. Tell me about yourself."

"Oh ... okay." I frowned, and then cleared my throat again, stalling while I tried to think. "I guess, I'm ... I'm trying to figure out what to do with my life. That's why I'm here."

"You think being a deathstreamer is what you want to do?"

"I think so," I said. "I mean, it scares me a lot."

"Sometimes it's good to be scared," Dev said. "It makes us grow."

"I guess so. And I'm getting better. About being scared, and ... well, fighting in general."

"You are getting better. And the fans have really taken to your 'worst to first' storyline. There are people who were born to be streamers, you know – they grew up hunting, or just have a knack for combat that you can't teach. But you – you have a different appeal. Folks like to see hard work being rewarded. You've got karma on the battlefield. And the purist approach – just fighting with the basic load, no upgrades – it complements your arc well."

"Thanks," I said, wondering what an "arc" was.

"What do you think about StreaMercs?" Dev asked. He gestured with one hand, waving it over the ship behind me. "All of this."

"In general? I think it's an opportunity to serve our planet," I said. "I think we're saving the human race."

Dev cocked his head to one side. "I hope so," he said. His eyes lost focus for a moment. "There are days when I feel like we're destroying humanity, but … I hope it's as you say." He seemed to see me again, and smiled. "So: what plans do you have for Team Valkyrie?"

"Um, plans?" I asked.

Dev nodded. "If you're going to be a contract streamer, I want to know that you're going to continue to push the envelope out there."

"You're offering me a contract?" I asked. It might have come out as a squeak. Maybe.

"I am," Dev said.

"Thank you so much," I gushed.

Dev smiled. "You're welcome. You've earned it."

I exhaled, shaking my head in disbelief.

"Now," Dev said, clapping his hands together. "What does this mean? For starters, it means we'll be featuring your feed on the main page at the start of the next battle, and supporting that with a heavy ad push on other properties, introducing you as our newest contract streamer. So you can expect to see a lot of new viewers."

"Got it," I said.

"Winning a contract," Dev continued, "also means you'll be permanently on our 'Featured Streamers' list, and our search algorithms will prioritize showing your stream to viewers. And of course, you'll be able to keep seventy percent of tip money and ad revenue now, as opposed to the standard fifty percent. Finally, I believe we have a suite available for you. No more barracks life for you."

I thought, for a moment, about Naja and Taalib, and felt a pang of guilt. *Do I really deserve this more than them? Or have I just been lucky?*

"Sound good?" Dev asked, watching me.

"Yes," I said, nodding. "Sounds great."

"Good. Being on contract comes with responsibilities, too. As part of your contract, you'll be expected to participate in regular PR and recruiting efforts for StreaMercs, both here on the *Final Hope*, and when we return to Earth. And we'll be assigning you some products to use and feature in your stream when you're on board. Clothing, some personal care brands, that kind of thing. You'll be able to veto anything that doesn't fit your brand or tastes, if you choose. Okay?"

"Absolutely," I agreed.

He stood up. "Then, congratulations, Sam."

"Thank you," I told him, standing and shaking his hand. "I … I won't let you down."

"You'll do fine," he told me. "Just remember: you're getting a contract because you're entertaining, yes, but also because you're an innovator. The essence of all good streamers is to experiment with the medium." He smiled again, but there was sadness in his smile this time, as he looked into my eyes. "Be well, Sam."

* * *

Avery met me outside Wagyu, where I was standing in my socks, doing my best not to hop up and down in excitement. Avery was wearing a sarong that honestly wouldn't have looked out of place on a man or a woman, but her hair was braided and tucked up in a neat, feminine bun.

"It's a little early for lunch," she said.

"It's never too early to celebrate," I said.

"Celebrate?" Avery frowned, and then her eyes went wide. "Did you …?"

171

"Yes!" I squealed, and wrapped my arms around her neck. She laughed and hugged me back, squeezing hard.

"Ah, congrats, girl. That's awesome. We are *definitely* celebrating."

And we did. We started with a bottle of champagne and some caviar, and then Avery went into full gourmand mode and planned a five-course meal with the holographic waiter's help. Three sumptuous hours later, I flopped onto Avery's bed, groaning and holding my stomach.

"Oh, god I'm full," I said, and hiccupped.

"Mmm," Avery agreed collapsing beside me. "What was the bill?" she asked.

"Astronomical," I said.

"We'll split it," she said.

"Damn right we will," I said, and we laughed.

She turned and looked at me. "I forgot to ask you: what did you think of Dev, and that crazy apartment of his? Wild, right?"

"I mean, I was impressed," I said. "I walked in and thought I was about to fight the final boss, or … meet the wizard of Oz, or something."

"Right? And then you see Dev, and he's like, this nerdy little coder who looks like he got lost trying to find the server room, and ended up on a warship." Avery shook her head. "The funny thing is, I don't think Dev designed that room. I think someone at Stellarus said, 'The CEO needs an awe-inspiring suite where he can command the ship,' and then Dev moved in and was like, 'Um, I'll just put a couple sofas here, and my bed here, and I'll be all set.'"

"He's one of the richest men in the galaxy, right?"

Avery nodded. "Mm-hm. Over a hundred billion."

I whistled. "If I had that much money, I'd at least have some cool toys," I said.

Avery rolled onto her stomach, propping herself up on her elbows. "Like what?"

"I don't know. A shit ton of vintage video games. And

I'd put in a hot tub or something, under that big dome. That'd be nice."

Avery laughed. "Hot tubbing under the stars, in the CEO suite. They probably wouldn't let him – wouldn't fit in with the StreaMercs brand."

"Who wouldn't let him?" I asked.

"The Stellarus board of directors. The rumor is that they call most of the shots. They give Dev a lot of leeway to run StreaMercs, but ultimately, he doesn't own this ship, or the company. They do."

"Huh. Dev was hard to get a read on," I mused. "He was nice, but he seemed a bit … distracted."

"Yeah, I read a bio of him once. He's a total cipher."

"A what?" I asked.

"A cipher – an enigma. It's ironic, if you think about it. He's made his fortune broadcasting our personal lives to the world, but he's a very private man. It took some paparazzo like three years of stalking him to figure out that he was gay, even." Avery pulled the circlet off her head. "… and speaking of privacy," she said, and shut the camera off, then reached across and shut mine off, too.

I felt my heart skip a beat. She took my face in her hands and kissed me.

"Why'd you turn off our cameras?" I asked, playfully. "I thought you said we should always be streaming, all the time."

"You need to read the terms and conditions of your new contract," Avery told me, mock seriously. "Specifically the section about contract violations, and streaming inappropriate content." She kissed me again. Her voice dropped to a whisper. "And we need to save some part of ourselves that's just for us."

"Just for me?" I asked her.

"Just for you."

CHAPTER 22

"Well, merc-heads, that's a wrap on Pentares. The *Final Hope* is headed back to Earth orbit, which means some of you lucky streamer fans might just spot your idol out and about town in a few days, at least if you live near a space hub. It also means that we'll soon meet the latest crop of recruits, which is always a fun time. (Friendly reminder: our forum policy prohibits organizing noob death pools for betting purposes. Yeah, a lot of 'em are gonna die. But let's not gamble on it, m'kay? That's just tacky.)

"Personally, I felt the last batch of recruits was a bit lame – sure, there were a couple promising young 'uns who might amount to something, but nobody really grabbed me (all you Valkyrie fans can hate on me in the comments if you want, I don't care). You know what we need? We need a BAD BOY. Or bad girl, whatever. Somebody you love to hate, but can't stop watching, and can't stop talking about. Fingers crossed!"

-StreaMercsFans.com blog post, December 5th, 2233

The ramps closed, and the streamer next to me on

the elevator flipped them the bird. "Sayonara, Pentares," he said, with feeling. "Fuck this muddy little shithole; we're out of here."

The elevator swayed, and I steadied myself against an ammo locker. *So tired I can barely stand up straight.* I checked that my e-rifle was clear, blowing a drop of sweat off the tip of my nose.

"Well, team, I am officially gassed," I told my fans. "Man, how long was that last assault?"

>>>*FOREVER.*

>>>*Dunno, missed the first half, had to go to school.*

>>>*Eight hours, fifty minutes.*

"Yeah, thought so. Felt like forever and a day. Well, I'm headed up for a hot shower and then I think I might sleep the whole way back to Earth. But rumor has it they have our next planet IDed already, so stay tuned. We'll be back in action soon."

I ended up skipping the shower – once I had turned my weapons in and climbed out of my vac-suit, it was all I could do to drag myself down the hall to my suite. They gave me the same suite we toured during our orientation – my contract had said I could have it redecorated if I wanted, but I don't know the first thing about interior decoration, and it looked fine to me, so I had just left it as is. As I found my room, the ship's PA system congratulated us for liberating another planet, and announced that we were headed back to Earth. *Hooray,* I thought. The door opened after scanning my face barcode, and I stumbled inside, kicking my pants off, and fell on the bed, still half-dressed.

Sleep.

I dreamed about streaming, of course. Ever since my first battle, I had been dreaming about combat. At first, the dreams were nightmares – vivid explorations of all the awful ways I could die at the hands of an Ocho. Those never really went away, but more and more, my dreams centered around a different anxiety. Now when I arrived on the planet, I watched my viewer count drop, my name fall off the leaderboard. I would stand, frozen, trying desperately to think of some stunt I could pull to get my fans back, to keep them entertained. Sometimes in my dreams I was simply summoned to Dev's living quarters again, where he shook his head sadly and took away my contract.

* * *

"... and what's your name?" I asked, plastering a smile on my face.

The man's jaw worked for a moment, then he finally managed to say: "Ford. Make it out to 'Ford,' please."

"Sure," I said. I took another glossy headshot off of the stack on the table in front of me and wrote: *To Ford. Love, Valkyrie6.*

Ford reached down to take the autograph, but grabbed my hand instead, and in a swift movement, brought it to his lips, kissing my fingers. I cringed, and pulled my hand back.

"Sir, no touching," the security bot behind me said, stepping forward.

"Uh, sorry," Ford said, and scuttled away with his photograph before the bot could detain him.

"Well, that was gross," Avery said, from the chair next to me.

"Yeah," I agreed, squirting sanitizer onto my hands and rubbing it in vigorously.

"That's why I never meet fans as a girl," Avery said, signing one of his own headshots for the next fan in his line. "Folks like Ford are less likely to try that crap with a man. Thanks for coming!" Avery told the fan, with a brilliant smile. "But I still have the pleasure of getting to deal with the odd Zealot who spends three hours in line just to tell me I'm going to hell for my gender choices."

"Charming," I said, and smiled at the next fan in my

line. I had known a few Zealots growing up – as the popularity of the major religions declined, some of the faithful had reacted by forming a new meta-religion, based on a mishmash of radical elements of Christianity and Islam. They basically picked the most reactionary rules from each and called it Zealotry, and set about loudly criticizing anyone that didn't join up. It was a weird recruiting strategy. I was never sure how they were still around, but if history tells us anything, it's that people will do some weird shit just to feel like part of a group.

I have to sever ties with all of my friends and give you my life savings? Cool, just so long as there's a secret handshake.

"You guys are just the cutest couple ever!" My next fan said. She was young, no more than thirteen or fourteen, and wore a bright pink knit cap.

"Aw, thanks," I replied. "Thanks for watching. See, Avery: some fans are awesome."

The StreaMercs PR rep let us have a solid hour for lunch, so rather than sneak a sandwich in the convention center's backstage area, Avery and I caught a taxi down to the Sydney Harbor Bridge and ate at an outdoor café overlooking the Opera House.

"This is nice," I said, after we had ordered. I took a deep breath of salt air, and gazed out at the harbor, dotted with white sails.

"You said it was your first time in Australia, right?" Avery asked.

"Yeah – my family never traveled much. I'm kinda glad corporate sent us here and not somewhere stateside. I like Australia. Except for that hand-kissing creep." I made a face.

Avery shook his head. "Plenty of creeps back home, too. Hell, if you haven't been harassed on your stream yet, you've got that to look forward to, sorry to say. Happens to us all."

"I've seen it," I replied. "How is it that some men still think women streamers are all sex objects? You would think it would be obvious if they're watching a StreaMercs feed that I'm not a sex worker. So, no ... dickhead. I'm *not* gonna send you my panties, or show you my tits."

"You're not gonna show me your boobs again?" Avery pretended to pout, looking crestfallen.

"Ugh, all men *are* the same," I laughed.

"Naw, just report them, and move on. Only thing you can do," Avery said, turning serious again.

"Yeah," I said. A robo-waiter appeared, and set a panini in front of me, along with a glass of white wine.

"Smiter!" a middle-aged woman waved at Avery from the sidewalk. "I love you!" she yelled, still waving.

He smiled and blew her a kiss. "Are you okay?" he asked me, taking a bite of salad. "You seem down."

"Just worried about stuff," I said.

"What stuff?"

"Work," I said.

Avery exhaled loudly and rolled his eyes, exasperated.

"I've had fewer viewers in each of my battles since signing a contract," I told him.

"Happens to everybody," Avery said, sipping his water. "You get a huge boost initially from being the newest contract winner, then things settle down."

"Mm," I said, unconvinced.

"Listen, contracts are great," he said. "But yeah, they're keeping a close eye on how each of us performs. If you're struggling and they think they've got better prospects out there, they'll drop you."

"This is supposed to make me feel better?" I asked.

Avery gave me a wry smile. "No, but it's reality. You can't just coast now that you've got your contract. That pressure to go out, to fight, to *entertain*, to do better than the last time? It never stops."

* * *

On the second day of the convention, Avery and I had

to do a panel where all the fans got to ask us questions. Are you guys gonna get married? Do you get scared before every battle? What would it be like if the Ochos ever attacked Earth? Answers: (1) we *just* started dating, (2) damn skippy I get scared, and (3) the word cataclysmic comes to mind.

In the afternoon we did photoshoots for a few hours, posing with fans who had paid extra. We got a cut, of course, but most of the revenue went to StreaMercs. Then, as soon as our official duties were done, I dragged Avery up to the Gold Coast, and we went snorkeling on the Great Barrier Reef, out among the rainbow-hued fish and craggy coral heads. I stayed shallow. Avery got a sunburn. But we had fun.

Avery flew home to Louisiana the next day, but after I'd given my parents an obligatory check-in video call, I didn't really feel like heading back to New York. I wandered around Sydney for half a day, spent a couple hours in a vintage arcade, got bored, and then caught the next shuttle back up to SouthEast Station, and from there, transferred over to the *Final Hope*.

I immediately regretted it. The *Final Hope* was a ghost town – everyone was planetside, getting some fresh air and sunlight, catching up with friends and family. Avery had warned me it would be lonely, and I had pooh-poohed him, assuring him I could keep myself entertained. I could have flown back down to Earth again, but that would have been admitting he was right, and damn it, I was tired of him being right about everything, all the time. So I stayed up there, alone and self-righteous.

By my second day back on the *Final Hope*, I had already done two swim workouts and one set of weights, completed six more training modules in the VR sim (gotta keep sharp), watched three movies, and completed a speed-run on Super Mario. On my way back from the deli with a sandwich for lunch, I heard voices and walked over to the balcony by the statue-fountain-thing. A gaggle of noobs stood at the boarding hatch below, starting their orientation. Something in their wide-eyed expressions struck a chord in me – they reminded me of … me, just a short time ago. Of Arliss, and Dhia, and Johnny. I thought about it for a moment, and then marched over to the hatch marked *Crew Area – Authorized Personnel Only* and knocked on it a couple times. Eventually, a confused crew member showed up.

"Can I help you?" he asked, frowning.

"How do I volunteer to train the noobs?" I asked.

"You *want* to train them?" he asked, his frown deepening. "It doesn't pay much."

"I'm bored," I said. *And maybe if someone halfway competent trains them, they'll stand a better chance of surviving more than a few minutes on our next drop.*

"I'll get back to you," he promised.

So it was that the following morning, I found myself standing on the ramp in the landing bay and watching a dozen noobs gather in front of me, waiting to be trained.

"Alright, everybody here?" I asked.

"Uh, no," a tall guy near the back said.

"No? Did somebody quit already?" I asked.

"No … Sofia just said she's not going to come to training."

"Sofia said she wasn't going to come?" I asked, putting my hands on my hips.

"Uh … yeah," he said, sheepishly.

"I think I better have a word with this Sofia. Wait here."

And that's how I met SoSo.

SoSo. You know how scientists think that everyone is genetically predisposed to be attracted to a certain type of person? As if your body can somehow sense that they'd be a good mate for you, because of pheromones and bone structure and facial symmetry and all these physical cues that get synthesized in your brain into lust, basically? Well, I buy it, but I think the opposite is true, too. Some people you see, and in a split second, you know you just want to punch them in the mouth.

Sofia Pajuelo – SoSoYummy to her fans, SoSo for short – from Lima, Sudamerica. SoSo was a natural at everything, everything came easy to her. Looks? Check. Taller than me by about three inches, with natural red hair cut in a bob. Allergic to exercise but thin nonetheless (I'm not jealous – you're jealous). Money? Yup – born into a wealthy family, had one of those blowout quinceañera parties that look more like a state fair than a teenager's birthday party. Popular? You better believe it. I don't know if they have prom queens in Sudamerican high schools, but she would have won, hands down. And SoSo would have acted shocked – me? I don't believe it! – when they handed her the tiara, before bestowing a gracious smile on the adoring crowd.

I found Sofia in the barracks bathroom with a panoply of cosmetic products spread across three sinks, carefully applying mascara as she streamed a makeup tutorial to her fans. She had even used lipstick to draw hearts on one of the mirrors. A tiny brown dog – a chihuahua – sat in one of the sinks, watching her expectantly.

"What. The. Actual. Fuck," I said.

"Excuse me?" Sofia asked, turning to me. "Oh, hi!"

"Sofia, I assume?"

She held out a hand, smiling. "My friends call me SoSo. And you are?"

"Valkyrie," I told her, ignoring her outstretched hand.

Sofia turned to the dog. "Say 'hi' to Valkyrie, Brutus!" The dog yipped at me obediently.

I wanted to ask her how the hell she had convinced StreaMercs to let her bring a dog on board, but instead, I forced myself to remain calm, and asked: "Why aren't you at training, Sofia?"

"Oh, that's right now? Oh, shoot. I scheduled this streaming sesh for my fans, and I just can't let them down." She tossed her hair, radiating concern. "I'm not going to get in trouble for missing training, am I?"

I opened my mouth, and then realized that I actually had no idea if training was required or not. *And it's not like I have any authority over her, either.*

"You're not …," I shook my head, trying to order my thoughts. "It's not about you getting in trouble. It's a question of you getting killed once we land on Ciprax."

"Oh, phew," SoSo said, breathing a sigh of relief. "In that case, I'm not worried. But thank you so much for checking in on me, Valkyrie. That was *so* sweet of you." Before I knew it, I was being hugged, and, I realized belatedly, politely but firmly dismissed.

I watched in stunned disbelief as SoSo patted Brutus on the head, turned back to her mirror, and returned to prattling about eyeliner. *Fuck it*, I thought, after a moment. *If she wants to get killed, that's not my problem.*

I clomped back down the hall to the landing bay.

"She still didn't want to come?" the tall kid asked me.

"No," I growled. "Apparently she had a prior engagement. Anybody else want to blow off training?" I glowered at them, but no one volunteered.

"Good," I told them. "Then let's get started. Lesson number one: you have about a hundred and ninety-two hours before we land on Ciprax and you're in combat. Every minute of that time that you spend in training increases the likelihood you'll survive. And this is it – there is no other training. We're going to start by going through the first ten modules in the VR sims. I'll be in there with you, and I'll pull out anyone I see that needs extra help for some one-on-one training. Questions?"

"When do we get to shoot real guns?" a girl in front asked.

"When I'm satisfied you're ready," I told her. "Suit up."

CHAPTER 23

"In blossom today, then scattered;
Life is so like a delicate flower.
How can one expect the fragrance to last forever?"
-Admiral Onishi Takijiro, composed during the Second
World War

I made those noobs *sweat*. A few of them complained, at first. Hell, one guy took a page out of SoSo's book and stormed off the range when I told them we were staying in the vac-suits all day – no lunch except for energy supplements from the suits. But he came back, sheepishly, an hour or so later, and slurped down his lunch from the tube while shooting, like everybody else. They weren't ready when we arrived above Ciprax, at least not to my eye, but they were a whole lot more ready than I had been.

Ciprax. Just thinking about it makes me shiver. Ice planet, zero atmosphere, a little below Earth's gravity. And far enough away from its sun that it was perpetually twilight on the surface, regardless of what day/night phase we were in at the time. We fought by starlight, with thermal imaging overlays on our heads-up displays, and crampons on our boots for traction. And no matter how high I turned up the climate control in my vac-suit, some of the planet's cold seemed to seep in through the seams.

I ducked, flattening myself against the ice, as a plasma beam passed overhead, then peered along my e-rifle's sights. *Where are you …?* Out among the ice crystals and snow drifts, a dark form detached itself from the shadows, heading toward me. *Ah. There.*

I fired, and the Ocho toppled over, skidding across the ice for several feet.

>>>*Third wave ETA: ten minutes.*

"Thanks," I acknowledged the fan who had sent me the message.

>>>*Noobs in trouble.*

I inhaled sharply, sitting up. "Which clan?"

>>>*Gladiators. Ten o'clock position.*

I took my bearings and then stood up, and ran across the middle of our position, passing the great anchor chain on the way. Ahead, flashes of plasma fire lit up my field of view, throwing the broken terrain into sharp relief.

"Gladiators, Valkyrie. What's going on over there?"

"We got out ahead of the main perimeter, and now there's a whole mess of them, coming at us!"

"Fall back. Buddy teams – one covers, the other runs."

"I think they're past us already!"

God damn it. I picked up my pace, until a shape loomed out of the darkness ahead. I fired, and then vaulted over the dying Ocho. Two more to the left: I sent an extended burst their way.

On my heads-up display, I could see the clan's positions ahead – their streamertags seemed to be clustered around a large outcropping of ice. They were surrounded – backs to the iceberg, a ring of Ochos pressing in on them from all sides. A line of tracers snaked out and away from the iceberg, tracking in my general direction.

"Watch your fire! Friendly coming in, from the anchor cable."

I knocked down two more Ochos who were concentrating on the noobs and never saw me coming. Then I turned and worked my way, methodically, around the perimeter of their position, slowly rolling up the Ocho line, until the clan was able to break out and join me. It took us nearly ten minutes, but eventually, we beat the Ochos back.

"Anyone hurt?" I asked, reloading my e-rifle, as the clan gathered around me in the dark.

"Don't think so," a wide-eyed noob said, shaking his head.

I exhaled in relief. At some point during training, I had come to the decision that I was going to keep this noob class alive, at least through their first battle. They were going to be the noob class that made it, damn it – every last one of them. Well, except for SoSo. *SoSo's on her own.*

"Thanks, Valkyrie. If you hadn't—"

"Save it," I told them. "You guys should be setting a perimeter right now. Everybody got a fresh mag in their weapon?"

A commotion a few hundred meters off to our left caused us all to look up. Several dozen Ochos had emerged from a tunnel in the ground, and were running at full speed toward us, their long, sinewy bodies undulating as they crossed the ice field.

"Okay," I said, keeping my voice even. "Everybody spread out, take cover, and wait for my signal to open up."

"Can we handle that many?" one of the noobs asked, a tremor in his voice.

"We'll find out," I said, with more confidence than I felt. *Either way, we're gonna get a hell of a lot of views out of this.*

Suddenly, a streamer ahead of us stepped out from behind an ice formation and opened up on the Ochos with an under-barrel grenade launcher. The grenade detonated among the first rank of Ochos, throwing their advance into sudden confusion. The streamer pressed forward, walking straight at the Ochos, firing in sustained, controlled bursts, the tracers wreaking havoc among the densely-packed mass of Ochos. They were shooting an upgraded rifle, I saw – one of the more expensive models that used a belt linked to a backpack full of ammunition, allowing them to fire hundreds of rounds without reloading. In the space of fifteen seconds, the Ocho assault had turned into a rout, and the streamer cut down a surviving alien as the rest of the Ochos scrambled back down their hole.

Well, shit, I thought, as the streamer turned to face us. *Thanks for stealing our thunder, asshole.*

"Whoa," one of the noobs commented. "Who is that?"

I zoomed in on my heads-up display, noticing for the first time that the streamer's armor was painted a custom, neon pink. Then their streamertag popped up on my screen.

No. Fucking. Way.

SoSo sauntered up to us, smiling prettily. "Hey, guys! Oh my gosh, this is crazy right? Can you believe we're fighting aliens halfway across the galaxy right now?"

* * *

My bad mood lingered all throughout the rest of that battle, and I was still fuming when I got back to my suite. Not even a long, hot shower accompanied by a glass of wine made me feel better. Angrily, I flipped on my computer's holographic screen as I toweled my hair dry, and called up SoSo's replay from the battle. Then I sat and watched, my frown deepening.

She's had training – a lot of it – before she got here, I realized, watching her dispatch Ochos with practiced ease. Begrudgingly, I admitted that she was strong tactically (great, even), and she was entertaining, too. She infused her battle narration with emotion at every turn, and even singled out a few fans to talk with directly during the battle. *And she's got money – that's a ten thousand dollar weapon upgrade, at minimum. Maybe fifteen. And she bought it before her first battle. Somebody's bankrolling her.*

I swiped her feed to one side, and spent some time searching the web. The Pajuelos, it turned out, were an Old Money family from what was once Peru. Daddy had inherited control of a copper mining company from Sofia's grandfather. I read a few translated news articles: the company had run afoul of recent environmental regulations, and was in the midst of paying some stiff government fines. *She has to be loaded, though – so why would SoSo even want to join StreaMercs?*

I checked out SoSo herself next. She had had a stream before joining up – several years ago, she'd been a moderately popular fashion vlogger, everything from clothing to makeup tutorials, as I'd seen.

So why the switch to deathstreaming?

I shook my head. *Maybe she's just in it for the fame. But either way, she's been prepping for this for months.* I swore quietly. *And I stormed into the bathroom, calling her out on skipping training … she made me look like an idiot. Hell, she probably planned that whole thing out, just so she could cause a scene with me and make fans think she was a ditzy bimbo. And I played right into it for her.*

I switched back to her replay, and watched as she took up a position in a freshly-dug trench on the perimeter. With her automatic rifle's relentless rate of fire, she quickly dominated the activity in her sector, swiping kills from streamers on either side of her. *Just like she stole our kills.*

A few of the streamers nearby yelled at her, but SoSo feigned ignorance, and in one case, had the gall to tell a veteran streamer that she was sorry that he had been having trouble, but he looked like he was about to be overrun, so she just *had* to help him. *#sorrynotsorry*

I'd seen enough; I shut the replay and checked the time – Avery and I had a reservation at Giuseppe's in a few minutes. I pulled on a pair of jeans and a t-shirt, tugged my hair back into my usual ponytail, slipped on my streaming rig, and then jogged down the corridor and through the casino to the restaurant.

Avery saw me as I walked in and waved – I saw that she was wearing a skirt and a silk blouse, with a set of pearls around her neck. Her long blonde hair was done up in buns on either side of her head, Princess Leia-style. I smiled to myself. *She's way better at hairstyling than I am.*

Then I got closer, and saw that she was sitting with someone else. Someone with a little brown dog sitting on the seat next to her.

You have got to be kidding me.

Avery laughed, and SoSo leaned across the table, putting one hand on Avery's arm, laughing with her.

"What's so funny?" I asked, drawing up next to the table, smiling with an effort.

"Nothing," Avery said, chuckling. "SoSo's a trip, that's all. Have you two met?"

SoSo looked up at me. "I'm not sure …?" she said.

Oh, that's how you're going to play this? I got you. I shook my head. "No, I don't think so," I said. I stuck out my hand. "Valkyrie6. Sam."

"SoSo," she said, smiling.

"Cute dog," I said.

"Thanks!" SoSo flashed me a million-watt smile.

I sat down next to Avery, forcing her to scooch over on the bench. It took every ounce of my being not to kiss her on the cheek and casually mention that this was meant to be a date. *Our date.* Instead, I smiled at SoSo again. "Are you joining us? I'm sure the restaurant won't mind."

"Oh, I'm not interrupting something, am I?" SoSo asked, glancing between the two of us.

"No, no," I said, and was dismayed to see Avery shake her head, too. "Join us, it'll be fun," I told her. "I always like meeting the noobs."

"SoSo posted a pretty impressive score today," Avery

said. "Noob or not, those are contract-level numbers you put up."

"Aw, thanks," SoSo said. "How did you guys do?"

"Solid," Avery said.

"Decent," I lied.

"Sam, I'm hugely impressed at what you're able to do with just the basic issue weapons," SoSo said. *So you do know who I am*, I noted, silently. "I can't help thinking you'd be amazing with some upgrades."

I shook my head. "Nope. I'm an ER-forty-five girl, all the way."

"Really? I'd be happy to lend you my kit for a battle," SoSo offered. "We could swap, it'd be fun!"

"I'm all set, thanks."

"Okay," SoSo shrugged. "Avery and I were discussing a team-up in the next battle. What do you think, should we do a crossover stream?"

I turned to Avery. "Really?"

She demurred. "SoSo was pitching me on it. I'm not sold on the idea. Yet."

"I'll get you to come around," SoSo said, batting her eyelashes at Avery. Avery laughed. I threw up in my mouth a little.

"Shall we order?" I asked, grasping for a way to change the subject. "I'm starving."

"Oh, I can't stay," SoSo said, sliding off of her bench and gathering her chihuahua up in her arms. "Italian food always makes me feel so bloated." She wrinkled her nose. "All those carbs, right Brutus?" She tapped the dog on the nose.

"You sure?" Avery asked, and I nearly kicked her under the table.

"Yes, thanks," SoSo said, and blew us both an air kiss. "Bye, ladies. So great to chat."

* * *

Alice watched me impassively from her chair.

"You're awfully quiet tonight," I told her.

"I don't think this topic of discussion is particularly productive," Alice said. "I'd like to talk to you about your friend Lucie. The one who died."

"No," I said. Then, after a moment of awkward silence: "You're not gonna say anything about the whole SoSo situation?"

Alice shrugged her holographic shoulders. "What would you like me to say?"

"I don't know. How about validating my feelings."

"Your feelings are always valid," Alice said. "But the question is: *why* do you think you feel so angry about her?"

"You're the neural net with all the answers," I said. "You tell me."

"Do you think you're jealous of her?"

I snorted. "Of SoSo? Ugh, no. What's the opposite of jealousy? That's how I feel about her."

"Mm-hm," Alice said. "But you're still angry with her."

"I think she's a manipulative little brat. And I think she's going to try to make a move on Avery," I said. "And I know that sounds petty and insecure, but ... I don't care."

"So what are you going to do about it?" Alice asked.

I rolled my eyes. "Alice, you're the one that's supposed to tell me what I should do."

"Telling patients what to do is not at all what I'm programmed to do, as you know," Alice said, patiently. "But if you're asking my advice, I would suggest that you talk to SoSo about how you're feeling. That's the best way for the two of you to establish a more healthy relationship."

"You know," I said, standing up, "I think I will." I headed for the door.

"Sam, not while you're angry," Alice called, but I was already in the corridor at that point.

SoSo was in the barracks bathroom, applying

moisturizer before bed. She was not wearing her streaming rig, I noted, but the moment she saw me, she perked up, flashing me a million-watt smile.

"Sam! What are you doing here?" she asked.

I set my streaming rig down on the sink, deliberately shutting it off.

"We need to talk," I said. "Offline."

SoSo looked up from my circlet, and I watched her aspect change, like an actor peeling off a mask after a show. Her posture slouched, her smile faded, and there was a hardness to her eyes that I had not seen before.

"Offline? Sounds serious," SoSo said, with a smirk.

"I know what you're doing," I said.

"Oh? What's that?" SoSo said, turning back to the mirror, and inspecting her face.

"Cut the crap, Sofia," I said. "You know Avery and I are dating."

"Ah," she said, smiling knowingly. "The old, 'stay away from my man,' speech. How refreshingly original."

"Original or not … stay the fuck away from Avery."

SoSo rolled her eyes, and then turned to face me. "Sweetie, I don't owe you any explanations, okay? But I'm going to give you one, because I'm feeling generous, and that way maybe you'll let me go to bed in peace." She crossed her arms over her chest. "The only reason I gatecrashed your little date tonight was to introduce myself to Avery's fans. And – spoiler alert – Avery's not the only person I was flirting with tonight. Ask around: I spent all evening tracking down the top contracted streamers, chatting them up. Do you get it now? I'm not stealing your boyfriend. I'm stealing his *fan base*."

"Good luck," I told her. "The fans can see through your little act."

"We'll see," she shrugged. "Anyway, I'm not here to make friends."

"That's patently obvious," I told her. I grabbed my streaming rig, and left.

I went straight to Avery's suite, and the hatch slid open for me, as Avery had programmed it to do. He was in the shower, the steam filling the bathroom. He must have caught sight of my reflection in the mirror – he wiped an arm across the droplets on the glass of the shower, peering through.

"Hey," he said, smiling.

"Hey." I didn't bother getting undressed, I just dropped my streaming rig on the counter and stepped in, slipping my arms around him as the water soaked through my clothes.

"Mm, this is nice," he said, and kissed me.

"I got jealous, I'm sorry," I said, after a moment.

"Jealous? Of what? Or who?"

"You and SoSo," I said. "I thought she was trying to get between us."

Avery glanced down at my body, pressed against him. "There's not much room between us, at the moment," he said, smiling. "Although we could get even closer if you took your clothes off, too."

I kissed him again.

* * *

In the morning, Avery had the bakery deliver breakfast to his suite. He set the tray down on the bedside table, and then handed me a hot croissant.

"I don't like her," I said, sitting up, and propping a pillow against the headboard behind me.

"Are you still stuck on SoSo?" Avery asked, pouring himself a coffee.

"Yeah. She doesn't bug you?"

Avery shrugged. "I kinda like her."

"You *like* her?" I asked, incredulous. "Remember the part where she said she's trying to steal your fans?"

"Sure. But I respect the hustle. And I have to give her credit: she saw a niche and staked out a hell of a claim to it."

"What niche?" I asked. "Being a bitch?"

"Being a villain. Who's the more interesting character in comic books: the pure, uncomplicated superhero, or the flawed, evil villain? She's got subscribers signing up in droves. Have you seen her numbers?"

"They're hate-watching her?"

"I don't know, maybe. But listen: we've all been running around pretending to play nice with each other like this is some big frat party, or a road trip with guns, right? But not SoSo. SoSo said, 'No, fuck that – we're not all in this together, we're business competitors. I'm here to kill Ochos and make money, period.' "

"But good luck to all the other streamers, fake smile, winky face," I pointed out.

"Right!" Avery said, sitting back down on the bed. "It's a brilliant play."

"You're not going to team up with her, are you?" I asked.

Avery scoffed. "Hell no. Lone wolves, always." He held out a fist, and I bumped it with my own.

"Lone wolves."

CHAPTER 24

"Ride on down, ride on down,
Ride on down to the killin' ground,
Lock and load, laugh and joke,
Make some bank (but don't get smoked),
Ride back up, spend it all,
Final Hope's got a fucking shopping mall.
Whooooo!
...and then you ride on down, ride on down,
Ride on down to the killin' ground."
-Lyrics from *Let's Take a Ride* by the *Vac-Suit and Ties*, a popular deathstreamer band

My ER-45 had picked up a nick in the barrel grip sometime during the previous battle on Ciprax – scratched against a piece of ice, or clipped by an Ocho's forearm, I wasn't sure. I picked at it, absentmindedly, as the elevator descended. A streamer standing next to me nudged me with his elbow, watching me fiddle with the e-rifle.

"You're not getting nervous, are you? Not Valkyrie!"

"Naw," I said, and I realized with a sudden shock that it was true. *I'm not nervous.* In my memory, Pentares was a big, fear-soaked blur. I still dreamed about it. But something had changed on Ciprax. Sure, I was still scared from time to time, when things got hairy and the Ochos really pressed us. And the pressure to perform was omnipresent, as bad as ever. But I didn't feel that gut-churning terror anymore, that helplessness.

I feel ... confident. I'm good at this shit. I shook my head, smiling. *And I feel something else, too: excited.*

I knew, when the ramps dropped and the battle started, I would feel that adrenaline rush again. And I was looking forward to it.

In a minute, I get to fight for my life, to save my planet and maybe some other streamers' lives, too ... and a couple million people are gonna be cheering me on.

War is a hell of a drug.

The ramps dropped a minute later, and I took a deep breath, letting the feeling flood through me.

* * *

I put my boot on the writhing Ocho's neck, and fired into the general area of its head at point blank range.

"Clear!" I heard one of the members of the Gladiator Clan call, as he finished off another Ocho nearby, one of nearly a dozen that had fought their way up to this section of the perimeter, closing with the streamers at hand-to-hand range.

"I'm getting tired of bailing you guys out," I observed, reloading my e-rifle. "I thought I trained you better than this."

"We're getting better," one of the girls protested. Her streamertag floated over her head in my display: *FoxyHole.*

"Better is a relative term," I said. "You didn't exactly set the bar high in your first battle."

"We're just looking out for your fans," Foxy joked.

"They'd get awfully bored if you didn't have to swoop in and rescue us rookies every battle."

Fair enough, I thought. *Valkyrie, Savior of the Noobs … not a bad brand to stake a claim to.* I checked my heads-up display. *Forty minutes into the fight. The main Ocho counter-attack will be hitting us soon. Where's our third wave? They should be down already …*

On a whim, I pulled up SoSo's feed, just to see how she was doing. She was reloading at the moment; wherever she was on the perimeter, the fight had died down. She was chatting with a fan about a new makeup line, or something.

Got more kills than me, I noted, grimacing.

And then, suddenly, there were Ochos *everywhere*.

Ochos can dig, it turns out. Those razor-sharp armored forearms can hack through ice like nobody's business. We had set up our standard circular perimeter around the base of the elevator cable, and while we were waiting for the usual frontal assault, the Ochos' main force was busy tunneling right under us, until they burst out of a dozen holes inside the perimeter, behind our lines.

One minute I was standing across from FoxyHole, thinking of an appropriate quip, and the next, an Ocho loomed over her and two forelegs sprouted through the front of her chest, leaking blood. The Ocho tossed Foxy aside, but by then I had recovered from my shock, and I holed it through the thorax. I got two more, killing one a split second before it could decapitate another member of Gladiator Clan. Then something massive crashed into my back, and I fell forward onto my face. I caught a glimpse of a foreleg – an Ocho, on top of me. My e-rifle was pinned under me, so I let go of it and drew my pistol, twisting it to fire blindly past my hip, into the space above me. At the same instant, something sharp and heavy and unbearably cold punched into my lower back. I screamed in agony.

The Ocho died – I have no idea if I killed it or

someone else did, but either way, it keeled over with its foreleg still firmly embedded in my back.

"Fentanyl," I gasped. "Jesus Christ, fentanyl."

As the drug coursed through me, I pushed myself off the ground, grunting from the effort of lifting half of a dead Ocho, as well. I could feel the sharp edges of its leg sliding in the wound in my back, cutting me deeper. I yelled in anger and pain, and then, with a final push, I managed to make it topple off of me.

My heads-up display started flashing warning symbols immediately – something about blood loss and inability to place an automated tourniquet, due to wound location. I lay on my side for a moment, just catching my breath, and then pulled a plug bandage out of a pouch. Gingerly, I located the wound in my back and then braced myself. I depressed the bandage release, which propelled the plug deep into the wound.

"Fuck me!" I nearly passed out from the pain this time, despite the fentanyl – my vision went dark for a moment, and when it came back, it was filled with little white flashes that I mistook for snow. I spent a moment just lying there, panting, recovering my senses.

>>>*Get up!* one of my fans urged me.

>>>*Hurry!*

"Yeah, you guys try doing this crap," I gasped.

At last, I managed to get into a kneeling position, pick up my e-rifle, and take stock of the situation.

The battlefield was pure chaos. Gone were the ordered trenches and clear front lines of our typical battles, replaced by confused knots of streamers, locked in close quarters combat with Ochos, wherever I looked.

I stumbled over to FoxyHole's body and leaned down, wiping a coating of ice crystals off of her visor.

"You alive?" I asked.

Her face was sheet-white, but she blinked as I watched, and then nodded.

"Good." I tore open her medical kit and pulled two

more plug bandages out. "This is gonna hurt a lot. Sorry."

I jammed the bandages into her wounds without waiting for a response. I saw her scream, but none of the sound reached me – she was in shock, and must have left her microphone switched to the setting for talking to her fans. I pulled a grappling hook off of my belt and hooked it onto an exterior handle behind Foxy's neck.

"Hang in there," I said. Then I set off toward the anchor, the grappling line pulling her across the ice behind me.

Three different Ochos spotted us as I made the trek, but only one of them managed to get off a plasma shot before I saw it. It missed. I didn't. As we neared the anchor, I saw a streamer jog up to us carrying a submachine gun.

"Sam!"

"Taalib," I said. "How's your day been so far?"

"Busy," he said, gesturing to a cluster of wounded streamers waiting near the anchor. "We're gonna have a hell of a butcher's bill when this one's over." (He was right. We ended up losing twenty-four streamers in that counter-attack, plus another thirty-two injured. The bloodiest battle in StreaMercs history. At least until that point.)

Taalib caught sight of the blood leaking out of my back. "Are you okay?"

"Dunno," I said. "I'm gonna let the robo-surgeons figure that out."

"Let me help," he said.

"I'm good," I said. "But take her. I can make it to the anchor from here."

"Got it," Taalib said. He bent and unhooked my grappling line, and then hauled Foxy up over his shoulder. "Cover me?"

"With pleasure," I said, turning with an effort and shuffling backwards, my e-rifle up. I could feel the strength sapping out of me, so I took a quick sip of energy supplement, before remembering about the hole in my back. *Wonder if it'll just leak out of me, like in the cartoons?*

The next half hour seemed to take forever, but afterwards I could only remember pieces of it, like snippets in a highlight reel. Trauma does weird things to your memory of events; I think it's a self-protection thing, as if your mind doesn't want you to be able to recall just how awful it was. I remember kneeling on the ice, struggling to keep my e-rifle lined up as a group of Ochos closed in. I remember firing and reloading. I remember glancing up into the sky again and again, waiting for the elevator to emerge from the darkness. I remember the third wave appearing, finally, and someone hauling me onto the elevator, laying me on my back. And I remember feeling my face against a hospital pillow, and the metallic clank of pieces of my armor falling to the floor, as the robo-surgeons lasered me out of my vac-suit.

They work fast, those surgeons. They knocked me out for the surgery, but when they were done, they must have given me something to wake up quickly – I guess being conscious speeds up the healing process. When I went back and checked the timestamps in my livestream, less than forty minutes after I passed through the doors of sick bay, I was awake again, staring at a humanoid robot standing next to my bed.

"How do you feel?" it asked.

"Sore," I said. I spotted my streaming circlet on the table next to my bed and slipped it on, activating it. "How's FoxyHole doing? Did she make it?"

The surgeon paused for a second, scanning its databanks. "FoxyHole sustained major damage to her heart. She went into cardiac arrest during surgery, but has been given an artificial heart, and was successfully revived several minutes ago. Her prognosis is improving." (She made it, but it was her last battle – one near-death experience was one too many for her).

"Good," I said. "What about me?"

"You were much luckier," the robot told me. "The puncture wound nicked your kidney, but not deeply. It managed to miss all the other major organs."

"So I can fight?" I asked.

The robot tilted its head to one side. "Undoubtedly," it said. "You'll be fully healed within a few weeks. You should limit your physical activity until that time."

"I'm not bleeding, right?" I asked.

"No," the robot agreed.

"Good," I said. "So I can fight." I pushed myself up in bed.

"Now?" the robot asked.

"Yeah, now."

Something seemed to short-circuit in the robo-surgeon's programming, because it had to think about that for a minute. "You want to go back out? Now?" it asked, finally.

"My friends are down there," I said, and swung my legs over the edge of the bed.

"I'm not sure I can authorize that," the robot said.

"Well, go figure out who can," I told it.

It turned and disappeared out into the hallway, and a moment later, I had myself unhooked from the various IV lines and monitoring devices in the room. They started beeping in alarm, but I found a power button and shut them down. I padded silently to the room's entrance, and stuck my head through the doorway.

Coast's clear, I thought, and set off.

Walking hurt – my new wound throbbed with every step, but it was bearable. I probably wouldn't have been able to sneak out of sick bay under normal conditions, but they were operating at max capacity, flooded with other casualties from the surprise Ocho attack. I managed to avoid the attention of the robots I did see, and a minute later, I was standing in front of my locker in the equipment bay, pulling a fresh under-suit on. A brand new vac-suit stood waiting for me, delivered into place by some helpful automated process that must have been triggered by my old suit's computer as it was being torn apart in sick bay. I stepped in, the seals closed, and I clunked across the hall to draw my basic load. My ER-45 had even been cleaned by the bots in the armory. *Still got the nick in the hand-grip, though.*

I made it into the landing bay just in time to board the elevator before it dropped to the surface for its first resupply run. I was the only streamer on board. As the ramps closed, I checked my viewer count.

Two-point-six million. And rising fast.

"You guys ready for some more action?" I asked.

>>>Hell yeah!

I smiled and loaded a fresh magazine.

CHAPTER 25

"Happy New Year, fellow streamer addicts! Ciprax is in the books, but that does NOT mean the action is over. In case you missed it yesterday, there was a bit of a kerfuffle on the *Final Hope* ... a good old fashioned donnybrook, if you will. Check out Smiter's feed for the best POV."

-StreaMercsFans.com blog post, January 2nd, 2234

On the screen in the cafeteria, a starmap showed the *Final Hope's* progress from Ciprax along the galactic arm, back toward our solar system, and Earth.

"We're eating lunch somewhere else," I told Avery, eyeing my tray with disdain. "Being frugal is nice and all, but ... ugh."

He shrugged. "You're paying, then."

I clucked my tongue. "They were right: chivalry is truly dead."

"... and good riddance," Avery said. "If I'm paying for your meal, or holding the door open for you, or whatever, it's because I'm being polite, not because you're a woman."

"I was just kidding," I told him.

"I know." He smiled, and took an exaggerated bite of egg casserole. "Mm-mm. Bland but healthy, and can't beat the price."

I snorted. "If I didn't like you so much, I'd punch you in the face right now."

Avery cocked an eyebrow at me. "You 'like me so much,' huh? Sounded for a second like you were about to use another 'L' word."

"Nope," I said, grinning. "You first."

"Okay," Avery said, shrugging. "Be that way."

I sipped my cranberry juice and scratched at the wound on my back.

"How're your stitches?" Avery asked.

"Itchy," I said, biting into a slice of toast. "I keep wanting to pick them out."

"When did you last take a painkiller?"

"Last night," I said. "Don't worry, I'm dialing them back – Alice is making me."

"Still hurts?"

"Yeah," I said. "But not as bad."

"I remember my first puncture wound," Avery said, frowning. "I thought I was gonna die on the elevator back up."

"How long did you make it before you first got injured?" I asked him. "How many battles?"

Avery thought for a moment, tapping the end of his fork against his chin. "Eight or nine? I'd have to go back and check. Definitely during my first campaign, I remember that much."

"I can't believe that's two campaigns down," I told him. "Ten battles already. I still feel like I'm faking it."

"Imposter syndrome," Avery said, nodding. "It's a real bitch. You know—"

A burst of raucous laughter from the table next to ours interrupted him, and we both looked over. Two young men were horsing around with their food for the benefit of their viewers, tucking pieces of bacon over their lips like mustaches.

"Rice and beans!" one of them demanded, holding out an empty bowl.

"You moron! That's Sudamerican. Khanna's a curry eater."

"Whatever, they're all the same," the first one replied.

His companion doubled over, laughing.

"Hey, folks?" Avery asked. He was smiling, but I could see the cords standing out in his neck. I put my hand on his arm.

They turned and looked at Avery. "What?"

"Go ahead and make fun of Dev if you want, but cool it with the ethnic stuff," Avery said. "Aim higher, huh?"

"We can stream whatever we want," the first one said.

"Yeah, fuck you, contract boy," the second said. "We're not interrupting your boring-ass stream. Butt out."

"Let's just move," I told Avery.

He shook his head.

"Please?" I said, standing up, with my tray in hand. "Just ... we'll move."

Avery sighed and picked up his tray.

"Aw," the first streamer said, in mock disappointment. "You guys are gonna miss my bit about fags."

My tray was right there, right at the level of his stupid, bigoted face. I clocked him in the jaw with the edge of the tray, knocking out a tooth and spilling shitty egg casserole all over the place. I wound the tray back for another good strike, but a security bot snatched it away from me and slammed me down on the table, face first. *Sneaky fucking robots. Must have seen things getting tense and rolled over while we weren't looking.*

I didn't see what happened with Avery and the other streamer, but he told me later he got a couple good licks in before the bots broke it up. He got a nice shiner under his right eye, too.

They took away our streaming rigs and hauled us into

the crew area – I figured we were headed for some kind of detention cell, but the bots just kept going, all the way up to Dev's suite. The hatch slid open, and there was Dev, waiting for us with arms crossed, brow furrowed. Behind him, the stars streaked past the canopy in long white blurs, as if we were flying through a snowstorm.

Dev ignored the four of us and spoke to one of the security bots. "Show me the footage," he said. A hologram appeared in the air between us, and we watched the scene unfold, starting from when Avery had interrupted the two assholes. Dev listened in silence.

"Stop," he said, when the fight was over. The hologram disappeared. He eyed each of us in turn, mustache bristling. "Well?" he asked.

Well, what? I thought. *You saw what happened.*

The asshole I had hit spoke first, and I had the satisfaction of hearing a slight lisp from his missing tooth. He had blood on his chin, too. "We were just making a joke. We were doing a bit, for the viewers. And then Mr. Confused over there—"

"You insensitive asshole," Avery spat.

"—gets all huffy and interrupts our stream, and his girlfriend clocks me in the jaw out of nowhere. She broke my tooth!"

Dev turned to me. "Do you deny hitting him?"

I frowned. "No …? I mean, you saw the video, right?"

Dev turned to Avery. "Did you hit this other man?" he asked.

"Yes, but—" Avery started, but Dev held up a hand for silence.

"You're both contract streamers," Dev said, "which means you're well aware of our policy on fighting. You're each fined fifty thousand dollars for code of conduct violations."

"Fifty …? We were defending *you*!" Avery said.

"I've seen the feed, Mr. Desmiter," Dev said. "I'm aware of what was said. That doesn't excuse your actions."

A look of smug satisfaction spread across the face of the streamer I had hit. *Motherfucker,* I thought.

Then Dev turned to face them. "Gentlemen, joking or not, your language was not acceptable."

The streamer Avery had hit huffed. "Whatever, man. We have a right to say what we want. Free speech."

"You absolutely do have that right," Dev agreed.

Are you fucking kidding me? I thought.

"… but this is a private corporation – *my* corporation," Dev continued. "And I am under no obligation to give you a forum in which to broadcast your views. Your streaming privileges are revoked for life."

* * *

Stellarus had sent thousands of long-range probes out to scour the galaxy, trying to find other planets with Ochos on them. But the galaxy's a big place, and the probes were all coming up empty. Back at Earth, we took on a fresh crop of noobs and waited in orbit for almost three weeks. Then somebody at StreaMercs finally got frustrated watching us twiddle our thumbs, and they decided to throw together a "Hero's Tour," as they dubbed it. Officially, the tour was designed to help us drum up new recruits (the latest batch hadn't brought us back up to full strength – we still had a lot of holes in the ranks), and let us show our appreciation to the fans. But it was mostly a way for StreaMercs to sell tickets and merch, and keep generating revenue until the next campaign.

Avery and I both got picked, along with all of the other contract streamers, but they split the tour into two and some jerk assigned us to different teams – Avery ended up on the Asia/Pacific tour, while I got the Americas. Probably StreaMercs' passive-aggressive way of telling us they were still pissed about me decking that bigoted jerk back in the cafeteria.

I kissed Avery goodbye and boarded a Stellarus rocket

headed to Rio de Janeiro, along with ten other streamers ... and SoSo, with her own shiny new contract.

Fuck my life.

I took a seat on the rocket next to Petro and Aleksa, a Ukrainian couple in their mid-thirties who had earned their contracts not long after Avery had – they were old timers, by streamer standards. The Demevskayas had joined up together, and carved out a nice audience for themselves by being the first married couple on StreaMercs. Their success attracted imitators, over the years – going into battle with your spouse by your side proved a pretty compelling narrative – but no one fought as well as the two of them, and as a result, no one survived as long as they did. I had seen their feed: individually, they were more than proficient. Together, they were downright lethal; they had an uncanny ability to anticipate each other's movements and coordinate their tactics with minimal communication. I wondered if Avery and I would make as good a team.

"Where's Avery?" Petro asked, seeming to read my mind.

I sighed, and shook my head. "The other rocket. They split us up," I said, strapping myself in.

"What?" Lexy asked, frowning. "No, that's not fair."

"Tell me about it," I said. "This tour is going to suck."

I stayed in a funk for the whole flight down, and the limo ride to the stadium, and barely paid attention to the StreaMercs rep as he walked us through a rough rehearsal that afternoon. But that evening, I walked out onto a stage in front of eighty thousand screaming fans, and the adrenaline rush was nearly as overwhelming as being in combat.

I could get used to this.

For each show, they got a marquee local band to open for us, and then once the crowd was riled up, we came out and each took turns narrating a highlight reel of our best moments, as the crowd cheered us on. Then a local entertainer interviewed us as a group, and took some questions from the audience, too. We signed autographs afterwards, and hung out backstage with fans who had paid extra. And in every city, the local corporations fought over who could throw us the biggest after-party.

After our third appearance, I found myself sincerely hoping the Stellarus probes took their sweet time finding any more Ochos.

CHAPTER 26

"Passed, unanimously: a bill allocating $200 million for a memorial statue to be erected in the home town of every deathstreamer who gives their life in service of the planet. Chair notes that debate was limited to the amount that should be allocated; the final approved amount being double what the original bill had called for."

-Meeting notes from the 289th Session of the United Nations General Assembly

Our final appearance on the *Hero's Tour* was back home in New York, to another sold-out stadium crowd. Afterward, limos whisked us to a club where they had a literal red carpet waiting for us, paparazzi included. The camera flashes were blinding, but I smiled and posed, showing off a loaner gown that Avery had helped me pick out – I can't even remember the designer, but Avery had assured me it was on trend.

"Valkyrie! Here!"

"Hey! Sam!"

"Valkyrie! What's the best part about being a

streamer?"

"Not paying for your drinks at parties like this," I told the reporter, grinning.

"What's next for your feed?" another reporter asked.

"Watch and see," I said, winking. *AKA: I have no clue.*

"Valkyrie, what do you think of the rumors that Smiter went on a date with a fan in Japan?"

"It's not a rumor, it's true," I said, raising my voice over the hubbub. "And I think it was really sweet of Avery to give back to the fans like that." *Thanks, StreaMercs PR team, for prepping me for this one.* Avery had told me about it ahead of time; it had been a recruiting lunch, he'd been pitching a film starlet on joining up.

"You're not jealous?"

I smiled. "Not at all. But I do miss him."

Farther down the carpet, I heard a peal of laughter – SoSo, gushing at a reporter's joke, as she signed a fan's VR goggles. I crossed to the other side of the carpet, intending to pass by her.

"Valkyrie!" A somewhat over-eager fan was leaning over the metal barricade, extending a book toward me with outstretched arms. His dark hair was plastered to his forehead with sweat. "Sign this? Please?!"

I walked over and took the young man's pen. "Who should I make it out to?" I asked. The book turned out to be a scrapbook – it looked handmade, and featured pictures of me from the StreaMercs website, plus a few screenshots from my feed.

"Uh, Seth. My name's Seth," the man said, blushing. "I'm your biggest fan!"

"Aw, thanks," I said.

I wrote: *To Seth, my biggest fan – love, Valkyrie6.* I planted a kiss on the page next to my autograph.

"You made this?" I asked, taking a closer look at the scrapbook.

Seth nodded. Out of curiosity, I flipped the page, and found more pictures of me, but this time, they were from college, and even high school. *Someone's been doing some serious web-searching,* I thought, my smile frozen in place. On the next page, I saw a picture of my parents' house. There was a leaf taped to the page, and a flake of paint. *A chip of paint …? Paint that matches the color of their house.* I tapped it. "Where did you get this?"

"I, um, took it," Seth said.

My smile froze. I handed him the book. "Stay away from my family, Seth."

Inside, having run the gauntlet of the red carpet, the dozen of us waited in a darkened foyer, until the deejay announced us. The music reached a crescendo – I recognized it as the popular anthem *Thank You For Your Service,* but the DJ had sped it up and set it to a thumping bass track.

"Ladies and gentlemen! It's my honor and privilege to present … the men and women of the hour, the heroes of Earth … your deathstreamers!"

We ducked past a curtain and out onto a narrow stage at the front of the club, to thunderous applause from the packed crowd. I waved with the other streamers, the StreaMercs rep took a minute to thank our corporate sponsors, and then a host led us to a roped-off section of couches. Suddenly tired, I flopped onto a couch, next to Petro and Lexy.

"You look as tired as I feel," Lexy said, smiling.

"I could go to sleep right here," I told her.

"Well, buck up – they'll start letting the fans in in a minute, and then we've gotta be on our best behavior." Lexy nodded at the security bot standing by the rope, where the fans were already lining up. "What do you want to drink? Petro will go get it."

"Champagne?" I asked. "Thanks, Petro."

"I'll have a cosmo," Lexy said.

Petro stood and crossed to the private bar. I took a closer look at the waiting fans, who had purchased a VIP pass to be able to meet us. Seth was near the front.

Watching me. The StreaMercs rep passed by at that moment, and I grabbed him by the arm.

"Hm?" he asked, bending down to couch level. "What's up, Sam?"

"Sweaty-looking guy with the dark hair, third or fourth in line," I said. He turned to look, but I held his arm tight. "No, don't look. But he's creeping me out."

Lexy frowned, glancing past me. "He does look a bit off," she agreed. "Stalker vibes?"

"He scraped a piece of paint off my parents' house for a scrapbook," I said.

The StreaMercs rep nodded seriously. "I'll take care of it."

Petro came back with our drinks then, and I took a sip and relaxed, the cool champagne tickling my throat. The StreaMercs rep spoke with a security robot, and I watched as the android politely but firmly took Seth in hand and led him away, out of the club.

Bye, I thought, with relief.

Then the other security bot started to let fans into our section, and we soon found ourselves surrounded.

"Oh, man – Valkyrie, I can't believe it. Can I take a picture with you?" my first fan asked.

"Of course!" I said. I took another sip of champagne and put my biggest smile back on.

* * *

I ran into Petro at the bar about an hour later, stealing a quiet moment to himself.

"Hanging in there?" he asked me.

"Yeah. It's tiring, but … kinda fun, too?" I said. "I dunno. My mom would say I just like the validation."

He sipped at a tumbler of clear liquor – vodka and tonic, I guessed. "There is plenty of that to go around," he said, cocking an eyebrow.

"What, validation?" I asked. "You don't enjoy this?"

"I do," he said. "Hard not to. But ... are we really that special?"

"I mean, we're fighting a war – for all of them," I said, gesturing at the crowded club.

"And we're getting paid handsomely," Petro pointed out. "It's not entirely selfless, what we do."

I frowned. "I guess so. But none of them volunteered."

Petro pursed his lips. "No, but—" Suddenly, Lexy appeared, and draped an arm over her husband.

"Hey, mylashka. Another drink?" Petro asked her.

"I better not," Lexy said, stifling a yawn. "You two look like you're having a debate over the meaning of life. Come on! This is a party!"

I laughed. "Says the girl who wants to take a nap."

Petro turned to me, not ready to let it go. "This is what I'm saying: one of the fans asked me earlier if he could name his son after me. Not 'Petro,' mind you. That ... okay, I could see ... maybe. No, he wants to name his son 'PayDay,' my streamertag."

"So?" I asked. "I'd be flattered."

Petro shook his head. "It feels wrong. We're not gods. I don't even like the word 'hero.' And yet they put us on a pedestal, without even thinking, because that's the socially acceptable thing to do. 'I Support the Troops,' blindly and without question. It's the unthinking idolization that gets me."

Lexy sighed, and rubbed his back. "Okay: enough, grumpy. You've earned a little admiration, I think. But you need to earn your keep, too, and you need to stop letting your wife do all the talking. Now, come on."

She pulled him back into the crowd. I watched them go, and then scanned the fans still waiting outside the rope.

Waiting for hours, just to meet us. I better get back out there, too.

Suddenly, I frowned.

"Mom? Dad!"

I rushed over to the security bot, and after some brief

yelling to be heard over the music, finally convinced the machine to let my parents through, though neither of them held a VIP pass. It felt good to hug them again. I pulled them over to the end of the bar, the nearest thing I could find to a quiet, private spot.

"I was going to come see you, tomorrow – now that the tour is over. I missed you guys," I said, and meant it.

Mom touched my face. "We missed you. How are you feeling? How's your injury?"

"You know about that? You've been watching my stream?" I asked.

Dad shook his head. "Remember Joey, the kid next door? He watches your stream."

"Religiously," Mom added.

"He sends us an update after each battle, letting us know what happened, that you're okay. We still can't watch," Dad admitted. "I tried to watch a replay or two, but it's too much."

"He says you're doing well," Mom said, with a twinge of pride.

"When I'm not getting mauled by Ochos, yeah," I said. "It's … it's complicated. But I like it. So far."

"You mean to keep going?" Mom asked.

I nodded. "I think so. Sorry."

"Can I ask why?" Dad asked. "You've made a nice little bundle, Joey says."

"The money's nice," I said. "But mostly I like feeling like I belong, like I'm doing something meaningful."

And … I kinda like the feeling of being in combat. I almost said it, but bit my tongue.

"Well, I'm never going to like it," Mom said. "But I'm happy you've found something that makes you happy."

Dad squeezed my shoulder. "Proud of you, kiddo," he said.

"Thanks," I said.

"Now," Mom said, taking my hands in hers. "Tell me all about this Avery character."

* * *

Mom and Dad stayed until closing time, after all the other fans had left. I had to get back to the meet-and-greet, of course, but they hung out at the bar while I chatted with fans, and whenever I took a break we caught a few more moments to ourselves. When the party had wrapped up, Mom insisted I go home with them, and Dad sealed the deal with a promise to cook blueberry pancakes in the morning. The three of us walked out to the sidewalk together to catch a ride back out to Long Island, and Dad wrapped his pea coat around my shoulders in the chill winter air.

As the car pulled up, the door to the club swung open – it was the StreaMercs rep, hand held to one ear. He saw me and waved, beckoning.

"Thanks, I'll tell her."

He ended the call on his watch, and strode over.

"Thought you'd want to know," he said. "The stalker guy, Seth? StreaMercs' legal team just secured a restraining order against him on your behalf."

"At this hour?" I asked, eyebrows raised.

The rep grinned. "Come on, this is StreaMercs. You think we can't get hold of a friendly judge just because it's one a.m. on a Saturday? If Seth comes within five hundred feet of you or your family, he goes to jail. We're suing him in civil court too, for emotional damages. We won't win, but that's not the point – the point is to bleed him with lawyer fees. Anyway, that's the last you'll see of him."

I sighed with relief. "Thanks."

The rep's watch buzzed again. He held his hand to his ear. "Yeah?"

"Sam?" my dad called, from the backseat of the taxi. "Are you coming?"

"Yup," I said, but the rep caught my elbow.

"Okay, got it," he told his phone. "Yeah, we're just

215

finishing here. Launch deck seven, understood." He hung up. "Sorry, Sam," he said.

"What?" I asked.

"Full recall," he said. "All streamers to the *Final Hope*. They found another Ocho planet. It's back on."

CHAPTER 27

"Though the professional militaries of Earth would have scoffed at the thought of self-taught amateurs being effective on a battlefield, the Ocho Wars demonstrated combat's Darwinian natural selection process with brutal clarity. Veteran deathstreamers became extremely proficient fighters after logging ten or fifteen rides – they had to; the incompetent simply did not survive. And the truly elite streamers – the SRD Team, in particular – would not have been out of place among the top tiers of the 21st century's special operations forces."

-Harriet Seldon, "Free-for-All: Strategy and Tactics in the Octipede War"

I shifted my weight in my vac-suit, watching impatiently as my fellow streamers filed into the *Final Hope's* main lobby. They eyed us curiously.

"Feels weird to be wearing all our gear outside the ready room and landing bay," I commented to Lexy, standing next to me.

"Mm," she said, nodding. "I feel like I'm going to

break something by accident. Or ruin the carpet."

I caught sight of Avery, leaning against the marble banister of the stairs leading up to the casino level. She gave me a bemused smile. Other familiar faces dotted the crowd – Naja and Taalib, up on the balcony. The Gladiator Clan was gathered in a knot at the foot of the fountain. And I saw SoSo halfway up the other staircase, looking bored.

At least they didn't ask her to be part of this, I thought. *Score one for Valkyrie.* Then a thought occurred to me. *Maybe they DID ask her. Maybe she turned them down … and I was their second choice.* I frowned. *Shut up, brain. You're not helping.*

Finally, Dev appeared – he threaded his way down through the streamers on the left staircase, then joined the six of us in our vac-suits, facing the crowd. The CEO touched his watch, and I heard his amplified voice come through the ship's PA system.

"Test, test," Dev said. "Okay. We'll be starting the deceleration process in about six hours, and I expect the first wave will have boots on the ground tomorrow morning, assuming all goes well with anchoring. We'll be trying something a little different on Venatur, debuting a concept I've been working on for some time, along with StreaMercs' hardware engineers. I think the fans are really going to love it, and it should give us a distinct tactical advantage on the battlefield." He gave the crowd a tight smile. "If we're lucky, it might even help bring this war to a close sooner rather than later," he added, almost as an afterthought.

Dev turned and gestured at us.

"Meet the Strategic Research and Development Team. These contract streamers have been hand-picked by StreaMercs to beta test advanced weapons and armor before we roll them out to the full complement of streamers. For the benefit of our viewers, I'll ask them to introduce themselves, starting with Foo. Foo?"

Foo stepped forward. "Hey, I'm Junior Kotze. My tag's

'SNAFUBAR,' or 'Foo' for short." Foo's vac-suit had a South African flag sewn on his left shoulder. His ancestors had been poachers, but later generations had become trackers for safari tours, and Foo had made the leap from there to hunting Ochos. He carried a semi-automatic grenade launcher with an integrated submachine gun. "Really pumped to be part of this team. Thanks to Dev for the opportunity." He nodded at the CEO, then stepped back into line.

We glanced down the line.

"Me next?" Jack asked. "Oh, sorry!" he laughed. "Uh, hi, everyone. I'm Pan Jung-Hee, 'FullMetalJackass' but everyone calls me 'Jack.' Proud to be from the JKR. I'm a Sagittarius, and I like long walks on the beach—"

"Not everyone knows what 'JKR' is," Dev interrupted, amidst growing laughter from the streamers.

"Huh?" Jack said.

"Please explain to your colleagues – and the viewers watching at home – what 'the JKR' is," Dev said.

"JKR's 'The Joint,' " Jack said, helpfully.

Dev waited, and then rolled his eyes. "The Joint ... Korean Republic."

"Yeah, but no one calls it that anymore, bro," Jack said, leaning on the bipod of his sniper rifle. "It's just 'The Joint.' "

Dev sighed. "Thank you for the geography lesson. Lexy, PayDay?"

Lexy and Petro introduced themselves next, as a couple – not for the first time, I was struck by how similar they looked to one another.

Both slim with blonde hair and blue eyes – if they weren't married, they could pass for brother and sister.

Lexy finished with a long phrase in Ukrainian, which one or two native speakers in the crowd smiled at, and then I stepped forward.

"Hey, Samentha Ombotu-Chen – Sam, or 'Valkyrie6' if you're looking for my stream. I'm from New York – the one on Earth, not the colony. Like Lexy and Petro, I'll be a plain old rifleman on the team. Basic kit, for the win," I said, patting my weapon.

"Thank you, Sam. And finally ... Darth," Dev said.

To my left, a tall, heavily-built Maori stepped forward – the tattoos on his face wrinkled when he smiled.

"DarthSnuggles," he said. "Tangaroa Tui, to my mum and dad. When these blokes get in trouble, I'll be there bail them out, yeah?" He hefted a belt-fed machine gun and smiled, menacingly.

"Do the haka!" someone in the crowd yelled.

"Naw," Darth said. "Only before a battle." That was Darth's thing (well, aside from being one of the few streamers physically capable of carrying the heaviest machine gun in the StreaMercs arsenal): on the elevator ride down, he performed a traditional Maori war dance. I hadn't seen it yet, so when he broke it out on our first ride down together, it got me all fired up, after I got over my initial shock. It's not often that you see a two hundred and fifty pound dude in combat gear yelling, beating his chest, and sticking his tongue out.

"Okay, that takes care of introductions," Dev said. "Now for the fun part. Earlier I mentioned this team's primary objective will be testing out new hardware." He eyed us, nodding carefully. *Get ready.* "The first invention we'll be testing ... is this."

On cue, the six of us touched a control pad mounted on the sleeves of our vac-suits. Nothing happened ... at least from my perspective. From the startled looks of the streamers watching us, the tech had worked as intended.

"This is GhostSkin," Dev said, beaming. "Active camouflage, visual stealth, cloaking technology ... call it what you like, the effect is the same: it absorbs ninety-eight percent of all light waves reflected off of each streamer, rendering them effectively invisible. And yes, it eliminates light in the spectra that Ochos can perceive, not just in the human-perceptible wavelengths."

Dev gestured to us, and we de-ghosted, flickering back into existence ... but while hidden, we had brought our (empty) weapons up, pointing them menacingly at our friends. Horrible muzzle discipline, but Dev had insisted, and it was very theatrical – the viewers loved it.

"How are we gonna know where they are?" a streamer asked.

"We'll be outlined in your heads-up display," Foo said, tapping his helmet visor. "Highlighted in neon yellow, so you can't miss us."

"I hope they do miss us," Jack pointed out. "If they're shooting near us, at least."

"Other questions?" Dev asked.

"When can the rest of us get this Ghost-stuff?" a girl up on the balcony asked.

"To be determined," Dev said. "Sorry I can't be more precise. The SRD team needs to test it in combat first, and then we need to conduct a thorough assessment for how best to deploy it ... and whether we deploy it more broadly or not. It may prove too unwieldy to manage with large numbers of people using it all at the same time. So we have to see, basically."

"Are you gonna charge us to buy it?" she asked.

"We haven't decided yet," Dev said. "I'd like to make it free, but I'm still negotiating with the StreaMercs board on that point. And for all the fans watching, I'll note that we're looking to develop a commercial, mass-produced version for you to purchase at home, as well. Stay tuned."

"How are they going to fight?" another streamer asked.

"In traditional clan structure," Dev said. "They'll ride down on the first wave, and fight as a unit, supporting each other. Otherwise we've left it up to them to determine what role they will play on the battlefield." He turned to us. "Have you discussed that in any more detail yet?"

We looked at each other for a minute, and when no one spoke, I stepped forward. "Uh, no ... we're still hammering it out. But we're leaning toward operating outside the main perimeter. That means serving as a reconnaissance element, giving you guys early warning of Ocho movements, and then intervening where we see the most need."

"We're going to try to ambush them when they're massing, break up their big attacks, that kind of thing," Lexy added.

"Right," I said. "And we'll see how it goes. If you guys have suggestions, we're all ears."

A crewmember, standing to one side, raised her hand. "Dev, fan question."

"Go ahead," Dev said.

The crewmember raised her wrist, reading off her watch. "You said the SRD team has a primary objective of testing out new tech," she said.

"Mm-hm," Dev agreed.

"What's their secondary objective?"

Dev nodded. "Good question. Once they feel comfortable with the advantages – and limits – of GhostSkin, I've asked the team to attempt a rather radical mission. I'd like them to try to penetrate an Ocho colony while it's still inhabited."

There was a murmur of disbelief from the crowd. *I know*, I thought. *It's totally fucking crazy.*

Dev held up his hands. "Again, only once the team has a good feel for what they can do with this new technology. But the only way we've seen the inside of an Ocho colony is through exploratory drones, well after all of the inhabitants are dead. I think there's a chance that the team could learn something critical about Ochos – a weakness perhaps, some vulnerability, or even recover a piece of working alien technology. Something that could help us end the war."

There he goes again with the "ending the war" talk, I thought. *The bigwigs at Stellarus headquarters can't be happy about him saying stuff like that, live on air. If the war ends he'd be out of a job*

222

... we all would. So why does he seem so determined to do it?

* * *

"First order of business," Darth said, stepping out of his vac-suit, after the announcement ceremony. "We need a better name."

"Ugh, yes – 'SRD' is totally lame," I agreed. "It feels like we should be wearing lab coats instead of armor." I clipped my boots into the deck and waited while the servo-arms uncoupled my back plate, my ears popping as the suit depressurized.

"I kinda like 'Ghosts,' " Lexy said. "Why not just 'Ghosts'?"

Darth shook his head. "It doesn't make sense," he said. "Ghosts can be seen, but not felt. We're the opposite – we need something that's tangible but invisible."

"'Mirage'?" Jack asked.

"Naw, mate, that's just like 'Ghosts,' " Darth said.

"It doesn't have to make sense," Lexy pointed out.

"What about 'Chameleon'?" Jack tried.

"Yeah, sorta …," Darth agreed, hanging his under-suit up in his wall locker. "But chameleons are pretty sedentary, right? They're not, like, apex predators or anything."

We debated it for a few more minutes, but couldn't agree on a suitable alternative, so ultimately decided that "SRD Team" would have to do, for the time being. *Weaksauce.*

"I'll see you guys," I told the other five, heading for the ready room bathroom, as they prepared to leave.

"Team dinner at seven," Petro reminded me.

I flashed him a thumbs-up over my head. "I'll be there."

In the bathroom, I pushed on the door to the first stall and it swung open, and I found myself face-to-face with SoSo.

"Get out!" she screamed, tears streaking her makeup.

"Whoa, sorry," I said, backing up hastily.

What ... was that?

"Uh, are you okay?" I asked, through the closed stall door.

SoSo sniffed. "Fine. Please leave."

"You're sure?" I asked.

"Go away!"

"Okay," I said. "Sorry again."

I turned and left, heading for my suite, my mind spinning. Avery was waiting for me, feet tucked up on the couch, under her skirt.

"That was quite the show," she said.

"Hm?" I said, distracted.

"The big reveal. The fan forums are going nuts over the SRD Team and this GhostSkin," she said.

"Oh, yeah?" I asked, flopping onto the couch next to her. "That's good. Are you mad that you didn't take them up on it, now?"

Avery shook her head. "No. I've never played well with others. I'm still surprised you signed on. What happened to 'lone wolf forever'?"

"I know, I know," I grumbled. "But the contract enhancements, the royalty rate, front page placement ... hell, you know all the perks – you saw the terms of the deal," I said. "And that GhostSkin is pretty legit."

"It is cool," Avery admitted. "And Dev seems to be pretty stoked about it. All that talk of ending the war ...."

"Right? What was up with that?"

Avery shrugged. "I dunno. Maybe he wants out, for some reason. But it's a strange time for him to get an attack of conscience."

"I don't think I'm ready for the war to end," I said, a frown creasing my brow. "It's just getting good."

"It's not over. Not yet," Avery said. "I need another campaign or two before I cash out. So I hope Stellarus is out breeding lots more Ocho colonies for us to fight on undiscovered planets."

"You think?" I asked, sitting up. "Like, seriously – would it be that farfetched, Stellarus doing that?"

Avery laughed. "Take your tinfoil hat off, killer. That rumor's been bouncing around since the very first campaign."

"You hear a rumor enough times …" I said.

"Naw, repetition doesn't make it true," Avery said. "If it was true, why'd they take so long to find Ciprax? Time is money: that's just lost revenue, they should have had another planet lined up for us."

"That's true," I agreed.

"And what, they bribed a ton of Earth's scientists to go on record saying we don't understand Octipede biology, while at the same time, some Stellarus scientists at a secret base understand them well enough to breed them? I don't think so."

"Okay, okay," I said. "Forget I asked."

"What are we doing for dinner?" Avery asked.

"Can't," I said, pursing my lips. "SRD Team dinner. You're on your own." Suddenly, I remembered SoSo. "Hey, a weird thing happened to me just before. I walked into the bathroom in the ready room, and SoSo was in there, in one of the stalls, crying."

"Crying? Why, did she lose a friend on the last campaign?" Avery asked.

"I don't think she has friends," I said, and winced. *That came out a bit meaner than I intended. But maybe it's true …?* "Anyway, I don't think it was sad crying."

"What kind of crying was it?" Avery asked.

"I don't know, it looked like stressed out, angry crying."

"She did great in the last campaign. She just got a contract," Avery said. "What's she angry about?"

"Beats me," I said. "She yelled at me when I tried to help."

"Hm," Avery said, frowning. "Maybe the stress is getting to her."

CHAPTER 28

"I'm calling it now: someone on this 'SRD Team' is going to get smoked by friendly fire. And I'll tell you what: if I tag anyone, I'm not gonna feel bad about it for one second. Those invisible motherfuckers get in my field of fire, that's on them."

-Unidentified deathstreamer, prior to the first battle of Venatur

So … GhostSkin is *amazing*.

We hit the ground running on Venatur, and found ourselves in the midst of a thick jungle, which surrounded the elevator on all sides. I use the term "jungle," but it wasn't like any jungle back on Earth. Our briefing had said the "trees" were actually a type of tiny, unintelligent aliens that lived together in colonies, like coral. And they were purplish-brown, with little white fronds that extended out to filter food particles from the air. Compared to Pentares and Ciprax, it was pretty, in a claustrophobic, these-colors-are-all-wrong kind of way. Like we were fighting inside a Dr. Seuss book. Either way,

the terrain turned our usual battles with the Ochos –
where they appeared in the distance, and made a long
charge at us, trading fire out in the open – into something
a lot more up-close and personal. A lot more *intimate*.

But for once, they weren't waiting for us when we
landed. The rest of the first wave pushed out and
established a perimeter, but the SRD Team went into
Ghost mode and kept going, navigating deeper into the
forest with the help of a StreaMercs controller up on the
Final Hope. He was watching us via orbital camera, guiding
us toward the nearest Ocho nest, which had been located
the night before by the recon drones. I still wasn't sure
about climbing down any holes, but that wasn't our
mission yet, anyway – this first battle was all about testing
the equipment.

And hoo boy did it work.

Our first clue that it was a game-changer was when Foo
got literally knocked over by an Ocho that came around a
tree and ran smack into him. The confused creature
righted itself and spun in a circle, trying to find what it had
run into, but by then Foo was back up on one knee, and
sprayed it with his submachine gun at point-blank range.

Three other Ochos appeared a moment later, hearing
the gunfire.

"Wait!" Lexy said. "Cover them, but don't shoot yet.
Let's see if they can spot us."

It was certainly an odd sensation, standing there,
watching our mortal enemies look right past us. "I'm
getting goosebumps," I told my fans. "And not in a good
way. This is weirding me out."

Foo stood up then, and the slight rustling noise caused
all three of the Ochos to veer their heads toward him.

"Oh, crap," Foo said, freezing in place. They couldn't
hear our internal comms, sealed as our heads were inside
our helmets. But they could certainly hear us when our
suits touched the foliage, or whatever it was called.

"They're looking, like, *right* at me," Foo whispered.

"Move," I told him. "But try not to brush up against anything."

In my visor, I saw Foo's highlighted outline take a tentative step forward, then another.

"Still looking at you?" Petro asked.

"Nope," Foo said. "Wait! Yeah, one of them glanced at me for a second, it's kinda … I think he might have me."

"Lexy …," Petro warned.

"Drop 'em!" Lexy called.

A brief hail of bullets later, and we stood looking at three more holed carcasses.

"So … they can see us?" Jack said.

"Kinda," Foo said. "Like we're a shadow, or the hint of a shadow."

"… and only if we give them a lot of time to try to figure it out," Darth said.

"This is gonna be fun," I observed.

We found the tunnel down into the Ocho nest soon afterwards, and set up a linear ambush along the main route from the tunnel back to the anchor. Soon enough, the Ochos came pouring out … and died in droves. We had stripped the tracer rounds out of our ammo, so with no way to tell where the fire was coming from, the Ochos had barely enough time to realize they were under attack, and no hope of locating us before we cut them down. It was starting to feel unsportsmanlike, but then, fighting fair in a war is a great way to guarantee that you lose.

We were getting ready to pull up stakes after a half hour or so – the SRD Team unanimously agreed that sitting still for too long could lead to discovery – but then we heard that the main Ocho counter-attack had just hit the perimeter, and we kicked our butts into high gear. Our controller up on the *Final Hope* walked us in to the fight: about a thousand Ochos were converging on the four o'clock section of the perimeter, and we managed to get ourselves in position right on their flank as they turned to face our comrades. The battle had taken its toll on the jungle by this time – between plasma blasts and human fires, a fair number of "trees" had been downed, opening up the sightlines somewhat. So when Darth let loose with his machine gun, it was immediately devastating. The front line of Ochos had reached the trenches by this point, but we took their reinforcements by complete surprise.

I was swapping in my fifth magazine when the Ochos finally figured it out and managed to get a sizable force headed in our direction.

"They're locked in on us!" Lexy announced, firing into a packed mass of Ochos to our left as they wove through the fallen tree trunks.

"Took them long enough," Jack said. "We've been making a hell of a racket over here."

"Displace?" Petro asked. "If we stop firing and move …"

"All well and good, but some ammo would be choice right now," Darth warned.

"Running low? I'll stay with Darth," I said. "We'll cover you guys, then when you're clear, we'll break contact and hit the elevator for a resupply run."

"Roger," Foo said. "Moving."

I let my bolt ride forward and took aim at an Ocho heading toward us.

CHUNK-CHUNK-CHUNK.

… and down it went. Two other Ochos turned toward me, and I shifted to my right instinctively. The Ochos fired, blindly, their plasma beams missing well to my left. *They're shooting where I just was …*

"I bet they're spotting our muzzle flashes," I said, with sudden insight. "The GhostSkin makes us disappear, and hides the guns themselves – but not the flash. They see us firing."

"Better pick up some suppressors before the next battle, eh?" Darth grunted. "But I might be buggered. Don't think they make anything that can hide this bad boy's signature."

He ripped off another sustained burst from his machine gun, tearing into a pack of Ochos headed up the hill toward the perimeter.

"Your gun's too big? Never thought I'd hear a man complain that he was packing too much," I joked.

"It's a pain, sometimes, really," Darth protested. "Lugging it around all day. Putting all the other men to shame."

I laughed. "For the record, and my viewers, it's not what you're packing that matters – it's how you use it."

"Oh, I can use it, too," Darth assured me, firing again. "See?"

"Ooo … be still my beating heart," I said, grinning. "I might have to consider getting a new boyfriend."

"Whoa," Darth said. "Hold up. I am not about to start a fight with Smiter."

"What? You've gotta have at least a hundred pounds on him. You don't think you could take him?"

"Smiter? Pfft. Only an idiot would pick a fight with someone who's confident enough to dress up as a woman whenever they choose. I'll stick to Ochos, thanks."

I smiled. *Wise words.*

"… but I'm not gonna be able to fight Ochos for much longer at this rate," Darth said, checking his fire. "SRD Team, you fellas clear?"

"Clear," Petro said. "We looped clock-wise, we're down around the six right now, no enemy contact."

I saw Darth stand up next to me – I followed suit. "All streamers vicinity four o'clock, this is Valkyrie6 and DarthSnuggles. We're inbound to the perimeter in approximately two minutes. Watch your fire."

We cleared the perimeter fine and de-ghosted, just to avoid any friendly fire incidents. Darth's gun barrel was glowing a dull, angry red, and my own ER-45 was hot to the touch, even through my vac-suit's gloves. *That's what happens when you post a record-breaking kill count,* I thought.

The elevator was still at ground level; inside, I pulled a

few extra mags off the supply rack and sipped some energy supplement. Then, while Darth fed a fresh belt of ammo into his backpack mount, I flipped through a couple feeds. Avery was out on the perimeter beating back an Ocho assault – as usual, in the thick of it, but holding his own just fine. I sent him a kissy face emoji and was about to close the view but decided to check out SoSo's feed, on a whim.

SoSo was not on the perimeter. It took me a moment to locate her, and I realized that she was out well past the perimeter.

She's halfway out to the Ocho nest. And totally on her own.

I'd pulled some crazy solo stunts of my own – straying outside the perimeter on your own was a surefire way to boost your viewer count.

And, eventually, get killed, I thought. *Especially that far out. She's really pushing the envelope.*

From the looks of things, she was being pursued by a decent number of Ochos, too.

"SoSo, Valkyrie: you okay out there?"

"Fine. Why?" SoSo asked, panting slightly. "Is being invisible getting boring?"

Ouch. "Just offering a hand, if you need it," I said.

"Aw … bless your heart," SoSo said, sweetly. "But please don't patronize me."

I swear to god, I thought. *This girl could make being bitchy an Olympic sport.* But beyond the usual arrogance and casual indifference, there was something brittle in her tone, too.

Is the ice queen … cracking?

* * *

"Has it been hard?" Alice asked.

"What?" I asked.

"Working with a team," the virtual psychiatrist said, her holographic smile unwavering.

"It's been a little weird," I admitted. "But not too

crazy. It helps that we get along. We work well together."

"You can credit Dev and his team for that," Alice observed. "I'm sure they considered your different personalities and the overall team dynamic before deciding who to invite into the SRD program."

"I'm sure they asked for your input, too," I said.

"They did," Alice said.

"Are you … fishing for a 'thank you'?" I asked her.

"No," Alice said.

Do AI programs get huffy? I studied Alice closely, but if she was annoyed or offended, I couldn't tell.

"Okay," I said, letting it go.

"What else is on your mind?"

"Avery and I were talking the other day. About what would happen if the war ended."

"How would you feel if that happened?" Alice asked.

"I don't know. Upset, I guess."

"Why?"

"Because I only just found this. I feel like I fit in here, and I don't … I don't want to lose it. And like Avery said, I still want to make some more cash."

"You'll always have the satisfaction of knowing what you've accomplished here, right?" Alice asked.

"I guess?" I sighed. "It's more that I don't …" I stopped, and looked at the floor. "I don't know what I would do with myself, if this was over. What if this is all I'm good at?"

"What about freediving?" Alice asked, quietly. "You were good at that, once."

I chewed the inside of my cheek.

"We have to talk about it eventually, Sam," Alice told me. "About Lucie."

"Not today," I said.

CHAPTER 29

"Archaeological and forensic analyses of Octipede colonies that have been abandoned following StreaMercs operations have yielded extremely limited results. Either the Octipedes live in stark simplicity, completely eschewing tools, artifacts, artwork, etc. ... or they take care to destroy all evidence of their society prior to engaging in combat with human forces. A reconnaissance of a living, working colony is recommended in order to continue this research."

-Memo from Stellarus Extraterrestrial Science Division

We really stepped in it, during the fourth battle of Venatur. After the SRD Team's overwhelming success during the first three battles, we got cocky, complacent. We forgot that the Ochos weren't mindless enemies – they could adapt, just like us. And they adapted fast.

We pushed out beyond the perimeter, just like the first three times, patrolling our way toward one of the Ocho nests. This time, however, we encountered no Ochos on the way there, and indeed, their tunnel appeared to be empty when we finally found it, hidden amongst the gnarled roots of a tall tree. After we had watched the tunnel over the sights of our weapons for a few minutes, Foo got up and dropped a grenade down the hole.

"Knock, knock," he said, scrambling back to our line.

WHUMP.

A cloud of dust puffed out of the tunnel entrance, but another minute dragged by and no Ocho appeared.

"Nobody home?" Jack guessed.

"Nobody at this tunnel," Petro said. "It's one big colony, each tunnel is just a separate entrance. But they all connect up underground."

A message from the *Final Hope* flashed on our heads-up displays.

>>>Dev wants you to enter the colony.

I groaned. "For the record, I've got a really bad feeling about this."

But we made our way over to the hole and stood in a semi-circle around it.

"First one in gets all the viewers," Petro said.

"First one in gets all the enemy fire, too," Lexy said.

"Rock, paper, scissors?" Jack suggested.

"Yeah, but does the winner get to go in first, or do they *not* have to go first?" Lexy asked.

"I don't wanna go in there," Jack said. He had slung his sniper rifle over one shoulder, drawing his pistol instead. "Winner gets to stay up here as lookout."

Darth lifted his machine gun. "No worries. I'll go."

I put my hand on his arm. "You go first, and none of us are gonna be able to see around you, big guy. I'll go."

Nobody seemed to object, so I started down into the hole without further ado, my ER-45 at the ready. My e-rifle was heavier than normal, with a long cylindrical suppressor weighing down the end of the barrel. I had caved and purchased the upgrade after the first battle – the whole SRD team had equipped ourselves with suppressors to try to keep our visual signatures concealed during firefights. It was a big change from my "basic kit only" philosophy, so I had agonized about it for a while and even sent a poll to my fans. But at the end of the day, they seemed to agree that it was a good idea.

The tunnel had a sloped floor – steep, but not too steep to walk down. I had to duck under the tree roots at the entrance, but a few feet after that, the hole enlarged, and was wide enough that I could stand easily in it, and neither of my arms could touch the sides. The curved earthen walls were scored with long, deep gashes – slash marks from the Ochos' digging arms, I guessed. I stopped, listening, but the only sound I could hear was my own breathing.

The light dimmed as I stepped deeper into the hole, and my visor automatically cycled through several visual modes, eventually settling on infrared. I glanced over my shoulder – Darth's highlighted outline was right behind me, and I could see the others starting into the tunnel behind him. The GhostSkin seemed to shimmer more than usual where two streamers overlapped, and I frowned.

"We're a lot easier to see when we're all lined up like this," I noted. "The GhostSkin doesn't handle overlap well."

"I'll be sure to complain to Dev when we get back to the ship," Jack said.

Knowing Dev, he's probably already firing off a message to his engineers to improve the software, I thought.

I shifted my e-rifle, snugging it into my shoulder, and continued down the tunnel. Shortly, we reached a junction – the tunnel split, one section angling off to the left, the other to the right.

"Uh, which way?" I asked.

"Beats me," Darth said.

>>>*The majority of other tunnel entrances are northeast of you,* the *Final Hope* sent. *It's likely that that's where the center of the*

235

colony lies, too.

I rolled my eyes. "… m'kay. So, again, which way?"

>>>*Left.*

"Thank you."

"We need some breadcrumbs," Foo commented. "Some way to tell where our exit is, if we get split up or have to get out, fast."

I ejected a round from my e-rifle and set it on the ground, pointing up the tunnel toward the entrance hole. "Follow the bullets," I said.

And so we went, deeper into the colony, navigating via infrared in the dark, and leaving a trail of bullets behind us. After nearly twenty minutes, I saw something on the ground up ahead – as I drew closer, I realized we were at a three-way intersection, and the object on the ground was one of my own bullets.

"What the fuck, *Final Hope*," I said, exasperated. "You just led us in a big-ass circle."

>>>*Sorry. Don't have a map, just trying to guide you toward the center. Take middle tunnel this time.*

"We keep this up, we're going to end up in Kiev in a little while," Lexy said.

"I hear it's lovely this time of year," Jack said.

"What, March?" Lexy snorted. "Sure. It's just like the French Riviera."

March, I thought. *I've been at this for half a year now. Time flies.*

Suddenly the middle tunnel opened up – one minute I was standing in a tunnel, and the next I had stepped out into a massive cavern, the openness yawning all around me. I swept my e-rifle around the room, shifting quickly to one side of the tunnel to allow the rest of the team to enter with me.

"Clear," I noted. "I think. I can't see all the way across the room."

"Clear this side," Darth echoed.

We stopped and stared for a moment. In contrast to

the rough-hewn tunnels we had been traveling through, every surface in this room – with the exception of the dirt floor – was smoothly polished stone. The ceiling far above was held up by a series of delicate columns, each of which twisted upward in an intricate spiral pattern. Some of the columns were joined together midway along their height by narrow rock arches, while other arches curved gracefully up to the ceiling.

"It's almost like standing in a forest carved of stone," Petro said.

"It's beautiful," Darth said.

"What are all those holes in the wall?" Jack asked.

"Living spaces for the Ochos," Petro said. "Like beds, sort of, cut out of the rock. Didn't you read the research paper on colony structure StreaMercs sent us?"

"Yeah, Jack," I said. "Didn't you read the ...what was it, Petro?"

"You guys are useless," Petro said, sighing. "This is one of their living chambers. One of several, probably – a few thousand Ochos live in each."

"Split up," Lexy said. "Let's see what we can find."

Darth and I headed around the wall to the right, while Jack and Foo went left. Lexy and Petro crossed the center of the room. When we reached the row of holes, I stooped down and pointed my e-rifle into the first one. *Empty.*

"Kinda look like honeycombs in a beehive," Jack said, after a while. "No honey, though."

"Well, duh," Foo said.

"What do they eat?" Jack asked. "Each other?"

"Nothing," Lexy said. "They're self-sustaining. They get their energy from their fusion reactors, remember?"

"I'm not seeing anything," Darth said. "Like, this room is completely bare. Forget food, there's absolutely no tech, not even rudimentary tools."

"That's consistent with exploratory drone findings," Foo said. "What? I read the briefings, too."

The six of us converged on the far side of the room,

where another tunnel led out of the chamber. We stood staring at each other in the dark for a moment.

"This is anticlimactic," I remarked.

"Yeah, where the hell are they?" Darth asked.

"Fighting, probably," Lexy said.

>>>*They're massing outside the landing zone perimeter, yes.* The *Final Hope* sent us.

>>>*The Ocho main effort appears to be in place, but they haven't launched their attack.*

"Well, we should get going, then," Darth said. "We snuck in, we found bugger all, the battle's about to start – let's get the hell out."

>>>*Yes. But we may have a problem.*

CHAPTER 30

"The Octipedes demonstrated tactical patience, long-range coordination between units, and a willingness to sacrifice short term gains in order to achieve overall objectives. The evidence is now incontrovertible: they are more intelligent than we have given them credit for. And they are fighting harder – and smarter – than ever."

-Excerpt from the official StreaMercs after action report on the fourth battle of Venatur

Deserted or not, it was a relief to get out of the Ocho colony – a relief to have clear sky overhead, and sunshine, and the semi-familiar sights of Venatur's coral jungle. But our relief lasted only long enough for us to cover the two miles back to the landing zone, where we took a knee in a line, peering through the jungle, and confirmed exactly what the *Final Hope* had warned us of.

The Ochos were waiting for us.

Instead of attacking the perimeter, they had simply surrounded it, staying far enough back that they remained hidden, unseen by the streamers dug in several hundred meters away through the jungle. The ring of Ochos was packed dozens deep in places – some faced the perimeter, but many were faced *outward*, clearly expecting an attack from the rear. *An attack from us*. And now, they were waiting.

"We're cut off," Jack remarked. "Son of a bitch."

Their plan was plain: once we attacked them, they'd locate us from the noise of our weapons, and half of the Ochos would keep our friends bottled up in the perimeter, while the other half surrounded and destroyed us.

"How did they know?" Petro asked. "They're expecting us. How did they know?"

"Telepathy?" Lexy guessed. "Either that or a survivor from one of the last battles made it out to warn them about us."

"Either way, we're screwed," I said.

"Okay, ideas?" Lexy said.

We knelt in silence for a few moments, thinking. I checked the map in my heads-up display – all four waves were down in the perimeter, our full strength entrenched just a few hundred meters away.

"What are the chances we can get some help from the perimeter?" Petro asked, apparently reading my mind.

"Low," Lexy said. "Would you want to come out of your nice, cozy trench to assault the Ochos in the open?"

"If everyone came out of the trench and attacked, we'd stand a decent chance of getting clear," Petro said.

"They're gonna take heavy casualties in an open fight like that, though," I said. "Like on Ciprax, when the Ochos tunneled up inside the perimeter. We can't ask them to do that for us."

"We could split up," Jack said. "They're expecting an attack at one point along their perimeter, not multiple points." He cleared his throat. "Actually, scratch that. They might be a little confused at first, but the end result is gonna be the same."

"We could try to sneak through their line," Foo said. "Hold our fire and just hope they don't see us."

I watched the Ochos nearest us – they were moving restlessly, their sinewy forms looping and doubling back on themselves, pacing. Packed as they were into a thick ring of bodies, it made them resemble a brown river, or a teeming den of snakes.

"I don't think we'd make it," I said.

"What's your idea, then?" Jack asked, testily.

"I don't know," I admitted.

"We could do what we did in the first battle," Darth said. "Someone creates a noisy diversion, draws heaps of them away, and then the others try to sneak through the gap."

"*If* they leave a gap," Lexy said. "And what happens to the person creating the diversion?"

"They'd be on their own," Darth said, and left it at that.

"Petro?" Lexy asked.

"I'm thinking," he said.

After another minute, I sighed. "I think we just pick a spot and assault them. Spam them with grenades, hit them hard, try to punch through, and make a dash for the perimeter."

The team digested that for a moment.

"We could coordinate with the perimeter," Petro said. "They could shift forces to that area in advance, so they could cover us once we're in sight."

"It means we get to stick together," Jack said. "Nobody has to draw the short straw and sacrifice themselves."

"If nothing else, we'd go down fighting," Foo said.

In the end, we voted, and my assault plan was the unanimous winner.

"Lead the way, Valkyrie," Lexy said.

"Right. Smiter, this is Valkyrie," I said into my radio mic.

"I'm tracking; I've been watching your feed," Avery

responded. "Give me five minutes, I'm corralling volunteers and moving to your section of the perimeter."

"I love you, babe," I said. *Oh, shit.*

"Did you just use the 'L' word?" Avery asked, and I swear I could hear the grin on his face.

"That depends," I said, "on whether you get us back inside the perimeter in one piece. All of us."

"Will do what I can," Avery said, turning serious. "And in case I can't … love you, too."

I expected some flak from the rest of the SRD Team for all of the PDA on the tactical net, but they refrained – I guess it was a sign of exactly how dire our situation was. We discussed the plan one more time, made our final checks, and waited. When Avery had his team in place, we stood, and started toward the ring of Ochos, moving slowly and carefully.

"Stay close," I said. "But don't bunch up too much."

If they saw or heard us, the Ochos didn't let on. We closed to within about fifteen meters of the Ochos, and then stopped.

"Grenades," I said, trying to keep my voice calm. I pulled a grenade off my tactical vest and armed it.

"Ready," Darth said, and I heard the others echo him.

"Ready. See you guys back on the ship," Jack added.

"Toss 'em!" I yelled.

I threw my grenade, then hit the dirt, prostrating myself on the ground. The seconds ticked by—

BOOM! BOOM! BADABOOM!

"Go!" I yelled, jumping up, as chunks of earth and trees rained down on us from above.

I ran, headlong, toward the Ocho line – a tree was toppling, lazily, in the center of where our grenades had landed. Ocho carcasses littered the ground wherever I looked, but for every dead Ocho, I saw three or four live ones, and more rushing toward us from either side. I heard more flat explosions to my right – Foo, opening fire with his grenade launcher. I took down two Ochos in my path with quick bursts, and saw a group to my left catch a long burst of machine gun fire from Darth.

"They're closing the gap!" Lexy cried.

I clubbed an Ocho in my path with my e-rifle's butt, not bothering to stop and finish it, and fired left, then right, still running.

"Keep going!" I said, reloading.

For a split second, it looked like the Ochos were going to close the gap – I could see them pressing in on both sides. Then, just as I brought my e-rifle up, we all seemed to fire at once, and the mass of Ochos in front of us parted, falling under the withering fire.

"Run!" Jack yelled. "I can see the trench from here!"

The Ochos – now behind us – seemed to realize that we had broken through, and all at once, the jungle was lit up with a thick grid of plasma beams, tracking back and forth across the ground, seeking us. I threw myself down and rolled onto my back, pointing my e-rifle between my legs and firing rapidly. I saw three more Ochos fall, but as I turned to get up again, something sparked on the ground behind me. A cloud of black smoke and flames erupted off of Darth's outline – a plasma beam had connected with his life support pack. His GhostSkin shorted out a moment later, exposing him to view.

"Shit, Darth!" I called. "Darth, come in!"

His radio must be hit. I scrambled onto my hands and knees and crawled toward him, staying low as more plasma beams sizzled past. *How the hell am I gonna drag him out of here?? This volume of fire is insane.*

"Avery, do you have a visual on me?" I panted.

"No!" he replied. "Wait! No, I just picked up Petro and Lexy, they're crawling in under heavy fire."

"Same!" Jack added. "Foo and I are about fifty meters short of the perimeter."

"Darth's down," I said. "I'm trying to reach him. Can anyone give me covering fire?"

"No. Can't see you, can't see the Ochos," Avery

replied. "Hang on."

I reached Darth then, and craned my neck to see in through his helmet. He was alive and conscious, but his tattooed face was sweating heavily – he looked to be in some pain. When his mouth moved, I couldn't hear him. I shook my head, as more plasma beams reflected off the plastic of his visor.

"Can't hear ya," I told him, in case he was still receiving. I shifted and looked over his back – the plasma blast had detonated an ammo pouch, and I could see shrapnel holes along his lower back and legs.

An Ocho appeared, lunging toward us – I fired, one-handed, and it reared back, its legs flailing in shock and pain.

Is it even possible to pull him behind me, while crawling? Better find out, I guess. I yanked out my grappling cable and hooked it onto his armor over one shoulder. Then I turned and pulled myself along the ground. When the cable went taut, I felt Darth move several inches, but it was slow going. A plasma beam glanced off my forearm, singeing the skin under the vac-suit.

Ow, fuck! And now that part of my armor is visible. Shit.

I checked my heads-up display – we were still almost seventy meters from the perimeter.

We're not gonna make it.

"Valkyrie, status?" I heard Avery ask.

"Trying to haul Darth in," I said. "I don't, uh … I don't know if I'm gonna be able to pull this off."

I inched forward another foot, as another plasma blast gouged into the earth ahead of us.

"I'm coming down there," Avery said.

"Don't you dare," I said. "Too hot."

I checked back over my shoulder: *no Ochos following us, at least. But they're still firing like crazy, and Darth looks like he's losing consciousness.*

When I turned back to face the perimeter, I found a set of armored feet standing over me.

"God damn it, Avery!" I cursed. "I said not to …" I looked up, but the vac-suit was bright pink.

"Go!" SoSo said, letting loose with her auto-rifle. She pumped her grenade launcher, and launched a round toward the Ocho lines, ignoring a plasma beam that narrowly missed her head. "Quit gawking and go, already!"

"Yeah," I said, confused. "Right."

I stood and ran, bent over at the waist, tugging Darth behind me. Suddenly the load lightened. I looked back: SoSo had clipped her own cable to Darth and was pulling him, too, jogging backwards, firing all the while. A plasma beam licked across her left thigh, but she snarled and fired back. We reached the perimeter trench a minute later, and then two streamers grabbed Darth and hustled him back toward the elevator. I fell down into the trench, gasping. Avery found me a moment later, and wrapped me in a hug. Then he pushed me away, inspecting me at arm's length.

"I'm okay," I said, still catching my breath.

"You're damn lucky," he said. He nodded toward the trench. "They're coming for us now, in force. We're gonna need you on the line."

"I know," I said. "I just need a second."

Avery nodded and stood up, turning back to the battle. I took a sip of water as Lexy squatted next to me, grabbing me by the arm.

"You made it," I said, relieved.

"We all did, somehow. How's Darth?" she asked.

I shook my head. "Shrapnel, lower back. Hard to tell the damage."

"Nice job getting him here," she said. "Your plan worked."

"Only because of SoSo," I said. "Where is she?" I stood up, scanning the streamers in the trench, but none of them were wearing neon pink armor. "Where'd she go?"

"I dunno, why?" Lexy asked.

"She saved us," I said, still dazed by what I had seen. "She just walked right out there, in the middle of that firestorm, and … saved us."

CHAPTER 31

"Male Veterans: 1.5 times more likely to commit suicide (vs. civilian males)

Female Veterans: 5.5 times more likely to commit suicide (vs. civilian females)."

-Hoffmire, Kemp, and Bossarte: "Changes in Suicide Mortality for Veterans and Nonveterans by Gender and History of VHA Service Use, 2000–2010"

I couldn't find SoSo.

I rode the third elevator back up after the battle ended, following the crowd of streamers through the landing bay. After I turned my weapons in and climbed out of my vac-suit, I ran across the hall to the medical bay, eager for the latest report on Darth. Prognosis: good. It had taken us nearly six hours to subdue the Ochos after the SRD Team broke through their lines, so he was already out of surgery, lying on his stomach and eating an ice cream cone.

"Got a couple extra holes in my bum," he said, between licks. "But the docs say I'll be right in a couple weeks."

"Good," I said, tousling his short, black hair. "We're gonna need that machine gun of yours soon, I'm sure."

"Yeah. Listen, thanks for sticking with me out there. I owe you one."

"You'd do the same," I told him, knowing it was true. "And speaking of, I gotta go find SoSo. She saved both of us."

"Well, thank her for me, too."

"Will do."

Back out in the main hallway, I ran into the last group of streamers, debarking from the elevator. I stepped aside, letting them clomp past in their vac-boots, headed to the armory. I scanned the crowd as they passed me, but did not spot a pink-armored streamer. I frowned.

Of course SoSo's gonna make it hard for me to find her. I just want to thank her.

I crossed over to the VR sim training rooms next – they were abandoned, not surprisingly, so it only took me a moment to pull on a headset and flip through feeds to find SoSo's.

Offline. That's … odd. SoSo's always online. Unless she's showering, or something.

I headed to her suite next, but when I touched the doorbell, the hologram panel next to the hatch reported that she was not in.

Maybe I just missed her, and she's back online now, I thought.

I ran into Taalib in the hallway.

"Hey, congrats!" he said.

"What, for making it back alive?" I asked.

"No, for the record," he said.

"What record?" I asked, confused.

"You guys set a new record today, you didn't know?"

I shook my head.

"The SRD Team posted the highest single battle clan earnings of all time today," Taalib said. "Ka-ching, girl." He punched me in the shoulder lightheartedly.

"Oh, nice," I said. *I haven't even checked my numbers.* "Hey, you know SoSo?"

"I don't really know her," Taalib said. "I know *of* her."

"Well, have you seen her around?"

"Nope," Taalib said. "Sorry."

I headed back toward the VR training rooms. I caught myself jogging, and frowned. *Why is this so damn urgent? Go shower and get some dinner, sheesh.*

But I didn't. I turned into the training center, grabbed the nearest headset, and accessed SoSo's feed. She was still offline, so I pulled up a replay of her last stream. Out of curiosity, I watched the part where she had saved Darth and me. It was even more incredible watching it from her point of view – up in the trench, she'd been able to see just how bad the fire was.

But she jumped out of the trench the minute I reported that Darth went down, I realized, with a start. *She knew we'd need help, and didn't even hesitate.*

I fast-forwarded, right to the end of the video. I watched as the elevator ramps dropped, revealing the inside of the landing bay. The streamers in front of her headed toward the arms room, but SoSo turned and faced the training ranges. Then the feed just stopped.

She's … on the range? A little practice, to use up the rest of her ammo, I guess? But that was over an hour ago.

I left the VR training center and headed back across the landing bay, where several maintenance robots were busy repairing damage to the elevator, the white-hot fire of their welding tools casting deep shadows around the bay. The hatch to the training ranges slid open as I approached it, but it was dark and eerily quiet inside. As the motion sensor lights clicked on across the ceiling, I caught sight of someone seated on the floor, slumped against one of the range lane dividers. SoSo's pink helmet sat upturned on the floor beside her, and a pistol lay in one hand.

I covered my mouth and turned away.

Oh, Christ. Not SoSo.

Not again.

* * *

SoSo's funeral was packed. StreaMercs set up an official feed for it, and promised to give half of the proceeds to a suicide prevention foundation. The other half would go to SoSo's family. I didn't want to go, but not going would have been far worse, so I gripped Avery's hand tightly throughout it, and then afterwards I dragged him to the Fiddler's Green, along with the SRD Team (minus Darth).

"I'm gonna get blackout drunk, because I don't want to feel right now," I told Avery. "And then you're going to carry me home."

"Okay," he said, and rubbed my back.

Later, after we had finished another round, Lexy nudged Petro, and he cleared his throat.

"I did some research," he said. "I didn't know her very well, but … I still wanted to know why."

"I think we all do," Avery said.

"A friend of SoSo's put up a long post on her memorial page," Petro said. "It was illuminating."

"A friend? A streamer?" Foo asked.

"No," Petro shook his head. "Someone she grew up with. According to this friend, Sofia's family was … not well liked. Her mom was okay, but her dad was a real piece of work. And they'd been having money trouble for some time."

"Hold on, I thought they were loaded," I said, frowning. "He was the CEO of a … utility company or something."

"They *were* loaded," Petro said. "Her father used to run a mining company. But he got caught bribing environmental officials, and did a short stint in jail. The government fines and legal fees basically wiped them out, but her father was too proud to admit it. He made them stay in their mansion, kept buying expensive stuff, and throwing lavish parties."

"With what money?" Avery asked.

"Well, exactly," Petro said. "He was just putting them deeper in debt. And then he saw Sofia doing well with her fashion stream, and he pushed her to monetize that. He pushed her very, very hard, according to this friend. Sofia basically had to quit school and focus on the stream full time. She was supporting her whole family."

"So why'd she join StreaMercs?" I asked.

"Daddy got greedy," Jack guessed.

Petro pointed at him. "Yes. He saw there was a lot more money to be made here, so he sold one of the properties they still had, enrolled her in combat classes, and ... there we are. She hated being a deathstreamer, but she was such a good actress, she never let anyone know."

I twirled my glass, watching the liquor at the bottom swirl from side to side.

"She didn't want to fight," Lexy said, quietly. "Her friend said it terrified her, every minute of it. But her father wouldn't let her quit."

I'm not here to make friends, I heard SoSo say, in my head.

"Well, her dad just made bank from her funeral with that official feed," Foo said. "He even profited off her death."

"Fucking asshole," Jack said, after a time.

I ordered another round.

* * *

I was nursing a nasty hangover when I went in to see Alice the following morning. The *Final Hope* had repositioned already, anchoring near the last colony left on Venatur, but on Dev's orders, there would be no battle today. They called it a "maintenance stand-down," but I don't think there was anything that actually needed to be fixed on the ship. It was more out of respect for SoSo. And, I suppose, to give us all a chance to get our heads back in the game.

"Can you turn down the lights?" I asked Alice, rubbing at the ache in my forehead.

"Of course," Alice said. The lights dimmed to a soft glow, leaving Alice's hologram the brightest thing in the room. "Why does it bother you that you didn't get a chance to thank SoSo?" Alice asked.

"I don't know," I said. "She saved my life. That deserves a 'thank you,' right?"

"Is it possible that you held some lingering antipathy toward her? That you didn't want to feel indebted to someone you disliked?"

"Yeah," I said, nodding. "But ... I also thought maybe we could put the past behind us. I thought this could be a new start. I guess I wanted to apologize to her, too."

"And now you feel regret because you never got to tell her that," Alice said.

"I feel regret because she's dead," I said. "And maybe me being a jerk to her is part of the reason why."

"Why she's dead? No, Sam," Alice said. "You can't take the blame for her decision."

"I should at least have seen the signs. God knows I know what to look for. If I'd been paying attention, or gotten to the range sooner ..." My voice faltered, and I felt tears on my cheeks, hot and wet.

"Sam," Alice said. "This isn't on you."

We sat in silence for a time. I sniffed, wiping at my face.

"You want to talk about Lucie," I said.

"I think it's time," Alice said. "It's been four years. I think you need to start the healing process, Sam. Denial has to end sometime. And maybe by talking about Lucie, you can properly grieve for SoSo, too."

I took a deep, ragged breath. "Damn it."

"Tell me what happened," Alice said, gently. "I've read the news articles, but I want to hear how you experienced it."

"Lucie was my freediving partner," I said. "We met in college – she started a freediving club the first week of freshman year, put up posts on every forum, flyers all over the school, but I was the only other person to show up to the first meeting." I smiled at the memory. "She had baked enough cookies for a couple dozen people, but it was just me and her. Just the two of us."

"You became friends," Alice said.

"Best friends," I said.

"She taught you how to freedive?" Alice asked.

I nodded. "In the pool at first, the diving well, when the springboard divers weren't using it. We'd practice breath holds and strokes, doing laps underwater. Then, later, we went out into the open water, off her folks' place on the Jersey shore. We started doing competitions that summer."

"What happened?" Alice prompted, gently.

"The summer after junior year we were training at her house – we'd go out on her boat all day, drop a line, and just dive. One morning I slept in and she wasn't home when I got up, and the boat wasn't in the marina. I checked my watch and found its GPS locator out at one of our dive sites, so I bummed a ride with a fishing boat, but she wasn't on board when we got out there. I thought she was down on a dive, that I had just missed her."

I took another deep breath. Alice waited.

"We never dove on our own, so I should have known something was up. I just figured she was mad at me for sleeping in, or something. So I suited up and waited, but she … didn't come up. I was watching the clock, waiting for her to pop up, and this pit was just growing in my stomach as the seconds ticked by. I realized that maybe something had gone wrong, so I jumped in, and dove down the line. She was at the bottom of the line, I saw her in the dark, just floating there, clipped to the line. And I knew she was dead, just from how still she was."

"What did you do?" Alice asked.

"I swam back up, and then I hauled up the line, and got her back on board. I called the Coast Guard, and did CPR for a while, and then just held her, until they took her away from me."

"That must have been hard," Alice said. "Being alone on the boat, waiting for help to come."

I shook my head. "The hardest part was going to her house with the Coast Guard, to tell her parents." I shivered involuntarily.

"I imagine so," Alice said. "The articles I reviewed said it wasn't an accident."

"No," I said. "We found her note later that day, up in her room. And it was like … all these pieces of who Lucie really was finally fell into place. All the things that I had seen but not understood, or had ignored, it all finally made sense. I should have realized."

"You think you could have prevented it?" Alice asked.

"Shouldn't I have?" I asked. "The signs were all there. Manic behavior, social withdrawal, sleeping all the time."

"Her parents didn't anticipate it, either," Alice pointed out.

"They weren't hanging out with her all day, every day. They weren't the ones she was sharing all her thoughts and dreams with," I said.

"She wasn't sharing *all* of her thoughts with you, either," Alice said. "Or else you would have known not to leave her alone; you would have tried to get her some help."

"I don't know," I said, shaking my head. "I don't think that makes me any less culpable. I'm still a shitty friend for missing it."

"Did she ever tell you she was hurting?" Alice asked. "Did she ever ask you for help?"

"No," I said.

"Would you have helped her, if she had?"

"Of course," I said.

Alice spread her hands wide. "Then I don't think you

can be angry with yourself. And you certainly shouldn't blame yourself."

I chewed the inside of my cheek. "That's easier said than done."

"I know," Alice said. "But let me ask you this: would the Lucie you knew and loved have wanted you to still be agonizing over her death today? Would she have wanted her suicide to cause you this much pain?"

"... no," I said.

"Then perhaps you should think about honoring her memory a different way," Alice said.

"I can't just flip a switch and decide to feel differently about all of it," I said.

"No, you can't," Alice said. "But over time, you can at least try to forgive yourself."

CHAPTER 32

"They did *what* to the elevator? Show me. Ventral camera, full magnification." [pause] "Oh god. Oh my god."

-Dev Khanna, CEO of StreaMercs. Transcript of security recording from the bridge of the *Final Hope*, immediately following the descent of the first wave during the final battle on Venatur

S omething felt wrong from the minute we boarded the elevator for the last battle on Venatur. Maybe I was still out of sorts from SoSo's death, or maybe it was the break in routine – the extra day off between battles. Or it could have been the fact that the SRD Team was a man down, with Darth still in recovery. Either way, I didn't feel right.

We nearly made it down: the touchdown timer was approaching twenty seconds when a massive shockwave crashed into the elevator, knocking us all to the floor. I heard screams, and then there was a hideous groan of twisting, shearing metal. The elevator tilted drunkenly to one side, throwing us into a giant pile of tangled limbs and weaponry, and then the power went out, bathing us in darkness. I screamed, then, because I could feel us falling again, only this time it wasn't the smooth, controlled descent of the elevator along the cable, it was a wrenching, tumbling free-fall that seemed to last an eternity.

We hit *hard*, though the thick jungle canopy slowed the elevator slightly, as did the emergency airbags that inflated around the elevator's exterior. I smashed into a ramp face-first, and something hard and pointy slammed into the left side of my rib cage, and I felt a distinct *crack* and gasped in pain. Don't ever break a rib – it makes literally every breath you take painful from that point on. Then everything was still, and dark. Somebody was lying on top of me, and I was pretty sure I was on top of somebody else. I gave myself a dose of painkiller to take the edge off.

Ouch.

Honestly, the next twenty minutes were a clusterfuck of epic proportions. Eventually, after much cursing and fumbling, we managed to disentangle ourselves from the pile of a hundred other streamers, and take inventory. The news was grim: eight streamers had been knocked unconscious and were still out for the count. Another seven were awake, but still reeling from severe concussions. A full thirty had broken limbs of some kind, meaning they either couldn't walk or couldn't fight, and in some cases, they couldn't do either. And nearly everyone else – myself included – had something sprained or badly bruised. About the only good news was that no one had been killed. *So far.*

Our first order of business was for everyone to retrieve their proper weapons – thank god for the locator beacons StreaMercs embeds in them, otherwise that would have taken us the rest of the day. Then we surveyed the elevator itself. Based on gravity, we deduced that we were sitting roughly upright, though the room had a noticeable lean to it. Finally, we managed to get a ramp partially opened, using a manual release handle. That proved to be a bad idea, because the second sunlight spilled in over the top of the ramp, a dozen plasma beams tore inside, promptly killing the two streamers standing in front of the ramp. We backed up, taking cover and moving our wounded streamers away from the ramp.

"We still need to see outside," someone noted, when the plasma beams stopped firing.

"So go look," someone else suggested.

There was a long pause, during which no one moved.

"Fuck, I will." A streamer I didn't recognize pushed his way through the crowd toward the ramp. In my heads-up display, his name appeared: *SantoClauso*. He had a camera mounted on his rifle's barrel, whose video feed linked to his helmet – it was supposed to allow him to hide down in a trench, hold up his gun, and shoot with some degree of accuracy without exposing himself. I'd seen them in the arms room catalogue but they always felt unsporting to me. In this case, though, it proved to be a lifesaver.

While the rest of us stayed back, Santo edged up to the open ramp and cautiously held his e-rifle up for a few seconds, then hastily withdrew it as a volley of plasma beams responded.

"We're on the ground," he said.

"No shit," someone commented. "Why are we tilted?"

"I dunno," Santo said. He ducked under the ramp's opening, repositioning himself, then held the e-rifle aloft. Again, the Ochos replied with plasma beams, scoring the elevator's ceiling, throwing sparks off the armored steel. Santo backed away.

"Ochos everywhere," he said. "Not the usual welcoming committee, it looks like all of them are out, and they're right on top of us. We're surrounded. The full colony."

Santo moved once again, and angled his e-rifle for a final glance.

"Oh, shit," he said.

"What?"

"I can see the elevator," he said.

"We're *in* the elevator," someone told him.

"No, I mean the cable," Santo said. "I can see the cable, it's swinging free. They cut the cable."

We pieced it together from satellite footage later on. When the elevator left the *Final Hope* with us aboard, the cable and anchor began to vibrate, as they always did. Several dozen Ochos had immediately formed a tight ring around the anchor. They had interlocked their forearms somehow – the same arms that emitted those deadly plasma blasts, fueled by their internal fusion reactors. Then they proceeded to pump plasma energy into each other through their linked arms, the entire ring a massive, energy-producing feedback loop. After a few minutes, their armored shells could no longer contain all that energy stored within them, and the whole chain detonated at once. The blast cut the cable right at ground level, leaving the anchor embedded in the earth and the cable swinging free. A few hundred feet above them, we were far enough away to survive the blast, but the elevator was still falling, and we simply slid off the end of the severed cable, landing several hundred meters away from the anchor.

After a few minutes of noisy argument about our predicament, we thought to call the *Final Hope*, and they confirmed that, yes, the cable was cut, and, no, they weren't sure yet how they were gonna get us back on board. Stand by. That's when the reality of our situation sunk in.

Stand by.

After the radio call, several loud arguments broke out among the streamers. I squatted down on the floor, next to Lexy, along with the rest of the SRD Team. Avery found us a moment later, and knelt next to me, giving my arm a friendly squeeze.

"You okay?" he asked.

I nodded. "Think I busted a rib, but I've got it under

control. You?"

"Bruised but not broken," he said.

Jack was helping Foo rig a sling around his neck – he had dislocated a shoulder in the crash, though luckily, it was not his dominant arm.

"I thought we were fucked last battle," Jack said. "But this is definitely worse."

"We've got food, water, and ammo," Foo said, nodding toward the resupply lockers in the center of the elevator. "We should be able to hold out for a while."

"Six days," Lexy said. "They've got six days to figure something out, and then we all go critical on oxygen."

"If those Ochos decide to try to get in here, I'm not sure we'll last six hours," Petro said, glancing over at the open ramp.

"You want to try to break out?" Lexy asked him.

Petro twisted his mouth. "No. They've got us outnumbered ten to one, and we'd have to leave the wounded behind. I just don't like being pinned down."

Someone tapped me on the shoulder, and I looked up.

"SRD Team?"

"That's us," I said.

"You guys up for some target practice?" the streamer asked. "We're gonna open up a few more ramps, start trying to take out some of those Ochos. We figured with your GhostSkin, you guys would want to be on the trigger. They can't see you, so you guys can shoot while we reload, kind of thing. Might keep them from trying to break in here."

I traded looks with the other SRD Team members. "Sounds like a plan," I decided, and pushed myself upward, groaning as the pain returned.

The rest of that first morning was a blur. The elevator had twelve ramps; we cracked open six of them and took turns manning the firing slits, shooting at anything that moved, and ducking when the plasma beams came in. Everyone who wasn't shooting lay on the floor, both for cover and to conserve oxygen. Jack dominated the kill count all day: he built himself a perch out of supply crates in the middle of the elevator and set his sniper rifle up, shifting his fire between ramps to keep the Ochos guessing. I wasn't far behind him – I fired damn near every weapon in our inventory, got the top of my helmet singed on several occasions, and snuck in a few sips of energy supplement in between firefights.

About mid-afternoon, the Ochos seemed to have had enough, and backed off, fading into the jungle. But the occasional plasma beam told us they were still there, still watching, still waiting. I sat, leaning my back against the ramp, my legs sprawled out on the floor of the elevator, resting. They let us catch our breath for about thirty minutes, and then a contingent of Ochos made a rush for one of the ramps, and we were back at it. The SRD Team stayed at the ramps the whole time, discarding empty weapons, taking fresh ones when they were handed to us. Shooting, always shooting. We weren't the only ones fighting, not by a long shot – plenty of other streamers took turns on the ramps when we needed a break, and when the Ochos got close, *everyone* near a ramp stepped up to help beat them off.

They assaulted during the night, too. I was sleeping, but our sentries sent out a general alarm to all streamers, and the piercing siren had me on my feet without a conscious thought, e-rifle at the ready. We held them off, but they just came again. And again.

When the sun rose, Avery organized an ammo check. We had all blown through our basic loads by that point, and had started to raid the resupply cabinets in the center of the room. With the help of a few lightly wounded streamers, Avery opened up every drawer and crate, laid the ammunition boxes out carefully for easier access, and then counted it. When he was done, he stood up.

"By my count, we've used over a third of our ammo. At that rate, we'll run out sometime tomorrow evening," he said, shaking his head. "Only fire when you're sure of a kill. Don't use two bullets when one will do."

I was catching a mid-morning nap between firefights on the second day when an "all hands" notification went out, and moments later, Dev's face appeared on my screen. He looked like he had gotten even less sleep than we had.

"We have a plan," he said. "I'd like to say it has a high likelihood of success, but I'm not going to lie to you, either." He cleared his throat, and I noted how bloodshot his eyes were. "We have a spare anchor, and we can repair the cable. We're in the process of doing so right now. So we can reestablish a physical link between the *Final Hope* and the ground. The problem we face is that we do not have a spare elevator – we never considered that the elevator itself could be detached like this. So we have to build one, by cannibalizing parts from the *Final Hope*. First we have to locate those parts, then we have to assemble them around the new cable. We're working as fast as we can, but it's going to take some time."

"How long?" Avery asked.

"Another five days," Dev said. "We think."

"That's going to put us at the extreme limit of our air supplies," Avery pointed out. "We're running low on ammo, too."

"I'm aware," Dev said. "Listen, we're monitoring you guys closely, we know what you're up against. But we don't currently have a way to get supplies down to you. The crisis team back at Stellarus is looking into it, but the reality is that any resupply attempt would just delay the main rescue effort."

I made a mental note to dial back my painkiller doses – I wasn't sure how much I had on board, but I was sure that it wasn't going to last another five days. I had used it fairly liberally through the night to combat the pain in my ribs.

Might need it for something worse later on, I thought.

I saw a flurry of activity on my feed – my fans were

upvoting a question so that I'd see it. "Oh, crap," I said, scanning the text. "Dev, if you repair everything and then drop anchor, the Ochos could just do the same thing they did yesterday. How are we going to make sure they don't just blow it again?"

Dev grimaced, and rubbed his forehead, mussing his hair. "I'm afraid it will be up to you guys to secure the anchor and cable, until the new elevator reaches the ground. We'll have that elevator full of streamers to reinforce you, but until they reach the ground ... you'll need to keep the Ochos away from the anchor."

More good news, I thought, frowning. *So ... IF the Ochos don't kill us all first, and IF you can build a new elevator, and IF our oxygen lasts, and IF we can break out of here and defend the anchor site long enough ... then MAYBE we've got a shot at making it back to the ship.*

Fantastic.

CHAPTER 33

"We've been looking for the enemy for some time now. We've finally found him. We're surrounded. That simplifies things."

-Colonel Lewis Burwell "Chesty" Puller, at the Battle of Chosin Reservoir, 1950

On the afternoon of the sixth day, they finished the replacement elevator capsule. Dev called to let us know that they had started lowering the cable. I reached up and grabbed Avery's hand – he pulled me upright, and I gasped out of habit, groaning at the now-familiar pain in my ribs. I hadn't been able to ration my painkiller supply as well as I had hoped, and as predicted, it had run out the day before. I looked around the elevator, which was lit dimly by sunlight filtering in through the tops of the ramps on one side of the room. Exhausted streamers stood at the ramps, waiting, weapons held limply in slack arms. I didn't look to my left, but I knew – because I had carried some of them there myself – that a neat stack of thirty-eight bodies lay blocking one of the damaged ramps. *Thirty-eight. Thirty-eight of our friends.*

The other survivors lay scattered on the floor, sleeping or resting, their weapons close at hand. Their armor – like my own – was streaked with plasma burns, sliced and torn in places from the night attack where the Ochos had managed to get inside the elevator for several terror-filled minutes. I shuddered, recalling that fight. My lasting impression was of screams and muzzle flashes in the dark, but I also remembered seeing two Ochos grab hold of a streamer, pulling him over the top of a ramp, almost as if they were trying to take him prisoner. They had gotten him out of the elevator, but the streamer had detonated one of his grenades before they got very far, killing the Ochos who had grabbed him.

"Strike team," Avery said, breaking me out of my reverie. "On me." His voice was hoarse from overuse. I'm not sure how or why he'd become the de facto leader over the past several days – it probably went back to him thinking to count the ammo, or being the first to reply to Dev. After that, he'd just kind of … directed us, and by unspoken agreement, we'd followed him. It fit him well – he was a natural.

He gathered us near one of the ramps – the SRD Team, Avery, and a couple dozen volunteers. We carried what ammo was left – for me, that meant three grenades and a grand total of four spare magazines. The rest of the survivors of the first wave would stay behind, locking the ramps shut behind us, in the faint hope that that would keep the Ochos out long enough, while we fought our way to the anchor site, and secured it.

"When the ramp drops, it's an all-out sprint, like we talked about, right?" Avery said, looking between us. "SRD Team first. Run, don't stop, no matter what. Even if we lose people along the way, we keep going. This whole thing fails if some of us don't reach that anchor and hold it."

Tired nods.

"Okay. Final checks, and then we go."

I knew my ER-45 was loaded, but I did a bolt-check anyway, and then settled the strap around my chest, watching as Avery loosened a magazine in one of its pouches. He looked strange under his visor – the light blonde scruff of a beard was showing on his face, the first time I'd ever seen him with facial hair. I hugged him, impulsively, and he patted me on the back.

"You want to stay at my place or yours tonight?" he asked, smiling faintly.

I touched my visor against his – the closest we could come to kissing in our vac-suits. "Love you," I said.

"Love you, too," he told me. He seemed about to say something else.

"What?" I asked.

"I … I'm done," he said, with a sigh. "If we make it back—"

"We will," I interrupted.

"I know," he said. "But … I'm just done with streaming, after this. I've got enough money. This is it."

I frowned. "You're gonna leave me?"

"Come with me," Avery said. "You could quit, too."

"And do what?" I asked. But I had to admit, at that moment, stranded down on the surface of Venatur, it was a compelling thought. *Is this really worth it?*

"Just think about it," Avery said, and I heard the crank of the ramp, starting to open.

I activated my GhostSkin, watching as my armor shimmered and disappeared. A flood of notifications arrived in my heads-up display – my viewers, wishing me luck. Then the sun hit my visor. I squinted, and took a deep breath.

Here we go.

We surprised them, somehow. After six days of siege warfare, holed up in our crashed elevator capsule, the Ochos weren't expecting us to come out. We made it several meters outside the elevator before they even responded, weakly, with a few plasma blasts. I burned through half a mag when we reached their line, taking down five Ochos in my line of sight, still running. On my visor, a large, orange arrow pointed the way toward the anchor site, several hundred meters ahead through the trees.

Then we were through their line – we'd done it. I allowed myself a brief smile of relief. I caught glimpses of my fellow streamers as I ran – Foo ahead of me, Lexy and Petro to one side, patches of their armor visible where the GhostSkin had taken damage.

"We lost DefconDon!"

"They're regrouping. On our six!"

"Keep going!" Avery urged us, panting.

Another Ocho appeared to my left – I shot it without thinking. My legs ached, and it felt like I was being stabbed in the ribs with each gasp of air. My breathing was ragged, my throat dry. I kept going.

And suddenly, we were there – the arrow disappeared from my heads-up display, replaced by a wide orange circle overlaid on the jungle floor, showing where the anchor would be. I glanced up. *No sign of it yet – a few more minutes, and then it'll be down. Then we just have to hold out five more minutes, and the second wave will be here to help.*

The rest of the SRD Team arrived a moment later, and then the other volunteers straggled in, breathing hard.

"How many?" Jack asked, counting heads quickly.

"We lost some," another streamer told him. "They caught up and cut a bunch of us off. Don't know how many."

"Where's Avery?" I asked, trying to locate him in the group.

"Get a perimeter going!" Petro rasped, pushing several people toward points outside the circle. "Come on – you, here. Go!"

"Where's Avery?" I yelled. I accessed the radio channel we had set up for the breakout team. "Avery, come in!"

There was no response.

"Sam! Perimeter!" Petro said, grabbing me by the elbow.

I felt my heart race. "No, Petro, Avery's not here," I sobbed. "I gotta go find—"

"Sam, I know!" Petro said. "But the Ochos are coming, and if we don't hold this site, there's no chance at all he'll make it. None of us will."

"It's *Avery*!" I pleaded. "What would you do if it was Lexy out there?"

"Lexy didn't make it either," Petro said, and somehow the quiet, simple statement cut through me like a knife. *Lexy …?*

I looked around the circle, wide-eyed, but it was true – the only SRD Team outlines I saw were Jack, Foo, and Petro.

"Perimeter," Petro repeated, as a shadow crossed overhead – the anchor, descending at last.

"Right," I said, swallowing hard. "Sorry."

I hurried to the edge of the circle and lay down, setting my three remaining magazines on the ground beside me, pointing my e-rifle out at the trees. I could see movement in the distance, among the waving white fronds of the trees – Ochos, inbound.

Avery!

"I've got a ten thousand dollar prize for whoever can locate Avery for me," I said aloud to my viewers, my voice still trembling. "Find him, and then send me grid coordinates. *Please.*"

Then the Ochos burst through the undergrowth. They came at us relentlessly, from all sides, driving at us, backing off, then crashing in again, like storm-tossed surf pounding a shoreline. But we held them off, the twenty of us. After the first attack, the anchor touched down behind us, rattling us in our vac-suits as it buried itself deep into the earth in the middle of our tiny perimeter.

"Anchor's set! Elevator should be down in five

minutes!" Petro yelled. "Five minutes!"

The streamer next to me took a plasma blast directly to the visor, the white-hot energy spearing him in a straight line from head-to-toe. He slumped over, dead. I pushed myself over toward him, pulled his e-rifle closer to me, and readjusted my fire to cover his sector, too.

"Tighten up," Petro warned. *Someone on his side of the anchor must have been hit, too.*

"Last mag!" someone called.

My vac-suit posted a warning notification.

>>>*Air supplies critical. One hour remaining.*

"Last mag!" the streamer yelled, again.

"We're *all* on last mag!" Foo replied.

A message rose to the top of my viewer feed.

>>>*Avery's not online. His last broadcast showed him running past an Ocho tunnel, and then something knocked him down, and seemed to drag him toward the tunnel. Then the feed died.*

"What?" I said, shaking my head. "They were trying to take him into the colony? Is he alive?"

>>>*Unknown – he's not broadcasting vitals, location, anything. Sending you the tunnel coordinates. I'm not gonna accept any reward money. Just get home safe.*

I didn't have time to thank the fan who had sent it – my bolt clicked on an empty chamber and I swore, dropping my e-rifle and picking up the dead streamer's weapon in its place. Without the GhostSkin and suppressor on my e-rifle, it would mark me as a clear target for the Ochos, but I didn't have time to worry about that right now.

Time!

I checked the time in my heads-up display.

Still three minutes until the elevator is down. Shit.

"They're massing," Foo warned. "I'm about to have more targets than bullets."

I looked up and saw that he was right – the Ochos had gathered, a hundred meters out. Abruptly, in unison, the outer ring of aliens stood upright, locking their forearms together, as if holding hands in a giant circle around the anchor.

"What the hell?" I breathed, trying to make sense of what I was seeing. Then realization dawned, and my stomach fell. "Take them down!" I yelled. "They're going to try to cut the cable again!"

But the rest of the Ochos were surging toward us, shoulder-to-shoulder, their sword-like forearms tearing up the ground as they ran. I fired at one of the Ochos in the far circle, trying to ignore the incoming threat.

Suddenly, a hail of bullets rained down from above – tracers tore into the Ochos, plunging down into their lines, sending them reeling, tumbling across the forest floor. Grenades erupted amongst the Ochos who had formed the outer circle, breaking their chain apart. I craned my neck, and saw the unfamiliar outline of the replacement elevator, dropping fast, its ramps open, streamers leaning out to provide covering fire.

Dev must have started them down the cable before the anchor was even set! Thank god.

I hauled myself to my feet – ignoring another shriek of pain from my broken ribs – and ran, headlong, through the chaos, not caring if I was hit by friendly or alien fire. The direction marker bobbed in my heads-up display – the tunnel was ahead, somewhere. *The tunnel … and Avery.* I dodged a final group of Ochos, and then the battle was behind me and I was alone, running through the trees.

The distance scrolled down on my display – fifty meters, twenty, five. I burst out of a group of trees and found three Ochos clustered around the tunnel. One of them was carrying something bulky, dragging it up out of the tunnel.

Avery.

I screamed in rage and fired, my finger convulsing around the trigger. The Ocho on the left gave a jerk, crashing into the one next to it, the two of them falling in a tangle of brown limbs and armored carapaces. I killed the one on the right next, pumping rounds into it until the e-rifle was empty. Then I hurried over to Avery, kneeling next to him. I shook him.

"Avery!"

No response. I searched, frantically, for signs of a wound.

"Come on …"

Something twitched in my peripheral vision. I realized, with sudden dread certainty, that the third Ocho wasn't dead. In my haste, I had assumed I had killed it along with the first one, but it had merely collapsed under the weight of its dying comrade. And now it was freeing itself. And it could see me, a hazy shadow, clutching a very visible e-rifle. I dropped the e-rifle and reached for Avery's pistol, pulling it out of his holster, but the Ocho tackled me from behind before I could bring the pistol to bear, and we tumbled down into the tunnel. I fumbled with the gun and fired a round – the Ocho was on top of me now, scrabbling. I fired again. The Ocho flicked its forearm, a quick strike that curved gracefully through the air. It cut through my upper thigh with shocking ease, amputating my left leg above the kneecap. I screamed and kept firing until the Ocho collapsed.

>>>*Tourniquet applied, left thigh*, my heads-up display reported. I saw stars as I felt the cord cinch tight around my leg.

"Fentanyl!" I ordered.

>>>*Supplies depleted.*

The pain was like a hot skillet, pressed against my leg, my body throbbing with every heartbeat. There was a shocking amount of blood on the dirt floor of the tunnel, though with my GhostSkin activated, it appeared to have sprung from thin air. I felt my eyesight dim.

Losing it. Gonna pass out.

I shook my head, trying to clear the cobwebs from my brain.

Gotta stay conscious.

I accessed my radio. "Valkyrie6 is down, requesting assistance," I said, my voice thin and weak.

Another message on my visor: >>>*Communications offline. Uplink damaged.*

The Ocho must have broken my radio when it tackled me, I realized. *I'm bleeding out ... in an Ocho tunnel ... that no one knows about. And I'm invisible.*

>>>*Air supplies critical. Fifty-five minutes remaining.*

I shivered, feeling suddenly cold. I forced myself to focus, lifting my right hand, my arm strangely heavy. I reached feebly for my control pad, trying to deactivate the GhostSkin. Then a wave of nausea rushed over me, and I felt myself falling, dizzyingly, into the dark.

CHAPTER 34

"StreaMercs' revenues from new enrollment rose in Q4 2233 on the back of an increased recruiting push, but streaming ad and transaction fee revenue continue to be the dominant income sources. The big question – as ever – is sustainability. How long can the war continue? Regardless, our recommendation remains: BUY."

-Sachs & Morgan, Co. analyst notes on Stellarus' public earnings call

I lived. Barely.

Thank god for my fans. They saw me go offline and rounded up a couple streamers in the second wave to come find me. And they couldn't find me, not at first – they spotted Avery, took a quick look down in the tunnel, didn't see me because my GhostSkin was still on, and decided that I could be anywhere in the colony, and the elevator was leaving soon – they had to get Avery back if he had a shot at making it.

Which, frankly, would have been an okay result in my book.

But one of my super-fans was watching their feed, and saw the puddle of blood, and sent a massive tip to that streamer begging them to take one more look, and … well, they got me out of there, along with Avery. They got all of our fellow first-wave streamers who were stranded in the downed elevator out, too.

By the time they woke me up, we were already on our way back to Earth. The first thing I noticed, sitting there in the hospital bed, was that my left leg was gone – the thigh ended abruptly above where my kneecap would have been, the whole area swaddled in white bandages. I touched it, gingerly.

Well, that … changes things. Fuck.

Then I noticed Darth, sitting in a chair next to the bed, petting a small, brown dog in his lap. He was in regular clothes, so I surmised that he had healed enough to be let out of the hospital.

"Hey," I said. My throat was sore.

Darth looked up. "G'day," he said, his broad, tattooed face wrinkling in a smile. "Welcome back."

"That SoSo's dog?" I asked.

Darth nodded. "Yeah, they asked if anyone wanted to adopt him, and I felt bad for the little bugger. He's a nippy little twat, but we're starting to get along."

"Avery?" I asked.

Darth nodded. I sighed, relief washing over me. A shadow crossed Darth's face.

"What?" I asked. Then I remembered the final minutes of the battle, our desperate last stand to protect the anchor and the cable. "What about the others?"

Darth looked at the floor. "Foo and Jack are fine." He cleared his throat. "Lexy and Petro didn't make it."

I sobbed, covering my mouth with one hand, the IV lines trailing beneath my wrist.

Darth plowed on, determined to get it over with: "… Lexy died on the way to the anchor, an Ocho caught her in the back with a plasma beam. After the elevator touched down, Petro went to look for her. He found her body, but in the confusion of trying to get everyone from the first wave back up to the ship, they lost track of him. He ran out of air."

"He didn't get up, or call for help?" I asked, sniffing.

Darth shook his head. "The third wave found him sitting next to Lexy, holding her hand."

I took Darth's hand and we sat in silence for a while, crying together.

"There's, uh … there's something else," Darth said, wiping at his eyes. "Avery's not … right."

"What do you mean?" I asked.

Darth pushed the call button on my bed. "I better let one of the robo-docs explain."

They couldn't find anything wrong with Avery, when they brought us back on board the *Final Hope*. He was unconscious, but all of his vital signs were normal. Finally, after they got him out of his vac-suit, the doctors found a microscopic puncture wound on his neck. His vac-suit had been punctured at the same spot, and then it had sealed itself, as it was designed to do. They scanned him with every medical device they had, and sampled everything they could think of, but found nothing physically wrong with him. And then, inexplicably, he woke up.

"Can I see him?" I asked the robo-doc, when it was done explaining Avery's condition.

"As far as we can tell, he is not dangerous," the doctor explained. "But given the nature of the attack and his symptoms, our fear is that this was an attempt at a bio-weapon. So he will have to remain quarantined."

"A bio-weapon?" I asked, incredulous. "The Ochos can't even build tools. They sleep in holes in the ground. How the hell are they going to cook up a bio-weapon?"

The robot shook its head. "We have to take precautions. For everyone's safety."

"For how long?" I asked.

"I don't know. It's up to a medical committee to

decide, not me."

"So I can't see him at all?" I asked.

"You may talk to him through a two-way hologram feed."

They brought me a keypad, and set it up. Darth excused himself, not wanting to intrude. A moment later, Avery's face appeared on the hologram, floating in front of me. The room behind him was blindingly white – it looked like a hospital room, but far cleaner than mine.

"Hi," I said, trying to smile through my tears. "Hi, Avery."

"Hi," he said, and smiled back. I thought my heart would break, seeing his smile again. Then his brow furrowed, and reminded me of all the times he had frowned at me in mock annoyance, before laughing at me.

"Do I know you?" Avery asked.

"Yes," I said, my voice cracking. "I'm Sam. We were friends. We *are* friends."

"Oh," Avery said, still frowning. "Really? When did we meet?"

My breath caught in my throat. "Last year," I told him. "You helped me get home after I had too much to drink one night."

"Mardi Gras?" Avery asked. "Tourists always get crazy drunk at Mardi Gras."

I shook my head. "No, it was here, on the *Final Hope*. In the casino."

Avery nodded, but his face was still a mask of confusion. "The psychiatrist program – Alice – tells me I've forgotten a lot of what happened recently. I'm sorry."

"You don't have to apologize," I told him, trying to hold it together.

"Why are you in the hospital?" Avery asked.

"I got hurt," I said.

"Oh. How did you get hurt?"

"Fighting the Ochos," I told him. "I'm a deathstreamer, just like you."

"Oh, okay," Avery said, looking down. "Alice shows me videos sometimes. She says I made them, but when I watch them, I forget them immediately. I can't remember any of it."

"You will," I told him. "I'll help you."

"It's frustrating," Avery said.

"Yeah," I said. *Talking to me bothers him*, I realized. *Because then he has to face everything he's lost.*

"I should go," Avery said. "It was nice to … talk to you."

"You too," I said. The connection ended, the hologram disappearing.

I set the keypad down on my lap, or what was left of it.

"It was nice to meet you," is what he almost said. I bit my lip. *I lost my leg, and my boyfriend, all in one day,* I realized. *Fucking Ochos. What did they do to us?*

I cried for a while, and when that didn't make me feel better, I thumbed the button to give me more painkillers. I fell asleep, and my dreams were filled with pain and loss.

And rage.

* * *

They fitted me for a standard cyber-prosthetic leg – it was neural-linked, so I could control it by thought, and "feel" when things touched the skin. Sort of. I could sense things, but … it wasn't the same. It didn't take me long to learn how to use it, at least, and I was up and walking by the time the *Final Hope* arrived back in Earth orbit. But my gait had an extra little hitch in it that annoyed me with every step, and every night, when I took it off to shower and let it charge, I had to stare at my pink-scarred stump, and remember just how changed I was. Just how … incomplete.

I talked to Avery three more times, but his frustration – both at being locked up in quarantine, and his amnesia in general – became more and more evident in each conversation. Finally, in our last conversation, he asked me why I kept calling him. I told him the truth: that we had loved each other, that I thought we could get that back, even if he never recovered his memory of our earlier time together. He was silent for a while, and then he asked me to stop calling him. I was angry, too ... and hurt, I guess. They transferred him to a secure Stellarus facility on the Moon soon afterward, to finish out his quarantine. I watched his shuttle thruster away from a viewport in the rec bay, then wiped my tears, and hobbled back to my suite.

While we waited for another campaign, most of the streamers headed down to Earth for leave. I stayed aboard the *Final Hope* and spent two weeks in physical therapy, sweating out my anger on various treadmills and weight sets, regaining my strength. StreaMercs gave me a full physical at the end of the second week, even making me put my vac-suit on to run a mile with full combat load. I passed. I think they were hoping I wouldn't. I hit the VR sims for training, too – there weren't many modules that I hadn't finished yet, but the completionist in me forced me to ace them all, just because.

We took on a fresh load of noobs – the company had a tough time with recruiting, after Venatur. StreaMercs had been forced to put out a five-minute video explaining the modifications they were making to the elevator cable, to make it resistant to future attacks. I didn't bother to watch. *I'll ride down anyway.* I trained the noobs for the next two weeks, pushing them hard, just like the last class. Between sessions, I found myself checking my watch often, looking for an all hands recall, a departure alert letting us know we'd be headed back out soon.

Bored, I checked my bank account one day, and sat staring at my money, wondering what to do with all of it. I had a bunch of vintage consoles shipped up to the *Final Hope* and went on an antique video game binge for a few days. I even set a new high score on the rec bay's Ms. Pac-

Man machine. I threw a party for the noobs when I decided they had "graduated," renting out Wagyu for the evening and showing them a thing or two about how real streamers drank. I found the suicide prevention charity StreaMercs had donated SoSo's funeral proceeds to, and made a sizable anonymous donation, too. Petro and Lexy's families were trying to raise money to build a small museum and park dedicated to their memory – I donated a bunch to them. Then I sent my parents a voucher for an all-expenses-paid round-the-world tour from a luxury tour company, including a stop on the Moon. They tried to refuse it, but I played the crippled veteran card and they relented. They had fun, from the pictures I saw.

And still, Stellarus couldn't find any more Ocho planets.

* * *

"Are you all packed up?" Alice asked me.

I nodded. "Mm-hm."

"Back to Long Island?" she asked. "You have an apartment there, right?"

"Yeah," I said. *I haven't seen the inside of that place for nearly a year.* "Still hard to believe they're kicking us all out, sending us home."

"I'm sure they'll find another planet soon," Alice said. "Let's hope this is just a temporary suspension of operations."

"Yeah."

"Have you been thinking about Lucie anymore? Or SoSo?"

"Some," I admitted.

"Any epiphanies?"

I sighed. "I still think I could have done something more to help them."

"But …" Alice prompted.

"… but I'm willing to admit it wasn't my fault."

"That's good, Sam. That's progress," Alice said. "Have you talked to Avery again?"

"No," I said. "He said not to call."

"It was hard for him," Alice told me. "He remembered everything from before the war. But nothing after he joined up. He said he felt like the memories were there, in his mind, he just couldn't grasp them. They kept slipping away. Memories are a big part of who you are, as human beings. To lose them can be … devastating."

"I thought you're not allowed to share your conversations with other patients," I said.

Alice shrugged. "When it's helpful for both patients' mental health, the rules can be relaxed a little." She settled her hands in her lap. "He's heading home soon."

I perked up. "They're letting him out?" I asked.

"Soon," Alice said. "They just want to observe him for a bit longer."

"They're going to let him go back to Earth?" I asked. "To Louisiana?"

"I believe so. Avery hired a lawyer. He's threatening to sue the company for wrongful imprisonment."

I laughed. "That sounds like Avery."

"Will you visit him?" Alice asked.

I shook my head, sobering again. "Maybe. Someday."

Alice smiled. "I hope you do. I think it would be good for both of you." She checked her watch, causing me to do the same.

"I better get going," I said.

"Yes," Alice said. "You don't want to miss your shuttle."

I stood up reluctantly, and then turned to face her. "Alice? Can we do these sessions after I go home?"

She shook her head sadly. "No, Sam. While the ship's in dry dock, I'll be deactivated. I'm sorry."

"Oh, okay," I said.

"Take care, Sam," Alice said.

CHAPTER 35

"I find I do not belong here anymore, it is a foreign world … I ought never to have come on leave."

-Erich Maria Remarque, "All Quiet on the Western Front"

I took the hypertube down to Philadelphia, and met Paul and Remy for drinks at The Dive the first Friday after flying home. It had only been a few years since graduation, but I expected The Dive to have changed for some reason. But when I pushed the door open, I smiled broadly at the smell of stale beer and bleach.

Hasn't changed a bit. Still a shithole.

"Sam!" Remy raised her hand from a booth along one of the walls, waving to me, and I saw Paul turn and look over his shoulder.

I waved back and walked over, grimacing inwardly and doing my best to hide my unnatural stride. Abruptly, a young man at one of the tables en route stood up.

"Holy shit, you're Valkyrie!" he said, his jaw dropping open. He turned to his friends at the table. "Guys:

Valkyrie. The deathstreamer."

"Uh, yeah," I said.

"You're … you're a goddamn legend. You led the breakout on Venatur. Can I take a photo?"

"Sure," I said, my face flushing. I looked over – Paul and Remy were watching the exchange, bemused smiles on their faces.

The student took a selfie, grinning. "Thanks!"

"Thanks for watching," I told him, automatically. I crossed over to my table, hugged Paul and Remy, and then sat.

"Well, Miss Legend," Remy said, smirking. "Thank you for joining us."

I frowned at her. "It gets old, being recognized," I assured her.

A waiter appeared, bearing a drink, and placed it in front of me.

"From the gentleman over there," he said, pointing to the fan I had taken a photo with.

Remy laughed. "Sure, tell me more about the burden of celebrity," she scoffed.

I saluted the fan with my drink, then took a sip, grinning. "It has some perks."

They laughed again, and we drank a toast to the Three Musketeers – reunited again. For a while, it was like old times – Remy was just starting another satirical novel, having done several months of research on the world of competitive eating, and Paul was finishing his PhD (already, the over-achiever). He regaled us with a story of the time he got two of his undergrad lectures mixed up.

"… so I was supposed to be talking about Freud with the one-oh-one class," Paul said. "But instead I gave them the four-oh-one Abnormal Psych lecture on genetic markers for sociopathy. And then in the afternoon, the opposite."

"Oops," Remy chuckled.

"The crazy part is, none of my students called me on

it!" Paul said. "Now I'm debating whether to own up to it, or just keep going back on the original syllabi. But do I change the final exams …? Hmm."

I laughed. "That reminds me of the time that one of my teammates selected the wrong ammo loadout before a drop," I said. "He meant to tell the armorer 'no tracers,' but ended up with 'all tracers' instead. So we get on the ground, GhostSkin on, the Ochos are coming at us, and Darth opens up, and there's just this bright orange line of bullets, basically a huge neon arrow saying 'I'm right here, shoot me!' "

Remy and Paul shared a look.

"What, uh … what's GhostSkin?" Remy asked, after a moment.

"Yeah, what are tracers?" Paul asked.

"Oh. Bullets that glow when you fire them," I said.

"Why do they glow?" Paul asked.

"So you can see what you're hitting," I said.

"Oh. Right," Paul said.

An awkward moment of silence passed. Then Paul smiled at me. "Look at you. Last time we were all here, you were bummed because you didn't know what you were going to do with yourself. Now you not only found something you enjoy, you're an international superstar. Good for you."

I cocked an eyebrow. "Actually, I'm back in the same boat again. If they don't find another Ocho planet, I have no idea what I'm going to do with myself."

"You'd want to go back?" Remy asked, surprised.

I nodded. "In a heartbeat."

"Why?" Paul asked, frowning.

"Because the job's not done," I said.

"But you've done your part, haven't you?" Remy asked. "Let somebody else take it from here."

"That wouldn't feel right," I said. "For starters, somebody else isn't as good as I am. If I stay here, somebody has to go in my place, maybe die for me. Why?

Why is my life worth more than theirs?"

Remy patted my hand. "I'm just saying … you've earned a break. You served, you did your time. We like having you home."

Paul looked down at the table. "Yeah. And a lot of people are saying …" I caught Remy shoot him a look of warning. He broke off.

"What?" I asked. "What are they saying?"

Paul sighed. "Well, they're saying that we should never have fought the Octipedes in the first place. I guess, there's a growing movement of people questioning if they were ever really a threat."

I crossed my arms over my chest. "You haven't seen what they can do to a person."

"No, no I haven't," Paul said, looking away.

"If we tried to set up a colony near one of theirs, it would be a massacre," I told him. "Just … they'd slaughter men, women, children. It'd be a nightmare."

"So we shouldn't colonize their planets," Paul said. "We could just leave them be."

"I think what Paul's trying to suggest is that maybe the Octipedes were only a threat because we made them one," Remy said.

I felt my teeth grinding together. I reached under the table and unclipped my cyber-prosthetic, then slammed it onto the table, spilling our drinks.

"Tell me again how much of a threat they are," I said.

Paul stared at my leg for a moment, blushing furiously. "I'm sorry. Forget I brought it up."

Paul and Remy both made excuses to leave not long afterwards. We all apologized to each other, and hugged it out, but … something had changed, and we all felt it. After they left, I strapped my leg back on and went and sat with the fan who had asked for my photo.

At least he appreciates me.

I bought him and his friends a round, and they made me tell them a few war stories, punctuated by a round of shots … which led to me buying the whole bar a round. At some point the fan tried to lay a kiss on me, which resulted in me knocking him on his ass. I decided to leave before I did anything else stupid, and caught the next hypertube back to New York, drunk and grumpy.

I miss Paul and Remy, damn it, I realized, as the forests of New Jersey slid by in a blur. *I miss how things were.*

* * *

The sun was dipping low over the horizon, and I rubbed my arms against my sides in the evening chill. Overhead, the town's Oktoberfest banner flapped in the autumn wind. Behind me in the booth, my helmet cam view of the battle of Venatur played out on a high-res hologram. We were preparing to fight our way out of the downed elevator, the SRD Team forming up for one last assault. I saw Lexy and Petro on the screen and looked away, a lump in my throat.

A civilian crossed the street, leaving a baked goods stand and heading directly for my booth. I sat up straighter in my chair.

"Hi," she said, smiling at me.

"Hi," I said. "StreaMercs fan?"

"Hm? Oh, no," she said, mildly confused. "Ah, do you know where the restrooms are?"

I pointed down the street. "Cafeteria, one block that way."

"Thanks," she said, and headed off.

Fuck this, I thought. I stood up, my prosthesis creaking. I pulled a set of plastic tubs out from under the folding table and started to pack up my stuff. Dad arrived as I was folding up the banner with my streamer logo.

"Need a hand?" he asked.

"Hey, Dad," I said. "Sure."

"Lot of fans today?" he asked.

I shook my head. "A few."

"They know the autographs are free, right?" he asked, cheerfully.

"That's what the sign says," I agreed.

He clucked his tongue. "Well, I don't get it," he said. "Nobody appreciates the streamers anymore. It's not right."

"It's human nature," I said, sliding the folding table into the back of my truck. "We've been out of the streaming game too long."

Dad helped me close the doors to the truck. "They're just streaming junk now," he said. "This LuxeLife stuff, have you watched it?"

"A little bit," I said. "Not really my thing."

LuxeLife had popped up to fill the gap StreaMercs left in the livestreamed VR entertainment space. They convinced a number of ultra-wealthy people to strap on streaming rigs and go around their daily lives, sharing their champagne brunches and yachting trips in the Med with the normal people of the world. I had seen a few hours of it, when it first came out, but after watching a bunch of trust fund kids debate whether it was better to invest in racehorses or Renaissance paintings from the comfort of a hot tub in Tahiti, I logged off and never looked back.

That's not entertainment. There's not even any skill involved.

My dad was looking at me expectantly. "Hm?" I asked. "Sorry, I missed what you said."

"Mom and I are going up to Maine next weekend, to see the foliage. Do you want to come?"

"I don't know," I said, shutting the truck's lift gate.

"Don't just stay here moping around your apartment," Dad said. "Come on, it'll be fun."

"Mm," I said. "I'll think about it."

"I need someone to talk to other than your mother," Dad said, smiling conspiratorially. "She'll just spend the whole time complaining about how high the hypertube fees have gotten."

"I saw they're thinking about raising them again," I

said.

"Are they?" Dad shook his head. "That's the third hike in the last year."

Hypertube fees. Two years ago I was waging war to protect the future of humanity. Now I'm bitching about hypertube fees. I sighed and looked out over the remnants of the town fest, the people moving from booth to booth. *It's all so god damn pointless.*

"I gotta go, Dad," I said. "Thanks for the help."

"You don't want to come over for dinner?" he asked.

"No," I said. "Maybe later in the week." I gave him a quick hug and then hopped in the truck without meeting his eye.

There was a case of wine waiting at my front door when I got home. *My monthly delivery.* I pushed it inside my front door and ripped open the box, carrying two bottles to the kitchen with me.

"Welcome home, Sam," Zoe said. "A package was delivered for you earlier."

"Yeah, found it, thanks," I told my assistant. I tore the wrapper off one of the bottles with my teeth and then removed the cork with practiced ease, tossing it into the sink. There was a red plastic cup on the counter already – a quick glance told me I had drunk out of it already. I sniffed it, and then shrugged and poured more wine in.

"Place an order for delivery, Zoe. Siam Kitchen. The usual."

"Ordering," Zoe said. "Spring rolls, pork satay, green curry chicken, and jasmine rice?"

"Uh huh," I said, sitting on the couch. "Play some music, Zoe."

I flipped through my e-mail on my keypad for a minute – all spam. Zoe had apparently sensed that I felt like wallowing again, because she put on some bluesy jazz. Over a mournful saxophone riff, the singer crooned, "Better to have loved and lost ... than never to have loved at all."

Bullshit, I thought. *If you lose what you loved, you learn just how painful life is without it.*

"Cancel, Zoe." *Little too on-the-nose.*

Zoe killed the music.

I put my keypad down, took another swig of wine and then pulled my VR headset on, surfing through the channels to see what was playing. *A ballgame. Improv comedy show. More LuxeLife crap – ugh, no thanks.* I navigated to the StreaMercs portal out of habit, and the familiar message greeted me:

The Stellarus fleet is still hard at work searching for additional Ocho planets! It's our goal to get the StreaMercs back online (and fighting!) soon. Click here to sign up for our mailing list and be notified of any new updates. StreaMercs – Ride to Glory!

Underneath, in smaller text, I read the words: *Last updated: two years ago.*

I hit refresh, and watched as the same message popped up again. And again. I slipped the headset off and let it fall to the floor. I finished the wine in my cup in three long gulps, coughing and wiping at my mouth. In the background, I could hear the steady *drip-drip* of my leaky sink. I stared at the wall.

"Is this how you felt, Lucie?" I asked the silence. "Like you were down at the bottom of a well, staring up, not knowing how to climb out? Like the well was getting deeper each day?"

I took a deep, ragged breath.

God help me.

CHAPTER 36

From: Novia, Lisbeta (Captain, *Dunedin II*)
To: Sloan, Jim (Commander, Stellarus Fifth Fleet)
Cc: Kinney, Archer (Chairman of the Board, Stellarus); Khanna, Dev (CEO, StreaMercs)
Subject: Pyrrhus preliminary exploration report

Jim-

We found them. Full report attached, but it's by far the most heavily populated Ocho world we've surveyed since the war began. My science officer thinks this is their homeworld. Short of landing and asking them myself (LOL no), she wants me to stress to you that there's no real way to confirm ... at least until they're all dead and the archeologists can take a closer look at things. But ... good bet this is where they came from originally. It's gonna take a hell of a lot to clear them out, though. Not just the usual four or five colonies, the damn things are everywhere – our surveying robots were eliminated before they'd been on the ground for two minutes. I've left airborne sensors in place to continue monitoring. The *Dunedin's* in orbit, awaiting further instructions.

-Lisbeta

From: Kinney, Archer (Chairman of the Board, Stellarus)
To: Khanna, Dev (CEO, StreaMercs)
CC: Kim, Dolton (Chief Marketing Officer, Stellarus)
Subject: Re: Pyrrhus preliminary exploration report

Dev-

How fast can you get things spun up again? Whatever you need, you got – just happy to have the StreaMercs revenue stream open again.

-Archer

p.s.- We're calling it their homeworld from here on out – I'm not gonna wait until the war's over, and miss out on all that PR, just so some damn archaeologist can confirm it after the fact. One final campaign, on the Ocho's home turf … come on! People are gonna go nuts.

-E-mail thread recovered from the Stellarus server archives

The snow was drifting across the road, piling up faster than the automated plows could clear it away. I stepped down out of my truck, blowing on my gloved hands, and headed for the stoop of my building, watching as the wind snatched the flakes into swirls that danced across the pavement.

"Sam?"

I looked up – a man was standing on the steps, waiting for me. Underneath the hat and scarf, his bearded face looked vaguely familiar.

"Yeah?" I asked.

"Hi," he said, extending a gloved hand and smiling briefly. "Can I come in?"

I shook his hand warily. "Do I know you?"

"It's Rolfe," he said, smiling again. "ROFLRolfe, your

recruiter? Remember?"

Rolfe! "Oh, right – sorry," I said. "Hard to recognize you with the hat and all."

I let us in the main door, and then we climbed the stairs to my apartment. My bad leg caught on the loose step by the landing, as it often did, and I tripped for a second, catching myself on the handrail.

"Sorry."

"No, don't worry about it," Rolfe said.

In my apartment, he hung his coat on a hook by the door, and then I showed him into the living room.

"Sorry about the mess," I said, lifting a pizza box off the coffee table.

"Don't worry about it," Rolfe said. "You should see my place."

He took a seat on the couch and I pulled up a chair across from him.

"So …?" I asked. "Trying to organize a reunion tour, get the old crew back together for one last fling?"

He looked at me, his face serious.

I sat forward on my chair. "Wait, you are?"

"Do you have a home assistant?" Rolfe asked.

"Sure," I said. "Zoe?"

"I'm here, Sam," Zoe said, helpfully.

Rolfe tapped on his watch. "Zoe, I just sent you a non-disclosure agreement. Can you record and enable us to verbally authorize?"

"Recording," Zoe said.

Rolfe looked at me. "This NDA prevents you from discussing any part of what I'm about to share with you, with anyone, until StreaMercs releases you to do so. You understand?"

"Okay," I said. "I agree to the terms."

Rolfe smiled, and spread his hands wide. "StreaMercs is coming back online."

"You're shitting me," I told him.

"I'm not," Rolfe said. "They're refitting the *Final Hope*

as we speak. They found them, Sam."

They found them.

"There's more: it's not just any old planet. It's their homeworld, Sam. Sixty-eight separate colonies, according to the drone survey."

"Sixty-eight?!" *Jesus Christ. Between seven and eleven thousand Ochos per colony ... that's a metric fuck-ton of Ochos.* My head spun.

"This is THE battle, Sam," Rolfe said. "The big one. The *last* one."

I rubbed at my forehead, thinking. "... and you're offering me the chance to go fight?" I asked, quietly.

Rolfe nodded, slowly. "They're going live with a global advertising campaign next week, in order to kick-start regular recruiting. But Dev and his team put together a list of superstars that they want back, to be part of the live announcement. Your name was at the top of that list."

"Who else?" I asked. "Darth, Jack, Foo?"

"Jack and Foo declined, I'm afraid," Rolfe said. "But Darth said, and I quote: 'If Valkyrie's going, I'm in.' " He grinned again.

"Avery?" I asked.

Rolfe shook his head. "No. Avery refused to meet with us." He cleared his throat. "I should note that there's a substantial signing bonus involved," he continued, "and Dev wanted you to know that StreaMercs will pay for a full limb replacement."

"What do you mean, 'replacement'?" I asked.

"Just what it sounds like. It's a new, experimental procedure where they clone and regrow your limb, and then reattach it," Rolfe explained.

I met his eyes then. "I'd have my real leg back? They can do that?"

"They can now," Rolfe said, nodding. "As long as you don't mind a little gecko DNA in you."

My fingers itched at the scar along my thigh.

"It's a five hundred thousand dollar signing bonus,"

Rolfe said. "Plus the limb replacement."

I stood up and walked across to the kitchen, pacing.

"It's been three years," I said. "How can you be sure I'm still a decent fighter?"

"Come on," Rolfe said, frowning. "That's not something you can forget."

No, I thought. *No, it's not.*

"Are you going back?" I asked.

Rolfe chuckled. "I dunno if they'd take me. I was never very good at it, honestly. Nowhere close to your level. Recruiting I can do. Fighting … let's just say I'm lucky I lasted as long as I did."

"Sixty-eight colonies. That could take … years," I said.

"It might," Rolfe said. "And StreaMercs knows it's gonna require a different approach. They're gonna start with the most remote colonies, to make sure they can't reinforce each other and overwhelm you guys. They're gonna take breaks every few battles, give you guys a chance to rest and recover."

They want to drag this out as long as they can, I thought. *Milk it.*

"… and they're building a ton more berths into the *Final Hope*. Basically tripling the ship's troop capacity," Rolfe finished. "It's a whole different ball game."

"More streamers means more competition … less viewers for each individual," I pointed out.

"They're giving you and some of the other old hands top billing," Rolfe assured me. "Front page placement, default stream for new viewers, the works. You're guaranteed to make a boatload."

I rubbed my thumb against the palm of my hand, thinking. *You've been dying to go back from the minute you set foot back on Earth. This is everything you wanted.* I looked at Rolfe, who was watching me eagerly.

… So why are you getting cold feet??

"If you're on the fence, I can talk to the StreaMercs team, and we can try to negotiate something more," Rolfe said. "No promises, but …"

"It's not about the money," I said. *It was never really about the money.*

"Then what's holding you back?" Rolfe asked.

I sighed. "Fear."

He scoffed. "What? Valkyrie, dominator of the leaderboard, legendary SRD Team member? What are you afraid of? Not the Ochos."

"Everybody's afraid of the Ochos," I told him. "Don't try to tell me you weren't."

"Fair," he admitted. "But you'd have GhostSkin. You'd have time to train up again before the ship is ready to leave, once your surgery is done—"

"I'm afraid," I said, cutting Rolfe off, "that another campaign on the *Final Hope* is going to mean I'm never going to feel at home on Earth again. It's been three years. I was just starting to … I dunno, fit back in. Reintegrate."

"Fit in? You'd be a hero," Rolfe said, frowning. "If you go back, and help wipe out the Ochos, we're talking ticker tape parades, talk show appearances, the whole nine yards."

"For a while, yeah," I said. "And then what? What happens when humanity moves on, but I don't?"

"I don't follow …" Rolfe said.

I gestured toward the front hall, out at the world. "They can – and do – forget about us, Rolfe. Once the war is over, everyone else goes back to their lives. But we don't. We can't. After combat life is just … bland. It's like eating oatmeal for breakfast, lunch, and dinner. Your whole life just feels muted. Nothing matters, and everything that civilians think *does* matter is just petty bullshit." I sighed and sat down on the chair again. "They don't understand me, and I don't understand them. I don't belong."

Rolfe watched me in silence for a time. "That's how you feel now?" he asked.

He wasn't in long enough, I realized, with a start. *It didn't change him, like it changed me. He doesn't get that he's just a dealer, offering a junkie one more hit.*

"Yeah, that's how I feel now," I said. "And it's only gonna get worse if I go back." I looked at the floor, my brows knit in concentration. Finally, I looked back up at Rolfe. "How many noobs did you say they're recruiting?"

"Over a thousand," Rolfe said.

A thousand new recruits, fighting their first campaign on the Ochos' home turf. They're gonna get slaughtered. I shook my head. *God damn it. I'll be damned if I let a bunch of noobs get killed in my place.*

I sighed again and crossed my arms over my chest.

"Where do I sign?"

CHAPTER 37

"Aerial surveillance of Pyrrhus indicates a thriving Octipede population, between fifty and seventy-five times typical density and size. That alone suggests a more protracted, bloody operation than any of the preceding ones. However, if initial estimates are correct that Pyrrhus is their planet of origin, the Octipedes can be expected to fight with unparalleled ferocity – the survival of their species is quite literally at stake. Simulations predict that the invasion will last upwards of eight months, and require multiple return trips to Earth to take on new recruits in order to replace losses."

-Excerpt from the official StreaMercs intelligence assessment of Pyrrhus

It was a strange feeling, after three years of using the prosthetic, to have my leg back. Exercising was great – it was a joy to be able to walk without concentrating on it, and kick underwater during my swim workouts. I had always hated running, but I found myself hitting the treadmill, just for the fun of it. What was weird was not taking it off at night – my bed felt oddly crowded all of a sudden, with two legs getting tangled up with each other. And I hadn't missed shaving it – I was kinda hoping the gecko DNA would mean it wouldn't grow hair, but of course, it did. Better that than scales, I guess.

With my surgery and recovery, I was one of the last streamers to board the *Final Hope*, a scant week before departure. I floated through Northwest Station, dropping down the central tube past the familiar shops and vending machines, catching glimpses of ships docking and refueling through the portholes. When I arrived back at the ship's dock, I paused a minute in the doorway, peering through at the giant streamer statue in the fountain, his spear glistening over the dying Ocho. I took a deep breath, then pushed on through, letting my feet settle down into the carpet as gravity took over.

Home again.

The first thing I did, before anything else, was head straight for the VR training sims, and book every available slot they had open. Then I shouldered my bag and made my way to my room.

They kept my suite exactly the way I left it – opening the hatch was like opening up a time capsule, the nostalgia almost a tangible force pressing on me. There was even a pile of Game Boy games on the coffee table, and one of my socks in a drawer where I had left it by accident.

Walking through the *Final Hope* was no different – I saw ghosts in every corridor. Lexy, Petro, SoSo … Avery. The ship was packed with streamers – Darth and some other old faces, but mostly all new recruits. They had strapped two extra berthing pods along the sides of the ship, attaching them via docking tubes. I took a spin through just to check them out, but they were pretty tight quarters, even worse than the regular barracks. If you've ever seen those capsule hotels they have in Japan, you'll have a good sense for what the new berths were like. And with three times as many streamers on board, there were lines for everything – the gym, the restaurants, hell, I had to wait thirty seconds at one point just to let a group of recruits walk past my door, so I could get back inside my suite. And there were security bots everywhere – I guess because there were so many more streamers aboard, StreaMercs was just playing it safe. But it seemed like there was a security bot at every hatch and staircase on the ship.

They gawked at me – the noobs, I mean. A few gathered up the courage to introduce themselves, but mostly they would stare at me wide-eyed, until I met their gaze, and they would look away, embarrassed, before talking to each other in hushed tones. It felt like high school all over again. StreaMercs had put them through some rudimentary training, wholly inadequate, I was sure … but there wasn't enough time left for me to run anything else, especially not with so many new recruits.

On my second day back, I vac-suited up and drew my ER-45 from the armory, where yet another pair of security bots stood guard. On the live fire range, a new kid took the lane next to mine, and I heard him popping away at a paper target with an upgraded e-rifle. After a few minutes, he stopped to watch me burn through one of my magazines.

"Wow," he said, when I was done.

I looked him over – he had a good six inches and seventy-odd pounds on me, but he looked like he was all of fifteen. I took his e-rifle from him and unscrewed the optics, sliding them forward to the correct mounting position, then tightened the sling and handed it back to him.

"It should be tight against you, not flapping around," I said. "And your ammo pouches are all jacked up. You put them on too close together: you're not gonna be able to get the magazines out of half of them."

"Thanks. Any other advice? For when we get to Pyrrhus?"

I shrugged. "Find a veteran and stick close to them. Do

what they do," I said.

"Anyone in particular?" he asked. "There aren't that many veterans."

I loaded another magazine, sighing. "Yeah. I know."

* * *

While we were en route to Pyrrhus, Darth and I had to do an interview with a reporter – a young woman who was actually a StreaMercs employee, part of their newly-formed Embedded News division. She would be dropping with us on Pyrrhus, reporting on the progress of the battles, and interviewing streamers both during combat and afterwards. We sat down on a couch beneath a pair of bright lights, set up on one side of the landing bay, with the newly-built, reinforced elevator behind us. Darth had brought Brutus – the little brown dog hopped up onto the couch and nuzzled happily into place on Darth's lap. A pair of security bots clomped through the bay as we got settled, one of the many now-ubiquitous security patrols around the ship.

On a chair next to us, the reporter faced the cameras briefly. "Hi, I'm Donata reporting for StreaMercs News, and it's my distinct privilege to be sitting next to two people who need no introduction. Both founding members of the SRD Team – Valkyrie and Darth! Thanks for talking to me. How are you guys?"

"Yeah, good!" Darth said, petting Brutus absentmindedly. "Really chuffed to be back, thanks, Donata."

I smiled. "Happy to be here."

"How crazy is this?" Donata gushed. "We're on our way to Pyrrhus, the Ocho homeworld. What does this mean to you guys, to be back for the final campaign of the war?"

Darth looked at me; I motioned for him to go ahead. "For me, it's a chance for some closure. We started this, many years ago, and we lost a lot of friends along the way, and now we have a chance to finish it. That will mean a lot to me."

"Valkyrie?" Donata asked me.

"Yeah, I agree," I said. "And I … well, I hope that people remember what we do here. I like to think this is the final part of our legacy, our contribution to humankind, if you will. Sure, we're making a good living here, no doubt. But at the end of the day, we saw a threat to our civilization, and we were the ones who stepped up and faced it. We volunteered to do this, so that others wouldn't have to. I want to go home knowing we made a difference."

"Well said," Donata agreed. "I don't think anybody can take that away from you." She checked the keypad on her lap, briefly, reading from a set of notes. "There's been a lot of speculation, maybe you guys can put the rumors to rest: are they re-forming the SRD Team?"

"Well, *we're* not," I said. "I don't know if StreaMercs is, you'd have to ask Dev that."

"You didn't want to try to get a clan together, maybe recruit some of the more senior veterans?" Donata asked.

"No," Darth said. "Out of respect for our former team members, mostly."

"I see," Donata said. "What about the two of you? Are you planning on teaming up?"

Darth and I shared a look. "Ah, no," I said. "Darth and I actually had dinner last night to discuss exactly that. I eventually convinced him that we should go lone wolf on this one. But I'm sure we'll see each other around when we get to the surface."

"I hope so. I know the fans would like to see that." Donata smiled and turned to Darth. "Any new tattoos, Darth?" she asked.

* * *

I went and saw Alice after the interview.

"You're looking good, Alice," I told her, relaxing into the armchair in front of the picture windows. Outside, the stars streaked by in a blur. "You haven't aged a day."

Alice smiled. "How are you doing, Sam?"

I shrugged. "You know me. I'm an adrenaline junkie with an ongoing existential crisis and a guilty conscience. Same shit, different day."

"Are you looking forward to the battle?" Alice asked.

"I'm here, aren't I?" I said. "I'd have come back even if they hadn't given me a wad of cash and a new leg."

"You're going to miss it, when it's over," Alice said.

I nodded. "I feel like a terrible person saying it, because this war's taken some of my closest friends, but ... I will miss it. What does that make me?"

"Human," Alice said.

I shook my head. "It makes me useless when I get back home, I'll tell you that much. Worse than useless." I sat up, pointing at Alice. "I was thinking about this, the other day. I'm a virus."

"A virus?" Alice frowned.

"A virus. An organism that feeds off of destruction."

"I don't think you're a virus, Sam," Alice said. "You just need to find something else to do with yourself, when you get home. Something else you can be proud of."

I sighed. "Like what?"

Alice pursed her lips. "I don't know. You've been an excellent teacher for the new recruits. Perhaps you should think about teaching."

I had a vision of myself standing at a hologram board in front of a room full of screaming kids. "Yeah, I don't think so," I said. "But who knows. I gotta survive this campaign first. Maybe the Ochos will solve my problem for me."

CHAPTER 38

"Historians love to ask the question 'what if?' What if Hitler had never invaded Russia? What if the United States had not needlessly antagonized the Kim regime into a second war on the Korean peninsula? In the Ocho War, we are drawn, inexorably, toward the question: what if StreaMercs CEO Dev Khanna had managed to execute his secret battle plan on Pyrrhus? How would the Octipedes have reacted? Would they still have sought to make contact, and if they did, how would Khanna's armed automatons have responded to the choice the Ochos laid before them? Instead a human made the decision, and for once, likely performed better than a machine would have."

-Harriet Seldon, "Free-for-All: Strategy and Tactics in the Octipede War"

I stood at the porthole in my living room, gazing out at the upper atmosphere of Pyrrhus.

Here we go. One last campaign. One last shot at glory. And it starts today.

Below the starfield, a thin blue haze of atmosphere

hung over the planet's oceans, which were speckled with emerald green islands and white clouds. But for the oddly-shaped land masses, it could have been Earth.

Several messages from my viewers appeared, superimposed via hologram over the glass of the porthole. I smiled.

"I was just thinking that," I said. "You guys are reading my mind. That island there almost looks like Italy, right?"

My watch buzzed, and I glanced down at it.

>>>*Video message from Avery Desmiter.*

I stared at it for a moment in disbelief, feeling my heartbeat quicken.

"Oh, geez" I said. "I don't know if I can watch this, guys."

>>>*What?! You HAVE to watch it!*

>>>*Come on!*

I smiled nervously. "Okay." I tapped the screen, and a hologram of Avery's face appeared in front of the porthole.

"Hey," he said. "Um, it's Avery. I know you're about to fight another battle, and I wanted to just say 'good luck.' Or break a leg – would that be more appropriate? And also … I'm sorry, for shutting you out." He sighed, rifling a hand through his long, blonde hair. "You have to understand, I watch videos of us together, from before, and the minute they're done, I can't remember them. It's like nothing from that time will stick in my head. I can't even say the name of the ship you're on, even though I know I just read it somewhere. And it's … really frustrating. But, Alice says I shouldn't be frustrated with you, and she's right. Anyway, I just wanted to let you know. And maybe, when you get back, we can meet up sometime. I don't want you to try to help me remember, if that makes sense. But maybe we can make some new memories together. Okay, that's it. Be safe, and give 'em hell for me."

The hologram derezzed, and Avery's face disappeared,

leaving only the gentle curve of Pyrrhus' atmosphere in the porthole.

I realized I had been holding my breath, and let it out in a long exhale.

"Whoa," I said.

My viewer feed was going bonkers – fan messages were pouring in faster than I could read them.

I laughed. "Yeah, of course I'm going to see him," I told them. "Duh!"

Then my doorbell rang. I nearly jumped out of my skin.

"Who is it?" I asked.

"It's Dev," the reply came, over the room's speakers. "May I come in?"

Dev? I had expected it to be Darth, coming to check in before we suited up. *Not Dev. What's he doing out of his CEO suite?*

"Uh, yeah," I said. "Of course."

I turned and faced the door as it slid open, revealing Dev. I hadn't seen him since coming back on board; he had aged considerably in the years StreaMercs had been offline. His salt-and-pepper goatee was now streaked with gray, and his face was lined with worry. But he smiled at me when he saw me. He touched his watch as he entered, and my own watch buzzed in response. I glanced down at it.

>>>Connection lost. Your stream is offline.

I took my streaming circlet off and set it down on the coffee table. "Hi, Dev," I said, sitting on the couch. "Private conversation, huh?"

"Hi, Sam," Dev said, taking a seat in an armchair. "It's good to see you again. And yes, I'd like to keep this between us."

I shrugged. "Okay. I gotta go suit up soon," I reminded him. "First wave drops in an hour."

"I know," Dev said. "I'll be brief." He glanced at my leg – my new leg. "How is it working?" he asked.

"Great," I said. "Thank you."

"It's the least we could do," Dev said, with feeling. He shifted in his seat. "Well, I will get right to it. I understand you're concerned about what to do with yourself after all of this is over."

I cocked an eyebrow at him. "Alice told me you don't watch recordings of our sessions," I pointed out.

"We don't," Dev said. "But Alice does give us summary reports, which my human resources team and I review carefully. We're responsible for your safety and well-being, which includes your mental health. And especially after what happened to SoSo, it's something I'm very much concerned with."

"I'm not going to kill myself," I told him.

"I'm glad to hear it," Dev said. "But the issue remains, no? What you'll do after the war?"

I nodded. "Yeah, I have no idea."

Dev cleared his throat. "Well, I thought I might make you a job offer."

"You want me to work for StreaMercs?"

Dev nodded.

"Doing what?" I asked. "Do you have an idea for another streaming entertainment concept?"

Dev smiled. "No. StreaMercs as it exists today will end with the war. But I recently secured the Stellarus board's approval to create a StreaMercs memorial."

"There are tons of StreaMercs memorials, all over the world," I pointed out.

"This isn't just a statue in a town square. This will be different. We are, in fact, sitting in it."

"The *Final Hope*?"

"Indeed," Dev agreed. "The ship will be placed in a geostationary orbit over Earth, so that anyone who wishes can visit. We'll keep the interior largely the same, but convert sections of the barracks and ready room into exhibits. It will be both a memorial and a museum. And, I hope, something to honor you and your colleagues. I intend to have a display for every streamer who fought in the war."

A memorial. Something to honor us – all of us.

"It could be a gathering place, too, for all of the veteran streamers," Dev continued. "A home away from home, if you will. A place they can come back to, to see their friends. I don't like the idea that after all they've been through, our streamers just go back home and never see their friends and comrades again."

Dev watched me in silence for a time. "What do you think?" he asked.

"I think ..." I started. I felt my throat tighten. "I think it's a wonderful idea. Truly." I sniffed, wiping at an eye. "I love it. But why are you telling me? You want me to work in the memorial?"

Dev shook his head. "I want you to *run* the memorial."

"You're not gonna run it?" I asked, taken aback.

"I've had enough of running things," Dev said, and a weight seemed to settle across his shoulders, his brow furrowing. "And I doubt Stellarus will let me, not after ..." he trailed off, shaking his head. "Never mind. This place doesn't need an aging manager who never lifted a weapon himself. It will need someone with your passion, someone who understands the terrible costs the streamers paid, and can pass on the lessons of this war to future generations. So that they may avoid our mistakes."

I frowned. "Mistakes?"

"Mistakes," Dev said, looking down at his hands, neatly folded in his lap. "My mistakes."

"What mistakes did you make?" I asked.

"This whole enterprise was a mistake, Sam. When we first met the Ochos, I was just an over-eager coder who saw a challenge and wanted to devise a solution to it. But I didn't realize – I should have foreseen – the consequences of turning war into a business. Of creating a mercenary force like this."

"I don't think I follow," I said. "StreaMercs has been a massive success. Are you saying the whole war wasn't necessary?"

"I'm saying the war should never have cost any human lives. If we had just used drones, we could have ended it far sooner," Dev said. "But we turned it into a profit-making exercise, and removed all the usual disincentives that have limited wars in the past. And several thousand young men and women are dead because of it. That is my legacy, and my greatest regret."

"Avery once joked that Stellarus was running around seeding random planets with more Ochos, so we could keep fighting," I said.

"No," Dev said, dismissing the accusation with a wave of his hand. "I would have known it if they had. And I would have put a stop to it, immediately. But the dead are still dead, and the task remains before us: we must never let it happen again."

Despite his tired demeanor, Dev's eyes showed an iron-hard resolve.

"The war will be over soon," I said. "Why would it happen again?"

"We thought humanity was done with war in the twenty-second century," Dev said. "Yet here we are. And this memorial, under your leadership, can ensure that humanity learns from my failure. You can ensure the lesson is learned, and passed on."

"Okay," I agreed, surprised at his sudden intensity. "I … I think I can do that. But you'll help, too. Right?"

"No," Dev said, standing. "I don't think I will be able to. For me, there is just one last chore to complete. A last chance to balance my ledger, as it were." He smiled at me. "I'm glad to know that StreaMercs' legacy rests with you, Sam. I told the Stellarus board you were the right choice; I wasn't wrong."

I stood, too, and shook his hand. "Thank you for the opportunity," I said. "Let's hope I make it through the campaign, huh?" I laughed uneasily.

"I don't think you need to worry about that," Dev said.

He made his way to the hatch, shook my hand again awkwardly, and left. I shut the door after him and then stood, staring at the closed hatch, my thoughts swirling.

This museum … it's everything I could have hoped for. Grinning, I took a deep breath, and let it out in a long exhale. For the first time in as long as I could remember, I felt … optimistic. Excited, even, about the future. *Samentha Ombotu-Chen, Director of the StreaMercs Museum.* It had a nice ring to it. *Captain of the Final Hope, both of us serving a new purpose in life.*

Another thought crossed my mind. *That was … really weird. Even for Dev, that was super awkward. He seemed … off. No, not just off. Depressed.*

As my sub-conscious chewed on the conversation, snippets came back to me, echoing in my ears.

You'll help, too. Right?

No. I don't think I will be able to.

StreaMercs' legacy rests with you, Sam.

I rubbed at my forehead, frowning. *He feels responsible for all of the streamers that have died. That's a lot of guilt. I felt responsible for just one person's death – Lucie's – and it tore me apart for years. It nearly killed me.*

What had he said?

One last chance to balance my ledger.

"Oh, fuck," I said aloud. *Dev's going to kill himself.*

I slapped the release pad for my door, and it slid open. The corridor was empty – Dev had already disappeared.

His suite, up at the bow. That's where he has to be.

I ran, headlong, through the ship, dodging around groups of confused streamers. Past the statue and fountain, up one of the winding staircases, through the casino to the hatch that led to the crew quarters and Dev's sprawling apartment. The hatch was open, and I could see the corridor beyond, a straight shot all the way to Dev's apartment. But a pair of security bots flanked the open outer entrance. As I skidded to a halt in front of the hatch, they shifted position, blocking my entrance.

"I need to see Dev, now," I told them. "It's an emergency."

"Mr. Khanna is not available," one of the bots told me. "He's not to be disturbed."

Damn it, Dev!

I stood there for a second, my mind racing, then turned and retraced my steps. I stopped in my suite briefly, grabbing and activating my streaming circlet, and then ran headlong to the equipment bay. All around me, other streamers were suiting up, preparing for the battle. I stepped into my vac-suit, waiting as the hydraulic arms bolted me in. As my heads-up display came online, I checked my viewer count. *Thirteen thousand. Shit. Need more.*

"Hey guys, I need your help," I told them. "I think Dev is about to do something really stupid. I need you to spread the word, get as many people watching this stream as you can. We need to get the attention of the Stellarus board ASAP."

>>>*What's he gonna do?*

>>>*What did you guys talk about?*

"Just do it! Flood the phone lines at Stellarus, and don't stop until someone high up is on my stream."

>>>*Kay.*

>>>*We're on it!*

I jogged out of the equipment bay and over to the arms room. "I need my e-rifle," I told the robot behind the counter.

My ER-45 showed up five seconds later, along with my usual loadout of spare magazines and grenades. "Good luck today," the robot told me, helpfully.

"Thanks," I said, grabbing the weapon. I slipped one magazine into a pouch on my vest and loaded the second, chambering a round.

"For safety, please wait until you are on the elevator—" the robot started, but I was already running down the hall, back toward the bow of the ship.

A group of noobs saw me coming. They frowned in

confusion, and then quickly stepped aside, their backs to the walls of the corridor. I ignored them, focusing on controlling my breathing, the sound of my metal vac-boots ringing on the ship's deck plating as I ran.

At the bottom of the staircase by the statue, I stopped to check my viewer count again. *Two hundred and twenty thousand. And growing.*

"Anyone been able to reach a member of the Stellarus board yet?" I asked.

>>>*Working on it.*

>>>*Got a couple Stellarus employees on the stream, but they haven't gotten the bosses on yet.*

>>>*Nearly.*

"Mkay," I said. "I'm gonna need their help overriding the lock to Dev's apartment. I don't think my vac-suit is gonna be sturdy enough to smash the hatch in."

>>>*WTF are you doing, Valkyrie?!*

>>>*Doesn't he have security bots guarding him?*

I started up the staircase. "Yeah, it'd be nice if someone could shut them down, too. But I don't have time to wait."

I paused just below the top of the staircase, took a deep breath, and then lunged forward, covering the final few steps in a rush. The bots' sensor-covered heads swiveled the second I appeared at the top, and I saw them bring their pistols up, tracking on me. But I had the drop on them, and fired first. I put three rounds into the bot on the left – it sparked and staggered backward, and then I shifted aim and hit the second one, knocking out its sensor suite with one round, before blasting it in the torso. I felt a pair of rounds impact my chest armor, knocking me off balance, the air forced out of my lungs in a rush. I staggered and fell to a knee.

Keep shooting!

The second bot had collapsed, twitching in a smoking heap on the floor, but the first bot was recovering, trying to get its weapon lined up despite a damaged arm. I fired another burst, then stood and advanced on it, firing all the while. It toppled over, emitting something between a groan and a whistle. I breathed a sigh of relief.

I could hear screams echoing in the casino behind me – streamers, surprised and panicked at the sudden firefight in their midst. I checked myself quickly, but though they had dented it, neither of the bullets had penetrated my armor.

Gonna have a nice pair of bruises tonight, though.

I kicked the bots' pistols away from them, and then proceeded down the corridor beyond. A crewman ducked his head out one of the side hatches, his eyes going wide when he caught sight of me. He backed up hastily and shut the door behind him. When I reached Dev's door, I pounded on it.

"Dev! Dev, open up!"

To my surprise, the hatch slid open, and I found Dev standing there, his hands held up.

"Sam … put the gun down," he said, eyeing me with concern.

I surveyed him quickly, then scanned the apartment beyond, but everything looked perfectly normal.

"What are you doing here?" Dev asked.

"Stopping you from doing something stupid," I told him.

His eyes narrowed. "What? How did you know …?" he asked, his voice quiet.

"I've seen the signs enough times, I told him. "I'm not gonna let your suicide be on my conscience, too."

"My suicide …?" Dev asked. Then he sighed. "You misunderstand, Sam."

I let my e-rifle fall to my side. "You're not gonna kill yourself?" I asked him.

"No."

A flicker of movement caught my eye. On the hologram screens at his desk, I saw lines of code, and a security camera view of the landing bay. The bay looked to be full of armed streamers, lining up to board the elevator.

I frowned, and brushed past Dev, walking up to the

desk.

"But ... the first wave's not supposed to drop for another hour," I said.

"They're not going to fight at all," Dev said.

As I neared the holograms, I saw that it was not streamers gathered in the landing bay, but security bots – hundreds of them. With a start, I remembered that in my sprint through the *Final Hope* to save Dev, I hadn't seen a single security bot, other than the two I had shot. *And the ship has been packed with them, all throughout this trip.*

"No more human casualties in this war," Dev said quietly, joining me at the desk. A slight smile of satisfaction crossed his lips.

"You brought all those extra bots on board to fight for us," I breathed.

Dev nodded. "They'll end the war. So you and all your friends can go home. Safely."

As I watched, the elevator ramps closed, and the vacuum warning lights came on in the landing bay. The elevator, bearing its complement of drone soldiers, shuddered, and then began to descend through the floor of the ship toward Pyrrhus, and the Ochos.

"But ... it was our fight to finish," I said.

Dev put a hand on my armored forearm. "Does it really mean that much to you?" he asked, his face full of pity. "That you'd risk your life, just to fight again?"

"I ... I don't know," I told him, shaking my head. I faced the screen, watching a schematic of the elevator sliding down the cable. *How is it possible to feel relieved and disappointed at the same time??*

Abruptly, the elevator stopped. Dev frowned, and bent over the computer's keyboard.

"What ...?"

"This is Stellarus Chairman Archer Kinney," a voice I didn't recognize said, booming from unseen speakers in the suite.

Dev looked up at me in surprise and dismay. "You're

streaming," he realized. "You warned them."

"I thought you were trying to kill yourself ..." I said.

"It's over, Dev," Kinney said. "I've assumed command of the *Final Hope* remotely, and I'm asserting my privilege as ranking member of the Stellarus board to terminate your employment."

Dev typed frantically at the keyboard, but on the screens, nothing responded to his inputs.

"Nooo ..." he groaned.

On the holograms, I saw the elevator open its ramps, out in the vacuum of space, well above Pyrrhus' upper atmosphere. After a moment, the security bots marched forward and out of the elevator, dropping silently toward the planet's surface.

"Sam, thank you for drawing this matter to my attention," Kinney told me. "I appreciate your loyalty to StreaMercs, and Stellarus."

I was too stunned to reply. The first of the security bots hit the atmosphere, and one by one, they burst into flames, a ring of meteors burning up on entry.

Dev turned to me, his face ashen.

"Sam, what have you done?"

CHAPTER 39

"Popular science fiction narratives undoubtedly played a part in shaping the early human strategies of the war. Early streamers were obsessed with locating the 'brain bug' or the alien 'queen,' convinced that a knockout blow to Octipede society's central nervous system or some as-yet-undiscovered leadership element would end the war. And then, just when humanity was on the verge of winning the war anyway, they were all proved right."

-Dr. Isabel Al-Alam, "Clash of Civilizations: Humanity's War on the Octipedes"

I barely made the first wave.

Under Chairman Kinney's orders, a pair of crewmen marched Dev out of his apartment and into a holding cell. I didn't even get a chance to tell Dev I was sorry; before I knew it, I found myself standing in his apartment alone, the canopy of stars stretching overhead. Then the automated landing bay announcement came on, warning the first wave to suit up. I hurried back to the equipment room, changed into a new vac-suit (one that *hadn't* taken a few pistol rounds to the chest), drew the rest of my ammo from the arms room, and pushed my way through the streamers crowding the landing bay.

Before I knew it, the ramps were closing, and we were headed down to Pyrrhus.

Pyrrhus. You're gonna get your final campaign after all. Happy, Sam?

I was staring into space, lost in my thoughts, when I felt someone shake me by the shoulder.

"Valkyrie!"

"Hm?" I focused and saw Darth staring at me, a look of concern on his face.

"My fans tell me you're totally spaced out, not responding to them or saying anything. What's up cuz? You okay?"

"Yeah," I said, shaking my head to clear it. "Fine. Just had a really weird morning."

"Someone said you shot up some security bots? And got Dev fired? What the hell happened?" Darth asked.

"Long story," I told him.

He cocked an eyebrow at me. "If you say so. Better get your head in the game, eh?"

"Right. I'm good."

I glanced at my viewer count – I was already at six million viewers, officially viral thanks to the drama at Dev's. Darth turned and fussed with his weapons; I took a deep breath and cued the audio channel for my fans.

"Well, everyone, it's been a hell of a strange day already, and we haven't even touched down yet. I'm … I'm not really sure how I feel about all of it. But I'll tell you this: in two minutes this elevator is going to hit the dirt on Pyrrhus, and we're gonna have the mother of all battles. I'm gonna shred some Ochos for you guys, just like I used to. Maybe teach these noobs how real deathstreamers do things. And live or die, I'll have seen this thing through to the end. We're gonna go out like legends."

The countdown timer above the ramps hit thirty

seconds, and continued downward. I felt the adrenaline start, deep in my core, spreading outward through my limbs, engulfing me in its warm, familiar embrace.

"Let's do this!" Darth said, slapping me on the back. His vac-suit shimmered and then disappeared. I activated my GhostSkin too, and flicked the safety off my e-rifle.

THUMP.

Touch-down, I thought.

The ramps dropped, and sunlight slanted into the dark elevator. We were at the top of a grassy hill, the green stalks waving in a gentle breeze. Beyond, the hillside curved down to a sparkling white sand beach, bordering the turquoise blue ocean. And all around the hillside, Ochos were already swarming toward us.

"Go! Get out!"

I shouldered past a hesitating noob as the first plasma beams sought the elevator, bringing my e-rifle up as I sprinted down the ramp. An Ocho in front of me reared up, its forearms opening to fire: I drilled it through the chest. To my left, I heard Darth open up with his machine gun, the storm of bullets tearing through a group of Ochos.

I saw an Ocho knock down a noob on my right, scoring a nasty gash on his arm with a claw swipe. I blasted it, and then hit a second that had turned to pounce on the wounded streamer as well.

"The landing zone's just chocka with Ochos today," Darth grunted to me.

"You can say that again," I told him.

"The landing zone's just chocka—" Darth started.

"Okay, haha," I said, cutting him off. I grinned. *Just like old times.* "Let's push out and try to start a perimeter," I suggested, finishing a magazine. I took a knee to reload. "Reloading. How about that low spot off to the left?"

"Looks right to me. But I thought you said we weren't going to team up on this one?" Darth said.

"Yeah, well – I didn't think we'd be fighting *all* of the

Ochos right from the start," I commented. I checked over my shoulder – the elevator was already rocketing skyward again, to retrieve the second wave. The ground was littered with corpses already, both human and alien. I gritted my teeth. *They're gonna make us pay for every inch.*

"Moving," I told Darth.

A plasma beam glanced past my shoulder, but I was already running, heading for the shallow dip in the ground we had spotted. It wasn't much, but it might be enough cover for us to start to make a stand, the kernel of a defensive perimeter that could be solidified when the digging drones arrived.

I slid into the low spot, firing down onto the Ochos climbing the hill below us. "Set," I told Darth.

"Moving," he replied.

I lobbed a grenade toward a particularly thick cluster of Ochos. *Jesus, they're coming on fast. Too many. Too many of them.*

Several Ochos, unable to see me, ran near my hole; I killed two of them, but the others were gone before I could stop them, passing me by, headed for other streamers' positions. *We're already overrun.*

I heard Darth land next to me. "I'll take this side," he told me, and his machine gun opened up again with a tearing roar.

We fought back-to-back, as the Ochos swarmed up the hill, pouring themselves at us. It was only five minutes, but it felt like five hours, every second an eternity, every decision life-or-death. I jammed in my sixth magazine and risked a quick look around the landing zone. There was no perimeter, not as such – just pockets of surviving streamers, huddled together, pressed on all sides by Ochos. As I watched, one such pocket was overrun, the handful of streamers disappearing under an angry wave of Ochos.

"We're not gonna hold them," I told Darth. "The second wave is still too far out."

I saw Darth's highlighted outline turn as he glanced around the landing zone. A surge of plasma beams converged on a pocket of streamers off to our left, and their weapons fell silent. Ochos outnumbered the streamers ten to one, and the ratio was only getting worse by the second.

"Shit," Darth said. "I thought they were supposed to pick a remote colony for the first landing site. How'd it go to shit, already?"

"Dunno," I said. "But I don't think we're gonna be able to rally the others and make a stand."

"No," Darth agreed. "I don't think we'd reach 'em. GhostSkin's the only thing keeping you and me alive right now."

I grunted, killing another Ocho with a burst. "They can't see us, but they can sure hear that noisy-ass weapon of yours. They're gonna find us."

Darth mowed down an Ocho. "What do you want to do?"

"Run," I said. "Bust out of here, head down the hill."

"*Down* the hill?" Darth asked. "That's where they're all coming from."

"Yeah, and they won't expect us to run at them," I pointed out. "We run, find a quiet spot and hunker down until the second wave hits the beach, and then we can surprise the Ochos, hit them from the rear."

Darth considered this in silence for a second. "Okay," he said, finally. "Better split up, so there's less chance of them spotting us."

"Uh huh," I agreed, firing at two Ochos. "I'm going. Stay safe."

"Right," Darth agreed. "You too."

I scrambled to my feet and ran, headlong, down the hill, past clumps of Ochos crawling through the grass. They heard me, but I was moving too fast, and they were too surprised or confused to turn and attack me. I ran, zig-zagging to avoid the aliens, until their ranks began to thin out. I had hoped to break out entirely, but there were groups of them in front of me as far as I could see, all the way down to the beach.

Shit. Well, there's fewer of them here, this'll have to do.

I spotted a clump of grass and threw myself down, rolling onto my back and lying still. Behind me, I could see the cable rising out of the top of the hill. The hill itself was thick with Ochos, moving inexorably upward, toward the survivors on the summit. Several Ochos passed close by me, their heads up and searching, questing forward, but I held still, and in a moment, they were gone. A grenade detonated in the distance. I could hear gunfire coming from the hill's peak still, but it was tapering off.

God damn it!

A pit of anger and fear settled in my stomach. "Darth, status?" I called quietly.

"Making like a hole in the ground," he replied, panting. "And crossing my fingers."

At least Darth made it out.

Another Ocho stopped off to my left, pausing for a moment, and then continued up the hill.

>>>*Ochos are mopping up*, a fan messaged me.

I couldn't hear any more gunfire now.

>>>*You two are now sole survivors from Wave 1. :-(*

>>>*Eight minutes until second wave touches down. Hang in there!*

Eight minutes, I thought. *We can hide for eight minutes.*

As I watched, the Ochos milled about the crest of the hill, picking positions to wait for the second wave, hunkering down in the waving grass. It was strange, seeing them moving about normally, instead of rushing toward me. The way they lay down reminded me of a pet dog, settling itself down at its master's feet to wait. But a large group of Ochos was still moving – they continued around the hillside, and came to a stop at the position Darth and I had recently occupied. They inspected it briefly, heads close to the ground, and then several heads swiveled, facing downhill.

Oh, shit.

"Darth …" I called.

"I see them," he said.

The group split into two, joining up with several other bands of Ochos on the hillside. One group headed off at an oblique angle to my right. The other headed straight for me, surveying the ground ahead of them slowly and methodically.

"Our footprints," I said. "They're tracking us!"

"I know," Darth said. "You head for the beach. Maybe they can't swim."

"The beach?" I frowned.

I heard Darth grunt, as if he was standing up. "Valkyrie, it's been an honor."

"What? Darth—"

He appeared suddenly a hundred meters to my right, the GhostSkin flickering off to reveal his hulking frame.

"Yoo-hoo, ya bastards!"

He fired – not at the group coming for him, but at the others, the ones tracking me. I saw the front rank of Ochos tumble to the ground, his bullets throwing up clouds of dirt as they impacted among the pack. Then he disappeared again, reactivating his GhostSkin.

"Damn it, Darth!" I yelled. I stood, hesitating.

"Go, Valkyrie!"

"No! I'm not gonna let you do this."

The Ochos above me were hesitating, and seemed to be on the verge of breaking off and heading toward Darth. I flicked off my GhostSkin and shot two of them, then ghosted myself again and ran several meters to my left. Over my shoulder, I saw that the pack had my trail again – they were running now, chasing me.

I stopped and fired again, killing another Ocho, then ran, reloading. Darth's machine gun opened up, well behind me. I looked up – the Ochos were closing in. I lifted my e-rifle, and then a massive weight crashed into my back, knocking me to the ground.

I screamed and rolled to one side, bringing my e-rifle

back up. The Ocho slammed down again, pinning my e-rifle to the earth beneath its writhing body. I fired, killing it, but another Ocho appeared. It couldn't see me, but it clambered over me, feeling along my body with its legs, trying to get a sense for where I was. As I tugged my e-rifle free, the second Ocho delivered a lightning-fast claw swipe that knocked the weapon several meters away. I snarled and pulled my pistol out as the Ocho scrambled on top of me.

Fine, I thought, *you'll die there, then.*

I shot it, repeatedly, and felt its weight settle down over me, the creature dying with a shiver. I killed the third Ocho that appeared, and the fourth, and then my pistol was empty, my spare magazines trapped under the Ocho on top of me. I started to try to push it off when another Ocho appeared. When I didn't immediately fire at it, it walked around me and the other Ochos corpses in a tight circle, as if inspecting a crime scene. Then it stepped closer, feeling the Ocho on top of me with its forearms, tracing the outline of my vac-suit, locating my invisible pistol and flicking it away from me. My heart was pounding in my chest.

I hope Darth made it, I thought. But I didn't hear his machine gun anymore. *Darth! I hope you took a ton of them down with you.*

"Thanks for watching, guys," I told my fans. It seemed like a lame way to end my stream, but I wasn't feeling particularly creative. "Tell my parents I'm sorry, and tell Avery I love him."

The Ocho took my helmet in its forearms, lifting my upper body off the ground.

"Do it," I told it.

It slammed me down to the ground, and my head rocked against the helmet padding, and everything went dark.

CHAPTER 40

"It is somewhat shocking, in retrospect, how much of humanity's understanding of Octipede biology comes from a brief span of minutes that a single deathstreamer experienced during the final battle on Pyrrhus."

-Dr. Aiko Clemson, "Extraordinary Extraterrestrials: Octipede Evolution and Lifecycles"

For a second, I thought I was back on Venatur. My visor had switched automatically to infrared mode. When I opened my eyes, I found myself lying on my back, staring up at a high, vaulted ceiling in the darkness above me.

Ow, fuck. My head hurts. Where am I?

I rolled onto my side and pushed myself up to a sitting position. I was in a domed cavern, the ceiling held up by a grove of thin stone columns, all intricately carved. The walls were lined with a honeycomb of thousands of cylindrical holes.

I'm … in the colony.

I scrabbled in the dirt for my e-rifle, then searched my

tactical vest for my pistol, a grenade, *anything*. But my weapons were gone, my armor stripped bare. I looked around again. The chamber was larger than the colony on Venatur, by three or four times at least. And it seemed older, somehow – the rocky floor was smooth, polished by countless Ochos passing across it over the centuries.

I scanned my vac-suit's control panel briefly: batteries at ninety-six percent, a hundred and thirty hours of air remaining, all food and water fully stocked. No ammo or weapons detected. *No shit.* My viewer feed was frozen, though. I frowned.

>>>*Unknown communications error. Feed is offline.*

Alone in the Ocho colony, with no weapons, and no comms, I thought. *Fantastic.* I checked the time.

I was out for ... almost fifteen minutes. So the second wave should be down. They're on the ground.

"Hey, if anyone's receiving this and you can track my location, I could use some help," I tried, testing out the main streamer radio channel. "I'm gonna try to—"

Scritch-scritch-scritch.

I looked up, and saw Ochos beginning to emerge from their burrows, their long, sinewy bodies sliding out of the holes in the rock. I stood hastily, but they surged forward, filling the cavern. There were hundreds of them, and they made sure to block the exit tunnel ahead of me first. Then they surrounded me, but stayed back, leaving me standing in the center of a circle of open ground. I balled my hands into fists.

"Okay," I said. "Who wants to go first?"

The Ochos stayed where they were, unmoving. I shifted my weight, and took a step toward the tunnel. The aliens in front of me reared up menacingly, their forearms pointed at me. But they held their fire, and when I stepped back again, they dropped back down to the floor.

Nothing more happened for several seconds. Then, like the first rays of dawn, a far-off light appeared in the exit tunnel. It wavered, and then grew stronger, casting long shadows across the colony chamber.

Please please please be a clan of streamers with barrel-mounted flashlights …

The light passed around a final curve of the tunnel, and my visor blanked out for a second at the sudden, blinding brightness. When it came back on, I saw that my helmet had polarized itself, attempting to shade my eyes from the light. But even at the visor's maximum shading, I had to squint to see the object that emerged from the tunnel.

It looked like a miniaturized sun – a white-orange ball of flame, from whose surface miniature flares of energy arced and extended at random intervals. It was perhaps three feet in diameter, and it hung, floating, several feet above the ground. It was blisteringly hot – I could feel the heat radiating off it, even from several meters away. And I had the distinct impression it was watching me.

I felt all of the hairs on my arms stand straight up, and then there was a sudden pressure at my temples, as if my forehead had been gripped in a vice.

"Ah!" I gasped. The glowing orb seemed to pulse, and I felt the pressure increase.

Then a torrent of images flooded my brain, too fast to see. A galaxy, stars, space. The rapid images slowed, and I saw a green-blue planet.

Earth! I thought. *No, it's not. It's Pyrrhus.*

The view zoomed in, taking me down to the planet's surface, skimming across the grassy plains, until I saw the same sun-like orb hovering over the beach. As I watched, time seemed to speed up – the clouds flitted by rapidly, the tides ebbed and flowed, and the sphere changed, its colors deepening to a dark, angry red.

A phrase popped into my head, unbidden: *>We are star children.<*

The orb turned black and solidified, and then it broke apart, suddenly, fracturing into many smaller pieces, which fell to the ground. The little brown shards lay there for a time, and then I saw them unfold tiny legs, eight each. The tiny pieces wriggled for a time, and then righted themselves and began to move through the grass. As time passed, they grew, and I recognized them for what they were: Octipedes. More time passed – decades, centuries, I could not tell. Then two of the Ochos met in the grass in front of me, and circled each other in an elaborate kind of dance. At the end, they intertwined, locking themselves into a tightly-knit armored ball, their forearms clasped. They remained that way for a time, and then slowly, the pair began to rise from the ground, floating. I saw cracks in their armor, bright light shining through from within. Then the armor crumbled away, revealing a shining ball of light-energy.

>*Our lifecycle. We are star children.*<

The Ocho-sun rose up into the sky and then, with shocking speed, rocketed toward the upper atmosphere, and outer space.

That's how they reproduce, I thought. *And how they travel and colonize other planets. They didn't kill off a more advanced alien species – they ARE a more advanced alien species!* I shook my head. Then another thought occurred to me. *Which means they can reach Earth, and replicate there. We were right to fear them.*

>*No.*< Suddenly the vision disappeared, and I was staring at the glowing Ocho in the colony chamber again. >*No.*< The thought in my mind was clear, as if someone had spoken the word to me directly. >*No. We do not wish this.*<

I cleared my throat. "You're not going to attack Earth?" I asked.

>*No.*<

"You attacked our explorers," I said. "Why should I believe you?"

The orb floated back, over the heads of the worm-like Ochos on the ground. It dipped and bumped into one of the Ochos, which reared up in fear and anger, and swung its forearms at the orb. They passed through the orb's outer surface without effect, and emerged red-hot and glowing on the other side.

>*They are juveniles. They react. In self-defense.*<

"Why can't they communicate?"

>*They are juveniles,*< the orb repeated. >*They have only instincts, not knowledge, or wisdom. When they mate and mature into this form, they will inherit the intelligence of our species.*<

"If you don't want to attack us, what do you want?" I asked.

>*I want to preserve what is left of my kind.*<

"Why didn't you come to us before?" I asked. "Why wait until now?"

>*The time was not right. I have matured well before my appointed time, in order to treat with you. The rest of my generation needs many more years to mature.*<

"… so they can mate, and travel to Earth, and kill us all," I said.

>*No.*<

Again, the crushing pressure on my head. I saw an orb flying through space, entering orbit over a turquoise planet, and this time I recognized the continents immediately. The orb flew through Earth's sky, and passed over a city, located on an island between two peninsulas of rolling forests. The buildings were low and made of wood, and smoke rose from their chimneys. In the cobbled streets, horses trotted in front of carriages; out in the harbor, several wooden ships lay at anchor, their tall masts rising up into the overcast sky. The orb paused in the air, surveying the city, and then curved gracefully upward, back through the clouds and into space.

They've visited Earth before. They came, and could have stayed – they could have invaded – and destroyed us easily. But they didn't.

And I knew it was true. I could feel the truth of it, deep in my bones. The orb was waiting, watching me.

"I … I'm sorry," I said, at a loss for words.

>*Will you help us?*<

"How?" I asked. *How can I possibly stop a thousand streamers from tearing this planet apart? Especially after their friends in the first wave have all been slaughtered.* "I don't think I can."

I felt the pounding in my forehead once again: this time, I saw a vision of Avery, quarantined in his room in the sick bay, just after the final battle of Venatur. *After he had been captured.*

>*Forget us,*< the orb said, in my head.

"What …?" I shook my head, frowning. "I don't understand. I can't choose to—"

The vision changed; time seemed to reverse. Avery lay down on a bed, and the robo-docs bent over him for some time, examining him. Pieces of vac-suit sprang from the floor, encasing him. I saw two streamers carry Avery's limp form backward into the elevator, then back across the alien terrain of Venatur and into the hole where I had found him. The streamers disappeared; Avery stood up, and the time reversal stopped. He was fighting, hand-to-hand, with an Ocho. The creature grappled him to the ground, and I saw it strike Avery in the neck, quickly, with a tiny filament extended from its forearm. Avery grabbed at the wound in his neck, yelping, then the Ocho skittered away.

That's right … they injected him with something. And it made him forget.

>*Forget us.*<

"You want to infect me, too … give me amnesia, like Avery." I said.

>*Yes. It is a mind contagion. A memory virus. It will take away memories of us.*<

I shook my head. "But … there are videos. Books. Historical records. The virus would have to erase those, too."

>*No, it will not. But it will prevent you from retaining them.*<

Just like Avery, I realized. *When he watches videos of himself streaming, his mind can't grasp them. He forgets again as soon as the video is over.*

"But it will only work for me," I said. "I could forget, maybe, but all of the other streamers will still remember. They'll still keep coming, to fight you. And all of the people watching this right now on Earth will remember, too."

>*It will spread this time, if you help us.*<

"How?"

>*Your friend fought the virus. We forced it on him, and he fought it – he did not want to forget. If you accept it, if you submit to it, then it will spread. Via thought and energy, to the rest of your race. The rest of the soldiers here, and the millions from your home who will be watching you soon. And they will all forget us, and the war.*<

The millions watching me, I thought. *But they won't have heard what the orb told me. They won't have seen what it showed me. If something goes wrong, they'll never understand why I would have chosen to help the Ochos.*

"Will we ever remember?" I asked.

>*The virus will die out, after several generations,*< the orb told me. >*Your race will remember the war, and what happened here. But not in your lifetime.*<

The full weight of what the orb was asking finally hit me. *Everyone will forget the war. They'll forget me. Who I was, all that I did. The war will be over, and I'll return home to … nothing. No StreaMercs memorial, no museum …*

I looked up, my eyes wide.

"Everything? We'll forget *everything* from the war – not just you and the Ochos, we'll forget about the friends we made here?"

>*Yes.*<

I sank to my knees.

Avery. I'll forget Avery, too.

Movement caught my eye: the communications indicator in my heads-up display had flipped from red to green. Nothing happened for a moment, and then messages rushed into my feed, piling up on top of each other. I heard radio chatter in my ear from the streamers in the second wave. My viewer count – which had started at zero – began spinning up at an alarming rate, until it stopped showing individual additions entirely, and just began to show the new additions in massive blocks.

Two million viewers … nine million.

Twenty-two million viewers.

And the numbers kept climbing. I looked up, and found a juvenile Ocho laying a bundle on the ground in front of me: my ER-45, my pistol, all of my remaining ammunition and grenades. The Ocho withdrew, back into the waiting crowd. I picked up the e-rifle. The orb rose higher in the air. Silently, the Ochos parted, clearing a passage to the exit tunnel. Then the juvenile aliens lay down on the floor, prostrating themselves, watching me.

>*You must choose. You can return to your people, and lead them here. You can continue the war, and end our race. We will fight you, but we will not win.*<

I imagined myself at the head of a pack of steely-eyed streamers, thundering down into the colony, weapons blazing, my fans cheering as we swept through the tunnels, avenging our fallen friends.

I could do it. My heart was pounding already in anticipation. *I could do it for Darth. For Johnny, and Dhia, and SoSo. For Lexy and Petro. For Avery. For me.*

A lone Ocho stood up. It held a single forearm out, and I saw a tiny filament extend from the tip of its armored claw.

>*Or you can end the war. You can save our race. You can choose to forget.*<

I looked at the orb, then over to the Ocho with its forearm held out, plaintively.

Choose to forget. And choose to be forgotten.

God help me.

CHAPTER 41

"In the year 2237, the first battle of Pyrrhus was an Event, capital 'E.' Many businesses closed for the day, there were viewing parties in city parks and theaters, and sales of StreaMercs' proprietary VR sets skyrocketed in the weeks ahead of the landing. There were thus approximately eight hundred and sixty-two million humans, spread across Earth and her colonies, watching various deathstreamer feeds at the moment that Valkyrie6's feed unexpectedly came back online. An unknown employee aboard the *Final Hope* immediately recognized that Valkyrie6 had stumbled into a dramatic and unprecedented situation, and made the on-the-spot decision to blank all other feeds, and show every single viewer what Valkyrie6 was seeing. Over the next few minutes, as word spread among citizens both in person and via social media, over a billion more humans tuned in. And Sam would have *known* it. Imagine, then, what she must have felt, facing the biggest decision of her life, and knowing that a significant percentage of humanity was watching her."

-Dr. Isabel Al-Alam, "Valkyrie: The Life of Samentha

Ombotu-Chen"

At the top of the hill, I could see digger drones excavating trenches, tossing clods of black-brown earth into the air. I saw streamers, too – the noobs in their pristine vac-suits, gathered around the perimeter, waiting for the next wave of Ochos. The Ochos who had surrounded the hill earlier had disappeared.

They were only there to buy enough time for the others to talk to me. They must've gone back to their colonies now.

I put my head down and climbed up the hill, back to the elevator. Back home.

"Valkyrie!"

"Hey!"

A group of streamers in front of me had stood up – I didn't recognize them, but they all had a matching skull insignia on their chest plates. *A noob clan*, I guessed.

"My viewers are saying you were in the colony!" one of the noobs said, as I drew near.

I paused, catching my breath.

"Yeah," I said.

"What happened?" the noob asked.

"They let me go," I said.

"They what?!" Through his visor, his eyes went wide. More streamers were congregating, gathering around us.

"Well, can you take us back there?" someone asked, when I declined to explain any further.

I looked them over – bundles of eager nervousness, fingers itching at triggers. Corporate sponsor logos splashed on their armor. Suddenly I felt very tired.

"Lead the way, Valkyrie," someone else urged.

"No," I said, and slung my e-rifle. I pushed through the group and headed toward the anchor, where the third wave of streamers was just beginning to disembark.

* * *

I was the only one who rode the elevator back up after the third wave – just me, and the bodies of several dozen streamers.

All that's left of the first wave, I thought.

When the ramps dropped, I found the fourth wavers waiting patiently for their turn around the landing bay, but word must have reached them that I wasn't in a chatty mood, and they stepped aside to let me pass. The way they parted ranks looked so similar to the way the Ochos had moved to let me leave the colony that I had a sudden feeling of deja vu.

Keep it together, Valkyrie, I scolded myself. *They already think you're going crazy.*

I turned my weapons in, giving my ER-45 a final, affectionate pat before handing it off to the robotic armorer. When I turned around, two robo-docs were waiting for me, blocking my path back to the equipment room.

"Let me guess," I said. "Quarantine?"

"For your own safety," one of the robots told me.

I nodded. "Uh huh. Wait a minute." I didn't wait for them to answer, but turned on my heel and headed down the hallway toward my suite, my vac-boots ringing on the steel deck.

"We need to examine you," one of the robo-docs protested, falling in behind me.

"I feel lightheaded," I told them. "My mouth is dry. And my neck hurts. Otherwise I'm fine."

"But we need samples," the robot whined. "Blood, tissue—"

A pair of crewmembers bustled down the hall toward us, looking worried. One of them was hurriedly strapping some kind of belt holster in place over his uniform, the weapon banging awkwardly against his thigh.

"Sam!" he called. "Sam, we need you in the sick bay, right now."

I met them at the door to my suite. Still in my vac-suit, I towered over them, which, judging by their faces, was all too evident to them, too. I realized, suddenly, that all of the security bots on board had been destroyed – either by me, in my rush to save Dev, or by Chairman Kinney, when he pulled the plug on Dev's plan to finish the war with an army of drones.

These two guys are all that StreaMercs can muster in terms of security forces right now.

The crewman finished buckling his belt, and let his hand rest uneasily on the stun weapon in its holster.

"You really think that thing's gonna penetrate my armor?" I asked, looking down at him.

"I'd rather not have to find out," he said, earnestly.

He's just doing his job, I reminded myself.

"Look," I told him. "I'm going to go into my suite. I need to take care of one thing, quickly, and then I'll come with you. I promise."

He shook his head reluctantly. "We gotta get you quarantined, ASAP. Whatever it is you need to do, can't it wait?"

"No," I told him. "I don't have much time." I touched the hatch release with my gloved hand, and the door slid open. "Five minutes," I told him, and stepped inside.

It was odd being inside my room in the vac-suit – everything looked smaller, shorter than usual, like I was in a funhouse version of the world. My keypad was lying on the coffee table, where I had left it; I picked it up, gingerly, willing myself not to damage it with my suit-enhanced strength. Then I sat down on the couch, which creaked and groaned, protesting at the weight of my vac-suit. After a few false starts, I got the keypad's communications app opened, and dialed Avery.

The screen showed the connection icon for what seemed an eternity. Then over my external microphones, I heard a pre-recorded message.

"This is Avery. Must have missed you, sorry! Leave a

message."

Beep.

I tapped on the screen again, and it tried to make the connection again.

"This is Avery. Must have missed you—"

Damn it! Avery, where are you!

I could feel myself sweating – my eyesight was starting to blur, as well.

No! Not yet!

Finally, I switched apps on the keypad, pulling up my journal. My fingers weren't nearly dexterous enough to type, so I mashed the video *Record* button, and ensured that the camera was pointed at my face.

"This is my final journal entry," I said. "I don't know how much longer I have, but it's important that I get this down. I need to make a record of what happened on Pyrrhus, when the Ochos captured me."

I licked my lips – concentrating was becoming difficult, the room was starting to swim around me.

Focus!

"… I hope, someday, that I can remember what happened here. But if not … maybe someone else will find this journal, and understand what I've done. And why."

I took a deep breath.

"They were waiting for us," I began. "When we landed, Darth and I were the only ones to make it out of the perimeter …"

EPILOGUE

"Undoubtedly, the situation was the most jarring for the streamers on Pyrrhus, and those aboard the *Final Hope* waiting to deploy. Imagine waking up, as if from a dream, but not being able to recall what that dream was. Not being able to remember how you came to be standing on an alien planet, armed for war. But war with who? And why? None of them would have had the answers. All they could do was return to the ship, and return home to Earth, full of questions that would never be answered."

-Dr. Isabel Al-Alam, "Clash of Civilizations: Humanity's War on the Octipedes"

The emptiness is my constant companion.

"The Gap," we call it, for lack of a better term. Nearly everyone is missing some of their past. For most, it's just a few hours, from time to time, that they can't account for. But some people have it worse than others, and we don't understand why. I'm one of the ones that have it worst of all. For me, whole *years* are missing. It's just easier not to talk about it, I find.

But not talking about it doesn't take away the emptiness.

My friend Paul, from college, studied the phenomenon for nearly a year, along with a number of other prominent academics – psychologists, neurologists, sociologists. Trying to figure out what had caused all of mankind, spread across a number of star systems, to suffer from simultaneous collective amnesia, or a mass neurosis, or whatever technical label they've settled on now. It was *the* burning question that everyone wanted to solve, for a while. They studied me, too: they brought me to a lab, and did all kinds of physical and mental tests. They didn't find anything, other than the scars and barcode tattoos that I can't explain. I gave them my keypad with my old journal entries – reading them frustrated me, because the words just seemed to disappear off the page as I scanned them. I think they put them in some kind of historical archive. For a while, Paul would call me every few weeks, giving me updates on their progress. But eventually, the academics let it go, and Paul did, too.

Modern science has limits, he said. We can't explain everything, even now.

I have money – a *lot* of money. It's nice, but I have no clue how it got into my bank account, because I can clearly remember a time when I would burn through my government stipend before the month was out. After I stopped trying to figure out what had happened to me, I bought a boat, and all the equipment I needed, and started freediving again. It's the only place I feel somewhat free, or … unburdened, at least. I can slip down the line, pushing deeper underwater, and stop trying to remember.

Later, the emptiness comes back.

I've thought about killing myself. At night, usually, when I'm alone in my apartment, and I can hear the married couple downstairs laughing at something, a shared joke, or a comedy show they're watching. I'm not going to go through with it – I think Lucie would be mad at me, if I did. If there's an afterlife, she'd be waiting for me, and she'd be pissed.

Did you learn nothing from my mistakes? she'd say.

I learned, Lucie.

I still think about doing it, though, lying there waiting for sleep to come. I sigh, and face the window, and watch the headlights of cars cast window-shaped pools of light on the ceiling as they pass by.

* * *

I'm out on the boat, after a good dive – not a personal best, but close. I haul up the line, with its neon depth markers every ten meters, pooling it on the deck at my feet. Something bright catches my eye: I look up, squinting.

The sun? No, the sun should be … behind me.

It sure looks like a sun, though – a small one, coming down through the sky toward me. It's like nothing I've ever seen before, but is somehow at the same time strangely familiar to me. I search my mind, but the memories just slide away from me, elusive. The glowing orb stops, hovering, several feet away from the boat. I can feel my heart racing.

The surface of the orb pulses, and I see miniature solar flares arcing across it. Suddenly I feel a vice-like pressure at my temples. I gasp, grabbing my head in both hands. When I look up, the orb and the ocean beyond have been replaced – I'm looking at a red-painted farmhouse, atop a hill by the sea. Fields of various crops roll gently down the hillside toward a small beach, with a wooden dock jutting out into a harbor. It looks warm, humid – I can see someone standing in one of the fields, tending to a trellis of some kind. Several drones hover in the background, spraying the crops with a gentle mist that forms rainbows in the sunlight.

>*Louisiana,*< a voice says in my mind. >*Go there.*<

The view changes, pulling back, over the roof of the farmhouse. I catch a glimpse of a mailbox, with peeling black numbers painted on its rusted metal sides. Then a green road marker: *Mayberry Rd.*

>*Go,*< the voice urges me.

The vision fades, the pressure in my head recedes. The orb is moving again, accelerating south across the waves, the swiftness of its passing leaving a ripple on the ocean's surface in its wake.

* * *

I finish packing the bed of my pickup truck and pull the cover tight over it, snapping it shut. It occurs to me, not for the first time, that it would make more sense to catch a hypertube to Louisiana, that packing up my entire life and driving there based on what was likely a hallucination is not only inefficient but borderline insane. But it feels right, in a way I can't explain. It's something to do, at least, something to break the routine, so I don't mind.

Worst case I just take a long road trip, find nothing, come home, and ... go back to doing nothing.

I drive to the marina first, where I back down the ramp, dipping the trailer into the water under my waiting boat. It doesn't take long to haul the boat out and secure it down for the trip, and then I'm on the highway, heading west. I consider stopping by my parents, but I saw them last night for dinner – another goodbye isn't necessary. I punch in the destination on the truck's autopilot, put my feet up on the dash, roll the window down, and let the summer wind blow through my hair.

The autopilot takes me through Brooklyn and over the bridge into Staten Island, leaving the gleaming skyscrapers of Manhattan in my rearview mirror. After that, it's a long slog south through New Jersey, past Lucie's old exit, where we'd go each summer to dive and hang out on the boardwalk in the evenings, flirting with boys and watching the seniors play shuffleboard.

A brief jog through Maryland, then around the outskirts of D.C., where the autopilot navigates afternoon rush hour without complaint, and then we head up into the rolling green hills of Virginia, traveling southeast along the West Virginia border. When it gets dark I stop for dinner and stretch my legs, checking the tie-downs on the boat to ensure everything is still secure. Then I push on for another few hours, stopping at a motel outside Chattanooga. I park at the back corner of their lot, the boat and truck taking up a handful of spaces, but instead of sleeping inside I grab the blankets and a couple pillows off my bed and stretch out on one of the loungers on the boat. I fall asleep looking up at the stars.

I shower in the morning, grab some breakfast at a diner up the street, and then it's back on the road. The morning grows noticeably hotter as we traverse Alabama, heading east from Birmingham to Jackson, Mississippi. I pass the time playing Game Boy and listening to the radio, though it's getting progressively harder to find a station that isn't playing Country music. At last a green road sign welcomes me to Louisiana, and not long after, the truck switches to a highway heading south toward Lake Charles.

The sun is setting by the time I can smell the sea again. I disengage the truck's auto-pilot and stop at a gravel and dirt T-junction. A dusty green sign at the intersection reads *Mayberry Rd.* I'm not sure whether to be surprised or relieved. I turn right onto Mayberry and in the distance, I can see a red farmhouse atop a small hill, with a battered mailbox out front. When I pull into the driveway, a tall, blonde woman is sitting on the porch, watching the road expectantly. I park the truck, my heart racing, then open my door and step down. She stands, her sundress ruffling gently in the breeze, and then she walks down the steps toward me, her ponytail flicking from side to side with each step. She stops a few feet away, watching me with a bemused half-smile.

"I'm sorry," I say, suddenly doubting myself. "I'm not quite sure why I'm here."

"That's okay," she says. "I've been expecting you."

"You have," I say.

She nods. "Don't ask me why or how," she says. "I'm not sure I could explain it." Her voice is deeper than I expected, but warm, with a rich Southern drawl. She holds out a hand. "Avery," she says. "Avery Desmiter."

"Sam," I say. "Nice to meet you."

She smiles again. "Nice to meet you, Sam. Come on in."

* * *

I am down at the dock, tying up the boat after my morning dive, when I see a taxi turn onto the road. A lazy plume of dust follows the taxi down to the farmhouse, where it stops. I frown, and then climb up past the sweet potatoes, skirting the corn field, enjoying the relative coolness of the shade under the peach trees. Avery had been working in the strawberry patch this morning, but he's not there anymore – just a weeder robot trundling through the undergrowth.

Maybe he went into town? I hope he remembers to swing by the marina this time to pick up those spare batteries for the boat.

I step inside the farmhouse through the back porch; down the hallway, I see Avery already letting someone into the kitchen.

The stranger is a huge bull of a man, his hair jet-black, with tattoos covering his bare arms and part of his face. But I see a barcode tattoo under his eye, just like mine and Avery's.

"G'day," the newcomer says, when he catches sight of me.

"Hey," I say.

A small, brown dog – a chihuahua, I think – runs from

between the newcomer's legs and up to me, where it yips twice. I crouch down and let it sniff my hand, but the dog licks it immediately, and then nuzzles against my leg.

"Seems like he knows you already, eh?" the man says, chuckling.

"I guess so," I admit, scratching the dog behind one ear. I stand up.

"Well, I'm Tangaroa," the man says, smiling. "That's a mouthful, though, so my mates call me Darth."

"Hi, Darth," Avery says. "Avery."

"Sam," I say, and we all shake hands.

"You've got the tattoo, too," Darth comments, touching his cheek briefly.

Avery and I nod.

"You guys are gonna think I'm taking the piss, but … a strange little light in the sky told me to come here, all the way from New Zealand," Darth says.

Avery and I share a look. "I believe you," I say.

Darth looks relieved.

"It told me you could help me," Darth says, looking at me.

"Help you?" I ask.

"Yeah," Darth says. "I'm not sure what it meant either."

"Well, is something wrong?" I ask him.

Darth shrugs. "Shouldn't be. I've got a couple million in the bank and nothing but time to spend it all." His smile fades, slightly. "But … I've also got a dog whose name I can't remember, and no idea what I did with myself the past few years. It … it bothers me, at times. A lot of the time."

"Do you talk about it?" Avery asks.

Darth shakes his head. "No. Nobody really understands."

"We do," I say.

"I think Sam *can* help you," Avery says. "I think that she's meant to, if that makes sense."

"Yeah?" Darth says, hopefully. "Are you a shrink?"

I'm about to say "no," but Avery beats me to it: "Close enough," he says. "She studied psychology, and her mother was a social worker. And I always feel better after talking to her."

Darth smiles. "No worries, then. Mind if I crash here a bit?"

Avery looks at me, inquiring. I nod. "Yeah. Of course," I say.

"Make yourself at home," Avery says to Darth. "We've got plenty of room."

Avery loops an arm around my hip, pulling me close. He smells like freshly-turned earth and strawberries. I look up at him and smile contentedly.

"You're gonna help us remember, Sam?" Avery asks.

I shake my head. "No. I'm gonna help us let go," I say. "I think it's time to stop mourning for the memories we've lost, and just start making new ones."

"Too right," Darth says.

Avery is looking over Darth's shoulder, and I follow his gaze – out on the road, another taxi is approaching, and in the distance, I see two more cars driving toward the farmhouse.

"Looks like you're not the only one joining us, Darth," Avery says.

Darth turns and looks. "More? Yeah, I suppose that would make sense, eh?"

Avery gives my hip a squeeze. "You up for it?"

I look into his eyes. "Yeah," I say.

The three of us go out onto the porch and wait, watching as a line of cars winds its way down to the farmhouse on Mayberry Road.

ABOUT THE AUTHOR

Piers Platt grew up in Boston, but spent most of his childhood in various boarding schools, including getting trained as a classical singer at a choir school for boys. He graduated from the University of Pennsylvania and joined the Army in 2002, spending four years on active duty. He lives with his family in New York.

To be the first to hear about his new releases and get a free copy of his *New York Times* bestselling Iraq War memoir, *Combat and Other Shenanigans,* visit:
www.piersplatt.com/newsletter

CPSIA information can be obtained
at www.ICGtesting.com
Printed in the USA
LVHW110025051118
595952LV00001B/1/P